غـايــة المــريــد في شــرح كتــاب التــوحيــد

Ghayatul-Murid

(The Destination of the Seeker of Truth)

Interpretation of Kitab At-Tauhid

First Edition: May 2003

Supervised by:

ABDUL MALIK MUJAHID

Headquarters:

P.O. Box: 22743, Riyadh 11416, KSA
Tel: 00966-1-4033962/4043432
Fax: 00966-1-4021659
E-mail: darussalam@naseej.com.sa
Website: http://www.dar-us-salam.com
Bookshop: Tel: 00966-1-4614483
Fax: 00966-1-4644945

Branches & Agents:

K.S.A.

- Jeddah: Tel & Fax: 00966-2-6807752
- Al-Khobar: Tel: 00966-3-8692900
  Fax: 00966-3-8691551

U.A.E.

- Tel: 00971-6-5632623 Fax: 5632624

PAKISTAN

- 50-Lower Mall, Lahore
  Tel: 0092-42-7240024 Fax: 7354072
- Rahman Market, Ghazni Street
  Urdu Bazar, Lahore
  Tel: 0092-42-7120054 Fax: 7320703

U.S.A.

- Houston: P.O. Box: 79194 Tx 77279
  Tel: 001-713-722 0419
  Fax: 001-713-722 0431
  E-mail: sales @ dar-us-salam.com
  Website: http:// www.dar-us-salam.com
- New York: 572 Atlantic Ave, Brooklyn
  New York-11217
  Tel: 001-718-625 5925

U.K.

- London: Darussalam International Publications Ltd., 226 High Street, Walthamstow, London E17 7JH U.K.
  Tel: 0044-208 520 2666
  Mobile: 0044-794 730 6706
  Fax: 0044-208 521 7645
- Darussalam International Publications Limited, Regent Park Mosque,
  146 Park Road, London NW8 7RG,
  Tel: 0044-207 724 3363

FRANCE

- Editions & Libairie Essalam
  135, Bd de Ménilmontant 75011
  Paris (France)
  Tél: 01 43 381956/4483 - Fax 01 43 574431
  Website: http: www.Essalam.com
  E-mail: essalam@essalam.com

AUSTRALIA

- Lakemba NSW: ICIS: Ground Floor
  165-171, Haldon St.
  Tel: (61-2) 9758 4040 Fax: 9758 4030

MALAYSIA

- E&D BOOKS SDN. BHD.
  321 B 3rd Floor, Suria Klcc,
  Kuala Lumpur City Center 50088
  Tel: 00603-216 63433 Fax: 459 72032

SINGAPORE

- Muslim Converts Association of Singapore
  Singapore-424484
  Tel: 0065-440 6924, 348 8344
  Fax: 440 6724

SRILANKA

- Darul Kitab 6, Nirmal Road, Colombo-4
  Tel: 0094-1-589 038 Fax: 0094-74 722433

KUWAIT

- Islam Presentation Committee
  Enlightenment Book Shop, P.O. Box: 1613 Safat 13017 Kuwait
  Tel: 00965-244 7526 Fax: 240 0057

Ghayatul-Murid

(The Destination of the Seeker of Truth)

Interpretation of

Kitab At-Tauhid

By the Noble Shaikh

Sâlih bin 'Abdul-'Aziz bin Muhammad bin Ibrahim Aali Shaikh

Minister of Islamic Affairs, Endowments, Da'wah and Guidance, Kingdom of Saudi Arabia

Translated by

Aqeel Walker

DARUSSALAM

GLOBAL LEADER IN ISLAMIC BOOKS

Riyadh, Jeddah, Sharjah, Lahore

London, Houston, New York

King Fahd National Library Cataloging-in-Publication Data

Al Shaikh, Salih bin Abdulaziz
Interpretation of Kitab At-tauhid: The destination of the seeker of truth -/ Salih bin Abdulaziz Al Shaikh. - Riyadh, 2003
325 p.; 14x21 cm
ISBN: 9960-892-38-7
1 - Islamic theology 2- Faith (Islam) I - Title
240 dc 1424/1011

Legal Deposit no. 1424/1011
ISBN : 9960-892-38-7

Contents

At-Tauhid (The Oneness of Allâh) 11
The Virtue of *At-Tauhid* and what Sins it Expiates 19
Whoever Actualizes *At-Tauhid* will enter Paradise without a Reckoning 25
Fear of *Ash-Shirk* 32
The Invitation to Testify that there is Nothing Worthy of Being Worshipped Except Allâh 38
The Explanation of *At-Tauhid* and the Testimony that None has the right to be Worshipped but Allâh 44
It is from *Ash-Shirk* to Wear a Ring, String or Anything Similar in Order to Remove Affliction or Prevent it ... 51
What has been Related Concerning *Ar-Ruqaa* and *At-Tamaa'im* 59
Whoever Seeks Blessings in Trees, Stones and Similar Things 66
What has been reported Concerning Slaughtering for Other than Allâh 76
A Sacrifice Should not be Made to Allâh at a Place where Sacrifices are Made to other than Allâh 84
It is from *Ash-Shirk* to Make a Vow to other than Allâh 89
It is from *Ash-Shirk* to Seek Refuge in other than Allâh . 91
It is from *Ash-Shirk* that one Seeks Help in other than Allâh or Supplicates other than Him 94
The Statement of the Allâh, the Most High, ... 102
The Statement of the Allâh, the Most High, ... 109

The Intercession 114

The Statement of Allâh the Most High, ... 124

What has been Narrated Regarding the Cause of the Disbelief of the Children of Aadam and Their Leaving Their Religion is Exaggeration Concerning the Righteous People 129

What has been Narrated Regarding the Condemnation of Whoever Worships Allâh at the Grave of a Righteous Man — So How About if He Worships the Man in the Grave? 137

What has been narrated Regarding Exaggeration Concerning the Graves of the Righteous People making them Idols that are worshipped besides Allâh 146

What has been Narrated Regarding Al-Muṣtafaa's ﷺ Protection of *At-Tauhid* and His Closing Every Path that Leads to *Ash-Shirk* 149

What has been Narrated Regarding the Fact that Some of this *Ummah* (Nation) will Worship Idols 153

What has been narrated Regarding *As-Siḥr* (Sorcery or Magic) 163

A Clarification of Some of the Types of *As-Siḥr* (Sorcery or Magic) 168

What has been Related Concerning the Fortunetellers (Soothsayers) and the like 173

What has been related Concerning Curing Magic Spells (*An-Nushrah*) 179

What has been related Concerning Belief in Omens (*At-Tatayyur*) 182

What has been related Concerning Astrology (*At-*

Tanjeem) 189
What has been related Concerning Seeking Rain by the Stars (*Al-Anwaa'*) 193
The Statement of Allâh the Most High 199
The Statement of Allâh the Most High, ... 204
The Statement of Allâh the Most High 209
The Statement of Allâh the Most High 213
A Part of Faith in Allâh is Being Patient with the Decrees of Allâh and the Statement of Allâh the Most High 216
What has been Related Concerning Showing Off (*Ar-Riyaa'*) 221
It is from *Ash-Shirk* that a Person Seeks Worldly Gain by his Deeds 225
Whoever Obeys the Scholars and the Rulers in Forbidding what Allâh has Allowed or Allowing what He has Forbidden, then He has Taken Them as Lords Besides Allâh 228
The Statement of Allâh the Most High 232
Whoever Denies Anything from the Names and Attributes (of Allâh) and the Statement of Allâh the Most High, ... 237
The Statement of Allâh the Most High, ... 241
The Statement of Allâh the Most High, ... 244
What has been related concerning Whoever is not Satisfied with the Oath taken by Allâh's Name 248
The Statement, "What Allâh willed and (what) you willed." 250

Whoever Curses Time, Then He has Offended Allâh..... 253
Using the Name "Judge of Judges"..... 256
Respecting the Names of Allâh and Changing One's Name for the Sake of that..... 258
Whoever Makes Fun of Anything that Contains the Mention of Allâh or the Qur'ān or the Messenger..... 261
The Statement of Allâh the Most High,..... 264
The Statement of Allâh the Most High,..... 270
The Statement of Allâh the Most High,..... 274
The statement "*As-Salaam* (Peace and Security) be upon Allâh" Should not be Said..... 277
The Person's saying, "O Allâh, forgive me if You wish."..... 279
The Person's Should not Say, "My male slave (*'Abdee*) or my female slave (*Amatee*)."..... 281
Whoever Asks by Allâh Should not be Denied..... 284
Nothing but Paradise Should be Asked for by Allâh's Face..... 286
What has Been Related Concerning Saying Law (If only...)..... 288
The Prohibition of Cursing the Wind..... 291
The Statement of Allâh the Most High,..... 293
What has been related concerning the Deniers of *Al-Qadar* (Decree)..... 296
What has been related concerning Those Who Make Pictures..... 300
What has been related Concerning Swearing Oaths Frequently..... 304

What has been related concerning the Protection of Allâh and the Protection of His Prophet 308
What has been related Concerning Declaring an Oath on Allâh 313
Intercession by Allâh Should not be Sought from His Creation 315
What has been Related Concerning the Prophet's Protecting the Sacredness of *At-Tauhid* and His Closing the Paths of *Ash-Shirk* 317
What has been related Concerning Allâh the Most High's Statement, ... 320

In the Name of Allâh,
the Most Gracious, the Most Merciful

At-Tauhid (The Oneness of Allâh)

Allâh the Most High said,

﴿وَمَا خَلَقْتُ ٱلْجِنَّ وَٱلْإِنسَ إِلَّا لِيَعْبُدُونِ﴾

"And I (Allâh) created not the jinn and mankind except that they should worship Me (Alone)."(51:56)[1]

And His Statement,

﴿وَلَقَدْ بَعَثْنَا فِى كُلِّ أُمَّةٍ رَّسُولًا أَنِ ٱعْبُدُوا۟ ٱللَّهَ وَٱجْتَنِبُوا۟ ٱلطَّٰغُوتَ﴾

---

[1] Concerning the Statement of Allâh the Most High,

﴿وَمَا خَلَقْتُ ٱلْجِنَّ وَٱلْإِنسَ إِلَّا لِيَعْبُدُونِ﴾

"And I (Allâh) did not create the jinn and men except that they should worship Me (Alone)." (51:56)

This means: And I never created the jinn and men for anything or any purpose from the purposes, except for one single purpose, which is that they worship Me (Allâh). This Verse contains the explanation of *At-Tauhid*. This is from the aspect that the *Salaf* explained the statement,

﴿إِلَّا لِيَعْبُدُونِ﴾

"Except that they should worship Me (Alone),"

as meaning: "...except that they should worship Me Alone in *At-Tauhid*." The proof of this understanding is that the Messengers were only sent for the purpose of singling out Allâh Alone for worship (*Tauhid ul-'Ibaadah*).

The reality of worship is submission and humility. When love and compliance are added to these two characteristics, it becomes legal (religious) worship. According to the Islamic Law, worship is to observe the commands and prohibitions (of Allâh) with love, hope and fear. Shaikh-ul-Islam said, "It (worship) is a comprehensive noun for what Allâh loves and is pleased with of statements and actions, both apparent and hidden." Therefore, the implication of this Verse is that every single act from the acts of worship must be for Allâh Alone, besides all else.

"And verily, We have sent among every *Ummah* (community, nation) a Messenger (proclaiming): 'Worship Allâh (alone), and avoid (or keep away from) *At-Tâghût* (all false deities, etc.)." (16:36)[1]

And His Statement,

﴿وَقَضَىٰ رَبُّكَ أَلَّا تَعْبُدُوٓا۟ إِلَّآ إِيَّاهُ وَبِٱلْوَٰلِدَيْنِ إِحْسَـٰنًا﴾

"And your Lord has decreed that you worship none but Him. And that you be dutiful to your parents." (17:23)[2]

---

[1] Concerning His Statement,

﴿وَلَقَدْ بَعَثْنَا فِى كُلِّ أُمَّةٍ رَّسُولًا أَنِ ٱعْبُدُوا۟ ٱللَّهَ وَٱجْتَنِبُوا۟ ٱلطَّـٰغُوتَ﴾

"And verily, We have sent among every Ummah (community, nation) a Messenger (proclaiming): 'Worship Allâh (alone), and avoid (or keep away from) *At-Tâghût* (all false deities, etc.)." (16:36)

This Verse is the explanation (*Tafseer*) of the meaning of worship and *At-Tauhid*, and that the Messengers were sent with these two statements: "Worship Allâh and avoid *At-Tâghût*." This is the meaning of *At-Tauhid*. In Allâh's Statement,

﴿ٱعْبُدُوا۟ ٱللَّهَ﴾

"Worship Allâh (alone),"

is the *Tauhid* of Affirmation (*At-Tauhid Al-Muthabbit*), and in His Statement,

﴿وَٱجْتَنِبُوا۟ ٱلطَّـٰغُوتَ﴾

"...and avoid (or keep away from) *At-Tâghût*",

is the negation of associating partners with Allâh (*Nafyi Al-Ishraak*). The word *At-Tâghût* is a derivation of the word *Ṭughyaan*, which is everything by which a worshipper transgresses his limit, whether it is something (or someone) that is worshipped, followed or obeyed.

Concerning His Statement,

﴿وَقَضَىٰ رَبُّكَ﴾

"And your Lord has decreed..."

[2] This means that He has commanded and ordained.

And His Statement,

﴿قُلْ تَعَالَوْا أَتْلُ مَا حَرَّمَ رَبُّكُمْ عَلَيْكُمْ أَلَّا تُشْرِكُوا بِهِ شَيْئًا وَبِالْوَالِدَيْنِ إِحْسَانًا﴾

"Say (O Muhammad ﷺ): Come, I will recite what your Lord has made forbidden for you; that you do not associate anything as partner with Him...' (6:151)[1]

And His Statement,

﴿وَاعْبُدُوا اللَّهَ وَلَا تُشْرِكُوا بِهِ شَيْئًا﴾

"Worship Allâh and do not associate anything as a partner with Him." (4:36)[2]

﴿أَلَّا تَعْبُدُوا إِلَّا إِيَّاهُ﴾

"...that you worship none but Him." (17:23)

This means: Restrict worship to Him Alone, besides all else. Allâh has commanded and ordained this. This is the meaning of the statement *"Lāilāha illallāh (None has the right to be worshipped but Allâh) in conformity. Thus, the implication of this Verse is clear in that At-Tauhid* is to single out the acts of worship for Allâh, or the realization of the statement, "None has the right to be worshipped but Allâh."

[1] Concerning His Statement,

﴿قُلْ تَعَالَوْا أَتْلُ مَا حَرَّمَ رَبُّكُمْ عَلَيْكُمْ أَلَّا تُشْرِكُوا بِهِ شَيْئًا﴾

"Say (O Muhammad ﷺ): Come, I will recite what your Lord has made forbidden for you; that you do not associate anything as partner with Him..." (6:151)

The intended meaning of the statement is, "Say (O Muhammad ﷺ): Come, I will recite what your Lord has made forbidden for you; He has ordained that you do not associate anything with Him as a partner." This means that He has commanded you, and the ordainment here is legislative (religiously). Thus, when the ordainment from Allâh is legislative (religiously), then it is an obligatory command. The Verse alludes to *At-Tauhid* just as that which preceded it.

[2] Concerning His Statement,

﴿وَاعْبُدُوا اللَّهَ وَلَا تُشْرِكُوا بِهِ شَيْئًا﴾

Ibn Mas'ud رَضِيَ اللهُ عَنْهُ said,

مَنْ أَرَادَ أَنْ يَنْظُرَ إِلَى وَصِيَّةِ مُحَمَّدٍ ﷺ الَّتِي عَلَيْهَا خَاتَمُهُ فَلْيَقْرَأْ قَوْلَهُ تَعَالَىٰ:

"Whoever wants to look at the will of Muhammad ﷺ, upon which is his seal, let him read the statement of Allâh, the Most High,

﴿قُلْ تَعَالَوْا۟ أَتْلُ مَا حَرَّمَ رَبُّكُمْ عَلَيْكُمْ ۖ أَلَّا تُشْرِكُوا۟ بِهِۦ شَيْـًٔا ۖ وَبِٱلْوَٰلِدَيْنِ إِحْسَٰنًا ۖ - إِلَىٰ قَوْلِهِ -: وَأَنَّ هَٰذَا صِرَٰطِى مُسْتَقِيمًا فَٱتَّبِعُوهُ ۖ وَلَا تَتَّبِعُوا۟ ٱلسُّبُلَ﴾ الآية

"Say (O Muhammad ﷺ): Come, I will recite what your Lord has made forbidden for you; that you do not associate anything as a partner with Him... (Up to) ...And verily, this is My Straight Path, so follow it and do not follow the (other) ways." (6:151-153)[1]

It is narrated that Mu'āth bin Jabal رَضِيَ اللهُ عَنْهُ said, I was riding behind the Prophet ﷺ on a donkey and he said to me:

"Worship Allâh and do not associate anything as a partner with Him." (4:36)

This Verse proves the prohibition of all the types of *Ash-Shirk* (associating partners with Allâh): Major *Shirk* (*Ash-Shirk ul-Akbar*), Minor *Shirk* (*Ash-Shirk ul-Asghar*), and Hidden *Shirk* (*Ash-Shirk ul-Khafy*). Likewise, it is not allowed to associate an angel, a Prophet, a righteous person, stones, trees, or a *Jinn* as a partner with Allâh, because these are (created) things.

[1] Ibn Mas'ud رَضِيَ اللهُ عَنْهُ said, "Whoever wants to look at the will of Muhammad ﷺ, upon which is his seal..."

This means that if it were decreed that he left a will and placed his seal on it, and then it was opened after his death - it would be these Verses that contain ten ordainments (or bequeathals). This statement of Ibn Mas'ud proves the great status of these Verses, which begin with the prohibition of *Ash-Shirk*. This proves that this is the most crucial, the first and the most important of matters.

«يَامُعَاذُ، أَتَدْرِي مَا حَقُّ اللهِ عَلَى الْعِبَادِ، وَ حَقُّ الْعِبَادِ عَلَى اللهِ؟».

"O Mu'āth, do you know what is the right of Allâh on his Slaves and what is the right of the Slaves upon Allâh?"

I responded, "Allâh and His Messenger know best." He said,

«حَقُّ اللهِ عَلَى الْعِبَادِ أَنْ يَعْبُدُوهُ وَلَا يُشْرِكُوا بِهِ شَيْئًا، وَحَقُّ الْعِبَادِ عَلَى اللهِ أَنْ لَا يُعَذِّبَ مَنْ لَا يُشْرِكُ بِهِ شَيْئًا»

"The Right of Allâh upon the Slaves is that they worship Him (alone) and not associate anything with Him. The right of the Slaves upon Allâh is that He does not punish whoever does not associate anything with Him."[1]

I said, "O Messenger of Allâh, shall I not give the glad tidings to the people?" He replied:

«لَا تُبَشِّرْهُم فَيَتَّكِلُوا»

"Do not inform them lest they rely (on this promise and lapse in their service to Him)."[2]

---

[1] He said: It is narrated that Mu'āth bin Jabal رَضِيَ اللهُ عَنْهُ said, "I was riding behind the Prophet ﷺ on a donkey and he said to me:

«يَامُعَاذُ، أَتَدْرِي مَا حَقُّ اللهِ عَلَى الْعِبَادِ، وَحَقُّ الْعِبَادِ عَلَى اللهِ؟ قَالَ: حَقُّ اللهِ عَلَى الْعِبَادِ أَنْ يَعْبُدُوهُ وَلَا يُشْرِكُوا بِهِ شَيْئًا».

"O Mu'āth, do you know what is the right of Allâh on his slaves and what is the right of the slaves upon Allâh?" ...He said, "The Right of Allâh upon the slaves is that they worship Him (alone) and not associate anything with Him."

This right is a right that is obligatory for Allâh, the Mighty and Majestic. This is because the Book (Al-Qur'ān) and the *Sunnah*, and even all of the Messengers, came with this right, its clarification and that it is the most binding of obligations upon the slaves (of Allâh).

[2] Then he said:

حَقُّ الْعِبَادِ عَلَى اللهِ أَنْ لَا يُعَذِّبَ مَنْ لَا يُشْرِكُ بِهِ شَيْئًا»

They (Al-Bukhari and Muslim) recorded this *Hadith* in the *Saḥiḥayn*.

Important issues of the Chapter

1) The wisdom behind the creation of the jinn and mankind.
2) That worship is *At-Tauhid*, since it is the subject in which there is dispute (between the Prophets and the polytheists).
3) That whoever does not come with it (*At-Tauhid*), then he does not (truly) worship Allâh. Concerning this is the meaning of Allâh's Statement,

   ﴿وَلَآ أَنتُمْ عَـٰبِدُونَ مَآ أَعْبُدُ﴾

   "Nor do you worship that which I worship." (109:3)
4) The wisdom behind sending the Messengers.
5) That the Message (of *At-Tauhid*) encompasses (i.e. has come to) every nation.
6) That the religion of the Prophets is one (and the same).
7) The major issue: That the worship of Allâh cannot occur except with rejection of *At-Tâghût*. Concerning this is the meaning of Allâh's Statement,

---

"The right of the slaves upon Allâh is that He does not punish whoever does not associate anything with Him."

"The right of the slaves upon Allâh..." This is a right that Allâh has enforced upon Himself according to the agreement of the people of knowledge. Allâh, the Mighty and Majestic forbids for Himself whatever He wills in accordance with His Wisdom, and He obligates upon Himself whatever He wills in accordance with His Wisdom. This is similar to His Statement in the sacred *Hadith* (*Al-Hadith ul-Qudsi*):

«إِنِّي حَرَّمْتُ الظُّلْمَ عَلَى نَفْسِي»

"Verily I have made oppression forbidden for Myself."

﴿فَمَن يَكْفُرْ بِٱلطَّٰغُوتِ وَيُؤْمِنۢ بِٱللَّهِ فَقَدِ ٱسْتَمْسَكَ بِٱلْعُرْوَةِ ٱلْوُثْقَىٰ﴾

"So whoever disbelieves in *At-Tâghût* and believes in Allâh, he has grasped the most trustworthy handle." (2:256)

8) That *At-Tâghût* is generally applicable to all that is worshipped other than Allâh.

9) The great importance that the *Salaf* (early generations of the Muslims) gave to the three decisive Verses of *Surah Al-An'âm* (6:151-153). This Verse contains ten issues, the first of them being the prohibition of *Ash-Shirk*.

10) The decisive Verses of *Surah Al-Isrâ'* (17:22-39). These Verses contain eighteen issues and Allâh begins them with His Statement,

﴿لَّا تَجْعَلْ مَعَ ٱللَّهِ إِلَٰهًا ءَاخَرَ فَتَقْعُدَ مَذْمُومًا مَّخْذُولًا﴾

"Do not set up any other *ilâh* (god) with Allâh, or you will sit down rebuked, forsaken." (17:22)

And He concluded them with His Statement,

﴿وَلَا تَجْعَلْ مَعَ ٱللَّهِ إِلَٰهًا ءَاخَرَ فَتُلْقَىٰ فِى جَهَنَّمَ مَلُومًا مَّدْحُورًا﴾

"And do not set up any other ilâh (god) with Allâh lest you be thrown into Hell, blameworthy and rejected." (17:39)

Allâh has alerted us to the tremendous importance of these issues in His Statement,

﴿ذَٰلِكَ مِمَّآ أَوْحَىٰٓ إِلَيْكَ رَبُّكَ مِنَ ٱلْحِكْمَةِ﴾

"This is (part) of the wisdom that your Lord has revealed to you." (17:39)

11) The Verse of *Surah An-Nisâ'* (4:36), which is called the verse of the ten rights. Allâh began these ten rights with

His Statement,

﴿وَٱعْبُدُوا ٱللَّهَ وَلَا تُشْرِكُوا بِهِۦ شَيْـًٔا﴾

"Worship Allâh and do not associate anything as a partner with Him." (4:36)

12) Drawing attention to the will of Allâh's Messenger ﷺ upon his death.

13) The knowledge of Allâh's right upon us.

14) The knowledge of the Slaves' right if they fulfil His right.

15) That this issue was not known by most of the Companions.

16) The permissibility of concealing knowledge for the common good.

17) It is recommended to give good news to the Muslim that pleases him.

18) The fear of depending solely upon the ampleness of Allâh's Mercy.

19) The statement of one who is asked about something that he does not know: "Allâh and His Messenger know best."

20) The permissibility of imparting knowledge specifically to some people rather than others.

21) The humbleness of the Prophet ﷺ in riding a donkey with another rider on the donkey behind him.

22) The permissibility of sharing a ride on an animal.

23) The virtue of Mu'āth bin Jabal.

24) The tremendous importance of this issue (i.e. *At-Tauhid*).

Chapter 1

The Virtue of *At-Tauhid* and what Sins it Expiates*

Allâh the Most High said,

﴿ٱلَّذِينَ ءَامَنُوا۟ وَلَمْ يَلْبِسُوٓا۟ إِيمَـٰنَهُم بِظُلْمٍ أُو۟لَـٰٓئِكَ لَهُمُ ٱلْأَمْنُ وَهُم مُّهْتَدُونَ﴾

"Those who believe and do not mix their belief with any *Dhulm*, for them there is security and they are guided ones." (6:82)[1]

---

* This means its expiation of sins. Thus, the more the slave increases in the actualization of *At-Tauhid*, the more he is likely to enter Paradise, whatever his deeds may be. For this reason the *Imaam* - may Allâh have mercy upon him - mentioned the Verse of *Surah Al-An'âm* (6:82).

[1] And Allâh the Most High said,

﴿ٱلَّذِينَ ءَامَنُوا۟ وَلَمْ يَلْبِسُوٓا۟ إِيمَـٰنَهُم بِظُلْمٍ أُو۟لَـٰٓئِكَ لَهُمُ ٱلْأَمْنُ وَهُم مُّهْتَدُونَ﴾

"Those who believe and do not mix their belief with *Zulm*, for them there is security and they are guided ones." (6:82)

The word *Zulm* (wrongdoing, oppression) here means *Ash-Shirk*. This is like what has been narrated in the *Hadith* of Ibn Mas'ud that the Prophet ﷺ said concerning this Verse when the Companions considered it to be something tremendous (i.e. too difficult). They said, "O Messenger of Allâh! Which of us does not wrong himself (i.e. by committing sins)?!" The Prophet ﷺ replied,

«لَيْسَ الَّذِي تَذْهَبُونَ إِلَيْهِ، الظُّلْمُ: الشِّرْكُ، أَلَمْ تَسْمَعُوا لِقَوْلِ الْعَبْدِ الصَّالِحِ: ﴿إِنَّ ٱلشِّرْكَ لَظُلْمٌ عَظِيمٌ﴾

"It is not that which you think. The *Zulm* is *As-Shirk*. Don't you hear the statement of the righteous slave (Luqmaan), 'Verily *Ash-Shirk* (associating partners with Allâh) is a great *Zulm* (wrongdoing, oppression and injustice) indeed.'" (31:13)

Thus, the meaning of the Verse according to what is appropriate for this chapter is: Those who believe and do not mix their faith up with any *Shirk*;

'Ubaadah bin As-Saamit رَضِـيَ اللهُ عَـنْـهُ narrated that Allâh's Messenger ﷺ said,

«مَنْ شَهِدَ أَنْ لَا إِلٰهَ إِلَّا اللهُ وَحْدَهُ لَا شَرِيكَ لَهُ، وَأَنَّ مُحَمَّدًا عَبْدُهُ وَرَسُولُهُ، وَأَنَّ عِيسَى عَبْدُاللهِ ورَسُولُهُ وَكَلِمَتُهُ أَلْقَاهَا إِلَى مَرْيَمَ وَرُوحٌ مِنْهُ، وَالْجَنَّـةَ حَقٌّ، وَالنَّارَ حَقٌّ. أَدْخَلَهُ اللهُ الْجَنَّةَ عَلَى مَا كَانَ مِنَ الْعَمَلِ».

"Whoever testifies that there is none worthy of being worshipped but Allâh, Who has no partner, and that Muhammad is His slave and Messenger, and that 'Eesa (Jesus) is the Slave of Allâh, His Messenger, and His Word which He bestowed in Maryam (Mary) and a spirit (created) from Him, and that Paradise is true, and that the Fire is true, Allâh will admit him into Paradise, whatever his deeds may be. [1]

---

for them there is security and they are guided ones. Thus, the virtue of the one who believes - meaning he singles out Allâh with *At-Tauhid*, and he does not mix his faith up with any *Dhulm*, meaning he does not mix his belief in *At-Tauhid* up with any *Shirk* - is that for him is complete security and guidance. Hence, the more *At-Tauhid* is decreased by the servant being covered with some types of *Dhulm*, which is *Ash-Shirk*, the more the security and guidance leaves him in relative proportion to that.

[1] He then said: 'Ubaadah bin Aṣ-Ṣaamit رَضِيَ اللهُ عَنْهُ narrated that Allâh's Messenger ﷺ said,

«مَنْ شَهِدَ أَنْ لَا إِلٰهَ إِلَّا اللهُ وَحْدَهُ لَا شَرِيكَ لَهُ، وَأَنَّ مُحَمَّدًا عَبْدُهُ وَرَسُولُهُ. . . الحديث»

"Whoever testifies that there is none worthy of being worshipped but Allâh, Who has no partner, and that Muhammad is His slave and Messenger..."

until he said:

«عَلَى مَا كَانَ»

«"Whatever his deeds may be."»

They (*Al-Bukhari* and *Muslim*) both recorded this *Hadith*.

They (*Al-Bukhari* and *Muslim*) also recorded the *Hadith* of 'Itbaan:

«فَإِنَّ اللهَ حَرَّمَ عَلَى النَّارِ مَنْ قَالَ: لَا إِلٰهَ إِلَّا اللهُ، يَبْتَغِي بِذَلِكَ وَجْهَ اللهِ».

"Indeed Allâh has forbidden for Hell the person who says: 'There is nothing worthy of being worshipped but Allâh,' seeking thereby the Face of Allâh."[1]

Abu Sa'eed Al-Khudri narrated that Allâh's Messenger ﷺ said,

«قَالَ مُوسَىٰ: يَارَبِّ عَلِّمْنِي شَيْئًا أَذْكُرُكَ وَأَدْعُوكَ بِهِ، قَالَ: قُلْ يَامُوسَى: لَا إِلٰهَ إِلَّا اللهُ، قَالَ: يَارَبِّ كُلُّ عِبَادِكَ يَقُولُونَ هَذَا. قَالَ: يَامُوسَىٰ، لَوْ أَنَّ السَّمٰوَاتِ السَّبْعَ وَعَامِرَهُنَّ غَيْرِي، وَالْأَرَضِينَ السَّبْعَ فِي كِفَّةٍ، وَلَا إِلٰهَ إِلَّا اللهُ فِي كِفَّةٍ، مَالَتْ بِهِنَّ لَا

This means, even if he was deficient in his deeds and he had sins and acts of disobedience. This is from the bounty of *At-Tauhid* upon its people.

[1] He then said: They (*Al-Bukhari* and *Muslim*) also recorded the *Hadith* of 'Itbaan:

«فَإِنَّ اللهَ حَرَّمَ عَلَى النَّارِ مَنْ قَالَ: لاَ إِلٰهَ إِلاَّ اللهُ، يَبْتَغِي بِذَلِكَ وَجْهَ اللهِ».

"Indeed Allâh has forbidden for Hell the person who says: 'There is nothing worthy of being worshipped but Allâh,' seeking thereby the Face of Allâh."

When a person says this statement, which is the statement of *At-Tauhid*, seeking the Face of Allâh by it, and he comes with its conditions and its requirements, Allâh favors him and gives him what He has promised him of making him forbidden for the Fire. And this is a great bounty and favor.

However, whoever comes with *At-Tauhid* and abstained from that which contradicts it, yet he had some sins and acts of disobedience, and he died without repenting, then he is under the Will of Allâh. If Allâh wills, He will punish him, then - after some time - He will make the Fire forbidden for him, and if He wills, He will forgive him and make the Fire forbidden for him initially (without punishment).

إِلٰهَ إِلَّا اللهُ».

"Mûsâ (Moses) said: 'O my Lord, teach me something by which I can remember You and supplicate to You.' Allâh answered: 'Say, O Mûsâ, *Lā ilāha illallāh* (none has the wright to be worshipped but Allâh).' Mûsâ said: 'O my Lord, all your slaves say this.' Allâh said: 'O Mûsâ, if the seven heavens and all of their inhabitants besides Me, and the seven earths were in a pan (of a scale), and *Lā ilāha illallāh* was in (another) pan, *Lā ilāha illallāh* would outweigh them.'"

Ibn Hibbaan and Al-Haakim recorded this, and he (Al-Haakim) graded it authentic (*Saheeh*).

At-Tirmithi recorded a *Hadith* that he graded good (*Ḥasan*), from Anas (who said): "I heard Allâh's Messenger ﷺ saying,

«قَالَ اللهُ عَزَّ وَجَلَّ: يَاابْنَ آدَمَ، لَوْ أَتَيْتَنِي بِقُرَابِ الْأَرْضِ خَطَايَا، ثُمَّ لَقِيتَنِي لَا تُشْرِكُ بِي شَيْئًا، لَأَتَيْتُكَ بِقُرَابِهَا مَغْفِرَةً».

'Allâh the Most High said, "O son of Aadam! If you came to Me with sins filling the earth, then you met Me without associating anything with Me, I would come to you with its (the earth's) fill of forgiveness."'[1]

---

[1] Abu Sa'eed Al-Khudree narrated that Allâh's Messenger ﷺ said,

«قَالَ مُوسَىٰ: يَارَبِّ عَلِّمْنِي شَيْئًا أَذْكُرُكَ وَأَدْعُوكَ بِهِ، قَالَ: قُلْ يَامُوسَى: لَا إِلٰهَ إِلَّا اللهُ...»

"Moosaa (Moses) said: 'O my Lord, teach me something by which I can remember You and supplicate to You.' Allâh answered: 'Say, O Moosaa, *Lā ilāha illallāh* (non has the wright to be worshipped but Allâh)..."

This means that if it is imagined that the sins of the servant reached the weight of the seven heavens and the weight of all that they contain of slaves and angels, and the weight of the earth, the statement *Lāilāha illallāh* would outweigh that weight of sins. This is the great virtue of the statement of *At-Tauhid* and it is only for whoever the statement becomes

Important issues of the Chapter

1) The abundance of Allâh's favor.
2) The numerous rewards of *At-Tauhid* with Allâh.
3) Along with this it expiates sins.
4) Explanation of the verse which is in *Surah Al-An'âm* (6:82).
5) Notice the five points in the *Hadith* of 'Ubaadah.
6) That when you combine it (the *Hadith* of 'Ubaadah) with the *Hadith* of 'Itbaan and that which follows it, the meaning of the statement *Lā ilāha illallāh* becomes clear to you, and the mistake of those who have been deceived also becomes clear to you.
7) Drawing attention to the condition which is in the *Hadith* of 'Itbaan.
8) The fact that the Prophets needed to be made aware of the virtue of *Lā ilāha illallāh*.
9) Drawing attention to its (the statement *Lā ilāha illallāh*) outweighing all of creation, along with the fact that many of those who say it lighten its weight in the scale.
10) The text which proves that the earths are seven just as the heavens (are seven).
11) That they have inhabitants.
12) Confirmation of the attributes, contrary to (the understanding of) the *Ash'ariyyah*.
13) That if you know the *Hadith* of Anas, then you know that

---

strong in his heart. Therefore, he becomes sincere in it and a firm believer in it, having no doubts concerning what it implies. He believes in what it contains and he loves what it implies. Thus, its effect becomes strong in the heart and it enlightens it, and as long as it is like this, it burns (away) whatever it meets of sins.

the Prophet's statement in the *Hadith* of 'Itbaan,

«فَإِنَّ اللهَ حَرَّمَ عَلَى النَّارِ مَنْ قَالَ: لاَ إِلٰهَ إِلَّا اللهُ، يَبْتَغِي بِذَلِكَ وَجْهَ اللهِ».

"Indeed Allâh has forbidden for Hell the person who says, 'none has the right to be worshipped but Allâh,' seeking thereby the Face of Allâh,"

that it is by abandoning *Ash-Shirk*, not simply saying it with the tongue.

14) Notice the combined mentioning of both 'Isâ (Jesus) and Muhammad as two Slaves of Allâh and His Messengers.

15) Knowing that 'Isâ was particularily as being the Word of Allâh.

16) Knowing that he ('Isâ عَلَيْهِ السَّلَام) was a spirit from Him (Allâh).

17) Knowing the virtue of belief in Paradise and the Fire.

18) Knowing his (the Prophet's ﷺ) statement,

"...whatever his deeds may be."

19) Knowing the *Al-Meezaan* (scale) has two pans.

20) Knowing the usage of the term "Face" (of Allâh).

Chapter 2

Whoever Actualizes *At-Tauhid* will enter Paradise without a Reckoning*

Allâh the Most High said,

﴿إِنَّ إِبْرَٰهِيمَ كَانَ أُمَّةً قَانِتًا لِّلَّهِ حَنِيفًا وَلَمْ يَكُ مِنَ ٱلْمُشْرِكِينَ﴾

"Verily Ibrâhîm was an *Ummah* (a leader having all the good and righteous qualities), or a nation, obedient to Allâh, *Hanîfa* and he was not one of those who were *Al-Mushrikûn* (disbelielievers in the Oneness of Allâh, and those who joined partners with Allâh)." (16:120)[1]

---

* This chapter holds a loftier status than the clarification of the virtue of *At-Tauhid* (i.e. the previous chapter). For verily all of the people of *At-Tauhid* share in the virtue of *At-Tauhid*. However, only the special people of this *Ummah* (nation) are the ones who truly actualize (i.e. fulfil and accomplish) *At-Tauhid*. The actualization of *At-Tauhid* is the subject of this chapter.

[1] Concerning the statement of Allâh the Most High,

﴿إِنَّ إِبْرَٰهِيمَ كَانَ أُمَّةً قَانِتًا لِّلَّهِ حَنِيفًا وَلَمْ يَكُ مِنَ ٱلْمُشْرِكِينَ﴾

"Verily Ibrâhîm was an *Ummah* (a leader having all the good and righteous qualities), or a nation, obedient to Allâh, *Hanîfa* and he was not one of those who were *Al-Mushrikûn* (disbelielievers in the Oneness of Allâh, and those who joined partners with Allâh)."(16:120)

This Verse contains the evidence that Ibrâhîm was one who truly actualized (and manifested) *At-Tauhid*. The proof is in the fact that Allâh, the Mighty and Majestic, described him with characteristics:

The first is that he was an *Ummah*, and *Ummah* means the leader who gathers all of the qualities of human perfection and attributes of goodness. This means that he was not lacking in anything of the characteristics of goodness, and this is the meaning of actualizing *At-Tauhid*.

The second description is that he was *Qaanit* (devoutly obedient) to Allâh. This contains confirmation concerning the necessity of obedience and the

And He said,

﴿وَٱلَّذِينَ هُم بِرَبِّهِمْ لَا يُشْرِكُونَ﴾

"And those who join not anyone as partners with their Lord." (23:59)[1]

---

necessity of the particulars of *At-Tauhid*.

In His saying *Ḥaneef* is a rejection of the way of the polytheists and turning away from them. That way (of the polytheists) contains *Ash-Shirk, Al-Bid'ah* (religious innovation) and disobedience (i.e. sin). These three things are from the manners of the polytheists (*Mushrikūn*): *Ash-Shirk, Al-Bid'ah* and disobedience without repentance or seeking forgiveness.

Then He said,

﴿وَلَمْ يَكُ مِنَ ٱلْمُشْرِكِينَ﴾

"...and he was not of those who ascribed partners to Allâh."

This means that he did not commit *Ash-Shirk* with its various types and he stayed away from the polytheist (*Mushrikūn*).

The Shaikh - may Allâh have mercy upon him - brings forth these meanings from the Verse. Hence, the Verse indicates to the Shaikh that its meaning is regarding the actualization of *At-Tauhid*.

[1] And concerning His Statement,

﴿وَٱلَّذِينَ هُم بِرَبِّهِمْ لَا يُشْرِكُونَ﴾

"And those who join not anyone as partners with their Lord." (23:59)

This is a negation of *Ash-Shirk*. For indeed the participle of negation when its influence is over the present tense verb, it suggests the generality of the verbal noun that is concealed within the verb. Thus, the meaning is as if He had said, "They do not commit *Ash-Shirk* (associate partners) - not a major act of *Ash-Shirk*, nor a minor act of *Ash-Shirk*, nor a hidden act of *Ash-Shirk*." The person who does not associate partners with Allâh is a *Muwaḥhid* (true monotheist; one who practices *At-Tauhid*). Hence, we have a necessary conclusion in this, and it is that whoever does not associate partners with Allâh by any form of *Ash-Shirk*, then he does not abandon *Ash-Shirk* except for His (Allâh's) At-*Tauhid*.

The scholars have said, "Allâh has placed the word *'Rabbihim'* (their Lord) first here because *Ar-Ruboobiyyah* (Lordship) necessitates *Al-'Uboodiyyah* (Worship and Servitude)." This (what is mentioned in this Verse) is the

Ḥuṣayn bin 'Abdur-Raḥmaan said, "I was once with Sa'eed bin Jubayr when he said, 'Who among you saw the shooting star last night?' I answered, 'I did.' Then I said, 'I was not in prayer (at that time), but I was stung (by an insect or scorpion).' He said, 'What did you do?' I replied, 'I used *Ruqyah*.' He said, 'What compelled you to do that?' I said, 'A *Hadith* that Ash-Sha'bee related to us.' He said, 'What did he tell you all?' I said, 'He narrated to us from Buraydah bin Al-Ḥuṣayb that he (the Prophet ﷺ) said:

«لاَ رُقْيَةَ إِلَّا مِنْ عَيْنٍ أَوْ حُمَةٍ».

"There is no *Ruqyah* except from the evil-eye or a poisonous sting."

He responded, 'He has done well who stops on what he has heard (i.e. acts according to it). However, Ibn 'Abbaas narrated to us from the Prophet ﷺ that he said,

«عُرِضَتْ عَلَيَّ الْأُمَمُ، فَرَأَيْتُ النَّبِيَّ ومَعَهُ الرَّهْطُ، وَالنَّبِيَّ ومَعَهُ الرَّجُلُ وَالرَّجُلاَنِ، وَالنَّبِيَّ ولَيْسَ مَعَهُ أَحَدٌ، إِذْ رُفِعَ لِي سَوَادٌ عَظِيمٌ، فَظَنَنْتُ أَنَّهُمْ أُمَّتِي، فَقِيلَ لِي: هَذَا مُوسَىٰ وَقَوْمُهُ، فَنَظَرْتُ فَإِذَا سَوَادٌ عَظِيمٌ، فَقِيلَ لِي: هَذِهِ أُمَّتُكَ ومَعَهُمْ سَبْعُونَ أَلْفًا يَدْخُلُونَ الْجَنَّةَ بِغَيْرِ حِسَابٍ وَلَا عَذَابٍ»

"The nations were displayed before me, and I saw a Prophet with a small group of people, and a Prophet

---

description of those who have manifested and actualized *At-Tauhid*, because by necessity, whoever does not commit *Ash-Shirk*, then his desires do not commit *Ash-Shirk*. And if the person commits *Ash-Shirk*, his desires come with innovations (i.e. religious heresies) or acts of disobedience (i.e. sins). Therefore, the negation of *Ash-Shirk* is a negation of *Ash-Shirk* in all of its types, a negation of *Al-Bid'ah* (innovation) and a negation of disobedience. This is the actualization of *At-Tauhid* for Allâh, the Mighty and Majestic.

> with a man or two, and a Prophet who had no one at all with him. Then a great mass of people appeared before me and I thought that they were my nation. But it was said to me, 'This is Mûsâ and his people.' Then I looked and there was another great mass of people. It was said to me, 'This is your nation and with them are seventy thousand people who will enter Paradise without any reckoning or punishment.'''

Then he stood and entered his house and the people began discussing those people. Some of them said, "Maybe they are those who accompanied Allâh's Messenger ﷺ." Some of them said, "Maybe they are those who were born in Islam and they never associated anything as a partner with Allâh." So they mentioned some other things (speculating about those people). Then, Allâh's Messenger ﷺ came out to them and they informed him (about what they had been saying). So he said,

«هُمُ الَّذِينَ لاَ يَسْتَرْقُونَ وَلَا يَكْتَوُونَ وَلَا يَتَطَيَّرُونَ وَعَلَى رَبِّهِمْ يَتَوَكَّلُونَ»

> "They are those who do not seek *Ruqyah*, they do not get themselves branded (cauterized), they do not follow omens and they put their trust in their Lord."

Then 'Ukkaashah bin Miḥsan stood and said, "Supplicate to Allâh that He makes me of them." He (the Prophet ﷺ) said,

«أَنْتَ مِنْهُمْ»

"You are of them."

Then another man stood and said, "Supplicate to Allâh that He makes me of them." He replied,

«سَبَقَكَ بِهَا عُكَّاشَةُ».

"Ukkaashah has beaten you to it."[1]

---

[1] In reference to the *Hadith*, the point of evidence in it is the Prophet's

statement,

«نَظَرْتُ فَإِذَا سَوَادٌ عَظِيمٌ، فَقِيلَ لِي: هَذِهِ أُمَّتُكَ وَمَعَهُمْ سَبْعُونَ أَلْفًا يَدْخُلُونَ الْجَنَّةَ بِغَيْرِ حِسَابٍ وَلَا عَذَابٍ»

"Then I looked and there was another great mass of people. It was said to me, 'This is your nation and with them are seventy thousand people who will enter Paradise without any reckoning or punishment.'"

Then he stood and entered his house and the people began discussing those people. Some of them said,

"Maybe they are those who accompanied Allâh's Messenger ﷺ." Some of them said, "Maybe they are those who were born in Islam and they never associated anything as a partner with Allâh." So they mentioned some other things (speculating about those people). Then, Allâh's Messenger ﷺ came out to them and they informed him (about what they had been saying). So he said,

«هُمُ الَّذِينَ لاَ يَسْتَرْقُونَ وَلَا يَكْتَوُونَ وَلَا يَتَطَيَّرُونَ وَعَلَى رَبِّهِمْ يَتَوَكَّلُونَ»

"They are those who do not seek *Ruqyah*, they do not get themselves branded (cauterized), they do not follow omens and they put their trust in their Lord."

The mentioning of these characteristics is not meant to suggest that those who manifest and actualize *At-Tauhid* do not seek the means (for their needs), as some people understand it. These people think that it is from perfection that one does not seek the means (for his needs) at all or that one should not seek medical treatment at all. This is a mistake because the Prophet ﷺ had *Ruqyah* performed for himself, he treated ailments, he commanded for illness to be treated, and he also commanded one of the Companions to use cauterization and other similar things as well. Therefore, this *Hadith* does not contain a suggestion that these people do not seek the means of cure. These three things are only mentioned in particular because they often become attached to the heart and cause the person to turn (with total reliance) to the one who performs the *Ruqyah*, or to the cauterizing, or the one who performs the cauterization or to the belief in omens. Thus, in these things is that which may cause a decrease in *At-Tawakkul* (reliance upon and trust in Allâh). Yet, treating ailments is Islamically legal. In some situations doing so may be obligatory, or recommended or simply allowed. The Prophet ﷺ said,

Important issues of the Chapter

1) Knowing the (various) levels of the people in *At-Tauhid.*
2) What is the meaning of its actualization (or fulfillment)?
3) Allâh's praising of Ibrâhîm due to his not being of the *Mushrikūn* (polytheists).
4) Allâh's praising of the foremost of the *Awliyaa'* for their being safe from committing *Ash-Shirk.*
5) The fact that avoiding *Ar-Ruqyah* and cauterization is from traits of actualizing *At-Tauhid.*
6) That which gathers all of these traits is *At-Tawakkul.*
7) The depth of the companion's knowledge in their awareness that they could not achieve the actualization of *At-Tauhid* except with deeds.
8) Their (the Companion's) eagerness for that which is good.
9) The virtue of this *Ummah* (nation) in both quantity and quality.
10) The virtue of the followers of Mûsâ.
11) The nations being presented before him (Prophet Muhammad ﷺ).
12) That every nation will be gathered individually with its Prophet.
13) The small number of those who responded to (the call of) the Prophets.
14) That whoever (of the Prophets) did not have anyone respond to him (i.e. his call), he will come alone (on the

---

«تَدَاوُوا عِبَادَ اللهِ وَلَا تَتَدَاوُوا بِحَرَامٍ»

"Treat your ailments, O slaves of Allâh, but do not treat with what is forbidden (*Ḥaraam*)."

Day of Resurrection).

15) The fruit of this knowledge is that one should not be deceived by great numbers, nor should he renounce the few.

16) The permission to perform *Ar-Ruqyah* to treat the evil eye and poisonous stings.

17) The deep knowledge of the *Salaf*. This is understood by his (Sa'eed bin Jubayr) saying, "He has done well who stops on what he has heard (i.e. acts according to it). However..." Thus, it is known that the first *Hadith* does not contradict the second.

18) The *Salaf's* refraining from praising a person for a quality that he did not possess.

19) The Prophet's statement, "You are of them", is a sign from the signs of Prophethood.

20) The virtue of 'Ukkaashah.

21) The usage of allusions in speech without being direct.

22) The excellent character of the Prophet ﷺ.

Chapter 3

Fear of *Ash-Shirk**

Allâh the Mighty and Majestic said,

﴿إِنَّ ٱللَّهَ لَا يَغۡفِرُ أَن يُشۡرَكَ بِهِۦ وَيَغۡفِرُ مَا دُونَ ذَٰلِكَ لِمَن يَشَآءُۚ﴾

"Verily Allâh forgives not that partners should be set up with Him, but He forgives except that (anything else) to whom He wills;" (4:48, 116)[1]

---

* The actualization (and fulfillment) of At-Tawheed with its people is accompanied by the fear of Ash-Shirk. He who fears Ash-Shirk will strive to avoid it by knowing its meaning and its types so that he will not fall into it.

[1] Concerning the Statement of Allâh, the Mighty and Majestic,

﴿إِنَّ ٱللَّهَ لَا يَغۡفِرُ أَن يُشۡرَكَ بِهِۦ وَيَغۡفِرُ مَا دُونَ ذَٰلِكَ لِمَن يَشَآءُۚ﴾

"Verily Allâh forgives not that partners should be set up with Him, but He forgives except that (anything else) to whom He wills;" (4:48, 116)

Some of the people of knowledge have said, "This proves that *Ash-Shirk* that is mentioned here (in this Verse) is the major, minor and hidden forms of *Ash-Shirk*. Thus, Allâh will not forgive all the forms of *Ash-Shirk*, except with repentance. This is due to the magnitude of the sin of *Ash-Shirk* since Allâh is the One Who creates, provides sustenance, gives and favors (His creatures) with bounties. Therefore, how can the heart turn away from Him to other than Him?" This is the view preferred by Shaikh ul-Islam Ibn Taymiyyah, Ibn Al-Qayyim, *Al-Imam* Muhammad bin 'Abdul-Wahhab and most of the scholars of the *Da'wah* (i.e. the call to *At-Tauhid*, the authentic *Sunnah* and the way of the *Salaf*).

Hence, if *Ash-Shirk* with its various types will not be forgiven, this necessitates that it should be feared with the utmost of fear. If *Ar-Riyaa'* (showing off), or swearing by other than Allâh, or hanging amulets, or using rings or string (as charms), or attributing blessings to other than Allâh will not be forgiven, then it necessitates the utmost of fear from it. Likewise is the case with the major *Shirk* (*Ash-Shirk ul-Akbar*). If *Ash-Shirk* occurs in the category of the hearts of the slaves, then the slave should seek to know its types, its categories and its particulars so that he will not fall into it.

And *Al-Khaleel* (Prophet Ibrâhîm) عَلَيْهِ السَّلَام said,

﴿وَٱجْنُبْنِي وَبَنِيَّ أَن نَّعْبُدَ ٱلْأَصْنَامَ﴾

"And keep me and my sons away from worshipping idols." (14:35)[1]

And in the *Hadith*,

«أَخْوَفُ مَا أَخَافُ عَلَيْكُمُ الشِّرْكُ الْأَصْغَرُ»

"The thing that I fear most for you all is the minor *Shirk* (*Ash-Shirk ul-Asghar*)."

He was asked about it (i.e. what it was) and he said,

«الرِّيَاءُ».

"Ar-Riyaa' (showing off)."[2]

---

[1] Then, after this Verse, the Shaikh - may Allâh have mercy upon him - mentioned the statement of Allâh, the Mighty and Majestic,

﴿وَٱجْنُبْنِي وَبَنِيَّ أَن نَّعْبُدَ ٱلْأَصْنَامَ﴾

"And keep me and my sons away from worshipping idols." (14:35)

And this is the statement of perfection of those who have actualized *At-Tauhid*. They are not complacent; rather they fear *Ash-Shirk* and those things that lead to it. The word *Aṣnaam* (idols) is the plural of *Ṣanam*, and it is that which is in the form of something that is worshipped other than Allâh. It may be in the form of the face of a man, or the body of an animal, or the head of an animal. It may also be in the form of the sun, and the moon and other similar things. The word *Wathn* (another word for idol) means everything that is worshipped besides Allâh, whether it is in the form of an image - which includes *Aṣnaam* - or it is not in the form of an image; for example, a grave.

And in the *Hadith*,

«أَخْوَفُ مَا أَخَافُ عَلَيْكُمُ الشِّرْكُ الْأَصْغَرُ»

"The thing that I fear most for you all is the minor *Shirk* (*Ash-Shirk ul-Asghar*)."

[2] He was asked about it (i.e. what it was) and he said, *"Ar-Riyaa'* (showing off)." Why did the Prophet ﷺ fear it and why was it the greatest

Ibn Mas'ud رَضِيَ اللهُ عَنْهُ narrated that the Prophet ﷺ said,

«مَنْ مَاتَ وَهُوَ يَدْعُو مِنْ دُونِ اللهِ نِدًّا دَخَلَ النَّارَ»

"Whoever dies while calling upon a rival (god) other than Allâh will enter the Fire." Al-Bukhari recorded this *Hadith*.[1]

---

of the sins that should be feared? Due to its resulting consequence, which is that it would not be forgiven. It is also due to the fact that the people are heedless of it, and for this reason the Prophet ﷺ feared this for them. *Ar-Riyaa'* (showing off) is of two types:

The *Riyaa'* of the hypocrite, which is showing off regarding the foundation of the religion (*Deen* of Islam). This means that the person outwardly exhibits Islam while he is inwardly hiding *Al-Kufr* (disbelief). Allâh says,

﴿يُرَآءُونَ ٱلنَّاسَ وَلَا يَذْكُرُونَ ٱللَّهَ إِلَّا قَلِيلًا﴾

"They show off for the people and they do not remember Allâh but little." (4:142)

The *Riyaa'* of the Muslim who believes in *At-Tauhid* (which is the second type of *Riyaa'*) is like the person perfecting his prayer so that he may be praised or seen, and this is the minor *Shirk* (*Ash-Shirk ul-Asghar*).

[1] Ibn Mas'ud رَضِيَ اللهُ عَنْهُ narrated that the Prophet ﷺ said,

«مَنْ مَاتَ وَهُوَ يَدْعُو مِنْ دُونِ اللهِ نِدًّا دَخَلَ النَّارَ»

"Whoever dies while calling upon a rival (god) other than Allâh will enter the Fire." Al-Bukhari recorded this *Hadith*.

Calling upon a rival (god) other than Allâh is a form of major *Shirk* (*Ash-Shirk ul-Akbar*), because supplication is worship. Rather, it is the greatest form of worship. It has been narrated in an authentic *Hadith* that the Prophet ﷺ said, "*Ad-Du'aa* (supplication, invocation, etc.) is worship."

So whoever dies while directing this worship or anything of it to other than Allâh - such as a rival god from the (false) rival gods - then he deserves the Fire.

Concerning his statement, "...will enter the Fire," this is like the situation of the disbelievers, who will abide in it forever, because the major *Shirk* (*Ash-Shirk ul-Akbar*) nullifies deeds if it occurs with the Muslim. Allâh, the Mighty and Majestic, said to His Prophet ﷺ,

﴿وَلَقَدْ أُوحِىَ إِلَيْكَ وَإِلَى ٱلَّذِينَ مِن قَبْلِكَ لَئِنْ أَشْرَكْتَ لَيَحْبَطَنَّ عَمَلُكَ وَلَتَكُونَنَّ مِنَ ٱلْخَـٰسِرِينَ﴾

Muslim records from Jaabir رَضِيَ اللهُ عَنْهُ that Allâh's Messenger ﷺ said,

«مَنْ لَقِيَ اللهَ لَا يُشْرِكُ بِهِ شَيْئًا دَخَلَ الْجَنَّةَ، وَمَنْ لَقِيَهُ يُشْرِكُ بِهِ شَيْئًا دَخَلَ النَّارَ».

"Whoever meets Allâh (on the Day of Judgement) without having associated anything with Him will enter Paradise, and whoever meets Him having associated anything with Him will enter the Fire."[1]

"And indeed it has been revealed to you (O Muhammad ﷺ) and to those (Allâh's Messengers) before you: "if you join others in worship with Allâh, (then) surely your deeds will be in vain and you will certainly be among the losers." (39:65)

The wording (in the *Hadith*)

«مِنْ دُونِ اللهِ»

"...other than Allâh,"

according to the scholars of *Tafseer* (interpretation of the Qur'ān) and the scholars of *Taḥqeeq* (investigation and verification), includes whoever calls upon Allâh while calling upon some other besides Allâh, and whoever calls upon other than Allâh, while turning completely to that thing instead of Allâh.

[1] Muslim records from Jaabir رَضِيَ اللهُ عَنْهُ that Allâh's Messenger ﷺ said,

«مَنْ لَقِيَ اللهَ لَا يُشْرِكُ بِهِ شَيْئًا».

"Whoever meets Allâh (on the Day of Judgement) without having associated anything with Him..."

This means that the person does not commit *Ash-Shirk* in any of its forms, nor does he turn to anyone (as an associate with Allâh) - not an angel, a Prophet, a righteous person, or a *Jinn*.

Concerning his statement,

«دَخَلَ الْجَنَّةَ»

"...will enter Paradise,"

it means that Allâh, the Mighty and Majestic, has promised him entry into Paradise by His Mercy and Favor.

The statement,

Important issues of the Chapter

1) Fear of *Ash-Shirk*.
2) That *Ar-Riyaa'* (showing off) is a form of *Shirk*.
3) That it (*Ar-Riyaa'*) is a form of minor *Shirk*.
4) That it is thing most feared for the righteous people.
5) The nearness of the Paradise and the Fire.
6) The mention of their nearness being combined in one *Hadith*.
7) That whoever meets Allâh without associating anything with Him will enter Paradise, and whoever meets Him while associating anything with Him will enter the Fire, even if he was the most devout worshipper among the people.
8) The great issue is the request of *Al-Khaleel* (Ibrâhîm) that both he and his sons be protected from the worship of idols.
9) His (Ibrâhîm's) consideration of the situation of most people in his saying,

---

«مَنْ لَقِيَهُ يُشْرِكُ بِهِ شَيْئًا دَخَلَ النَّارَ»

"...and whoever meets Him having associated anything with Him will enter the Fire,"

includes the major *Shirk, the minor Shirk* and the hidden *Shirk*.

Does entry into the Fire here mean eternally or for a limited time? The answer is that it depends upon the *Shirk*. If the *Shirk* was the major *Shirk* and the person died upon it, then he will enter the Fire eternally and he will never come out of it. If the *Shirk* was less than the major *Shirk*, like the minor or hidden *Shirk*, then verily its practitioner - if he knows it is *Shirk* - is under the threat of entering the Fire and remaining in it for an amount of time that Allâh knows. Then, after this he will be taken out of the Fire because he was among the people of *At-Tawheed*.

﴿رَبِّ إِنَّهُنَّ أَضْلَلْنَ كَثِيرًا مِّنَ ٱلنَّاسِ﴾

"My Lord, they have indeed led astray many among mankind." (14:36)

10) This contains the explanation of the statement *"Lā ilāha illallāh* (none has the right to be worshipped but Allâh), as mentioned by Al-Bukhari.

11) The virtue of whomever is free of *Ash-Shirk*.

Chapter 4

The Invitation to Testify that there is Nothing Worthy of Being Worshipped Except Allâh*

Allâh the Most High said,

﴿قُلْ هَٰذِهِۦ سَبِيلِىٓ أَدْعُوٓا۟ إِلَى ٱللَّهِ ۚ عَلَىٰ بَصِيرَةٍ﴾ الآية

"Say (O Muhammad ﷺ): 'This is my way; I invite unto Allâh with sure knowledge,.''' (12:108)[1]

---

* The Shaikh - may Allâh have mercy upon him - arranged this chapter to show that it is from the perfection of fearing *Ash-Shirk* and the completion of *At-Tauhid* that a person invites to *At-Tauhid.* This is the reality of the testimony that none has the right to be worshipped but Allâh, because it means the person's belief, his stating it, and his informing others of what it (the testimony) means.

The invitation to *At-Tauhid* is the invitation to the details of *At-Tauhid,* its particular aspects and the prohibition of *Ash-Shirk* and its types. This is from the important matters and it is what the Imam - may Allâh have mercy upon him - is explaining in this book.

[1] Concerning the Statement of Allâh the Most High,

﴿قُلْ هَٰذِهِۦ سَبِيلِىٓ أَدْعُوٓا۟ إِلَى ٱللَّهِ﴾

"Say (O Muhammad ﷺ): 'This is my way; I invite unto Allâh,'''

Meaning, and not to other than Him. This contains two points of benefit:

The first is that the *Da'wah* (Islamic invitation) is to *At-Tauhid.*

The second is drawing attention to the matter of sincerity (*Al-Ikhlaaṣ*). This is because many people, even if they call to the truth, they really are only calling to (the worship of) themselves.

Concerning the Statement,

﴿عَلَىٰ بَصِيرَةٍ﴾

"...with sure knowledge."

This means that he invites with knowledge, certainty and awareness, and he does not invite to Allâh upon ignorance.

Then Allâh says,

﴿أَنَا۠ وَمَنِ ٱتَّبَعَنِى ۖ وَسُبْحَٰنَ ٱللَّهِ وَمَآ أَنَا۠ مِنَ ٱلْمُشْرِكِينَ﴾

Ibn 'Abbaas رَضِيَ اللهُ عَنْهُ narrated that when Allâh's Messenger ﷺ sent Mu'āth رَضِيَ اللهُ عَنْهُ to Yemen he said to him,

«إِنَّكَ تَأْتِي قَوْمًا مِنْ أَهْلِ الْكِتَابِ، فَلْيَكُنْ أَوَّلَ مَا تَدْعُوهُمْ إِلَيْهِ شَهَادَةُ أَنْ لَا إِلٰهَ إِلَّا اللهُ».

"Verily you will come to a people from the People of the Scripture, so let the first thing that you call them to be the testimony that none has the right to be worshipped but Allâh.

In another narration he said:

«أَنْ يُوَحِّدُوا اللهَ»

That they single out Allâh Alone.

«فَإِنْ هُمْ أَطَاعُوكَ لِذَلِكَ فَأَعْلِمْهُمْ أَنَّ اللهَ افْتَرَضَ عَلَيْهِمْ خَمْسَ صَلَوَاتٍ فِي كُلِّ يَوْمٍ وَلَيْلَةٍ، فَإِنْ هُمْ أَطَاعُوكَ لِذَلِكَ فَأَعْلِمْهُمْ أَنَّ اللهَ افْتَرَضَ عَلَيْهِمْ صَدَقَةً تُؤْخَذُ مِنْ أَغْنِيَائِهِمْ فَتُرَدُّ عَلَى فُقَرَائِهِمْ وَاتَّقِ دَعْوَةَ الْمَظْلُومِ فَإِنَّهُ لَيْسَ بَيْنَهَا وَبَيْنَ اللهِ حِجَابٌ»

If they obey you in that, then instruct them that Allâh has obligated them to perform five prayers (*Aṣ-Ṣalaah*) every day and night. If they obey you in that, then instruct them that Allâh has obligated them to give charity that is to be taken from their wealthy and distributed to their

---

"I and whosoever follows me. And Glorified and Exalted is Allâh (above all that they associate as partners with Him), and I am not of the polytheists." (12:108)

This means, I invite to Allâh with *Baseerah* (clear knowledge and evidence), and so does whoever follows me from those who have accepted my invitation. For indeed they invite to Allâh with *Baseerah*.

Thus, this is the characteristic of the followers of the Prophets. That is that they do not only fear *Ash-Shirk*, and they do not only know *At-Tauhid* and act according to it. Rather, they also invite (others) to this, and this is an inevitable matter.

poor. If they obey you in that, then beware of taking the best of their possessions, and fear the supplication of the oppressed, for there is no veil between it and Allâh." (Al-Bukhari and Muslim both recorded it).[1]

They (Al-Bukhari and Muslim) also recorded from Sahl bin Sa'd رَضِيَ اللهُ عَنْهُ that on the Day of Khaybar Allâh's Messenger ﷺ said,

«لَأُعْطِيَنَّ الرَّايَةَ غَدًا رَجُلًا يُحِبُّ اللهَ وَرَسُولَهُ وَيُحِبُّهُ اللهُ وَرَسُولُهُ يَفْتَحُ اللهُ عَلَى يَدَيْهِ»

"Tomorrow I shall indeed give the flag to a man who loves Allâh and His Messenger, and Allâh and His Messenger love him. Allâh will grant victory by his hands."

So the people spent their night discussing which of them it would be given to. When they awoke the next morning they came to Allâh's Messenger ﷺ and each of them was hoping to be given it (the flag). Allâh's Messenger ﷺ said,

«أَيْنَ عَلِيُّ بْنُ أَبِي طَالِبٍ»

"Where is 'Ali bin Abi Tâlib?"

It was said, "He is suffering from an ailment in his eyes." So they sent for him and he was brought. He (Allâh's Messenger ﷺ) spat in his eyes and supplicated for him, and he was cured as if there had not been suffering from any pain. Then he gave him the flag and said,

---

[1] Ibn 'Abbaas رَضِيَ اللهُ عَنْهُ narrated that when Allâh's Messenger ﷺ sent Mu'āth̩ to Yemen...

The point of concern here is that the Prophet ﷺ commanded Mu'āth̩ that when he invited (to Islam) to make the first matter of the invitation be to the testimony that none worshipped except Allâh. This is explained by another narration recorded by Al-Bukhari in the Book of *At-Tauhid* in his *Saheeh*, in which he said, "That they single Allâh out (for worship)."

«انْفُذْ عَلَى رِسْلِكَ حَتَّى تَنْزِلَ بِسَاحَتِهِمْ ثُمَّ ادْعُهُمْ إِلَى الْإِسْلَامِ وَأَخْبِرْهُمْ بِمَا يَجِبُ عَلَيْهِمْ مِنْ حَقِّ اللهِ تَعَالَى، فَوَاللهِ لَأَنْ يَهْدِيَ اللهُ بِكَ رَجُلًا وَاحِدًا خَيْرٌ لَكَ مِنْ حُمْرِ النَّعَمِ»

"Proceed with ease until you arrive at their encampment. Then invite them to Islam and inform them of what is obligatory upon them from the rights of Allâh, the Most High. By Allâh, if Allâh guides one man by you it is better for you than red camels."[1]

Important issues of the Chapter

1) That the invitation to Allâh is the way of whoever follows Allâh's Messenger ﷺ.

2) The emphasis upon sincerity (*Al-Ikhlaaṣ*), because many of the people, if they call to the truth, they (actually) are calling to themselves.

---

[1] They (Al-Bukhari and Muslim) also recorded from Sahl bin Sa'd رَضِيَ اللهُ عَنْهُ that on the Day of Khaybar Allâh's Messenger ﷺ said,

«لَأُعْطِيَنَّ الرَّايَةَ غَدًا . . .»

"Tomorrow I shall indeed give the flag..."

The point of concern here is the statement, "Then invite them to Islam." The invitation to Islam is the invitation to *At-Tauhid*, because the greatest pillar of Islam is the testimony that there is none worthy of being worshipped except Allâh and that Muhammad is Allâh's Messenger. The Prophet ﷺ added to it that he also invites them to the rights of Allâh in it. This means in Islam, from the aspect of *At-Tauhid* and from the aspect of the obligatory duties and avoiding the forbidden things. For this reason it is obligatory in the invitation to Al-Islam that the foundation of the invitation be *At-Tauhid* and the explanation of the meaning of the two testimonies (*Lā ilāha illallāh wa Muhammadur-Rasoolul-laah*), should be an explanation of the forbidden things and the obligatory duties, because the foundation of the foundations is given precedence, and thus it is the first obligation.

3) That *Al-Baseerah* (clear proof and knowledge) is from the obligations.
4) From the signs of the beauty of *Tawḥeed* (in one's belief) is that it removes Allâh, the Most High, from any blasphemy.
5) That from the ugliness of *Ash-Shirk* is that it is blasphemy against Allâh.
6) Among the most important issues is the Muslim distancing himself from the polytheists so that he does not become one of them, even if he does not commit *Ash-Shirk*.
7) That *At-Tauhid* is the first obligation.
8) That it precedes everything, even the prayer (*Aṣ-Ṣalaah*).
9) That the meaning of "That they single out Allâh," is the (same) meaning of the testimony that non has the wright to be worshipped but Allâh (*Lā ilāha illallāh*).
10) That a person may be of the People of the Scripture (i.e. Jew or Christian) and not know this (testimony of *At-Tauhid*), or he may know it but not act according to it.
11) Emphasis upon teaching step by step (in stages).
12) Beginning with what is most important first, and so forth in order of importance.
13) Distribution of *Az-Zakâh*.
14) The person with knowledge removing any doubtful matter for the one who is learning.
15) The prohibition of taking the best of the people's possessions (for *Az-Zakâh*).
16) Guarding against the supplication of the oppressed.
17) The information that it (the supplication of the oppressed) is not hindered (from acceptance).

18) From the evidences of *At-Tauhid* is that which happened with the leader of the Messengers and the leaders of the *Awliyaa'* (righteous believers) of difficulty, hunger and afflictions.

19) His saying, "I shall indeed give the flag..." is a sign from the signs of the Prophethood.

20) His applying spit to the eyes of 'Ali was also a sign from the Prophetic signs.

21) The virtue of 'Ali رَضِيَ اللهُ عَنْهُ.

22) The virtue of the Companions in their discussion during that night (as to who would receive the flag) and their being preoccupied with it instead of the tidings of the forthcoming victory.

23) Faith in the decree (*Al-Qadar*), due to its (the flag) being acquired by he who did not strive for it and its being withheld from those who sought it.

24) The etiquette in his statement, "Proceed with ease..."

25) The invitation to Islam before fighting.

26) That it (fighting) is legislated for whoever has been invited to Islam before and was fought.

27) The invitation should be with wisdom. This is due to his statement, "...inform them of what is obligatory."

28) Being aware of the rights of Allâh in Islam.

29) The reward of a person by whose hand a single man is guided.

30) Swearing (by Allâh) in relation to the issuance of a religious verdict.

Chapter 5

The Explanation of *At-Tauhid* and the Testimony that None has the right to be Worshipped but Allâh*

Allâh the Most High said,

﴿أُوْلَٰٓئِكَ ٱلَّذِينَ يَدْعُونَ يَبْتَغُونَ إِلَىٰ رَبِّهِمُ ٱلْوَسِيلَةَ أَيُّهُمْ أَقْرَبُ﴾ الآية.

"Those whom they call upon desire (for themselves)

---

* Testifying contains certain things:

First: The belief in what one is about to say and testify to. Belief is not called belief unless there is knowledge and certainty with it.

Second: To speak it (i.e. profess it verbally).

Third: To inform of that and announce it. Hence, one says it with his tongue from the point of necessity, and he also is not called a testifier until he informs others of what he has testified to.

Therefore, the word *"Ash-hadu"* (I testify) means: I believe, I say, I announce and inform. These three things are collectively mandatory.

Concerning the statement *"Lā ilāha illallāh"*, the word *"Laa"* negates the right of *Al-Uloohiyyah* (worship and servitude) from anyone other than Allâh, the Mighty and Majestic. When the word *"illaa"* comes after the negation, it is a participle of exception and hence it gives an increase in meaning, which is limiting and restricting. Thus, the meaning is, "True divinity (or god-hood), or the true God is Allâh, solely and restrictively. There is no true god other than Him, besides all else."

The word *"ilaah"* means that which is worshipped and the predicate *"Laa"* is placed generically for grammar and it is not understood to mean existence (as in no *Ilaah* exists...). This is because the gods that are worshipped along with Allâh exist (i.e. other gods are worshipped besides Allâh). Thus, the predicate becomes meaningful with your saying, "with a right (to be worshipped)," or "true". Hence, the meaning of the statement *"Lâilâha bi-haqqin"* means: There is none that has the right to be worshipped. Therefore, everyone who is worshipped other than Allâh the Mighty and Majestic is really being worshipped, but he is worshipped in falsehood, injustice, transgression and violation (of what is right). This is what is understood by the Arab who hears the statement *"Lā ilāha illallāh."*

means of access to their Lord." (17:57)[1]

And His Statement,

﴿وَإِذْ قَالَ إِبْرَٰهِيمُ لِأَبِيهِ وَقَوْمِهِۦٓ إِنَّنِى بَرَآءٌ مِّمَّا تَعْبُدُونَ ۝ إِلَّا ٱلَّذِى فَطَرَنِى﴾

"And when Ibrâhîm (Abraham) said to his father and his people, 'Verily, I am innocent of what you worship, except Him who did create me; and verily, He will guide me.'" (43:26,27)[2]

---

[1] Concerning the Statement of Allâh the Most High,

﴿أُو۟لَٰٓئِكَ ٱلَّذِينَ يَدْعُونَ﴾

"Those whom they call upon..." (17:57)

This means, (those whom) they worship.

Then He says,

﴿يَبْتَغُونَ إِلَىٰ رَبِّهِمُ ٱلْوَسِيلَةَ﴾

"...themselves seek a means (*Al-Waseelah*) to their Lord."

Al-Waseelah is the goal and the need. This means that they only seek their needs from Allâh and Allâh is specifically singled out for that. Thus, they do not turn to other than Him, and they restrict and limit their turning to Him, the Mighty and Majestic. This statement has come here with the wording of Lordship (*Ar-Ruboobiyyah*) because answering supplication and granting is from the particulars of Lordship. Hence, the explanation of *At-Tauhid* appears in the Verse, and it is that every need among the needs only comes by Allâh, the Mighty and Majestic. Then Allâh says, "And they hope for His Mercy and fear His Torment." And this is particularly the case of the worshippers (or slaves) of Allâh. That is that in their worship they combine love, fear and hope, and this is the explanation of *At-Tauhid*.

[2] Concerning His Statement,

﴿وَإِذْ قَالَ إِبْرَٰهِيمُ لِأَبِيهِ وَقَوْمِهِۦٓ إِنَّنِى بَرَآءٌ مِّمَّا تَعْبُدُونَ ۝ إِلَّا ٱلَّذِى فَطَرَنِى فَإِنَّهُۥ سَيَهْدِينِ﴾

"And when Ibrâhîm (Abraham) said to his father and his people, 'Verily, I am innocent of what you worship, except Him who did created me, and verily He will guide me.'" (43: 26,27)

And His Statement,

﴿ٱتَّخَذُوٓا۟ أَحْبَارَهُمْ وَرُهْبَـٰنَهُمْ أَرْبَابًا مِّن دُونِ ٱللَّهِ﴾ الآية

"They (Jews and Christians) took their rabbis and monks as lords besides Allâh." (9:31)[1]

And His Statement,

﴿وَمِنَ ٱلنَّاسِ مَن يَتَّخِذُ مِن دُونِ ٱللَّهِ أَندَادًا يُحِبُّونَهُمْ كَحُبِّ ٱللَّهِ﴾

"And among mankind are those who take others besides Allâh as rivals (to Allâh). They love them as they love

---

This Verse contains negation and affirmation and it is the implication of the statement of *At-Tauhid*. The statement *"Laa ilaaha"* corresponds with the statement in the Verse,

﴿إِنَّنِى بَرَآءٌ مِّمَّا تَعْبُدُونَ﴾

"Verily, I am innocent of what you worship."

The statement *"illal-laah"* corresponds with the statement in the Verse,

﴿إِلَّا ٱلَّذِى فَطَرَنِى﴾

"except the One Who created me."

Al-Baraa'ah (declaration of innocence) is that the person hates what is worshipped besides Allâh, he disbelieve in it and he stands opposed to it. Submission in Islam cannot be correct unless this position is held in the person's heart.

[1] Concerning Allâh's Statement,

﴿ٱتَّخَذُوٓا۟ أَحْبَارَهُمْ وَرُهْبَـٰنَهُمْ أَرْبَابًا مِّن دُونِ ٱللَّهِ﴾

"They (Jews and Christians) took their rabbis and monks as lords (*Arbaab*) besides Allâh." (9:31)

The word *Arbaab* is the plural of *Rabb* and *Ar-Ruboobiyyah* (Lordship) here means *Al-'Ibaadah* (worship). This means they took their rabbis and their monks as objects of worship (i.e. gods). The next phrase,

﴿مِّن دُونِ ٱللَّهِ﴾

"...besides Allâh,"

means with Allâh. That is because they obeyed them in making the forbidden lawful and making the lawful forbidden with belief (in its correctness). And obedience is from *At-Tauhid*.

Allâh." (2:165)[1]

In the *Saheeh* it is reported that the Prophet ﷺ said,

«مَنْ قَالَ: لَا إِلٰهَ إِلَّا اللهُ، وَكَفَرَ بِمَا يُعبَدُ مِنْ دُونِ اللهِ، حَرُمَ مَالُهُ وَدَمُهُ وَحِسَابُهُ عَلَى اللهِ عَزَّ وَجَلَّ».

"Whoever says, *'Lā ilāha illallāh'* and disbelieves in whatever is worshipped besides Allâh,[2] his wealth and

---

[1] Concerning His Statement,

﴿وَمِنَ ٱلنَّاسِ مَن يَتَّخِذُ مِن دُونِ ٱللَّهِ أَندَادًا يُحِبُّونَهُمْ كَحُبِّ ٱللَّهِ﴾

"And among mankind are those who take others besides Allâh as rivals (to Allâh). They love them as they love Allâh." (2:165)

This means that they make the love of these gods equal to the love of Allâh. Thus, they love Allâh with intense love, but they also love these gods with intense love. This equality in love is *Ash-Shirk*. This is the thing that makes them from the people of the Fire, just as Allâh the Mighty and Majestic said in *Surah Ash-Shu'araa'* while informing about the statement of the people of the Fire,

﴿تَٱللَّهِ إِن كُنَّا لَفِى ضَلَٰلٍ مُّبِينٍ ○ إِذْ نُسَوِّيكُم بِرَبِّ ٱلْعَٰلَمِينَ﴾

"By Allâh, we were truly in a manifest error when we held you (false gods) as equals (in worship) with the Lord of all that exists." (26:97-98)

Therefore, love is a type of worship, and when they did not single Allâh out with it, they began taking rival gods other than Allâh. This is the meaning of *At-Tauhid* and the meaning of the testimony that there is none worthy of being worshipped except Allâh (*Lā ilāha illallāh*).

[2] In the *Saheeh* it is reported that the Prophet ﷺ said,

«مَنْ قَالَ: لاَ إِلٰهَ إِلاَّ اللهُ، وَكَفَرَ بِمَا يُعبَدُ مِنْ دُونِ اللهِ...»

"Whoever says, *'Lā ilāha illallāh' and disbelieves in whatever is worshipped besides Allâh...*"

This *Hadith* contains a stipulation that is more than simply making the statement. Along with saying the statement *"Lā ilāha illallāh"* there must also be disbelief in whatever is worshipped besides Allâh. The statement *"Lā ilāha illallāh"* includes disbelief and renunciation of everything that is worshipped besides Allâh.

blood becomes sacred and his reckoning is with Allâh, the Mighty and Majestic."[1]

The explanation of this matter is in the chapters that follow it.[2]

This Chapter Contains the Greatest and Most Important issues

These issues are the explanation of *At-Tauhid* and the explanation of the testimony (*Ash-Shahaadah*) and between them there are certain clear matters:

Among them: The verse of *Surah Al-Israa'* (17:57) in which Allâh clarifies the refutation against the polytheists who call upon the righteous in supplications. It also contains a clarification that this is the major *Shirk*.

---

[1] Then he said,

«حَرُمَ مَالُهُ وَدَمُهُ وَحِسَابُهُ عَلَى اللهِ عَزَّ وَجَلَّ»

"...his wealth and blood becomes sacred and his reckoning is with Allâh, the Mighty and Majestic."

This is because whoever says *"Lā ilāha illallāh"* and disbelieves in whatever is worshipped besides Allâh becomes a Muslim, and the wealth and blood of the Muslim is not lawful (to be taken) except for one of three things. Thus, it becomes clear to you that the explanation of *At-Tauhid* and the explanation of the testimony *Lā ilāha illallāh* requires more attention, observance, care and deliberation from you so that you understand it according to its evidence (or its reasoning).

[2] The explanation of this matter is in the chapters that follow it. This entire book is the explanation of *At-Tauhid* and the explanation of the statement *Lā ilāha illallāh*, and it is a clarification of what opposes this. It is also a clarification of what contradicts the foundation of *At-Tauhid* and what contradicts is perfection. It is a clarification of the major *Shirk*, the minor *Shirk*, the hidden *Shirk* and the *Shirk* of words and statements. It is also a clarification of the necessities of *At-Tauhid* - particularly *Tauhid ul-'Ibaadah* (the *Tauhid* of Worship) - such as affirming Names and Attributes for Allâh, and clarifying what *Tauhid ul-'Ibaadah* includes of affirming Lordship (*Ar-Ruboobiyyah*) for Allâh, the Mighty and Majestic.

Among them: The verse of *Surah Baraa'ah* (*At-Tawbah*, 9:31) in which Allâh clarifies that the People of the Scripture took their rabbis and their monks as lords besides Allâh. He also explained that they were only commanded to worship One God. Along with this is the verse's interpretation, which contains no ambiguity, which is obeying scholars and devout worshippers in sinful disobedience (to Allâh), and not calling upon them (in worship).

Among them: The statement of *Al-Khaleel* (Ibrâhîm عَلَيْهِ السَّلَام) to the disbelievers,

﴿إِنَّنِي بَرَآءٌ مِّمَّا تَعْبُدُونَ ○ إِلَّا ٱلَّذِى فَطَرَنِى﴾

"Verily, I am innocent of what you worship, except Him who did create me." (43:26-27)

So he (Ibrâhîm) excluded his Lord (Allâh) from those others deities that were being worshipped. Allâh mentions that this disavowal (from false gods) and this loyal adherence (to Allâh alone) is the explanation of the testimony *Lā ilāha illallāh*. Hence, Allâh said,

﴿وَجَعَلَهَا كَلِمَةًۢ بَاقِيَةً فِى عَقِبِهِۦ لَعَلَّهُمْ يَرْجِعُونَ﴾

"And he made it (i.e. *Lā ilāha illallāh*) a Word lasting among his offspring that they may turn back (i.e. to repent to Allâh or receive admonition)." (43:28)

Among them: The verse of *Surah Al-Baqarah* (2:165) concerning the disbelievers, whom Allâh said concerning them,

﴿وَمَا هُم بِخَٰرِجِينَ مِنَ ٱلنَّارِ﴾

"And they will not come out of the Fire." (2:167)

He mentioned that they love their rival gods as they love Allâh. This shows that they have immense love for Allâh, yet that does not enter them into the fold of Islam. So how about someone who loves the rival god greater than his love for Allâh? And how about someone who only loves the rival god alone and he does not love Allâh at all?

Among them: There is the statement of the Prophet ﷺ,

«مَنْ قَالَ: لاَ إِلٰهَ إِلَّا اللهُ، وَكَفَرَ بِمَا يُعْبَدُ مِنْ دُونِ اللهِ، حَرُمَ مَالُهُ وَدَمُهُ وَحِسَابُهُ عَلَى اللهِ».

> "Whoever says, *'Lā ilāha illallāh'* and disbelieves in whatever is worshipped besides Allâh, his wealth and blood becomes sacred and his reckoning is with Allâh."

This is from the greatest things that explain the meaning of *Lā ilāha illallāh*. For verily he did not make the mere pronouncing of the words that which safeguards the blood and wealth. He also did not make mere awareness of the meaning with pronouncing its words sufficient, nor affirming that, nor the fact that the person does not invoke any but Allâh Alone without any partner. Rather, the wealth and the blood do not become sacred (forbidden to be taken) until disbelief in whatever is worshipped besides Allâh is added to this. So if the person has doubt or refuses (to reject belief in other false deities), then his wealth and blood are not sacred.

Thus, what an issue this is, as there is nothing greater or more important than this. And what an explanation this is, as there is nothing clearer than it, and there is no proof more decisive than it for the one who disputes.

Chapter 6

It is from *Ash-Shirk* to Wear a Ring, String or Anything Similar in Order to Remove Affliction or Prevent it*

Allâh said,

﴿قُلْ أَفَرَءَيْتُم مَّا تَدْعُونَ مِن دُونِ ٱللَّهِ إِنْ أَرَادَنِىَ ٱللَّهُ بِضُرٍّ هَلْ هُنَّ كَـٰشِفَـٰتُ ضُرِّهِۦٓ أَوْ أَرَادَنِى بِرَحْمَةٍ هَلْ هُنَّ مُمْسِكَـٰتُ رَحْمَتِهِۦ﴾ الآية

---

* This is an attempt to explain *At-Tauhid* by explaining its opposite. It is known that a thing is recognized and distinguished by two things: by its reality and awareness of its opposite. The *Imaam* - may Allâh have mercy upon him - begins to mention what is the opposite of *At-Tauhid.* That which opposes *At-Tauhid* also opposes its foundation, and it is the major *Shirk* (*Ash-Shirk ul-Akbar*). It (major *Shirk*) is that which if a responsible person comes with it, it nullifies his *Tauhid* and he becomes a *Mushrik* (polytheist) who commits the major *Shirk* that expels him from the religion of Islam. The second thing is that which contradicts the perfection of the obligatory *Tauhid*, and it is the minor *Shirk* (*Ash-Shirk ul-Asghar*). Hence, if a person comes with anything of it, he has contradicted by it the perfection of *At-Tauhid*. This is because the perfection of *At-Tauhid* can only be achieved by the removal of all forms of *Ash-Shirk*.

The Shaikh - may Allâh have mercy upon him - began expounding upon *Ash-Shirk* by explaining forms of minor *Shirk* (*Ash-Shirk ul-Asghar*) that often occur. He began with the minor *Shirk* before the major Shirk in order to move from that which is lower to that which is higher.

Concerning his statement, "Chapter: It is from *Ash-Shirk*", the word "from" here is for portioning. In other words, this form that is presented in this chapter is part of *Ash-Shirk*.

Then he says, "...to Wear a Ring, String or Anything Similar", which is like pearls, charms, a piece of iron, and anything similar that is worn. Also, similar to this is that which is hung in the homes, or in the cars, or on the small children, from that which is worn or hung along with a type of belief. All of this is included in this chapter and it is from *Ash-Shirk*. The Arabs used to have beliefs concerning the ring, the string and other similar items

"Say: 'Have you seen that which you call upon besides Allâh?[1] If Allâh wanted some harm for me, could they

---

like charms, etc. They used to believe that whoever hung one of these things would be affected by it and he would profit. This would either be by the removal of some affliction after it had occurred or preventing some affliction before its occurrence, and this was even greater (of an evil). The reason is that the person would believe that these worthless items that were placed could prevent the Decree of Allâh. Why was this a minor form of *Shirk*? Because the person's heart would be attached to it and he would make it a cause of removing affliction or preventing it. The principle in this chapter is that affirming the effective causes is not permissible unless it is a Islamically legislated cause or it is affirmed by actual experimentation that this thing truly has an obvious effect that is not hidden. An example would be the medicine administered by the doctor and some other causes, which have obvious benefits. For example, your being warmed by fire, or cooled by water or things similar to this. These apparent causes have clear effects. Then, verily all types of minor *Shirk* could be a major *Shirk* depending upon the condition of the person who committed it. Hence, whoever believes in the ring or the string - for example - that it is not a cause but it actually brings about the effects itself (i.e. it has powers), then this is a commission of major *Shirk* with Allâh. This is because in this case the person has given the control of matters in this existence to things along with Allâh, the Mighty and Majestic. Therefore, the pillar of this chapter is concerning the attachment of the heart.

[1] Allâh said,

﴿قُلْ أَفَرَءَيْتُم مَّا تَدْعُونَ مِن دُونِ ٱللَّهِ إِنْ أَرَادَنِىَ ٱللَّهُ بِضُرٍّ هَلْ هُنَّ كَـٰشِفَـٰتُ ضُرِّهِۦٓ﴾

"Say: 'Have you seen that which you call upon besides Allâh? If Allâh wanted some harm for me, could they remove His harm?'" (39:38)

This means: Say do you all confirm that the One Who created the heavens and the earth is Allâh alone, and then you turn to other than Him in worship?! This is the methodology of the Qur'ân. It argues against the polytheists (*Mushrikūn*) by that which they themselves affirm of *Tauhid ur-Rubûbiyyah* (the *Tauhid* of Allâh's Lordship) against that which they reject of *Tauhid ul-Ilaahiyyah* (the *Tauhid* of Allâh's Worship). This Statement,

﴿تَدْعُونَ﴾

remove His harm, or if He (Allâh) wanted some mercy for me, could they withhold His Mercy?''' (39:38)[1]

'Imraan bin Husayn رَضِيَ اللهُ عَنْهُ narrated that the Prophet ﷺ saw a man with a brass ring on his hand and he said to him,

«مَا هٰذِهِ؟»

"you call upon"

contains supplication of asking and supplication of worship, because they are two conditions among the conditions of the people who associate partners with Allâh. That which they call upon besides Allâh is of differing types. Among them there are those who turn to some of the Prophets, Messengers and righteous people. Among them there are those who take the angels (as objects of worship). Others turn to the stars (in worship). Others turn to trees and stones (in worship). And still others turn to idols and graven images.

[1] Allâh then said,

﴿إِنْ أَرَادَنِيَ ٱللَّهُ بِضُرٍّ هَلْ هُنَّ كَـٰشِفَـٰتُ ضُرِّهِۦٓ أَوْ أَرَادَنِى بِرَحْمَةٍ هَلْ هُنَّ مُمْسِكَـٰتُ رَحْمَتِهِۦ﴾

"If Allâh wanted some harm for me, could they remove His harm, or if He (Allâh) wanted some mercy for me, could they withhold His Mercy?" (39:38)

Allâh negates that there is for these gods, with their varying types, any ability to harm or bring benefit. Therefore, it is futile that there would be any attachment to these terrible gods that are thought to possess some positions of status with Allâh the Mighty and Majestic that necessitate their intercession. The *Salaf* presented the Verses that discuss the major *Shirk* in order to refute the minor *Shirk*, as there is collectively in both forms of *Shirk* an attachment to other than Allâh the Mighty and Majestic. Hence, if the attachment to that which is greater is futile, the attachment to that which is less then it is even more futile. This is also because the meaning that this issue is concerned with is the invalidation of anyone's power to cause harm other than Allâh, or that if Allâh afflicts anyone with some harm that there is someone who is able to remove it without the permission of Allâh. This meaning, which is the attachment to what harms and what benefits, is the meaning that causes the polytheist to be attached to the ring or string.

"What is this?"

The man replied, "It is (to protect) from *Al-Waahinah.*" The Prophet ﷺ said,

«انْزِعْهَا فَإِنَّهَا لاَ تَزِيدُكَ إِلَّا وَهْنًا، فَإِنَّكَ لَوْ مِتَّ وَهِيَ عَلَيْكَ مَا أَفْلَحْتَ أَبَدًا»

"Remove it, for verily it will not increase you except in weakness, and verily if you died with it on you, you would never be successful." Ahmad recorded this with a chain that has no problem with it.[1]

Ahmad also has a narration from 'Uqbah bin 'Aamir that is

---

[1] The Shaikh said, "Imraan bin Ḥusayn رَضِيَ اللهُ عَنْهُ narrated that the Prophet ﷺ saw a man with a brass ring on his hand and he said to him,

«مَا هٰذِهِ؟»

"What is this?"

His Statement "What is this", was made for severe rejection. The man said, "It is (to protect) from *Al-Waahinah*". *Al-Waahinah* is a type of illness that weakens the body. The Prophet ﷺ said, "Remove it." This is a command and if the person who is commanded obeys the command then you command him with the tongue and you do not rebuke him with the hand (i.e. physically). The Prophet ﷺ said,

«انْزِعْهَا فَإِنَّهَا لاَ تَزِيدُكَ إِلَّا وَهْنًا»

"Remove it, for verily it will not increase you except in weakness." This means that if it has any effect, its effect would only be harmful to the body. Also its effect is harmful to the spiritually and mentally, as it weakens the spirit and the soul from being able to deal with the weakness and illness. This is the situation of everyone who commits *Ash-Shirk*, for verily he goes from one harm to another that is more harmful than the first, even though he thinks he is benefiting. Then the Prophet ﷺ said,

«فَإِنَّكَ لَوْ مِتَّ وَهِيَ عَلَيْكَ مَا أَفْلَحْتَ أَبَدًا»

"and verily if you died with it on you, you would never be successful." The negation here means one of two things:

First: That the negated success is the absolute success, which is entry into

Marfoo' (attributed to the Prophet ﷺ) which states,

«مَنْ تَعَلَّقَ تَمِيمَةً فَلَا أَتَمَّ اللهُ لَهُ، وَمَنْ تَعَلَّقَ وَدْعَةً فَلَا وَدَعَ اللهُ لَهُ»

"Whoever hangs a charm (i.e. putting it on himself or others), may Allâh not fulfil (his objective) for him. And whoever hangs a sea shell (i.e. putting it on himself or others), may Allâh not grant him peace and tranquility."[1]

In another narration he said,

Paradise and salvation from the Fire. This is concerning the situation of the one who commits major *Shirk*, because he believes that this ring of brass or that string that is hung is independently capable of causing benefit.

Second: That what is negated here is some of the success. And that is if the person makes something a means from that which Allâh has not made a means, neither legislatively (in the Islamic Law) or by decree. This is concerning the situation of the one who commits minor *Shirk*.

[1] Aḥmad also has a narration from 'Uqbah bin 'Aamir that is *Marfoo'* (attributed to the Prophet ﷺ) which states,

«مَنْ تَعَلَّقَ تَمِيمَةً فَلَا أَتَمَّ اللهُ لَهُ»

"Whoever hangs a charm (i.e. putting it on himself or others), may Allâh not fulfil (his objective) for him."

The wording *"Ta'allaqa"* (hangs or attaches) includes the act of hanging or the attachment of the heart to what is hung. Thus, the person wears (something) and his heart becomes attached to what he wears.

The Prophet ﷺ said,

«مَنْ تَعَلَّقَ تَمِيمَةً فَلَا أَتَمَّ اللهُ لَهُ»

"Whoever hangs a charm (i.e. putting it on himself or others), may Allâh not fulfil (his objective) for him."

At-Tameemah (charm) is a type of pearls and things that are placed upon the chests in order to prevent the evil eye, or prevent some harm or envy, and things similar to that. Here the Prophet ﷺ supplicated against the person who hands *At-Tameemah* that Allâh not fulfil (his objective) for him. This is because *At-Tameemah* is called a *Tameemah* because it is believed that it *"Tutimmu"* (fulfils and completes) the affairs. Thus, the Prophet ﷺ supplicated against him that Allâh the Mighty and Majestic not

«مَنْ تَعَلَّقَ تَمِيمَةً فَقَدْ أَشْرَكَ».

"Whoever hangs a charm has committed *Shirk.*"

Ibn Abi Ḥâtim recorded from Huthayfah رَضِيَ اللهُ عَنْهُ that he saw a man who had a string on his hand (to protect him) from fever. So he cut it and recited Allâh's Statement,

﴿وَمَا يُؤْمِنُ أَكْثَرُهُم بِاللَّهِ إِلَّا وَهُم مُّشْرِكُونَ﴾.

"Most of them do not believe in Allâh without committing *Shirk.*" (12:106)[1]

---

fulfil his objective for him.

He then said, "And whoever hangs a sea shell (i.e. putting it on himself or others)..." *Al-Wada'ah* is a type of sea shell that is placed on people's chests or hung on the upper arm in order to protect against the evil eye and similar things.

Then he said,

«فَلاَ وَدَعَ اللهُ لَهُ»

"...may Allâh not grant him peace and tranquility."

This means may He (Allâh) not leave him in ease, tranquility and rest, because he has associated a partner with Allâh, the Mighty and Majestic.

[1] The Shaikh then says, "Ibn Abee Haatim recorded from Huthayfah رَضِيَ اللهُ عَنْهُ that he saw a man who had a string on his hand (to protect him) from fever." The word *"min"* (from) here is for justification. This means that he hung the string in order to remove the fever or in order to protect against the fever. Then he said, "So he cut it." This proves that this is a great evil that must be rejected and cut off.

The *Salaf* said concerning the Statement of Allâh the Most High,

﴿وَمَا يُؤْمِنُ أَكْثَرُهُم بِاللَّهِ﴾.

"Most of them do not believe in Allâh..."

This means that Allâh is the Lord, and He is the Supreme Provider, and He is the Protector and He is the One Who causes death. This means *Tauhid ur-Rubûbiyyah* (the *Tawḥid* of Lordship). Then He says, "...without committing *Shirk.* Meaning, they associate partners with Him in worship. Thus, *Tawḥid ur-Rubûbiyyah* does not save. Rather, it is necessary that Allâh be singled out in worship.

Important issues of the Chapter

1) The strict forbiddance of wearing rings, string and similar things for such purposes.
2) That if the companion had died with it on him he would not have been successful. This contains a proof for the statement of the Companions that the minor Shirk is greater than the major sins.
3) That this is not excused due to ignorance.
4) That it will not bring any benefit in this life, but it will cause harm. This is due to the Prophet's statement,

   «لَا تَزِيدُكَ إِلَّا وَهْنًا»

   "It will not increase you except in weakness."
5) The harsh rebuking of whomever does something like this.
6) The declaration that whoever hangs or attaches something will be entrusted to that thing.
7) The declaration that whoever hangs or attaches a charm (or amulet) has committed *Shirk*.
8) That hanging a string in order to prevent (or cure) fever is from this (*Shirk*).
9) Huthayfah's recitation of the verse is a proof that the Companions used the verses concerning the major *Shirk* as a proof against the minor *Shirk*. This is just like what Ibn 'Abbaas mentioned concerning the verse of *Surah Al-Baqarah*. (2:165)

This evidence is related to the major *Shirk*. The author - may Allâh have mercy upon him - said,

> "This shows that the Companions used to use that which was revealed concerning the major *Shirk* to refute the minor *Shirk*."

10) That hanging sea shells as a protection against the evil eye falls into this category.

11) Supplicating against whoever hangs a charm or amulet that Allâh not fulfil his objective for him, and for the one who wears a seashell that Allâh not grant him any tranquility. This latter supplication means may Allâh abandon him.

Chapter 7

What has been Related Concerning *Ar-Ruqaa* and *At-Tamaa'im**

It is recorded in the *Saheeh* from Abu Basheer *Al-Ansari* رَضِيَ اللهُ عَنْهُ that he was with Allâh's Messenger ﷺ during one of his journeys when he sent a messenger ordering,

---

* This chapter is related to the explanation of the ruling concerning *Ar-Ruqaa*. *Ar-Ruqaa* is the plural of *Ruqyah* and in actuality it is supplications and words that are said or recited and then they are blown (onto something or someone). Some types of *Ruqyah* have an effect upon the limbs of the body, some types have an effect upon the souls, some types of it are permissible and legislated, and other types are *Shirk*. The Legislator has allowed *Ar-Ruqaa* that is free of *Ash-Shirk*. The Prophet ﷺ said,

«لَا بَأْسَ بِالرُّقَى مَا لَمْ تَكُنْ شِرْكًا»

"There is nothing wrong with *Ar-Ruqaa* as long as it is not *Shirk*."

In reference to *Ar-Ruqaa* that contains *Shirk*, then it is that which contains seeking protection or help from other than Allâh, or it contains something from the names of the devils (*Ash-Shayaateen*), or the person who uses it believes that the *Ruqyah* itself has the power to bring about the desired effect. In this case the *Ruqyah* is not permissible and it is from the *Ruqaa* that is *Shirk*.

At-Tamaa'im is the plural of *Tameemah* and we have previously explained it. We mentioned that it is everything that is hung whether it is leather, pearls, words of remembrance (*Athkaar*), or words for protections. It may also be in the form of some shape, like the head of an animal, or a gazelle, or a horseshoe, or black shreds of paper, or charms in the form of an eye, or words of glorification in a particular shape. All of these are *At-Tamaa'im*. That which combines these things is that they are all things from which the fulfillment of some good is sought, or the fulfillment of the matter of preventing harm. This is something that is not been permitted according to the Islamic legislation or the decree. Some people say, "I hang (amulets) but I do not envision any of these meanings. I hang this (amulet) in the car for beauty, or in the house for decoration." A small group among the people say similar to this. We say, "If the person hangs

«أَنْ لَا يَبْقَيَنَّ فِي رَقَبَةِ بَعِيرٍ قِلَادَةٌ مِنْ وَتَرٍ، أَوْ قِلَادَةٌ إِلاَّ قُطِعَتْ».

"No necklace from a bow string should be left on the neck of a camel, or any type of necklace, except that it should be cut off."[1]

Ibn Mas'ud رَضِيَ اللهُ عَنْهُ said, "I heard Allâh's Messenger ﷺ saying,

«إِنَّ الرُّقَىٰ وَالتَّمَائِمَ وَالتِّوَلَةَ شِرْكٌ»

'Verily *Ar-Ruqaa, At-Tamaa'im* and *At-Tiwalah* are *Shirk*.'"[2]

Recorded by Ahmad and Abu Dawud.

At-Tamaa'im for protection or removal of affliction, then this is minor *Shirk* if he believes that it is a means (of bringing about what he seeks). If he hangs it for beautification, then it is forbidden because in doing so he resembles those who commit minor *Shirk*. The Prophet ﷺ said,

«مَنْ تَشَبَّهَ بِقَوْمٍ فَهُوَ مِنْهُمْ»

"Whoever imitates a people, then he is one of them."

[1] The command to cut the necklace was because the Arabs believed that it prevented the evil eye from effecting the camels and livestock animals, and this is a belief of *Shirk*.

[2] Ibn Mas'ud رَضِيَ اللهُ عَنْهُ said, "I heard Allâh's Messenger ﷺ saying,

«إِنَّ الرُّقَىٰ وَالتَّمَائِمَ وَالتِّوَلَةَ شِرْكٌ»

'Verily *Ar-Ruqaa, At-Tamaa'im* and *At-Tiwalah* are *Shirk*.'"

This *Hadith* contains emphasis and it means that all *Ruqaa* is a form of *Shirk*, and every *Tamaa'im* is a form of *Shirk* and every *Tiwalah* is a form of *Shirk*. This generality has been given a specific exception only in regards to the *Ruqaa* that is mentioned in the text. *Ar-Ruqaa* was given a specific exclusion by the Prophet's ﷺ statement,

«لَا بَأْسَ بِالرُّقَىٰ مَا لَمْ تَكُنْ شِرْكًا»

"There is nothing wrong with *Ar-Ruqaa* as long as it is not *Shirk*."

It was also given a specific exclusion by the fact that the Prophet ﷺ performed *Ruqyah* and he had *Ruqyah* performed on him. Therefore, the evidence shows that all types of *Ruqyah* are not *Shirk*. Rather, some types of *Ruqyah* are *Shirk*, and they are those types that contain *Shirk*. In

'Abdullah bin 'Ukaym narrated the following *Marfoo'* (i.e. attributed to the Prophet ﷺ) report:

«مَنْ تَعَلَّقَ شَيْئًا وُكِلَ إِلَيْهِ».

"Whoever hangs something is entrusted to it." (Recorded by Aḥmad and At-Tirmithi).[1]

---

reference to *At-Tamaa'im*, no types of it have been given a special exclusion from the type that is a form of *Shirk*. Therefore, all types of *At-Tamaa'im* are considered *Shirk*.

The Shaikh - may Allâh have mercy upon him - explains *At-Tiwalah* as being something that they make claiming that it makes the woman more beloved by her husband and the man by his wife, according to their belief. Hence, this is a type of magic. The common people call this *Aṣ-Ṣarf* and *Al-'Atf*. In reality it is a type of *At-Tamaa'im*, because it is made and the magician is the one who chants on it (the charm) some *Ruqyah* that is *Shirk*. This makes the woman love her husband or it makes the husband love his wife, according to their claims. Therefore, this is a type of magic, and magic is *Shirk* with Allâh, the Mighty and Majestic, and it is disbelief (*Kufr*).

[1] 'Abdullah bin 'Ukaym narrated the following *Marfoo'* (i.e. attributed to the Prophet ﷺ) report:

«مَنْ تَعَلَّقَ شَيْئًا وُكِلَ إِلَيْهِ»

"Whoever hangs something is entrusted to it."

The word "something" here is an indefinite noun used to present a condition. Therefore, it includes all things in general. Thus, every person who hangs something is entrusted to it. So whoever tries to exclude some form from the various forms of hanging items from this generality, then the proof stands against him, because this evidence is general. If the servant is entrusted to other than Allâh, the Mighty and Majestic, then verily loss surrounds him from all sides. The servant's only honor, success, prosperity, good intent, and deeds are when his attachment is to Allâh Alone. This is in regards to his actions, his statements, his future and averting harms from himself. His intimacy should be with Allâh, his happiness should be with Allâh and his attachment should be to Allâh. His affairs should be turned over to Allâh and his reliance should be upon Allâh, the Mighty and Majestic. So whoever is like this, and he trusts in

At-Tamaa'im (the plural of *Tameemah*)[1] is something that is hung on children to protect them from the evil eye. However, some of the *Salaf* allowed this to be done if what is being hung is something (i.e. verses) from the Qur'ān. Others of them did not allow it and they considered it from the prohibited matters. Among them was Ibn Mas'ud رَضِيَ اللهُ عَنْهُ.[2]

Ar-Ruqaa (the plural of *Ruqyah*) is that which is called *Al-'Azaa'im*. However, the evidence (i.e. other narrations) has excluded from this (prohibition) that which does not contain *Ash-Shirk*. Indeed Allâh's Messenger ﷺ allowed it to be used against the evil eye and to cure poisonous stings.

At-Tiwalah is something that the people make claiming that it will make the woman more beloved by her husband or the man by his wife.

Aḥmad recorded from Ruwayfi' that he said, "The Allâh's Messenger ﷺ said to me,

«يَا رُوَيْفِعُ لَعَلَّ الْحَيَاةَ تَطُولُ بِكَ؛ فَأَخْبِرِ النَّاسَ أَنَّ مَنْ عَقَدَ لِحْيَتَهُ

Allâh while expelling the creation from his heart, then even if the heavens and the earth plotted against him to harm him, Allâh would make a way out of them for him. This is due to his trust in Allâh and his turning his affairs over to the Most Mighty - Magnificent is His Majesty and Holy are His Names.

[1] The Shaikh said, "*At-Tamaa'im* is something that is hung on children to protect them from the evil eye.'' His Statement, "something'' is inclusive of anything that is hung without any specified description, in order to repel the evil eye or protect from harms or bring about some personal good.

[2] Then he said, "However, some of the *Salaf* allowed this to be done if what is being hung is something (i.e. Verses) from the Qur'ān.'' The evidence shows that the various types of *At-Tamaa'im* are prohibited, but when the person hangs the Qur'ān he has not committed *Shirk*. This is because he has hung something from the attributes of Allâh, which is His Words. So in this case he has not associated some creation with Allâh in order to repel His harm.

أَوْ تَقَلَّدَ وَتَرًا أَوِ اسْتَنْجَى بِرَجِيعِ دَابَّةٍ أَوْ عَظْمٍ فَإِنَّ مُحَمَّدًا بَرِيءٌ مِنْهُ»

'O Ruwayfi'! Perhaps you will live a long time, so inform the people that whoever ties a knot in his beard, or wears a necklace made of bowstring, or cleans himself (after using the toilet) with animal dung, or a bone, then very Muhammad is innocent of him.'''[1]

Sa'eed bin Jubayr رَضِيَ اللهُ عَنْهُ said,

«مَنْ قَطَعَ تَمِيمَةً مِنْ إِنْسَانٍ كَانَ كَعِدْلِ رَقَبَةٍ»

"Whoever cuts a *Tameemah* (charm or amulet) from a person, it will be equal to freeing a slave."

---

[1] Aḥmad recorded from Ruwayfi' that he said, "The Allâh's Messenger ﷺ said to me,

«يَا رُوَيْفِعُ لَعَلَّ الْحَيَاةَ تَطُولُ بِكَ؛ فَأَخْبِرِ النَّاسَ أَنَّ مَنْ عَقَدَ لِحْيَتَهُ أَوْ تَقَلَّدَ وَتَرًا أَوِ اسْتَنْجَى بِرَجِيعِ دَابَّةٍ أَوْ عَظْمٍ فَإِنَّ مُحَمَّدًا بَرِيءٌ مِنْهُ»

'O Ruwayfi'! Perhaps you will live a long time, so inform the people that whoever ties a not in his beard, or wears a necklace made of bowstring, or cleans himself (after using the toilet) with animal dung, or a bone, then very Muhammad is innocent of him.'''

His Statement,

«تَقَلَّدَ وَتَرًا»

"wears a necklace made of bowstring."

is restricting the wearing of a necklace to *Al-Watar* (the bowstring), and this has an understood meaning. The implication is that the prohibition does not refer to the necklace simply because it is a necklace. Rather, it refers to the necklace that is believed to prevent the evil eye, like the bowstring necklace. Concerning his statement, "then very Muhammad is innocent of him," this is from the wordings that prove that this act is from the major sins, and it proves the tremendous nature of this act of disobedience. The minor *Shirk* is from the major sins just as the major *Shirk* is from the major sins.

Wakee' recorded this.[1]

He (Wakee') also recorded from Ibrâhîm that he said, "They detested *At-Tamaa'im* of all types, whether it was from the Qur'ān or other than the Qur'ān."[2]

Important issues of the Chapter

1) The explanation of *Ar-Ruqaa* and *At-Tamaa'im*.
2) The explanation of *At-Tiwalah*.
3) That these three things are all forms of *Ash-Shirk* without exception.
4) That *Ar-Ruqyah* with truthful words used against the evil eye and poisonous stings is excluded from this (i.e. being *Ash-Shirk*).
5) That if *At-Tameemah* is from the Qur'ān the scholars have differed as to whether it is included in this (i.e. being *Ash-Shirk*) or not.
6) That hanging bowstrings on the animals (as necklaces) to ward off the evil eye is included in this.

---

[1] Sa'eed bin Jubayr said, "Whoever cuts a *Tameemah* (charm or amulet) from a person, it will be equal to freeing a slave." This means it will be like freeing a slave. This shows the virtue of cutting off *At-Tamaa'im* because it is *Shirk* with Allâh, and the minor *Shirk* will cause one to enter the Fire in view of the threat regarding it. If someone cuts a *Tameemah* from the neck of the person who is wearing it, then he is in the position of freeing that slave from the Fire, because by that action he deserves the threat of the Fire. So if the person cuts the *Tameemah*, his reward will be based upon the type of his deed. Thus, just as he has freed this Muslim slave from the Fire, he will be rewarded by having the reward like that of freeing a slave.

[2] His Statement, "He also recorded..." is referring to Wakee'. His saying, "from Ibrâhîm", is referring to Ibrâhîm An-Nakha'ee, the student of Ibn Mas'ud. He said, "They", meaning the Companions of Ibn Mas'ud. And he continued, "detested *At-Tamaa'im of all types, whether it was from the Qur'ān or other than the Qur'ān.*"

7) The sever threat against whoever hangs a bowstring (as a necklace).

8) The virtuous reward of whomever cuts a *Tameemah* off of a person.

9) That the statement of Ibrâhîm (An-Nakha'ee) does not contradict what was mentioned previously concerning the difference of opinion (regarding *At-Tamaa'im* from the Qur'ān), because he was referring to the Companions of 'Abdullah bin Mas'ud.

Chapter 8

Whoever Seeks Blessings in Trees, Stones and Similar Things*

Allâh the Most High said,

﴿أَفَرَءَيۡتُمُ ٱللَّٰتَ وَٱلۡعُزَّىٰ﴾ الآيات.

---

* This title means: What is the ruling concerning him? The answer is that he is a *Mushrik* (polytheist, idolater). *At-Tabarruk* is to seek blessing, which means to seek the abundant good, its affirmation and its necessity. The texts of the Qur'ān and the *Sunnah* prove that Allâh is the One Who provides blessing and that among the creation, no one may bless another.

﴿تَبَارَكَ ٱلَّذِي نَزَّلَ ٱلۡفُرۡقَانَ عَلَىٰ عَبۡدِهِۦ﴾

"Blessed is He Who sent down the criterion (of right and wrong, i.e. this Qur'ān) to His slave (Muhammad ﷺ)." (25:1)

This means: The good of the One Who has sent down the criterion to His servant is tremendous, abundant, everlasting and confirmed. Allâh said,

﴿وَبَٰرَكۡنَا عَلَيۡهِ وَعَلَىٰٓ إِسۡحَٰقَۚ﴾

"And We blessed him (Ibrâhîm - Abraham) and Ishaaq (Isaac)." (37:113)

And He said,

﴿وَجَعَلَنِي مُبَارَكًا﴾

"And He has made me blessed." (19:31)

Thus, the One Who blesses is Allâh and it is not permissible for the creation to say, "I blessed something", or "I will bless your deeds", or "Your coming is blessed." This is because the word "blessing", and the meaning of blessing is only that which comes from Allâh. The reason for this is that the good, its abundance, its necessity and its affirmation only comes from He in Whose Hand is (control of) all matters.

The texts of the Qur'ān and the *Sunnah* prove that the blessing that Allâh gives to things is either that those things are places or times, or that those things are creations from the human beings.

The first group: The places and the times. It is apparent that Allâh, the Mighty and Majestic, has blessed some places, such as the Sacred House of Allâh (*Al-Masjid ul-Ḥaraam*), and like that which is around Jerusalem

---

(*Al-Bayt ul-Muqaddas*) and similar places. The meaning here is that these places contain abundant, inherent and lasting goodness. This is so that it will be more encouraging for their people who have been called to these places to constantly attend them. However, this does not mean that the ground and walls of these places should be wiped, as this blessing is inherent and it does not move in itself. In other words, if you touched the ground, or you were buried in it, or you sought blessings in it, the blessings themselves do not transfer (to you). The ground is only blessed from the aspect of meaning, from the aspect of the hearts being attached to it - like the Sacred House of Allâh - and the abundance of good that is achieved by whoever seeks it, comes to it, makes *Ṭawaaf* at it and worships at it. Even the Black Stone (at the *Ka'bah*) is a blessed stone, but its blessing is due to the worship (of Allâh). This means that whoever touches it seeking to worship Allâh, and due to obedience of the Prophet ﷺ in his touching it, and in kissing it, then he achieves by it the blessing of following (the Prophet ﷺ). Indeed 'Umar رَضِيَ الله عَنْهُ said when he kissed the stone, "Verily I know that you are a stone; you do not give benefit nor do you cause harm."

His Statement, "You do not give benefit nor do you cause harm", means it does not carry anything of benefit to anyone, nor does it repel any harm from anyone.

In reference to the times, this means that the time is blessed, like the month of Ramadhaan or some of the virtuous Days of Allâh. This means that whoever performs worship during those times and he desires the good that is in them, then verily he will achieve an abundance of reward that he would not achieve in other times.

The second group: This refers to the blessing that is attached to the children of Aadam (i.e. human beings). And Allâh has made His blessing for the Prophets and Messengers, as an actual blessing in itself. This means that their bodies were blessed, and that if anyone of their people sought blessings in their bodies, either by wiping them, or taking some of their sweat, or seeking blessing from some of their hair, then this is permissible. This is because Allâh made their bodies blessed. Likewise with Muhammad ﷺ, his body is also a blessed body. For this reason it has been related in the *Sunnah* that the Companions used to seek blessings in his sweat, his hair and likewise in other various things. Therefore, their blessing is a blessing in itself and it is possible for the effects of this blessing, virtue and goodness to be transferred from their bodies to other than them. This is something particular to the Prophets and Messengers. In reference to other than them, there is no evidence that proves that there was anyone from the Companions of the Prophets who had such personal blessings. Even the best of this *Ummah* (the Muslim nation), Abu Bakr and 'Umar (did not have such personal blessings). It has been related through many definite reports that the Companions, their students and those of the earlier generations did not seek blessings through Abu Bakr, 'Umar, 'Uthmaan and 'Ali رَضِيَ اللهُ عَنْهُم in the way that they sought blessings through the Prophet ﷺ, by seeking blessings in the hair and the ablution water. The blessing of people like is only the blessing of (their) deeds. It is not a blessing in the person himself that is transferable as if it were the blessing of the Prophet ﷺ. Therefore, we say, "There is blessing in every Muslim, and this blessing is not a blessing in the person himself. Rather, it is a blessing of (good) deeds, and the blessing of what he has with him of Islam and faith, and what is in his heart of fear and reverence of Allâh and honoring Him. It is also in his following His Messenger (Muhammad ﷺ)." This blessing is the blessing of knowledge, or deeds, or righteousness, and it is not transferable (to others). Subsequently, seeking blessings by the people of righteousness is by following them in their righteousness. Seeking blessings by the people of knowledge is by taking from their knowledge and benefiting from their teachings. Likewise, it is not permissible for blessings to be sought through them by touching them or seeking blessings in their saliva. This is because the best of the creation from this *Ummah* - and they are the Companions - did not do this with the best of the *Ummah* after its Prophet ﷺ - who were Abu Bakr, 'Umar, 'Uthmaan and 'Ali رَضِيَ اللهُ عَنْهُم. This is a matter that is settled.

The way that the polytheists (*Mushrikūn*) seek blessings is that they hope for an abundance of good, its continuation, its necessity and its affirmation by turning to (false) gods. These methods of seeking blessings differ and all of them are forms of *Shirk*.

His Statement, "and Similar Things" means: Things similar to trees and stones, like the different locations, or a specific cave, or a grave, or a water spring, or similar things from the things that the people of ignorance believe in.

Seeking blessings in a tree, a stone, a grave or various locations is major *Shirk* if the one who seeks their blessings believes that this tree, stone or grave will be a means of intercession for him with Allâh if he wipes it, rubs himself against it or clings to it. So, if the person believes that this thing is a

"Have you seen Al-Laat and Al-'Uzzaa." (53:19)[1]

---

means of mediation to Allâh, then this is taking a god along with Allâh, the Mighty and Majestic, and it is major *Shirk*. This is that which the people of *Al-Jaahiliyyah* (pre-Islamic days of ignorance) used to claim in reference to the trees and stones that they used to worship and the graves by which they used to seek blessings. They believed that if they performed religious devotions at places, or wiped these things, or sprinkled dirt on them, then this spot, or the person buried at this spot, or the soul that served this spot would intercede on the person's behalf with Allâh. Verily Allâh said,

﴿وَٱلَّذِينَ ٱتَّخَذُوا۟ مِن دُونِهِۦٓ أَوْلِيَآءَ مَا نَعْبُدُهُمْ إِلَّا لِيُقَرِّبُونَآ إِلَى ٱللَّهِ زُلْفَىٰٓ﴾

"And those who take *Awliyaa'* (protectors, supporters, lords, gods) besides Him (say): 'We only worship them so that they may bring us nearer to Allâh.'" (39:3)

Seeking blessings may also be minor *Shirk*. This is - for example - when a person takes the dirt of the grave and sprinkles it on himself due to his belief that this dirt is blessed, and if it touches his body, his body will become blessed as a result of the dirt. This is minor *Shirk* (and not major *Shirk*) because he has not directed worship to other than Allâh, the Mighty and Majestic. Rather, he has only believed that something is a means that is not an Islamically allowed means.

[1] Concerning the Statement of Allâh the Most High,

﴿أَفَرَءَيْتُمُ ٱللَّٰتَ وَٱلْعُزَّىٰ ○ وَمَنَوٰةَ ٱلثَّالِثَةَ ٱلْأُخْرَىٰٓ﴾

"Have you seen Al-Laat and Al-'Uzzaa? And Manaat the third other one?" (53:19,20)

Al-Laat was a white stone the people of At-Ṭâ'if had and it was not torn down until after the *Thaqeef* tribe accepted Islam. The Prophet ﷺ sent Al-Mugheerah bin Shu'bah to them and he tore it down and smashed it. There was a house built over it and it had custodians and slaves (who looked after it).

Al-'Uzzaa was a tree that was between Makkah and Aṭ-Ṭâ'if. It originally was one tree, but then a building was built over three trees. It had custodians there who cared for it and a woman who was a soothsayer was the one who served that object of *Shirk*. Then, when the Prophet ﷺ conquered Makkah he sent Khaalid bin Al-Waleed to cut down those three trees and kill the soothsayer woman who was using the jinn to misguide the people. In actuality, the attachment of the people was to that

Abu Waaqid Al-Laythee said, "We went out with Allâh's Messenger ﷺ to Ḥunayn and we had just recently left disbelief (*Kufr*). The *Mushrikūn* (polytheists, idolaters) had a lote tree, which they used to frequent for devotion and hang their weapons upon, and it was called *Tḥaatu Anwaat*.[1] So

---

tree and the woman who served that *Shirk*.

﴿وَمَنَوٰةَ ٱلثَّالِثَةَ ٱلْأُخْرَىٰٓ﴾

"And Manaat the third other one?"

The word other here means the lowly and despised, and it was also a stone that was called Manaat. This was due to the great amount of blood that was poured over it out of reverence for it.

Hence, the appropriate angle of interpretation for the Verse would be that Al-Laat is a stone, and Manaat is a stone and Al-'Uzzaa is a tree. And what the idolaters (*Mushrikūn*) used to do at these three idols is exactly the same as what the idolaters (*Mushrikūn*) do in these later times with the stones, trees and caves. What is even worse than this is the taking of the graves as gods to be turned to and places at which worship is performed!

[1] Abu Waaqid Al-Laythee said, "We went out with Allâh's Messenger ﷺ to Ḥunayn and we had just recently left disbelief (*Kufr*)."

This *Hadith* is a great authentic *Hadith*. The idolaters had a lote tree, which was a tree in which they held a belief. Their belief included three things. The first: That they used to have great esteem and reverence for this three. The second: They used to make religious devotions at this tree. This devotion meant that they would adhere to it due to reverence and seek to be near to it. The third: That they used to hang their weapons at it hoping that the blessing would transfer from the tree to the weapon. This was so that the weapon would last longer and would have more goodness for its carrier. This deed of theirs was major *Shirk* due to these three things collectively.

Those who were new converts from disbelief (i.e. new Muslims) among the Companions said, "O Allâh's Messenger! Make a *Tḥaatu Anwaat* for us just like their *Tḥaatu Anwaat.*" They thought that this was not included in *Ash-Shirk*, and that the statement of *At-Tauhid* does not annihilate this deed. For this reason the scholars have said, "Some of the virtuous people are unaware of some issues of *Ash-Shirk*. This is because some of the Companions, who were the most knowledgeable of the people

we passed by a lote tree and said, 'O Allâh's Messenger ﷺ! Make a *Thaatu Anwaat* for us just like their *Thaatu Anwaat.*' Allâh's Messenger ﷺ replied,

«اللهُ أَكْبَرُ! إِنَّهَا السَّنَنُ، قُلْتُمْ وَالَّذِي نَفْسِي بِيَدِهِ كَمَا قَالَتْ بَنُو إِسْرَائِيلَ لِمُوسَىٰ:

'*Allâhu Akbar* (Allâh is Most Great)! Verily it is the ways (of earlier nations). By He in Whose Hand is my soul, you all have said the same as the Children of Israa'eel said to Mûsâ':

﴿ٱجْعَل لَّنَآ إِلَـٰهًا كَمَا لَهُمْ ءَالِهَةٌ قَالَ إِنَّكُمْ قَوْمٌ تَجْهَلُونَ﴾

'Make for us a god just like their gods.' He said, 'Verily you are a people who know not.' (7:138)

«لَتَرْكَبُنَّ سَنَنَ مَنْ كَانَ قَبْلَكُمْ»

'Certainly you all will follow the ways of those who were before you.'' (*At-Tirmithi* — and he graded it authentic — *Saheeh*). [1]

---

concerning the Arabic language, accepted Islam after the conquest of Makkah and they were unaware of some particulars of the *Tauhid* of worship.''

[1] So Allâh's Messenger ﷺ said,

«اللهُ أَكْبَرُ إِنَّهَا السَّنَنُ، قُلْتُمْ وَالَّذِي نَفْسِي بِيَدِهِ كَمَا قَالَتْ بَنُو إِسْرَائِيلَ لِمُوسَىٰ:

"*Allâhu Akbar* (Allâh is Most Great)! Verily it is the ways (of earlier nations). By He in Whose Hand is my soul, you all have said the same as the Children of Israa'eel said to Mûsâ:

﴿ٱجْعَل لَّنَآ إِلَـٰهًا كَمَا لَهُمْ ءَالِهَةٌ﴾

'Make for us a god just like their gods.''' (7:138)

The Prophet ﷺ - pay close attention to this point - likened their statement to the statement of the people of Moosaa, "Make for us a god just like their gods.'' Consequently, they (the Companions) did not do what they had

---

requested, and when the Prophet ﷺ forbade them they ceased. And if they had done what they requested it would have been a major *Shirk*. But when they said and requested without doing, their statement became a minor *Shirk*, because it contained a form of attachment to other than Allâh, the Mighty and Majestic. For this reason the Prophet ﷺ did not command them to renew their Islam. What is obvious from this is that the major *Shirk* that the idolaters were involved in was not only related to seeking blessings from *Thaatu Anwaaṭ*. It was only (considered major *Shirk*) by the reverence, the religious devotion and seeking blessings by hanging items (all together). It has already been mentioned that seeking blessings by trees, stones and similar things, if it contains the belief that this thing will bring one closer to Allâh and raise the need to Allâh, or that their needs are more likely to be fulfilled and their affairs will be better if they seek blessings at this place, then this is major *Shirk*. And this is what the people of *Al-Jaahiliyyah* (pre-Islamic ignorance) used to do. If you notice what the worshipers of graves and the people of superstitious beliefs did in the latter times and in our times, you will find that they do the same as the earlier *Mushrikūn* (idolaters, polytheists) used to do with *Al-Laat, Al-'Uzzaa* and *Thaatu Anwaaṭ*. For indeed they believe in the grave. They even believe in the iron that surrounds the grave! At the various tombs and shrines in the lands in which *Ash-Shirk* has spread or appeared you find that the people even believe in the wall which is around the grave or the metal fence that surrounds it. When they wipe it they think that it is as if they have wiped the buried person, and their soul has come into contact (with the person), and that he will intercede for them because they have shown reverence to him. This is major *Shirk* with Allâh, the Mighty and Majestic, because it goes back to the attachment of the heart in bringing benefit and repelling harm to other than Allâh. It also makes the thing a means of mediation with Allâh, just like the deed of the earlier people, about whom Allâh said,

﴿مَا نَعْبُدُهُمْ إِلَّا لِيُقَرِّبُونَا إِلَى اللَّهِ زُلْفَىٰ﴾

> "We only worship them so that they may bring us nearer to Allâh." (39:3)

In reference to the other situation, which we informed you of at the beginning of the discussion concerning this, it is that the person makes some wiping or touching a means, as you see with some of the ignorant people. For example, a person comes to the *Ḥaram* (in Makkah) and he

Important issues of the Chapter

1) The explanation of the verse of *Surah An-Najm* (53:19-20).
2) Awareness of the nature of the matter which they (the Companions) requested (i.e. a tree similar to *Thaatu Anwaaṭ*).
3) The fact that they did not do (what they requested).
4) The fact that they intended to gain nearness to Allâh by that, because they thought that He would love it.
5) That if they were unaware of this, then others besides them are more likely to be ignorant of it.
6) That they (the Companions) have good rewards and the promise of forgiveness that others besides them do not have.
7) That the Prophet ﷺ did not excuse them. Rather, he responded to them by saying, *"Allâhu Akbar* (Allâh is Most Great)! Verily it is the ways (of earlier nations). Certainly you all will follow the ways of those who were before you." So he expressed the weightiness of the matter with these three statements.
8) The major issue, and it is the intent, is that he informed

---

wipes the outer doors of the *Ḥaram*, or some of its walls or some of its pillars. So this person, if he believes that there is a soul in this pillar, or there is someone buried near to it, or that there is someone who serves this pillar from the good souls - as they say - and he wipes it in order to reach Allâh, then this is major *Shirk*.

However, if the person wipes something with the belief that this place is blessed and that it is a means that will cure him, then this is minor *Shirk*. Therefore, if a person wipes something in making it a means, then this person's *Shirk* is minor *Shirk*. If his heart is attached to this thing that he is wipes, or seeks blessings from, or reveres, and he adheres to it and believes that there is a spirit there, or that he can use it as a means of mediation with Allâh, then this is major *Shirk*.

that their request was like the request of the Children of Israa'eel when they said to Mûsâ,

﴿ٱجْعَل لَّنَآ إِلَـٰهًا﴾

"Make for us a god." (7:138)

9) That the negation of this is from the meaning of *"Lā ilāha illallāh"* with its faintness and its obscurity from those people.

10) That he (the Prophet ﷺ) swore upon giving the ruling, and he would not swear unless there was some benefit in doing so.

11) That there is major and minor *Shirk*, because they did not apostatize by this (request).

12) Their statement, "And we were newly converts from disbelief" contains an implication that others besides them were not unaware of this matter.

13) Saying *"Allâhu Akbar"* (Allâh is Most Great) to express surprise, in contradiction to those who consider it disliked.

14) Blocking means (that lead to evil).

15) The prohibition of imitating the people of ignorance.

16) Anger when teaching.

17) The encompassing principle in his statement, "Verily it is the ways (of earlier nations)."

18) That this is a sign from the signs of the Prophethood, due to the fact that it has occurred just as he informed.

19) That all of what Allâh has rebuked the Jews and Christians for in the Qur'ān, it also applies to us.

20) That it was established with them that the acts of worship were established upon commands. Therefore, it becomes a

reminder concerning the questions of the grave. Concerning the question, "Who is your Lord?" Its answer is clear. Concerning the question, "Who is your Prophet?" Then it is from his informing of news of the unseen. Concerning the question, "What is your religion?" Then it is from their saying, "Make for us a god."

21) That the way (*Sunnah*) of the People of the Scripture (i.e. Jews and Christians) is blameworthy just as the way (*Sunnah*) of the *Mushrikūn* (idolaters, polytheists).

22) That the person who moves from the falsehood that his heart was accustomed to is not safe from there being some remnants in his heart of that custom (i.e. belief). This is due to their statement, "and we had just recently left disbelief (*Kufr*)."

Chapter 9

What has been reported Concerning Slaughtering for Other than Allâh*

Allâh the Most High said,

﴿قُلْ إِنَّ صَلَاتِي وَنُسُكِي وَمَحْيَايَ وَمَمَاتِي لِلَّهِ رَبِّ ٱلْعَالَمِينَ ۝ لَا شَرِيكَ لَهُۥ﴾

---

* This chapter is concerning what threat has been reported concerning slaughtering for other than Allâh and that it is associating partners (*Shirk*) with Allâh, the Mighty and Majestic.

Atḥ-Thabḥ (slaughtering) is the shedding of blood. There are two important things concerning slaughtering, and they are the point and the outstanding issue of this chapter.

The first: Slaughtering while making an offering by some name.

The second: That a person slaughters in drawing near to what he wishes to draw near to. Therefore, there is the mentioning of a name, and there is the intent. The mentioning of a name over a sacrificial animal, in reference to its meaning, is for assistance. This is because the letter *Baa'* in your saying, *"Bismillaah"* (With the Name of Allâh) means: I slaughter seeking blessings and seeking help by every Name of Allâh, the Mighty and Majestic. In reference to the intent, then this is an aspect of servitude and aims. Hence, the situations that we have are four.

The first: That the mentioning of a name is done with the intention being for Allâh Alone. This is *At-Tauhid* and it is worship. Therefore, two matters are obligatory when slaughtering: That the slaughter is done for Allâh with the intent of drawing near — if the person has intended to draw near to Allâh with it — like the sacrifices of *Al-Adh-ḥaa*, of *Ḥajj* (*Hady*) and the birth of a child (*Al-'Aqeeqah*). Secondly, that the Allâh's Name is mentioned over the sacrificial animal. If Allâh's Name is not mentioned intentionally, then the sacrificial animal is unlawful (to eat). If the person did not intend to draw nearer to Allâh with the slaughter animal, nor did he intend drawing near to other than Allâh, and he only slaughtered it for some guests that he was hosting or so that he could eat it, then is permissible and allowed. The reason is that he mentioned the Name of Allâh and he did not slaughter for other than Allâh. Therefore, this is not included in the threat or the prohibition.

The second situation: That the person slaughters with the Name of Allâh and he intends with his act of drawing near that this sacrificial animal is for other than Allâh. For example, he says, "With the Name of Allâh," and he causes the blood to flow (by cutting the animal's neck). Yet, he intends with his shedding of blood to draw near to this great person who is buried, whether it is a Prophet or a righteous person. So even though he slaughtered with the Name of Allâh, *Ash-Shirk* has occurred from the point that he shed blood as an act of reverence to the buried person and not for Allâh. Also included in this is what happens in some of the desert regions and even in some of the cities, when the people intend to honor someone who has arrived. They meet him with camels or something else from the livestock animals, and they slaughter them in his presence. Thus, the blood flows upon his arrival. This slaughtering is intended for other than Allâh, even if Allâh's Name is pronounced over it, and the scholars have ruled that this is forbidden. This is because there is shedding of blood for other than Allâh, and therefore it is not allowed to eat it. Also, before this, it is most appropriate to mention that it is not permissible to honor these people with the likes of this practice, because shedding blood is only done in reverence of Allâh alone. The reason is that He is the One Who deserves worship and reverence with these things, and He is the one who causes the blood to flow in the veins.

The third situation: That the person mentions other than the Name of Allâh and he intends that the sacrificial animal is for other than Allâh, the Mighty and Sublime. For example, he says, "In the Name of Christ," and he moves his hand in slaughtering (the animal), and he intends with that to draw near to Christ. This *Shirk* combines *Shirk* in seeking help and *Shirk* in worship. Similar to this is that the person slaughters in the name of Al-Badawee, or Al-Ḥusayn, or As-Sayyidah Zaynab, or Al-'Eedroos, or Al-Margheenaanee, or similar people who are turned to by some of the creation (i.e. humans) in worship. Thus, the person will slaughter in these names and intend by it this created person. In other words, the person intends when slaughtering that he is shedding blood in order to draw near to this created person. So this is *Ash-Shirk* from two aspects. First: The aspect of seeking assistance. Second: The aspect of servitude, reverence, and shedding blood for other than Allâh.

The fourth situation: That the person slaughters with a name other than Allâh, and he makes that for Allâh, the Mighty and Majestic. This is rare, and it probably occurs by the person slaughtering for one who is honored.

"Say (O Muhammad ﷺ): Verily my prayer, my sacrifice, my living, and my dying are for Allâh, the Lord of the worlds (all that exits). He has no partner." (6:162,163)[1]

For example, the person slaughters for Al-Badawee, then he intends with that to draw nearer to Allâh. In reality this goes back to *Ash-Shirk* in seeking assistance and *Ash-Shirk* in worship.

The intent here is that *Ash-Shirk* with the intent of slaughtering for other than Allâh, is a form of *Shirk* in servitude (or worship), and *Ash-Shirk* by mentioning other than the Name of Allâh over a sacrificial animal is *Shirk* in seeking assistance. This is the reason that Allâh said,

﴿وَلَا تَأْكُلُوا۟ مِمَّا لَمْ يُذْكَرِ ٱسْمُ ٱللَّهِ عَلَيْهِ وَإِنَّهُۥ لَفِسْقٌ ۗ وَإِنَّ ٱلشَّيَـٰطِينَ لَيُوحُونَ إِلَىٰٓ أَوْلِيَآئِهِمْ لِيُجَـٰدِلُوكُمْ ۖ وَإِنْ أَطَعْتُمُوهُمْ إِنَّكُمْ لَمُشْرِكُونَ﴾

"Eat not (O believers) of that (meat) on which Allâh's Name has not been pronounced (at the time of slaughtering the animal), for surely it is *Fisq* (a sin and disobedience of Allâh). And certainly, the *Shayâtin* (devils) do inspire their friends (from mankind) to dispute with you, and if you obey them, then you would indeed be *Mushrikūn* (polytheists)." (6:121)

This means: If you all obey them in *Ash-Shirk*, then verily you would be *Mushrikūn* (idolaters, polytheists) just as they are *Mushrikūn*.

[1] Concerning the Statement of Allâh the Most High,

﴿قُلْ إِنَّ صَلَاتِى وَنُسُكِى وَمَحْيَاىَ وَمَمَاتِى لِلَّهِ رَبِّ ٱلْعَـٰلَمِينَ ۝ لَا شَرِيكَ لَهُۥ﴾

"Say: Verily my prayer, my sacrifice, my living, and my dying are for Allâh, the Lord of the worlds (i.e. all that exits). He has no partner." (6:162-163)

This Verse proves that slaughtering and prayer (*Aṣ-Ṣalâh*) are both acts of worship. This is because He made sacrificing for Allâh (in the Verse), and from the deeds of Allâh's creation that are for Him are the acts of worship. For this reason His Statement, "my sacrifice," contains a proof that sacrifice (of animals) is one of the acts of worship and that it is rightly for Allâh, the Mighty and Majestic.

Concerning His Statement, "for Allâh, the Lord of the worlds (i.e. all that exists)," The letter *Laam* here is the *Laam* of worthiness (*Istihqaaq*). In His Statement, "He has no partner," is a third point of evidence. He has no

and Allâh the Most High said,

﴿فَصَلِّ لِرَبِّكَ وَٱنْحَرْ﴾

"So pray to your Lord and sacrifice (to Him)." (108:2)[1]

'Ali رَضِيَ اللهُ عَنْهُ said, "Allâh's Messenger ﷺ related four words to me:

«لَعَنَ اللهُ مَنْ ذَبَحَ لِغَيْرِ اللهِ، لَعَنَ اللهُ مَنْ لَعَنَ وَالِدَيْهِ، لَعَنَ اللهُ مَنْ آوَى مُحْدِثًا، لَعَنَ اللهُ مَنْ غَيَّرَ مَنَارَ الأَرْضِ»

'Allâh curses whoever slaughters for other than Allâh, Allâh curses whoever curses His parents, Allâh curses whoever shelters an innovator (i.e. religious heretic), and Allâh curses whoever changes the borders of the land.'"[2]

---

partner in prayer (*Aṣ-Ṣalaah*), nor in sacrifice. Thus, the person should not turn in prayer and sacrifice to anyone else with Allâh or other than Allâh. For He (Allâh) deserves the acts of worship and He (alone) is the Owner of the Greatest Kingdom.

[1] Concerning His Statement,

﴿فَصَلِّ لِرَبِّكَ وَٱنْحَرْ﴾

"So pray to your Lord and sacrifice (to Him)." (108:2)

Whatever Allâh commands then it is included in the limits of worship, because worship is a name that includes all of what Allâh loves and is pleased with of statements and actions, both external (apparent) and internal (hidden). Allâh has commanded the (performance of) prayer, so therefore, it is loved by Him. Allâh has commanded the sacrifice, and it is loved by Him and it pleases Him. Therefore, the sacrifice is worship for Allâh, the Mighty and Majestic.

[2] 'Ali رَضِيَ اللهُ عَنْهُ said,

"Allâh's Messenger ﷺ related four words to me:

«لَعَنَ اللهُ مَنْ ذَبَحَ لِغَيْرِ اللهِ. . .»

'Allâh curses whoever slaughters for other than Allâh...'"

The witness from this statement, is his statement,

«لَعَنَ اللهُ مَنْ ذَبَحَ لِغَيْرِ اللهِ»

Ṭaariq bin Shihaab narrated that narrated that Allâh's Messenger ﷺ said,

«دَخَلَ الْجَنَّةَ رَجُلٌ فِي ذُبَابٍ، وَدَخَلَ النَّارَ رَجُلٌ فِي ذُبَابٍ»

"A man entered Paradise because of a fly and a man entered the Fire because of a fly."

The people said, "And how is that O Allâh's Messenger?" He replied,

«مَرَّ رَجُلَانِ عَلَى قَومٍ لَهُمْ صَنَمٌ لَايَجُوزُهُ أَحَدٌ حَتَّى يُقَرِّبَ لَهُ شَيْئًا، فَقَالُوا لِأَحَدِهِمَا قَرِّبْ قَالَ: لَيْسَ عِنْدِي شَيْءٌ أُقَرِّبُ، قَالُوا لَهُ: قَرِّبْ وَلَوْ ذُبَابًا، فَقَرَّبَ ذُبَابًا فَخَلَّوْا سَبِيلَهُ فَدَخَلَ النَّارَ وَقَالُوا لِلْآخَرِ: قَرِّبْ فَقَالَ: مَا كُنْتُ لِأُقَرِّبَ لِأَحَدٍ شَيْئًا دُونَ اللهِ عَزَّ وَجَلَّ، فَضَرَبُوا عُنُقَهُ فَدَخَلَ الْجَنَّةَ»

"Two men passed by a people who had an idol, and no one was allowed to pass by it until he had offered something (as a sacrifice) to it. So the people said to one of them, 'Make an offering!' He said, 'I do not have anything to offer.' They said to him, 'Make an offering, even if it is a fly!' So he offered a fly and they let him go. Thus, he entered the Fire. They said to the other man,

---

"Allâh curses whoever slaughters for other than Allâh."

This means for the sake of other than Allâh, seeking to draw near to him and in reverence of him. In reference to the curse, it is casting away and removal from the Mercy of Allâh. If Allâh is the One Who is cursing, then he casts away and removes from the special Mercy of Allâh. In reference to the general mercy, then it includes the Muslim, and the disbeliever and all species of the creation. From that which is known is that when a sin from among the sins is accompanied by the curse, this proves that it is from the major sins. This is clear from the aspect that slaughtering for other than Allâh is *Shirk* with Allâh, and the person who does it deserves cursing, repulsion and distancing from the Mercy of Allâh, the Mighty and Majestic.

'Make an offering.' He said, 'I do not offer anything to anyone other than Allâh, the Mighty and Majestic.' So they struck his neck and he entered the Paradise."[1]

(Recorded by Aḥmad)

Important issues of the Chapter

1) The explanation of the verse,

---

[1] Taariq bin Shihaab narrated that narrated that Allâh's Messenger ﷺ said,

«دَخَلَ الْجَنَّةَ رَجُلٌ فِي ذُبَابٍ، . . .»

"A man entered Paradise because of a fly..."

The point of evidence from this *Hadith* is that making an offering to the idol by sacrificing was a cause for entry into the Fire. That which is apparent is that the person who did this was a Muslim, yet he entered the Fire because of what he did. This proves that slaughtering for other than Allâh is *Shirk* with Allâh, and it is major *Shirk*, because the obvious meaning of his statement,

«دَخَلَ النَّارَ»

"entered the Fire"

is that he deserved it along with whoever will remain in it forever.

It is also a point of evidence that the offering of this worthless thing, which was the fly, proves that whoever offers a sacrifice of something of greater value, that is greater in its benefit, better with its people and more expensive, then it is a greater cause of entering the Fire.

His Statement, "Make an offering," here means: slaughter (something) as an act of drawing near (i.e. devotion). Note here that they did not force people to do the act. The apparent meaning of his statement, "no one was allowed to pass by it," means that they would not allow anyone to pass it from that road until he had offered a sacrifice. This is not considered compulsion, as it is possible to say, "I will return to where I came from." If it is said that their compulsion occurred in their murder, then (the reply is that) this *Hadith* is concerning those who were before us. And the removal of compulsion or the permissibility of saying a statement of disbelief or doing an act of disbelief while one's heart is settled upon faith, this is something that is particular to this *Ummah* (i.e. it was not allowed for those before us).

﴿قُلْ إِنَّ صَلَاتِي وَنُسُكِي﴾

"Say: Verily my prayer, and my sacrifice..." (6:162-163)

2) The explanation of the verse,

﴿فَصَلِّ لِرَبِّكَ وَٱنْحَرْ﴾

"So pray to your Lord and sacrifice (to Him)." (108:2)

3) The beginning (of the *Hadith*) with cursing whoever slaughtered for other than Allâh.

4) The curse of whoever curses his parents, and from it is that you curse the parents of (another) man, and thus (in response), he curses your parents.

5) The curse of whoever shelters a *Muhdith*, and he is the person who does something (a sin or heresy) that necessitates the right (punishment) of Allâh. Therefore he seeks refuge with someone who will protect him from that.

6) The curse of whoever changes the boundaries of the land, and they are the designated borders that separate between your right and the right of your neighbor of the land. So you change it by advancing it or withdrawing it.

7) The difference between the curse of a specific person and the curse of people who do acts of disobedience in general.

8) This tremendous story, which is the story of the fly.

9) The fact that the man entered the Fire because of that fly, which he did not intend (to offer). Rather, he did it simply to avoid their harm.

10) Knowing the (despised) estimation of Shirk in the hearts of the believers, seeing how that man was patient with being killed and he did not agree with them in their

request, even though they only requested an external action.

11) That the man who entered the Fire was a Muslim, because if he was a disbeliever the Prophet ﷺ would not have said,

«دَخَلَ النَّارَ فِي ذُبَابٍ»

"He entered the Fire because of a fly."

12) This contains a supporting witness for the authentic *Hadith,*

«الْجَنَّةُ أَقْرَبُ إِلَى أَحَدِكُمْ مِنْ شِرَاكِ نَعْلِهِ، وَالنَّارُ مِثْلُ ذَلِكَ»

"Paradise is closer to one of you than the lace of his sandal, and the Fire is similar to that."

13) Knowing that the action of the heart is the great aim, even with the worshippers of idols.

Chapter 10

A Sacrifice Should not be Made to Allâh at a Place where Sacrifices are Made to other than Allâh*

The statement of Allâh the Most High,

﴿لَا تَقُمْ فِيهِ أَبَدًا﴾ الآية

"Do not ever stand in it..." (9:108)[1]

---

* Concerning the statement (in the chapter heading), "at a Place", the letter *Baa'* (at) here has an increased meaning more than just the meaning of the word "in". This increased meaning is that it gives an understanding of both the meaning of containment at a place and the meaning of vicinity. These two meanings are both intended here. That is that a sacrifice should not be made to Allâh near the place where sacrifices are made to other than Allâh, nor should they be made in the same place where sacrifices are made to other than Allâh. This is because in both situations there is participation with those who slaughter to other than Allâh.

An image of this issue: That there is any place where sacrifices are made to other than Allâh, for example, at a grave, or a shrine or a place that is revered by the *Mushrikūn* (polytheists, idolaters) or the people who believe in superstitions. In other words, those whose slaughtering is for the sake of the person in the grave or similar things. For verily it is not allowed for the Muslim who believes in *At-Tauhid* to slaughter (an animal) in this place, even if his sacrifice is done solely for Allâh. This is because he will be resembling those *Mushrikūn* in revering the places at which they perform acts of worship with their various forms of worship that are directed to other than Allâh. So slaughtering for Allâh alone, and not for anything other than Him, in a place where nearness to others besides Allâh is sought, is not allowed and it is not permissible. Rather, it is from the means that lead to *Ash-Shirk*, and it is from that which is attached to reverence of that place. Its ruling is that is forbidden and a means from the means that lead to *Ash-Shirk*.

[1] Concerning the statement of Allâh the Most High,

﴿لَا تَقُمْ فِيهِ أَبَدًا﴾

Thaabit bin Adh-Dhaḥḥaak said, "A man vowed to slaughter a camel at a place called Buwaanah,[1] so he asked the Prophet ﷺ about it and he said,

---

"Do not ever stand in it..." (9:108)

This is the prohibition of standing in *Masjid udh-Dhiraar* (the Masjid of harm), which was built by the hypocrites.

Allâh then said,

﴿لَّمَسْجِدٌ أُسِّسَ عَلَى ٱلتَّقْوَىٰ مِنْ أَوَّلِ يَوْمٍ﴾

"The Masjid (mosque) whose foundation was established from the first day on piety..."

Masjid udh-Dhiraar was established as a place for spying (on the Muslims) and in opposition to Allâh and His Messenger. Hence, since this was the intent in the establishment of it, then indeed participating with them in prayer in it was not permissible. This is because it would have been an approval for them or an increase in their numbers and an incitement for the people to perform prayer in it. Therefore, Allâh, the Mighty and Majestic, forbade His Prophet ﷺ and the believers from praying in *Masjid udh-Dhiraar*. So Allâh forbade that the Prophet ﷺ pray in *Masjid udh-Dhiraar*, and it is known that his prayer and the prayer of the believers along with him was solely for Allâh and for none other besides Him. Yet they were still forbade (from praying their) even though they were those who devoted their worship to Allâh Alone, and they did not have any intention of harm, division or spying. However, they were forbidden because of this participation and resemblance that was attached to going to that place. And this is an image that is present among those who slaughter for Allâh at a place where sacrifice is performed for other than Allâh. For verily, even if the person is doing his worship solely for Allâh, he is calling others to honor that place in his action.

[1] Thaabit bin Adh-Dhaḥḥaak رَضِيَ اللهُ عَنْهُ said, "A man vowed to slaughter a camel at a place called Buwaanah, so he asked the Prophet ﷺ about it and he said,

«هَلْ كَانَ فِيهَا وَثَنٌ مِنْ أَوْثَانِ الْجَاهِلِيَّةِ يُعْبَدُ؟»

'Was there any idol there that was worshipped from the idols of *Al-Jaahiliyyah* (pre-Islamic days of ignorance)?' They answered, 'No.'"

The Prophet ﷺ asked him to give details because the matter necessitated expounding. This question proves that if this characteristic - there being an

«هَلْ كَانَ فِيهَا وَثَنٌ مِنْ أَوْثَانِ الْجَاهِلِيَّةِ يُعْبَدُ؟»

'Was there any idol there that was worshipped from the idols of *Al-Jaahiliyyah* (pre-Islamic days of ignorance)?''

They answered, 'No.' He then said,

«فَهَلْ كَانَ فِيهَا عِيدٌ مِنْ أَعْيَادِهِمْ؟»

'Was there any celebration held there from their celebrations?'

The answered, 'No.'[1] So Allâh's Messenger ﷺ said,

---

idol there that was worshipped from the idols of *Al-Jaahiliyyah* - is present, it is not allowed to perform a sacrifice in that place. This is the purpose of relating this *Hadith* in the chapter.

[1] Then he said,

«فَهَلْ كَانَ فِيهَا عِيدٌ مِنْ أَعْيَادِهِمْ؟»

"Was there any celebration held there from their celebrations?''

The answered, "No.'' The word *'Eed* (celebration) refers to the place or the time which returns or is returned to. Therefore, the *'Eed* may be in reference to place because it is the name of the place that people customarily come to and it is returned to during a customary time. Likewise, the times are *'Eed* because they return at a specific time. So he said, "Was there any celebration held there from their celebrations?'' This means an *'Eed* of a particular place. It also could mean an *'Eed* of a particular time. It is known that the *'Eeds* of the *Mushrikūn*, in reference to the places or times, were related to their religious practices and their polytheistic religion. Therefore, the meaning is that they performed worship during these *'Eeds* with their polytheistic acts of worship. From that which is done at the *'Eeds* of the *Mushrikūn*, and the major act that is done is seeking to draw near (i.e. devotion to their gods) by slaughtering and shedding blood. This proves that participating with the *Mushrikūn* in a place where they seek to draw near to other than Allâh in a way that outwardly resembles their action is not permissible. The reason is that is participation with them in the apparent action, even though the person may be doing his act solely for Allâh, and not slaughtering for anyone except Allâh, or he is only praying to Allâh.

«أَوْفِ بِنَذْرِكَ، فَإِنَّهُ لَا وَفَاءَ لِنَذْرٍ فِي مَعْصِيَةِ اللهِ وَلَا فِيمَا لَا يَمْلِكُ ابْنُ آدَمَ»

'Fulfil your vow, for verily there is no fulfilling of a vow in disobedience to Allâh, nor in that which the son of Aadam does not possess (i.e. what he's not capable of doing).'"

Recorded by Abu Dâwûd and its chain of narration meets their (Al-Bukhari and Muslim) conditions.[1]

Important issues of the Chapter

1) The explanation of His Statement,

﴿لَا تَقُمْ فِيهِ أَبَدًا﴾ الآية

"Do not ever stand in it..." (9:108)

2) That the acts of disobedience effect the land, as do acts of obedience.

3) Referring the problematic issue to the clear issue in order to eliminate the problem.

4) The *Muftee* (one who gives legal verdicts) seeking clarifying details if he needs to do so.

5) That there is no harm in specifying a particular spot for a

[1] So Allâh's Messenger ﷺ said,

«أَوْفِ بِنَذْرِكَ، فَإِنَّهُ لَا وَفَاءَ لِنَذْرٍ فِي مَعْصِيَةِ اللهِ»

"Fulfil your vow, for verily there is no fulfilling of a vow in disobedience to Allâh."

The scholars have said, "The arrangement of what comes after the letter *Faa'* is based upon what was before it that came with *Faa'*." This proves that the reason for the permission given to fulfil the vow is that what was before it was not an act of disobedience. The request for clarification proves that slaughtering for Allâh in a place in which there is an idol that is worshipped or a celebration (*'Eed*) from the celebrations of the *Mushrikūn* is an act of disobedience of Allâh, the Mighty and Majestic.

vow, as long as there no preventive factors involved.

6) The prohibition of doing so if there is an idol there from the idols of *Al-Jaahiliyyah,* even if it is after the idols removal.
7) The prohibition of doing so if there is a celebration (*'Eed*) there from their celebrations, even if it is after the celebration has been stopped.
8) That it is not permissible to fulfil the vow that was made at such a place, because it is a vow of an act of disobedience.
9) Being cautious of resembling the *Mushrikūn* in their celebrations, even though one may not intend it (i.e. what they intend).
10) There is no vow for an act of disobedience.
11) There is no vow for the son of Aadam regarding that which he does not possess (or is not capable of).

Chapter 11

It is from *Ash-Shirk* to Make a Vow to other than Allâh

The Statement of Allâh the Most High,

﴿يُوفُونَ بِالنَّذْرِ﴾

"They (are those who) fulfill (their) vows." (76:7)[1]

And His Statement,

﴿وَمَا أَنفَقْتُم مِّن نَّفَقَةٍ أَوْ نَذَرْتُم مِّن نَّذْرٍ فَإِنَّ اللَّهَ يَعْلَمُهُ﴾

"And whatever you spend for spendings (e.g. in *Ṣadaqah* — charity, etc. for Allâh's Cause) or whatever vow you make, be sure Allâh knows it all." (2:270)

And in the *Ṣaḥeeḥ*[2] it is narrated from 'Aishah رضي الله عنها that

---

[1] Concerning the Statement of Allâh the Most High,

﴿يُوفُونَ بِالنَّذْرِ﴾

"They (are those who) fulfill (their) vows." (76:7)

Allâh, the Mighty and Majestic commends those who fulfill the vows, and His commending those who fulfill the vows necessitates that this is an act of worship that is beloved to Him, and that it is legislated. Whatever is like this, then it is from the types of worship, and directing it to other than Allâh is major *Shirk*.

Likewise is His Statement,

﴿وَمَا أَنفَقْتُم مِّن نَّفَقَةٍ أَوْ نَذَرْتُم مِّن نَّذْرٍ فَإِنَّ اللَّهَ يَعْلَمُهُ﴾

"And whatever you spend for spendings (e.g. in *Ṣadaqah* — charity, etc. for Allâh's Cause) or whatever vow you make, be sure Allâh knows it all." (2:270)

[2] And in the *Ṣaḥeeḥ* it is narrated from 'Aishah رضي الله عنها that Allâh's Messenger ﷺ said,

This obligates fulfilling the vow and the obligation of this proves that it is a beloved act of worship. This is because that which is obligatory is from the types of worship, and whatever is a means for achieving it then it is also an

Allâh's Messenger ﷺ said,

«مَنْ نَذَرَ أَنْ يُطِيعَ اللهَ فَلْيُطِعْهُ؛ وَمَنْ نَذَرَ أَنْ يَعْصِيَ اللهَ فَلَا يَعْصِهِ»

"Whoever vows to obey Allâh, then let him obey Him, and whoever vows to disobey Allâh, then he should not disobey Him."[1]

Important issues of the Chapter

1) The obligation of fulfilling vows.
2) Since it is confirmed that it is an act of worship for Allâh, directing it to other than Him is an act of *Shirk*.
3) That it is not permissible to fulfil a vow of disobedience (to Allâh).

---

act of worship. The reason is that the means that leads to fulfilling the vow is the making of the vow itself. Was it not for the vow, there would be no fulfilling of the vow. So the fulfillment becomes obligatory, due to the fact that the responsible person is the one who has compelled himself to do this act of worship.

[1] The Prophet ﷺ then said,

«وَمَنْ نَذَرَ أَنْ يَعْصِيَ اللهَ فَلَا يَعْصِهِ»

"and whoever vows to disobey Allâh, then he should not disobey Him."

This is because the person's obligating himself to do an act of disobedience to Allâh opposes Allâh's prohibition of disobedience. However, he must expiate that (vow) with expiation for an oath, and the place of that discussion is in the chapters concerning vows in the books of *Fiqh*.

Making a vow to Allâh is a tremendous act of worship, and making a vow to other than Allâh is also an act of worship. Therefore, if the person making the vow turns to other than Allâh with his vow, then he has worshipped that other (person or thing). If the person making the vow turns to Allâh with his vow, then he has indeed worshipped Allâh, the Mighty and Majestic.

Chapter 12

It is from *Ash-Shirk* to Seek Refuge in other than Allâh*

The statement of Allâh the Most High,

﴿وَأَنَّهُۥ كَانَ رِجَالٌ مِّنَ ٱلْإِنسِ يَعُوذُونَ بِرِجَالٍ مِّنَ ٱلْجِنِّ فَزَادُوهُمْ رَهَقًا﴾

---

* The word "from" here is for portioning (i.e. it is a part of the thing), and this *Shirk* is the major *Shirk*. This is because the letters *Alif* and *Laam* that are included with the word *Ash-Shirk* refers to that which is well-known, which is that seeking refuge in other than Allâh is major *Shirk* with Allâh. Seeking refuge is to request protection, and the letters *Seen* and *Taa'* (in the word *Isti'aathah*) are usually used to mean seeking. Protection means to seek that which will give security against evil. Seeking is a type of turning to and supplication, as there is someone from whom something is sought. If the one from whom something is sought is higher in status than the one who is seeking, then the act that is directed towards him is called supplication. Hence, in reality, seeking refuge is a request for protection, which is a supplication that contains that (request). And if it is a supplication then it is worship, and worship is for Allâh (alone) according to the consensus (of the Muslim scholars) and that which the textual evidence proves. Allâh said,

﴿وَأَنَّ ٱلْمَسَٰجِدَ لِلَّهِ فَلَا تَدْعُوا۟ مَعَ ٱللَّهِ أَحَدًا﴾

"And the mosques are for Allâh (Alone): so invoke not anyone along with Allâh." (72:18)

And He said,

﴿وَقَضَىٰ رَبُّكَ أَلَّا تَعْبُدُوٓا۟ إِلَّآ إِيَّاهُ﴾

"And your Lord has decreed that you worship none but Him." (17:23)

Actually, every evidence which mentions singling out Allâh with supplication or worship, then it is a proof for the special nature of this issue. The reality of this seeking refuge — that is only suitable for Allâh — is that which combines between two things. The first is the apparent deed of seeking protection, which is that he is protected from this evil or saved from it. The second is the hidden deed, which is the turning of the heart, its tranquility, its necessity and need for this one from whom refuge and

"And verily there were men among mankind who took refuge with some men among the jinn, but they (the jinn) increased them (mankind) in foolishness and transgression." (72:6)[1]

It is narrated that Khawlah bint Hakeem said, "I heard Allâh's Messenger ﷺ saying,

«مَنْ نَزَلَ مَنْزِلًا فَقَالَ: أَعُوذُ بِكَلِمَاتِ اللهِ التَّامَّاتِ مِنْ شَرِّ مَا خَلَقَ، لَمْ يَضُرَّهُ شَيْءٌ حَتَّى يَرْحَلَ مِنْ مَنْزِلِهِ ذَلِكَ»

---

protection is sought, and turning the matter of his salvation over to him. Thus, this seeking refuge is not suitable for any but Allâh according to the consensus (of the Muslim scholars). And if it is said, "It is suitable to seek refuge in the creation in that which the creation is capable of," then this is due to what has come in some of the evidences that prove this. That which is meant here is that seeking refuge by a statement (in someone of the creation) with serenity of the heart (being reliant) upon Allâh, its turning to Allâh and his good thinking of Him. Also, the person knows that this slave (of Allâh) is only a means. Thus, seeking refuge here is apparent, yet the reality of seeking refuge has not been established in the (person's) heart. So if the matter is like this, then this is permissible. With this, what these superstitious people say is negated, in reference to seeking refuge in the dead, the jinn and *Awliyaa'*, and that seeking refuge in the creation is only in that which they are able to do, and that Allâh is the One Who gave them that ability.

[1]

﴿وَأَنَّهُۥ كَانَ رِجَالٌ مِّنَ ٱلْإِنسِ يَعُوذُونَ بِرِجَالٍ مِّنَ ٱلْجِنِّ فَزَادُوهُمْ رَهَقًا﴾

"And verily there were men among mankind who took shelter with the males among the jinn, but they (jinn) increased them (mankind) in sin and transgression." (72:6)

The meaning of the word *"Rahaqan"* here is fear and confusion in the heart, which necessitated for them *Al-Irhaaq* (oppression). This *Rahaq* occurs in the bodies and the souls. Thus, when the matter is like this, then it is from the punishment upon them and punishment is only for a sin. Therefore, this Verse proves the rebuke of these people. They were only criticized because they directed this act of worship to other than Allâh, and Allâh commanded that refuge be sought in Him besides all others. There is

"Whoever settles at a place and says: I seek refuge with the perfect words of Allâh from the evil of what He created, nothing will harm him until he departs from that place of his.'"[1] (Recorded by Muslim).

Important issues of the Chapter

1) The explanation of the Verse of *Surah Al-Jinn* (72:6).
2) The fact that it (seeking refuge in other than Allâh) is from *Ash-Shirk*.
3) Using the *Hadith* as an evidence for this because the scholars use it to prove that the words of Allâh are not created. They say, "Because seeking refuge in that which is created is *Shirk*."
4) The virtue of this supplication, despite its brevity.
5) That the fact that some worldly benefit may be attained by some (created) thing, such as preventing an evil or bringing about some benefit, does not prove that it (seeking refuge in other than Allâh) is not from *Ash-Shirk*.

---

another station, which is the statement of Qataadah and some of the *Salaf* that *Rahaqan* means sin. This is obvious because seeking refuge (in other than Allâh) necessitates sin.

[1] It is narrated that Khawlah bint Hakeem said, "I heard Allâh's Messenger ﷺ saying, 'Whoever settles at a place and says...'"

The point of evidence here is that the Prophet ﷺ clarified the virtue of seeking refuge in the words of Allâh, and He made the evil creations that which forgiveness is sought against and the words of Allâh that by which refuge was sought.

﴿مِن شَرِّ مَا خَلَقَ﴾

"From the evil of what You created," (113:2)

means from the evil of that which Allâh has created. The intent of this general statement is, "from the evil of the creations that contain evil", because there are creations that are good and that do not contain any evil, like Paradise, the angels, the Messengers, the Prophets and the righteous believers (*Awliyaa'*).

Chapter 13

It is from *Ash-Shirk* that one Seeks Help in other than Allâh or Supplicates other than Him*

The Statement of Allâh the Most High,

﴿وَلَا تَدْعُ مِن دُونِ ٱللَّهِ مَا لَا يَنفَعُكَ وَلَا يَضُرُّكَ فَإِن فَعَلْتَ فَإِنَّكَ إِذًا مِّنَ ٱلظَّٰلِمِينَ ○ وَإِن يَمْسَسْكَ ٱللَّهُ بِضُرٍّ فَلَا كَاشِفَ لَهُۥٓ إِلَّا هُوَ﴾ الآية

---

* This heading means that it is from the major *Shirk*. His Statement, "or Supplicates other than Him" after his saying, "that one Seeks Help in other than Allâh" contains a conjunction attaching the general to the specific. This is because seeking help is one of the individual methods of supplication, as it is a request and requesting is supplication.

Seeking help (*Al-Istighaathah*) is to seek aid (*Al-Ghawth*), and aid occurs for whoever falls into distress and calamity from which he fears some severe harm or destruction. Therefore, it is said, "I seek his help (*Agaathuhu*)," when a person seeks refuge in someone and that person helps him in what he has been afflicted with and removes it from him. Hence, seeking help (*Al-Istighaathah*) is to seek aid (*Al-Ghawth*). It becomes a form of major *Shirk* when the person seeks the help of the creation in that which no one has the power to do except Allâh. If it occurs in that which the creation is able to do, then it is permissible. This is due to what Allâh said in the story of Moosaa,

﴿فَٱسْتَغَٰثَهُ ٱلَّذِى مِن شِيعَتِهِۦ عَلَى ٱلَّذِى مِنْ عَدُوِّهِۦ﴾

"So the man of his (own) party asked him for help against his foe." (28:15)

Concerning his statement "or Supplicates other than Him", supplication is worship. Supplication is of two types. The first: *Du'aa'ul-Mas'alah* (The Supplication of Request). We mean by this that which contains a request and question for Allâh. The person raises his hands to Allâh and supplicates. This is called the Supplication of Request, and it is that which usually occurs with the common masses of the Muslims in what is called supplication (*Du'aa'*). The second: *Du'aa'ul-'Ibaadah* (The Supplication of Worship). This is just as Allâh said,

﴿وَأَنَّ ٱلْمَسَٰجِدَ لِلَّهِ فَلَا تَدْعُوا۟ مَعَ ٱللَّهِ أَحَدًا﴾

"And invoke not besides Allâh any such that will neither profit you nor hurt you, but if (in case) you did so, you shall certainly be one of the *Zâlimûn* (polytheists and wrongdoers). And if Allâh touches you with hurt, there is none who can remove it but He." (10:106-107)[1]

"And the mosques are for Allâh (Alone), so do not invoke anyone along with Allâh." (72:18)

This means do not worship anyone along with Allâh and do not ask anyone along with Allâh. This is also similar to what the Prophet ﷺ said,

«الدُّعَاءُ هُوَ الْعِبَادَةُ»

"Supplication is worship."

Between these two (types of supplication) there is a difference. In reference to the Supplication of Worship, it is like the situation of one who offers prayer (*Aṣ-Ṣalaah*) or gives *Az-Zakâh*. Every category from the categories of worship is called *Du'aa'* (supplication), but it is a supplication of an act of worship. If this is confirmed then this separation or division is extremely important regarding the proof in the Qur'ān and in understanding the proofs that the people of knowledge have related. This is because it has occurred with the people who follow superstitions and those who call to *Ash-Shirk* that they interpret the Verse regarding the request as meaning supplication. In reality there is no difference between the Supplication of Requesting and the Supplication of Worship. One of them is the same as the other, either by inclusion or by necessity. The Supplication of Requesting is one of the types of worship and the Supplication of Worship necessitates that one asks Allâh to accept it.

﴿وَلَا تَدْعُ مِن دُونِ ٱللَّهِ مَا لَا يَنفَعُكَ وَلَا يَضُرُّكَ﴾

[1] "And invoke not besides Allâh any such that will neither profit you nor hurt you..." (10:106)

His Statement,

"And invoke not" is a prohibition. This prohibition is directed towards the deed "*Tad'u*" (you invoke). Since this is the case, then it generally includes all types of supplication - the Supplication of Requesting and the Supplication of Worship. This is one of the goals of the Shaikh in using this Verse as evidence. This Verse proves the prohibition of someone turning to anyone other than Allâh with a Supplication of Requesting or a Supplication of Worship. The worst of this prohibition is that it

(supplication) is directed to Al-Muṣtafaa (i.e. Prophet Muhammad ﷺ), who is the *Imam* of the righteous and the *Imam* of the people of *At-Tauhid*.
His Statement,

﴿مِن دُونِ ٱللَّهِ﴾

"besides Allâh"

includes the meaning, "with Allâh" or "independently besides Allâh."

﴿مَا لَا يَنفَعُكَ وَلَا يَضُرُّكَ﴾

"What will neither profit you nor harm you,"

means one who will nether benefit you nor harm you. The word *Maa* (what) includes the intelligent beings, such as angels, Messengers, and righteous believers (*Awliyaa'*), and the inanimate things, such as idols, trees and stones.

Allâh then said to His Prophet ﷺ,

﴿فَإِن فَعَلْتَ﴾

"but if (in case) you did so."

This means if you called upon anyone besides Allâh, and that someone has the description of not being able to benefit you nor harm you,

﴿فَإِنَّكَ إِذًا﴾

"then you shall certainly be"

- meaning because of this supplicating

﴿مِّنَ ٱلظَّٰلِمِينَ﴾

"one of the *Zâlimûn* (polytheists and wrongdoers)."

The meaning of *Zulm* (wrongdoing) here is *Ash-Shirk*. So if this is the case in regards to the Prophet ﷺ, whom Allâh perfected for him (his belief in) *At-Tauhid*, if there occurred any *Shirk* from him, then he would be a wrongdoer (*Zâlim*) and a polytheist (*Mushrik*) — may Allâh forbid that such would happen to him. Thus, this is a threat for whoever is less than him (the Prophet ﷺ) of those who are not perfect and who have not be given any protection from that.

Then Allâh mentioned the general principle in this regard, which cuts the veins of *Ash-Shirk* from the heart, when He said,

﴿وَإِن يَمْسَسْكَ ٱللَّهُ بِضُرٍّ فَلَا كَاشِفَ لَهُۥٓ إِلَّا هُوَ﴾

"And if Allâh touches you with harm, there is none who can remove it but He." (10: 107)

And His Statement,

﴿فَٱبْتَغُوا۟ عِندَ ٱللَّهِ ٱلرِّزْقَ وَٱعْبُدُوهُ﴾ الآية

"So seek the provision from Allâh (alone) and worship Him (alone)." (29:17)[1]

And His Statement,

﴿وَمَنْ أَضَلُّ مِمَّن يَدْعُوا۟ مِن دُونِ ٱللَّهِ مَن لَّا يَسْتَجِيبُ لَهُۥٓ إِلَىٰ يَوْمِ ٱلْقِيَٰمَةِ﴾ الآية

If Allâh touches you with some harm, who can remove the harm? He Who decreed it and destined it upon you may remove it. This cuts off turning to other than Allâh. However, it still remains allowed - regarding what the human being has the ability to do — that he (the person) may be turned to in seeking aid or seeking drink or things similar to that. Verily this is from that which has been permitted, because Allâh has made the person a means in that he is able to remove it (the harm) by the permission of Allâh. Otherwise, the true remover of harms is Allâh.

The statement, "with harm" here is also non-specific. It has come in the form of a conditional clause, so it includes all types of harm, regardless of whether it is a harm in the religion or in the worldly affairs, and regardless of whether it is a harm in the bodies, the wealth, the children and so forth.

[1] Allâh said,

﴿فَٱبْتَغُوا۟ عِندَ ٱللَّهِ ٱلرِّزْقَ وَٱعْبُدُوهُ وَٱشْكُرُوا۟ لَهُۥٓ﴾

"So seek the provision from Allâh (Alone) and worship Him (Alone) and be grateful (thankful) to Him." (29:17)

The foundation of the arrangement of this statement is as follows: So seek the provision from Allâh. And concerning the word *'Ind* (from or with), the scholars of meanings have said that putting first that which should be made last is used for particularizing. In other words, seek the provision from Allâh and make that seeking specifically for Allâh. Do not seek the help of other than Him in seeking provision. Provision is a general noun that includes all that is suitable to be granted and given. This includes health, wellbeing, wealth and so forth. Then he said, "and worship Him", in order to combine the kinds of requesting with what is included in the Supplication of Requesting and the Supplication of Worship.

"And who is more astray than one who calls (invokes) besides Allâh, such as will not answer him till the Day of Resurrection?" (46:5)[1]

And His Statement,

﴿أَمَّن يُجِيبُ ٱلْمُضْطَرَّ إِذَا دَعَاهُ وَيَكْشِفُ ٱلسُّوٓءَ﴾

"Is not He Who responds to the distressed one, when he calls on Him; and Who removes the evil." (27:62)[2]

---

[1] And His Statement,

﴿وَمَنْ أَضَلُّ مِمَّن يَدْعُوا۟ مِن دُونِ ٱللَّهِ مَن لَّا يَسْتَجِيبُ لَهُۥٓ إِلَىٰ يَوْمِ ٱلْقِيَٰمَةِ وَهُمْ عَن دُعَآئِهِمْ غَٰفِلُونَ﴾

"And who is more astray than one who calls (invokes) besides Allâh, such as will not answer him till the Day of Resurrection and who are (even) unaware of their calls (invocations) to them?" (46:5)

The point of proof from the Verse is that Allâh uses the word "calls (invokes)". So the description has come with the most repulsive misguidance regarding whoever calls upon the deceased, who are not living, besides Allâh. The proof that Allâh intends the deceased and not the idols, stones and trees is that the lack of response (to the supplications) will be

﴿إِلَىٰ يَوْمِ ٱلْقِيَٰمَةِ﴾

"till the Day of Resurrection."

And this is regarding the deceased because the dead person will be resurrected and be able to hear on the Day of Resurrection. The word Man (who) is for whoever it becomes clear that he is known. These were people who addressed others and they were addressed and they were known and things were known from them.

[2] And His Statement,

﴿أَمَّن يُجِيبُ ٱلْمُضْطَرَّ إِذَا دَعَاهُ﴾

"Is not He Who responds to the distressed one, when he calls on Him?" (27:62)

This Verse contains the point that the response of the distressed one in invocation — the Supplication of Request — only comes from Allâh, the Mighty and Sublime.

Aṭ-Ṭabarâni recorded with his chain of narration that there was in the time of the Prophet ﷺ a hypocrite who used to harm the believers. So some of them said, "Come with us so that we can seek the help of Allâh's Messenger ﷺ against this hypocrite."[1] So the Prophet ﷺ said,

«إِنَّهُ لَا يُسْتَغَاثُ بِي وَإِنَّمَا يُسْتَغَاثُ بِاللهِ»

"Verily help is not sought from me, rather it is only sought from Allâh."[2]

﴿وَيَكْشِفُ ٱلسُّوٓءَ﴾

"And Who removes the evil?"

Removal of evil sometimes is by seeking help and sometimes by other than that.

﴿أَءِلَٰهٌ مَّعَ ٱللَّهِ﴾

"Is there any god with Allâh?"

This is a rhetorical question for rejection. Allâh rebukes them for taking another god besides Allâh. For what thing (action)? For the person's invoking other than Allâh or turning to other than Allâh for the removal of evil in that which none is able to do except Allâh.

﴿قَلِيلًا مَّا تَذَكَّرُونَ﴾

"Little is that you remember."

[1] The Shaikh said, "Aṭ-Ṭabarâni recorded with his chain of narration that there was in the time of the Prophet ﷺ a hypocrite who used to harm the believers. So some of them said..." The speaker (who spoke on behalf of the believers) was Abu Bakr Aṣ-Ṣiddeeq رَضِيَ اللهُ عَنْهُ, as has been mentioned in some of the reports.

"Come with us so that we can seek the help of Allâh's Messenger ﷺ against this hypocrite." This request from the Companions to the Prophet ﷺ was a permissible request because they were requesting assistance from the Prophet ﷺ in that which he was able to do in his lifetime. This is because in this situation he was able to help by commanding that the hypocrite be killed, or imprisoned, or punished or by some other method, as he was harming the believers. However, the Prophet ﷺ taught them the proper etiquette in this matter.

[2] So the Prophet ﷺ said,

Important issues of the Chapter

1) Attaching the supplication to seeking help is a form of conjunction that attaches the general to the specific.
2) The explanation of the Allâh's Statement,

﴿وَلَا تَدْعُ مِن دُونِ ٱللَّهِ مَا لَا يَنفَعُكَ وَلَا يَضُرُّكَ﴾

"And invoke not besides Allâh any such that will neither profit you nor harm you." (10:106)

3) That this is the major *Shirk*.
4) That the most righteous of people, if he does this in order to please others, he will become one of the *Zâlimûn* (polytheists and wrongdoers).
5) The explanation of the verse which comes after it (10:107).
6) The fact that this does not benefit in this world, along with its being an act of disbelief (*Kufr*).
7) The explanation of the third Verse (29:17).
8) That the provision should only be requested from Allâh, just as Paradise is only requested from Him.
9) The explanation of the fourth Verse (46:5)
10) That there is no one more astray than one who invokes other than Allâh.
11) That the one who is called is unaware of the invocation of

---

«إِنَّهُ لَا يُسْتَغَاثُ بِي وَإِنَّمَا يُسْتَغَاثُ بِاللهِ»

"Verily help is not sought from me, rather it is only sought from Allâh."

He said this because there had occurred from them a type of turning to the Prophet ﷺ in that which he was able to do. Therefore, he explained to them that it is obligatory upon them to seek help from Allâh first. What is in this *Hadith* is proven by the previous Verses (of Qur'ān).

the one who supplicates and he does not know about it.

12) This supplication will be a cause of the one who was invoked hating and despising the one who made the supplication.

13) Calling this supplication an act of worship (performed) for the one who was invoked.

14) The rejection of the person who was invoked of this worship.

15) That these matters are the cause of him being the most misguided of the people.

16) The explanation of the fifth Verse (27:62).

17) The astonishing matter, which is the confession of the idol worshippers that none answers (the invocation of) the distressed except Allâh. For this reason they invoke Him in hardships making their religious worship solely for Him.

18) Al-Mustafaa's (Prophet Muhammad ﷺ) protecting the sanctuary (i.e. sacredness) of *At-Tauhid* and proper manners with Allâh.

Chapter 14

The Statement of the Allâh, the Most High,

﴿أَيُشْرِكُونَ مَا لَا يَخْلُقُ شَيْـًٔا وَهُمْ يُخْلَقُونَ ○ وَلَا يَسْتَطِيعُونَ لَهُمْ نَصْرًا﴾

"Do they attribute as partners to Allâh those who created nothing but they themselves are created? No help can they give them, nor can they help themselves." (7:191,192)[1]

---

[1] Presenting this chapter after the previous chapters is an excellent (method) of presentation and it shows tremendous understanding and depth in knowledge. This is because the explanation of the necessity of Allâh's *Tawhid*, and His deserving to be worshipped in His Godliness is what is centered upon in the natures (of people), as He is One in His Lordship. Hence, the evidence of Allâh deserving worship alone besides all others besides Him is a natural (innate), realistic and intellectual evidence.

This chapter contains the explanation that He Who creates, provides sustenance and owns is Allâh Alone, and that others besides Allâh do not possess any share of creating, providing sustenance or the decision in matters. Others besides Allâh do not possess any real ownership in any matter from the affairs, not even the most exalted of the creation in status, who is the Prophet ﷺ. Allâh said to him,

﴿لَيْسَ لَكَ مِنَ ٱلْأَمْرِ شَىْءٌ﴾

"Not for you (O Muhammad ﷺ, but for Allâh) is the decision." (3:128)

This means, "You do not possess anything of the matter." So who is it that possesses it then? It is Allâh, the Mighty and Majestic. Thus, if this is negated from the Prophet ﷺ, then it is negated even more so from other besides him. Those who turn to people in the graves, or the righteous people, and pious believers and the Prophets, among them they have some claim that these people possess some things. Either they possess something of the (ability to provide) sustenance, or mediation, or intercession without the permission of Allâh and His will. In reality these people are only subjects who are created. They do not create anything and they themselves are created. They are not able to help those

The Statement of Allâh,

﴿وَٱلَّذِينَ تَدۡعُونَ مِن دُونِهِۦ مَا يَمۡلِكُونَ مِن قِطۡمِيرٍ﴾

"And those, whom you invoke or call upon instead of Him, own not even a *Qitmîr* (a thin membrane over the date-stone)." (35:13)[1]

---

who ask of them. They do not possess anything of the dominion. The Qur'ān contains many proofs that the One Who deserves worship is Allâh Alone, besides all others. From these evidences and proofs is that which is in the *Qur'ān* that proves that the *Mushrikūn* (idolaters, polytheists) affirm the *Tawḥid* of Lordship (*Tawhid ur-Rubûbiyyah*). From these proofs is what is in the Qur'ān that Allâh aids His Messengers and His *Awliyaa'* (the pious believers) against their enemies. From these proofs is that the creation is weak and that he (the created being) came to life by no choice of his own. Rather, Allâh is the One Who brought him into this life. He (the created being) will also be taken out of this life without him having any choice in the matter. Therefore, he is controlled and he knows without a doubt that the One Who controls him, subjugates him and places him in this situation is not these (false) gods. Rather, it is Allâh Alone, and He is the One Who gives life and causes death. This is a general affirmation that is known by everyone in his innate nature. From these proofs is that unto Allâh belongs the Best Names and the Most Lofty Attributes, and that He possesses the Perfect Characteristics and the Most Grand Characteristics. Unto Him belongs absolute perfection that is not subject to any deficiency in any way in regards to every Name, every Characteristic and every Description that belongs to Him.

[1] The Statement of Allâh,

﴿وَٱلَّذِينَ تَدۡعُونَ مِن دُونِهِۦ مَا يَمۡلِكُونَ مِن قِطۡمِيرٍ﴾

"And those, whom you invoke or call upon instead of Him, own not even a *Qitmîr* (a thin membrane over the date-stone)." (35:13)

This is the point of witness. Even the *Qitmîr*, which is the skin of the date-stone or the connected string that runs from the top of the date-stone to the skin of the fruit, they do not even own that. Thus, this applies even more so to things other than it (the *Qitmîr*), that are superior to it. The word *Allaṯheena* (those) is an *Ism Mawṣool* (connecting noun) that generally includes everything that is called upon besides Allâh: the angels, or the Prophets and Messengers, or the righteous people from those who are

And it is recorded in the *Ṣaḥeeḥ* that Anas رَضِيَ اللهُ عَنْهُ said, "The Prophet ﷺ was struck on the day of Uḥud (the battle of Uḥud) and his tooth was broken. So he said,

«كَيْفَ يُفْلِحُ قَوْمٌ شَجُّوا نَبِيَّهُمْ؟»

'How will a people be successful who strike their Prophet?' Then the verse (3:128) was revealed,

﴿لَيْسَ لَكَ مِنَ ٱلْأَمْرِ شَىْءٌ﴾

"Not for you (O Muhammad ﷺ but for Allâh) is the decision.'"

And in it (the *Ṣaḥeeḥ)* it is also narrated that Ibn 'Umar رَضِيَ اللهُ عَنْهُمَا said that he heard Allâh's Messenger ﷺ, saying when he raised his head from bowing in the last *Rak'ah* (unit of prayer) of *Al-Fajr* (the morning prayer),

«اللَّهُمَّ الْعَنْ فُلَانًا وَفُلَانًا»

"O Allâh! Curse so-and-so and so-and-so."

He said this after he had said,

«سَمِعَ اللهُ لِمَنْ حَمِدَهُ رَبَّنَا وَلَكَ الْحَمْدُ»

"Allâh hears whoever praises Him. Our Lord, and for you is all the praise."

So Allâh revealed (the verse),

﴿لَيْسَ لَكَ مِنَ ٱلْأَمْرِ شَىْءٌ﴾

"Not for you (O Muhammad ﷺ, but for Allâh) is the decision." (3:128)

And in another narration it was reported that he (the Prophet

---

dead, or the evil people, or the jinn, and so forth. Everyone and everything that is called upon does not possess even a *Qiṭmîr*. Then why should they be asked? Therefore, it is obligatory that the person turn to the One Who possesses that with his request.

ﷺ) supplicated against Ṣafwaan bin Umayyah, Suhayl bin 'Amr and Al-Ḥaarith bin Hishaam, so the verse was revealed,

﴿لَيْسَ لَكَ مِنَ ٱلْأَمْرِ شَىْءٌ﴾

"Not for you (O Muhammad ﷺ but for Allâh) is the decision." (3:128)[1]

---

[1] And it is recorded in the *Ṣaḥeeḥ* that Anas رَضِيَ الله عَنْهُ said, "The Prophet ﷺ was struck on the day of Uhud (the battle of Uhud) and his tooth was broken. So he said,

«كَيْفَ يُفْلِحُ قَوْمٌ شَجُّوا نَبِيَّهُمْ؟»

'How will a people be successful who strike their Prophet?' Then the Verse (3:128) was revealed,

﴿لَيْسَ لَكَ مِنَ ٱلْأَمْرِ شَىْءٌ﴾

'Not for you (O Muhammad ﷺ, but for Allâh) is the decision.''' (3:128)

And in it (the *Ṣaḥeeḥ*) it is also narrated that Ibn 'Umar رَضِيَ الله عَنْهُ said that he heard Allâh's Messenger ﷺ saying when he raised his head from bowing in the last *Rak'ah* (unit of prayer) of *Al-Fajr* (the morning prayer), "O Allâh! Curse so-and-so and so-and-so." He said this after he had said, "Allâh hears whoever praises Him. Our Lord, and for you is all the praise." So Allâh revealed (the Verse),

﴿لَيْسَ لَكَ مِنَ ٱلْأَمْرِ شَىْءٌ﴾

"Not for you (O Muhammad ﷺ, but for Allâh) is the decision." (3:128)

And in another narration it was reported that he (the Prophet ﷺ) supplicated against Ṣafwaan bin Umayyah, Suhayl bin 'Amr and Al-Ḥaarith bin Hishaam, so the Verse was revealed,

﴿لَيْسَ لَكَ مِنَ ٱلْأَمْرِ شَىْءٌ﴾

"Not for you (O Muhammad ﷺ, but for Allâh) is the decision." (3:128)

These *Ahadith* did not possess anything from the sovereignty of Allâh. Therefore, if the matter is such, then verily the Prophet ﷺ conveyed that and explained it, and this applies even more so to others besides him. Thus, this applies even more so to the angels that this (ownership or

And in it (the *Ṣaḥeeḥ)* it is narrated that Abu Hurayrah رَضِيَ اللهُ عَنْهُ said, "Allâh's Messenger ﷺ stood when it was revealed to him (the Verse),

﴿وَأَنذِرْ عَشِيرَتَكَ ٱلْأَقْرَبِينَ﴾

'And warn your tribe (O Muhammad ﷺ) of near kindred.' (26:214)

So he said,

«يَا مَعْشَرَ قُرَيْشٍ - أَوْ كَلِمَةً نَحْوَهَا - اشْتَرُوا أَنْفُسَكُمْ لَا أُغْنِي عَنْكُمْ مِنَ اللهِ شَيْئًا، يَا عَبَّاسُ بْنَ عَبْدِالْمُطَّلِب، لَا أُغْنِي عَنْكَ مِنَ اللهِ شَيْئًا، يَا صَفِيَّةُ عَمَّةَ رَسُولِ اللهِ ﷺ لَا أُغْنِي عَنْكِ مِنَ اللهِ شَيْئًا، يَا فَاطِمَةُ بِنْتَ مُحَمَّدٍ سَلِينِي مِنْ مَالِي مَا شِئْتِ لَا أُغْنِي عَنْكِ مِنَ اللهِ شَيئًا»

'O people of Quraysh — or words similar to that — purchase your own selves. I will not be able to benefit you anything against Allâh. O 'Abbaas bin 'Abdul-Muṭṭalib, I will not be able to benefit you anything against Allâh. O Ṣafiyyah, aunt of Allâh's Messenger ﷺ, I will not be able to benefit you anything against Allâh. O Faaṭimah, daughter of Muhammad, ask me of my wealth whatever you wish. I will not be able to benefit you anything against Allâh.'"[1]

---

control over affairs) would be negated from them, and likewise with the Prophets and the righteous people among the followers of the Messengers.

Hence, since the matter is such, all turning to other than Allâh is negated, and it is obligatory that worship and all it types, such as supplication, seeking help, seeking refuge, slaughtering, vowing, and other types of devotional acts be directed to *Al-Ḥaqq* (Allâh) alone besides all others.

[1] And in it (the *Ṣaḥeeḥ*) it is narrated that Abu Hurayrah رَضِيَ اللهُ عَنْهُ said, "The Allâh's Messenger ﷺ stood when it was revealed to him (the Verse),

﴿وَأَنذِرْ عَشِيرَتَكَ ٱلْأَقْرَبِينَ﴾

Important issues of the Chapter

1) The explanation of the two Verses (7:120 and 35:13-14)
2) The story of Uḥud.
3) The *Qunoot* (invoking Allâh while standing in the *Ṣalâh*) of the leader of the Messengers (Prophet Muhammad ﷺ) and behind the leaders of the righteous believers (the Companions رضي الله عنهم) saying *"Ameen"* in the prayer.
4) That those who were supplicated against were *Kuffâr* (disbelievers).
5) That they did things that most of the disbelievers did not do, such as striking their Prophet, their eagerness to kill him, their mutilating the bodies of the Muslims who were killed (in the battle) even though they were their own cousins (i.e. their relatives).
6) Concerning this Allâh revealed to him (the Verse),

﴿لَيْسَ لَكَ مِنَ ٱلْأَمْرِ شَىْءٌ﴾

"Not for you (O Muhammad ﷺ, but for Allâh) is the decision." (3:128)

7) Allâh's Statement,

"And warn your tribe (O Muhammad ﷺ) of (kindred) near.' (26:214)

And he said, 'O people of Quraysh...'''

This is a clear proof that the Prophet ﷺ was not able to do anything that would benefit his near relatives, except what Allâh had given to him of the Message and fulfilling the trust. However, in reference to him being able to benefit them with anything against Allâh - such as him saving them from the torment, or the chastisement, or the punishment - Allâh has not given anyone of His creation anything of His sovereignty. It is only He Alone Who possesses the sovereignty and omnipotence. He is Alone in perfection, beauty and magnificence.

﴿أَوْ يَتُوبَ عَلَيْهِمْ أَوْ يُعَذِّبَهُمْ﴾

"Whether He turns in mercy to (pardon) them or punishes them," (3:128)

so He turned to (pardoned) them and they believed.

8) The *Qunoot* (invoking Allâh while standing in the *Ṣalaah*) in the time of disasters.

9) Naming those who are supplicated against in the *Ṣalaah* by their names and their fathers' names.

10) Cursing a specific person in the *Qunoot*.

11) The Prophet's story when the verse was revealed to him,

﴿وَأَنذِرْ عَشِيرَتَكَ ٱلْأَقْرَبِينَ﴾

"And warn your tribe (O Muhammad ﷺ) of near kindred." (26:214)

12) The Prophet's ﷺ seriousness in this matter in that he did what caused him to be labeled as insane, and likewise is the situation if the Muslim does it (what the Prophet ﷺ did) now.

13) His saying to those distant from him and close to him, "I cannot benefit you anything against Allâh." He even said, "O Faaṭimah, daughter of Muhammad, I cannot benefit you anything against Allâh." Since he made this clear - and he is the leader of the Messengers - that he could not benefit the leader of the women of all the worlds (Faaṭimah), and the person believes that he only speaks the truth, then he looks at what has fallen into the hearts of certain special people today, *At-Tauhid* and the strangeness of the religion will become clear to the person.

Chapter 15

The Statement of the Allâh, the Most High,

﴿حَتَّىٰٓ إِذَا فُزِّعَ عَن قُلُوبِهِمۡ قَالُواْ مَاذَا قَالَ رَبُّكُمۡۖ قَالُواْ ٱلۡحَقَّۖ وَهُوَ ٱلۡعَلِيُّ ٱلۡكَبِيرُ﴾

"Until when fear is banished from their (angels) hearts they say: 'What is it that your Lord has said?' They say: The Truth. And He is the Most High, the Most Great.''' (34:23) [1]

---

[1] "Until when fear is banished from their hearts they say:

﴿قَالُواْ مَاذَا قَالَ رَبُّكُمۡۖ قَالُواْ ٱلۡحَقَّۖ وَهُوَ ٱلۡعَلِيُّ ٱلۡكَبِيرُ﴾

'What is it that your Lord has said?' They say: 'The Truth. And He is the Most High, the Most Great.''' (34:23)

The word *Fuzzi'ah* (in the Verse) means that the fear is removed from the hearts of the angels. Thus, the angels have intense knowledge of Allâh and tremendous knowledge of Him, the Mighty and Majestic. And from that which they know about Allâh is that He is Al-Jabbaar (the Almighty), He is Al-Jaleel (the Most Magnificent), glory be unto Him, and He is the Owner of the Dominion. Due to this, their fear of Him is intense, because they cannot do without Him for even the blinking of an eye.

The attributes that contain this proof are the attributes of magnificence for Allâh. This is because the attributes are divided into various divisions with considerations. From the divisions of the attributes is that they are divided into attributes of magnificence and attributes of beauty. The attributes that cause fear, terror and fright of the Lord in the heart are called attributes of magnificence. The One Who truly possesses the attributes of magnificence is Allâh, because He is perfect in His Attributes. So if this is the case, then the One Who is perfect in His Attributes is the One Who is truly deserving of worship. Concerning the created human beings, then they are deficient in their attributes. They know that their life is not a perfect life. It is only a life that if it is exposed to anything (disastrous) the created being becomes dead. If he is exposed to any disease, he becomes sick. Therefore, they are weak, poor and needy. They do not have the perfect attributes. This is an evidence of their deficiency and inability, and it is an evidence that they

In the Ṣaḥeeḥ, Abu Hurayrah رَضِيَ اللهُ عَنْهُ narrated that the Prophet ﷺ said,

«إِذَا قَضَى اللهُ الأَمْرَ فِي السَّمَاءِ ضَرَبَتِ الْمَلَائِكَةُ بِأَجْنِحَتِهَا خُضْعَانًا لِقَوْلِهِ، كَأَنَّهُ سِلْسِلَةٌ عَلَى صَفْوَانٍ يَنْفُذُهُمْ ذَلِكَ، ﴿حَتَّىٰٓ إِذَا فُزِّعَ عَن قُلُوبِهِمْ قَالُوا۟ مَاذَا قَالَ رَبُّكُمْ ۖ قَالُوا۟ ٱلْحَقَّ ۖ وَهُوَ ٱلْعَلِىُّ ٱلْكَبِيرُ﴾ فَيَسْمَعُهَا مُسْتَرِقُ السَّمْعِ، وَمُسْتَرِقُ السَّمْعِ هَكَذَا بَعْضُهُ فَوقَ بَعْضٍ - وَصَفَهُ سُفْيَانُ بِكَفِّهِ، فَحَرَّفَهَا وَبَدَّدَ بَيْنَ أَصَابِعِهِ - فَيَسْمَعُ الْكَلِمَةَ فَيُلْقِيهَا إِلَى مَنْ تَحْتَهُ، ثُمَّ يُلْقِيهَا الآخَرُ إِلَى مَنْ تَحْتَهُ، حَتَّى يُلْقِيَهَا عَلَى لِسَانِ السَّاحِرِ أَوِ الْكَاهِنِ، فَرُبَّمَا أَدْرَكَهُ الشِّهَابُ قَبْلَ أَنْ يُلْقِيَهَا، وَرُبَّمَا أَلْقَاهَا قَبْلَ أَنْ يُدْرِكَهُ، فَيَكْذِبُ مَعَهَا مِائَةَ كَذْبَةٍ، فَيُقَالُ: أَلَيْسَ قَدْ قَالَ لَنَا يَوْمَ كَذَا وَكَذَا:؟ فَيُصَدَّقُ بِتِلْكَ الْكَلِمَةِ الَّتِي سُمِعَتْ مِنَ السَّمَاءِ»

"When Allâh decrees the matter in the heaven, the angels strike their wings in submission to His Statement, as if it (the sound of Allâh's voice) were a chain being dragged upon smooth rocks and it penetrates them causing them to be terrified. "Until when the state of fear is banished from their hearts, they say, 'What has your Lord said?' They say, 'The Truth. And He is the Most High, the Most Great.''' (34:23) Then, the eavesdroppers (devils) hear this order, and these eavesdroppers are like this, one over the other (Sufyaan demonstrated that by holding his hand slanted and separating the fingers). Thus, an eavesdropper hears a word which he will convey to one who is below him, and the second will convey it one who is below him, until the last of them

---

are dominated and subjugated. Therefore, it is obligatory for the slaves to turn to the One Who has the perfect Attributes, and Characteristics of beauty and magnificence - and He is Allâh Alone. This is the intent of this chapter and it is obvious, by the praises of Allâh the Most High.

will convey it to the tongue of the magician or fortuneteller. Sometimes a shooting star may strike the devil before he can convey it, and sometimes he may convey it before the shooting star strikes him, whereupon the magician (or soothsayer) adds to it a hundred lies. Then it is said, 'Did not he (i.e. the magician) tell us such-and-such a thing on such-and-such date?' So that magician is said to have told the truth because of that statement which was heard from the heaven."

An-Nawwaas bin Sam'aan رَضِيَ اللهُ عَنْهُ narrated that Allâh's Messenger ﷺ said,

«إِذَا أَرَادَ اللهُ تَعَالَى أَنْ يُوحِيَ بِالْأَمْرِ تَكَلَّمَ بِالْوَحْيِ أَخَذَتِ السَّمٰوَاتِ مِنْهُ رَجْفَةٌ - أَوْ قَالَ: رَعْدَةٌ شَدِيدَةٌ - خَوفًا مِنَ اللهِ عَزَّ وَجَلَّ فَإِذَا سَمِعَ ذَلِكَ أَهْلُ السَّمٰوَاتِ صَعِقُوا وَخَرُّوا للهِ سُجَّدًا، فَيَكُونُ أَوَّلَ مَنْ يَرْفَعُ رَأْسَهُ جِبْرِيلُ، فَيُكَلِّمُهُ اللهُ مِنْ وَحْيِهِ بِمَا أَرَادَ، ثُمَّ يَمُرُّ جِبْرِيلُ عَلَى الْمَلَائِكَةِ: كُلَّمَا مَرَّ بِسَمَاءٍ سَأَلَهُ مَلَائِكَتُهَا: مَاذَا قَالَ رَبُّنَا يَا جِبْرِيلُ؟، فَيَقُولُ: قَالَ الْحَقَّ وَهُوَ الْعَلِيُّ الْكَبِيرُ، فَيَقُولُونَ كُلُّهُم مِثْلَ مَا قَالَ جِبْرِيلُ، فَيَنْتَهِي جِبْرِيلُ بِالْوَحْيِ إِلَى حَيْثُ أَمَرَهُ اللهُ عَزَّ وَجَلَّ»

"When Allâh the Most High wants to reveal a matter, He speaks with revelation that causes the heavens to shake - or he said: severe thundering - due to fear of Allâh, the Mighty and Majestic. So when the inhabitants of the heavens hear that, they are stunned and fall down in prostration to Allâh. Then, the first to raise his head is Jibreel, and Allâh tells him what he wants of His revelation. Then, Jibreel passes among the angels, and every time he passes through one of the heavens the angels ask him, 'What has our Lord said, O Jibreel?' Jibreel replies, 'He said the Truth, and He is the Most

High, the Most Great.' Then, all of them say what Jibreel said. So Jibreel takes the revelation to where Allâh, the Mighty and Majestic, has commanded him."

Important issues of the Chapter

1) The explanation of the Verse (34:23).
2) What the verse contains of evidence for the invalidation of *Ash-Shirk*. Especially regarding attachment to the righteous people. It is the Verse about which is said, "Verily it cuts the roots of the tree of Ash-Shirk from the heart."
3) The explanation of His Statement,

﴿قَالُوا۟ ٱلْحَقَّ وَهُوَ ٱلْعَلِىُّ ٱلْكَبِيرُ﴾

"They say, 'The Truth. And He is the Most High, the Most Great.'" (34:23)
4) The reason for their asking about that.
5) That Jibreel answers them after that by his saying, "He said such-and-such."
6) The mentioning that the first to raise his head is Jibreel.
7) That he (Jibreel) replies to all of the inhabitants of the heavens because they (all) ask him.
8) That the overwhelming shock covers all of the inhabitants of the heavens.
9) The shaking of the heavens due to the speech of Allâh.
10) That Jibreel is the one who delivers the revelation to where Allâh commands him.
11) Mention of eavesdropping of the devils.
12) The description of their mounting on top of each other.
13) The sending of shooting stars.

14) That sometimes the shooting star strikes the devil before he can convey the news and sometimes he conveys it to the ear of his partner from the humans before it strikes him.

15) The fact that the soothsayer (or fortuneteller) sometimes tells the truth.

16) The fact that he (the fortuneteller) tells a hundred lies along with it.

17) That his lying is not declared truthful except due to this word that is heard from the heaven.

18) The souls acceptance of falsehood, and how they are attached to one (statement) and do not consider one hundred!

19) That they convey this word, some of them from others, and they preserve it and use it as an evidence.

20) Affirmation of the attributes, contrary to the denying *Ash'ariyyah*.

21) The declaration that this quaking and overwhelming is due to fear of Allâh, the Mighty and Majestic.

22) That they fall down in prostration to Allâh.

Chapter 16

The Intercession*

And Statement of Allâh the Almighty,

﴿وَأَنذِرْ بِهِ ٱلَّذِينَ يَخَافُونَ أَن يُحْشَرُوٓا۟ إِلَىٰ رَبِّهِمْ ۙ لَيْسَ لَهُم مِّن دُونِهِۦ وَلِىٌّ وَلَا شَفِيعٌ﴾

---

* Bringing this chapter after the two chapters that have preceded it is extremely appropriate. That is because those who ask the Prophet ﷺ, seek help from him, or ask others besides him from the righteous believers (*Al-Awliyaa'*) or the Prophets, if you establish the proof against them by what has been mentioned of the *Tawḥid* of Lordship, they present another argument. They say, "We believe that, but these people are near to Allâh and revered, and they have the honored status with the Lord, thus they are allowed intercession with Allâh. And whoever turns to them, they will please him with intercession, because they have an honored status with Him (Allâh), and they are of those whom Allâh has elevated. For this reason He accepts their intercessions." The Shaikh (Ibn Taymiyyah) has brought forth the situation of the polytheists and their arguments and said, "Nothing remains for them except for intercession if you argue with them." So this is the chapter of intercession.

Intercession is supplication. If someone says, "I seek the intercession of Allâh's Messenger", it is as if he is saying, "I request from the Messenger ﷺ that he supplicate to Allâh for me." Thus, it is supplication, and it is also the request for supplication. Therefore, every evidence that has preceded for us, and every evidence in the Book (the Qur'ān) or the *Sunnah* that contains a negation of another god being supplicated along with Allâh, then it is suitable as an evidence for negating seeking intercession from the dead and those who are absent from the world of responsibility (i.e. this life). Turning to other than Allâh with requests of intercession is major *Shirk* if this person being turned to is among the deceased. If the person if living, then that is permissible, because they are in the world of responsibility and they are able to answer (respond to a request). Allâh has allowed seeking intercession from them (the living) by them making supplication (for the one who requests it). For this reason, in the time of the Prophet ﷺ some of the Companions would come to the Prophet ﷺ and request that he intercede for them. This meant that he would

"And warn therewith those who fear that they will be gathered before their Lord, when there will neither be a protector nor an intercessor for them besides Him." (6:51)[1]

And His Statement,

﴿قُل لِّلَّهِ ٱلشَّفَـٰعَةُ جَمِيعًا﴾

"Say: To Allâh belongs all intercession." (39:44)[2]

---

supplicate for them. Also, every intercession is not accepted. There is intercession that is accepted and there is intercession that is rejected. It is accepted with conditions and it is also rejected with certain characteristics. Therefore, we see that intercession is two types in the Qur'ān and the *Sunnah*: the intercession that is negated and the intercession that is affirmed. The intercession that is negated is that which Allâh has negated from the people of polytheism (*Ash-Shirk*), as the Shaikh has presented.

[1] The first evidence is his statement: And Statement of Allâh the Almighty,

﴿وَأَنذِرْ بِهِ ٱلَّذِينَ يَخَافُونَ أَن يُحْشَرُوٓا۟ إِلَىٰ رَبِّهِمْ ۙ لَيْسَ لَهُم مِّن دُونِهِۦ وَلِىٌّ وَلَا شَفِيعٌ﴾

"And warn therewith those who fear that they will be gathered before their Lord, when there will neither be a protector nor an intercessor for them besides Him." (6:51)

This is referring to the intercession that is negated from everyone except the people of *At-Tauhid*, for verily their intercession is accepted with certain conditions. The conditions are: The permission of Allâh for the interceded that he may interceded, Allâh's being pleased with the interceder and the person who is being interceded for, and actually, the real interceder is Allâh besides all others. This is why he (the Shaikh) followed this Verse with another Verse,

﴿قُل لِّلَّهِ ٱلشَّفَـٰعَةُ جَمِيعًا﴾

[2] "Say: To Allâh belongs all intercession." (39:44)

Thus, all intercession belongs to Allâh, and the people of faith and others besides them, in reality they do not have any *Waliyy* (protector, supporter) nor *Shafee'* (intercessor) besides Allâh. Rather, the intercession must be by Allâh, meaning by His permission and His pleasure. So intercession benefits, but with conditions. For this reason the Shaikh brought the two

And His Statement,

﴿مَن ذَا ٱلَّذِى يَشْفَعُ عِندَهُۥٓ إِلَّا بِإِذْنِهِۦ﴾

"Who is he that can intercede with Him except with His permission?" (2:255)

And His Statement,

﴿وَكَم مِّن مَّلَكٍ فِى ٱلسَّمَٰوَٰتِ لَا تُغْنِى شَفَٰعَتُهُمْ شَيْـًٔا إِلَّا مِنۢ بَعْدِ أَن يَأْذَنَ ٱللَّهُ لِمَن يَشَآءُ وَيَرْضَىٰٓ﴾

"And there are many angels in the heavens, whose intercession will avail nothing except after Allâh has given leave for whom He wills and is pleases with." (53:26)[1]

Verses after it,

﴿مَن ذَا ٱلَّذِى يَشْفَعُ عِندَهُۥٓ إِلَّا بِإِذْنِهِۦ﴾

"Who is he that can intercede with Him except with His permission?" (2:255)

[1] And His Statement,

﴿وَكَم مِّن مَّلَكٍ فِى ٱلسَّمَٰوَٰتِ لَا تُغْنِى شَفَٰعَتُهُمْ شَيْـًٔا إِلَّا مِنۢ بَعْدِ أَن يَأْذَنَ ٱللَّهُ لِمَن يَشَآءُ وَيَرْضَىٰٓ﴾

"And there are many angels in the heavens, whose intercession will avail nothing except after Allâh has given for whom He wills and is pleases with." (53:26)

The point of evidence from the Verse:

First: That it contains the restriction of permission. Hence, no one may intercede except with the condition that Allâh allows him to — not the angels, the Prophets or those near to Allâh. It is Allâh Alone Who possesses the intercession. It is He Who grants success and it is not for anyone to start with intercession. Likewise is the case with the other Verse,

﴿إِلَّا مِنۢ بَعْدِ أَن يَأْذَنَ ٱللَّهُ لِمَن يَشَآءُ وَيَرْضَىٰٓ﴾

"except after Allâh has given permission for whom He wills and pleases." (53:26).

Meaning from the intercessors. His Statement, "and pleases" means that

And His Statement,

﴿قُلِ ٱدْعُوا۟ ٱلَّذِينَ زَعَمْتُم مِّن دُونِ ٱللَّهِ ۖ لَا يَمْلِكُونَ مِثْقَالَ ذَرَّةٍ فِى ٱلسَّمَـٰوَٰتِ وَلَا فِى ٱلْأَرْضِ وَمَا لَهُمْ فِيهِمَا مِن شِرْكٍ وَمَا لَهُۥ مِنْهُم مِّن ظَهِيرٍ ۝ وَلَا تَنفَعُ ٱلشَّفَـٰعَةُ عِندَهُۥٓ إِلَّا لِمَنْ أَذِنَ لَهُۥ﴾ الآيتان.

"Say (O Muhammad ﷺ) Call upon those whom you assert (to be associate gods) besides Allâh, they possess not even an atom's (or a small ant), weight either in the heavens or on the earth, nor have they any share in either, nor is there for Him any supporter from among

---

He is pleased with the speech of the intercessor and He is also pleased with the person who the intercession is for. The benefit of these conditions - and they are the benefit of this chapter - are as follows: That no one should be attached to this creation from which intercession is sought. No one should think that he has a position with Allâh by which he owns or controls the right to intercede. This is like the people of *Ash-Shirk* believing that their gods have the absolute power to intercede and that Allâh cannot refuse their intercession.

These Verses also contain a nullification of the claims of these polytheists (*Mushrikūn*) that there is someone who possesses (the right of) intercession without the permission of Allâh and without His being pleased with the one for whom intercession is sought. When it is confirmed that he does not possess (the right of) intercession and that the one who is allowed to intercede is only allowed to do so by Allâh honoring him and permitting him, then how can the person be attached to this creation? Attachment should only be to the One Who possesses the (right of) intercession. For this reason, the intercession of the Prophet ﷺ on the Day of Resurrection will occur without a doubt. But from whom do we seek it? We seek it from Allâh alone. Thus, we say, "O Allâh, allow Your Prophet to interceded for us." This is because Allâh is the One Who will inspire the Prophet ﷺ to intercede for so-and-so and so-and-so, who asked Allâh to allow the Prophet ﷺ to intercede for them. For this reason, the Shaikh (Muhammad bin 'Abdul-Wahhaab) - may Allâh have mercy upon him - followed this Verse with the Verse of *Surah Saba'* where He said,

﴿قُلِ ٱدْعُوا۟ ٱلَّذِينَ زَعَمْتُم مِّن دُونِ ٱللَّهِ ۖ لَا يَمْلِكُونَ مِثْقَالَ ذَرَّةٍ فِى ٱلسَّمَـٰوَٰتِ وَلَا فِى

them. Intercession with Him profits not except for him whom He permits." (34:22,23)[1]

Abul-'Abbaas said, 'Allâh has negated from other than Him all

﴿ٱلْأَرْضِ وَمَا لَهُمْ فِيهِمَا مِن شِرْكٍ وَمَا لَهُۥ مِنْهُم مِّن ظَهِيرٍ﴾

[1] There are three situation:

The first situation: That they call upon those whom they claim besides Allâh and that they look - do those whom they call upon possess even the weight of an atom in the heavens or the earth? Allâh said,

﴿لَا يَمْلِكُونَ مِثْقَالَ ذَرَّةٍ فِى ٱلسَّمَٰوَٰتِ وَلَا فِى ٱلْأَرْضِ﴾

"They possess not even the weight of an atom (or a small ant), either in the heavens or on the earth."

Therefore, the independent ownership is negated for them.

The second situation: Allâh said,

﴿وَمَا لَهُمْ فِيهِمَا مِن شِرْكٍ﴾

"nor have they any share in either."

This also negates that they are partners with Allâh in sovereignty, control or ownership of anything of the heavens and the earth. After this Allâh said, "there is not for Him", the Mighty and Majestic, "from among them." This means among these gods, there is no minister or assistant for Him.

The third situation: A final negation of the last belief, which is that these gods posses's (the right of) intercession. Allâh said,

﴿وَلَا تَنفَعُ ٱلشَّفَٰعَةُ عِندَهُۥٓ إِلَّا لِمَنْ أَذِنَ لَهُۥ﴾

"Intercession with Him benefits not, except for him whom He permits." (34:23)

Thus, He negates the last of what He negates, which is the intercession. However, He affirms it with a condition. He said,

﴿وَلَا تَنفَعُ ٱلشَّفَٰعَةُ عِندَهُۥٓ إِلَّا لِمَنْ أَذِنَ لَهُۥ﴾

"Intercession with Him benefits not, except for him whom He permits."

If this is the case, then who is it that is permitted? And who is it that He (Allâh) is pleased with to intercede? And who is it that He is pleased with him that intercession be made on his behalf? The answer to these three questions is in the statement of Shaikh ul-Islam (Ibn Taymiyyah) where he - may Allâh have mercy on him — said,

of what the polytheists are attached to. So he negates that there is any ownership or share of it for other than Him, or that there is any assistant for Allâh. Therefore, nothing remains but intercession, so Allâh explains that it does not benefit anyone except whom the Lord permits. This is as He said,

﴿وَلَا يَشْفَعُونَ إِلَّا لِمَنِ ارْتَضَىٰ﴾

'And they will not intercede except for him with whom He is pleased.' (21:28)

So this intercession that the polytheists believe in is rejected on the Day of Resurrection, just as the Qur'ān has negated it. The Prophet ﷺ informed,

«أَنَّهُ يَأْتِي فَيَسْجُدُ لِرَبِّهِ وَيَحْمَدُهُ»

"That he will come and prostrate to his Lord and praise Him."

He will not begin with intercession first. Then it will be said to him,

«ارْفَعْ رَأْسَكَ، وَقُلْ يُسْمَعْ، وَسَلْ تُعْطَ، وَاشْفَعْ تُشَفَّعْ»

"Raise your head, and speak; it will be heard. Ask and you will be given. Intercede and your intercession will be granted."

Abu Hurayrah رَضِيَ اللهُ عَنْهُ said to him, "Who will be the most fortunate of the people to receive your intercession?" The Prophet ﷺ replied,

«مَنْ قَالَ لَا إِلَهَ إِلَّا اللهُ خَالِصًا مِنْ قَلْبِهِ»

"Whoever said *Lāilāha illallāh* (None has the right to be worshipped but Allâh), sincerely from his heart."

Thus, this intercession is for the people of sincere faith (*Ikhlaaṣ*) by the permission of Allâh, and it is not for those who associate partners with Allâh. In reality, it is that Allâh (Alone),

He is the One Who favors the people of sincere faith, and thus, He forgives them by the medium of the invocation of whomever He has allowed to intercede. This is so that He may honor him (the intercessor) and he may attain the Praised Station (*Al-Maqaam ul-Maḥmood*). The intercession which is rejected by the Qur'ān is that which contains any *Shirk*. This is why it (the Qur'ān) has affirmed the intercession by his permission in various places.[1] Indeed the Prophet ﷺ

[1] "Allâh has negated from other than Him all of what the polytheists are attached to. So he negates that there is any ownership or share of it for other than Him, or that there is any assistant for Allâh. Therefore, nothing remains but intercession, so Allâh explains that it does not benefit anyone except whom the Lord permits. This is as He said,

﴿وَلَا يَشْفَعُونَ إِلَّا لِمَنِ ٱرْتَضَىٰ﴾

'And they will not intercede except for him with whom He is pleased.' (21:28)

So this intercession that the polytheists believe in is rejected on the Day of Resurrection, just as the Qur'ān has negated it."

His Statement, "is rejected on the Day of Resurrection" means it is rejected unconditionally. This is because the polytheists (*Mushrikūn*) believe that intercession occurs without the permission of Allâh or His pleasure. This is because the intercessor - according to them - possesses (the right to) intercession. However, the intercession occurs with conditions, as is confirmed in the Book (the Qur'ān) and the *Sunnah*.

Concerning his statement, "That he will come and prostrate to his Lord and praise Him." This shows that he will not begin with intercession first.

Then it will be said to him, "Raise your head, and speak; it will be heard. Ask and you will be given. Intercede and your intercession will be granted." This is concerning the evidence of permission. The Prophet ﷺ will be permitted and others besides him will be permitted, but they will not begin with that. They will seek permission to intercede and then they will be allowed. This is because they do not possess it. The only one who possesses intercession with Allâh is Allâh Himself, Alone.

"Abu Hurayrah رَضِيَ الله عَنْهُ said", meaning to the Prophet ﷺ, "Who will be the most fortunate of the people to receive your intercession?" The Prophet ﷺ replied,

---

«مَنْ قَالَ لَا إِلٰهَ إِلَّا اللهُ خَالِصًا مِنْ قَلْبِهِ»

"Whoever said *Lā ilāha illallāh* (None has the right to be worshipped but Allâh), sincerely from his heart."

Therefore, the one whom He (Allâh) is pleased with will be allowed to have intercession made for him after Allâh's permission, and this is the person of sincere faith (*Al-Ikhlaaṣ*) and *At-Tauhid*. Thus, the permission for this intercession is negated from the people of *Ash-Shirk*. For this reason he (Ibn Taymiyyah) said, "Thus, this intercession is for the people of sincere faith (*Ikhlaaṣ*) by the permission of Allâh, and it is not for those who associate partners with Allâh." Hence, if this is the case, the one who turns to the deceased, or Messengers, or Prophets, or righteous people, or evil people, seeking intercession from them, then he is a polytheist (*Mushrik*). This is because he turned in supplication to other than Allâh and these people do not possess (the right of) intercession. They are only allowed to intercede after the permission and pleasure of Allâh, and He is pleased with the people of *At-Tauhid*. The people of *At-Tauhid* are those who do not ask for intercession from anyone from the deceased. Therefore, everyone who asks a deceased person for intercession, then he has made the intercession of *Al-Muṣtafaa* (Prophet Muhammad ﷺ) forbidden for himself, as he has committed *Shirk* with Allâh, the Mighty and Majestic.

His Statement, "In reality, it is" means the reality of intercession. In other words, the reality of its occurrence and how does it occur? The answer is in the statement of Shaikh ul-Islam Ibn Taymiyyah: "that Allâh (Alone), He is the One Who favors the people of sincere faith, and thus, He forgives them by the medium of the invocation of whoever He has allowed to interceded. This is so that He may honor him (the intercessor) and he may attain the Praised Station (*Al-Maqaam ul-Maḥmood*)." Thus, the forgiveness of Allâh here is by mediation and not initially granted. This is to show the virtue of the intercessor and Allâh's honoring him and being merciful with him. This is the reality of intercession; that Allâh favors and accepts intercession by His permission. He favors the intercessor and honors him by allowing him to intercede. He favors and shows mercy to the one whom the intercession is for and so He accepts the intercession. Therefore, it is all a proof for whoever has a heart to understand the magnificence of Allâh and His being Alone in sovereignty. He is the One to Whom belongs all of the intercession, and He is the One Who possesses all matters. Hence, it is likewise obligatory for the hearts to be clarified that it (the intercession) will only be for the people of *At-Tauhid* and sincere faith (*Al-Ikhlaaṣ*)."[1]

---

attached to Him in hoping for intercession.

"The intercession which is rejected by the Qur'ān is that which contains any *Shirk*." For example, in the Statement of Allâh,

﴿لَيْسَ لَهُم مِّن دُونِهِۦ وَلِىٌّ وَلَا شَفِيعٌ﴾

> "They do not have besides Him any Waliyy (protector, supporter) nor any *Shafee'* (intercessor)." (6:51)

This intercession is negated, and it is the intercession that contains any *Shirk*. Likewise, the intercession for the *Mushrikūn* (polytheists, idolaters) is negated. This is because Allâh is not pleased with them. Therefore, it is confirmed by this that the one who has the right to intercession is the one whom Allâh has blessed, helped to magnify Him, and whose heart is attached to Him alone besides all others. Hence, every polytheist (*Mushrik*) who commits major *Shirk*, then intercession is negated from him, because intercession is a favor from Allâh for the people of sincere faith (*Al-Ikhlaaṣ*).

After this, Shaikh ul-Islam Ibn Taymiyyah says, "This is why it (the Qur'ān) has affirmed the intercession by his permission in various places." This is referring to the confirmed intercession, meaning that it (the Qur'ān) has confirmed it with the condition of permission. Permission means permission of existence and legislated permission. Thus, the person for whom it is allowed, it is not possible that intercession may occur for him except that Allâh has allowed it to happen, by letting him perform intercession. Thus, if Allâh prevents him from interceding by not letting it take place, intercession will not occur from him and his tongue will not move with the request for it. Likewise is the legislated permission regarding intercession. That is that it must be an intercession that does not contain any *Shirk*, and that the person who is being interceded for is not from the people of *Ash-Shirk*. Abu Ṭâlib has been particularly excluded from that, as the Prophet will intercede for him to have his torment lightened (i.e. in Hell). So it is an intercession that will not benefit him (Abu Ṭâlib) in allowing him to be taken out of the Fire. It will only be to lighten the torment. This is something that is specifically for the Prophet ﷺ according to what Allâh has revealed to him and allowed for him.

[1] "Indeed the Prophet ﷺ clarified that it (the intercession) will only be for the people of *At-Tauhid* and sincere faith (*Al-Ikhlaaṣ*)."

Important issues of the Chapter

1) The explanation of the Verse (6:51).
2) The description of the negated intercession.
3) The description of the affirmed intercession.
4) Mention of the great intercession, which is the Praised Station (*Al-Maqaam - Maḥmood*).
5) The description of what the Prophet ﷺ will do and that he will not begin with intercession. Rather, he will prostrate and then when he is allowed, he will intercede.
6) Who will be the most fortunate of the people to receive it (the Prophet's intercession).
7) That it (intercession) will not be for the one who associates partners with Allâh.
8) The explanation of its reality.

The clarification in this chapter is that the intercession that the hearts of the superstitious people are attached to, and those who are attached to other than Allâh, is false. Also their saying,

﴿هَٰٓؤُلَآءِ شُفَعَٰٓؤُنَا عِندَ ٱللَّهِ﴾

"These are our intercessors with Allâh,"

is a false statement. This is because the intercession that benefits is only for the people of sincere faith (*Al-Ikhlaaṣ*). As long as they seek intercession from other than Allâh, they are asking other than Allâh for intercession, and this validates their being prohibited from intercession. For it (intercession) is only for the people of sincere faith (*Al-Ikhlaaṣ*).

The summary of the chapter is that the attachment of these superstitious people to intercession is only against them and not for them, because as they are attached to the intercession, they are prevented from it. The reason for this is that they are attached to something that Allâh has not allowed in the Islamic Law. That is that they use intercessions that contain *Shirk*, they turn to other than Allâh and their hearts are attached to other than Allâh.

Chapter 17

The Statement of Allâh the Most High,*

﴿إِنَّكَ لَا تَهْدِى مَنْ أَحْبَبْتَ﴾ الآية

"Verily, you (O Muhammad ﷺ) guide not whom you like." (28:56)

---

* The Statement of Allâh the Most High,

﴿إِنَّكَ لَا تَهْدِى مَنْ أَحْبَبْتَ﴾

"Verily you (O Muhammad ﷺ) guide not whom you like." (28:56) The word *Laa* (not) here is for negation and His saying *Tahdee* (you guide) is the negated guidance. Here it refers to the guidance of assistance, inspiration and special help. It is that which the scholars call *Hidaayat ut-Tawfeeq wal-Ilhaam* (the guidance of assistance and inspiration). It means that Allâh places in the heart of the servant special help in acceptance of guidance that he does not give to others. Thus, *At-Tawfeeq* (assistance) means special help for whoever Allâh wants to be assisted and successful, and this is by him accepting the guidance and striving for it. The placement of this in the hearts is not for the Prophet ﷺ, as the hearts are in the Hand of Allâh and He turns them however He wills. Even whomever the Prophet ﷺ loved, he was not able to make him a guided Muslim. From the most beneficial of his relatives to him was Abu Ṭâlib, yet he still was not able to guide him to the guidance of assistance (*Hidaayat ut-Tawfeeq*).

The second type of guidance is that which is connected to the responsible person. It is the guidance of leading (to guidance) and directing. This type of guidance is confirmed for the Prophet ﷺ in particular, and for every caller to Allâh, and every Prophet and Messenger. Allâh said,

﴿إِنَّمَآ أَنتَ مُنذِرٌ وَلِكُلِّ قَوْمٍ هَادٍ﴾

"Verily you (Muhammad ﷺ) are only a warner, and to every people there is a guide." (13:7)

And He said concerning His Prophet ﷺ,

﴿وَإِنَّكَ لَتَهْدِى إِلَى صِرَاطٍ مُّسْتَقِيمٍ ۝ صِرَاطِ ٱللَّهِ﴾

"And verily you (Muhammad ﷺ) guide to a Straight Path, the Path

In the Ṣaḥeeḥ, Ibn Al-Musayyib narrated that his father said, "When death came to Abu Ṭâlib, Allâh's Messenger ﷺ came to him while 'Abdullah bin Abi Umayyah and Abu Jahl were (already) with him. Allâh's Messenger ﷺ said to him,

«يَا عَمِّ، قُلْ لَا إِلَٰهَ إِلَّا اللهُ، كَلِمَةً أُحَاجُّ لَكَ بِهَا عِنْدَ اللهِ»

'O my uncle, say *Lāilāha illallāh* (None has the right to be worshipped but Allâh) - a statement with which I may plead your case with Allâh.'

So they ('Abdullah bin Abi Umayyah and Abu Jahl) said to him, 'Will you turn away from the religion of 'Abdul-Muṭṭalib?' So the Prophet ﷺ repeated his statement to him and they repeated their statement to him. Thus, the last thing that he (Abu Ṭâlib) said was that he was upon the religion of 'Abdul-Muṭṭalib, and he refused to say *Lāilāha illallāh*. So the Prophet ﷺ said,

«لَأَسْتَغْفِرَنَّ لَكَ مَا لَمْ أُنْهَ عَنْكَ»

'Verily I will seek forgiveness for you as long as I am not prohibited from (seeking it for) you.'

Then Allâh revealed,

﴿مَا كَانَ لِلنَّبِيِّ وَٱلَّذِينَ ءَامَنُوٓا۟ أَن يَسْتَغْفِرُوا۟ لِلْمُشْرِكِينَ﴾

'It is not (proper) for the Prophet and those who believe,

---

of Allâh." (42:52-53)

"You guide" means that you lead and direct to a Straight Path with the most profound type of instruction and the most profound type of direction that are supported by miracles and evidences. These miracles and evidences prove the truthfulness of that guide and the truthfulness of that director.

Thus, if the guidance of assistance is negated from Muhammad ﷺ - even with his tremendous status and position with his Lord - it is false for the hearts to be attached in important requests, guidance, forgiveness, pleasure, removing evils and bringing good, except to Allâh.

to ask Allâh's forgiveness for the Mushrikîn (polytheists, idolaters).' (9:113)

And He revealed regarding Abu Ṭalib,

﴿إِنَّكَ لَا تَهْدِى مَنْ أَحْبَبْتَ وَلَٰكِنَّ ٱللَّهَ يَهْدِى مَن يَشَآءُ﴾

'Verily you (O Muhammad ﷺ) do not guide he whom you like, but Allâh guides whom He wills.' (28:56)"[1]

---

[1] In the *Ṣaḥeeḥ*, Ibn Al-Musayyib narrated that his father said, "When death came to Abu Ṭâlib, Allâh's Messenger ﷺ came to him while 'Abdullah bin Abi Umayyah and Abu Jahl were (already) with him. The Allâh's Messenger ﷺ said to him,

«يَا عَمِّ، قُلْ لَا إِلٰهَ إِلَّا اللهُ، كَلِمَةً أُحَاجُّ لَكَ بِهَا عِنْدَ اللهِ»

'O my uncle, say *Lā ilāha illallāh* (None has the right to be worshipped but Allâh) - a statement with which I may plead your case with Allâh.'

So they ('Abdullah bin Abee Umayyah and Abu Jahl) said to him, 'Will you turn away from the religion of 'Abdul-Muṭṭalib?' So the Prophet ﷺ repeated his statement to him and they repeated their statement to him. Thus, the last thing that he (Abu Ṭâlib) said was that he was upon the religion of 'Abdul-Muṭṭalib, and he refused to say *Lā ilāha illallāh*. So the Prophet ﷺ said, 'Verily I will seek forgiveness for you as long as I am not prohibited from (seeking it for) you.'" The letter *Laam* here (in the word *La-astaghfiranna*) occurs in response to the oath. It means,

«لَأَسْتَغْفِرَنَّ لَكَ»

"By Allâh, I will seek forgiveness for you."

And it occurred that the Prophet ﷺ sought forgiveness for his uncle. But did the Prophet's seeking forgiveness for his uncle benefit him? That did not benefit him because the one for whom the intercession was sought was a polytheist (*Mushrik*). Seeking forgiveness and intercession does not benefit the people of *Ash-Shirk*. The Prophet ﷺ does not possess the power to benefit a polytheist (*Mushrik*) with forgiveness of his sins, or to benefit anyone from those who turn to him with *Shirk* for assistance in removing whatever afflicts of him suffering or bringing any good. For this reason the Prophet ﷺ said,

«لَأَسْتَغْفِرَنَّ لَكَ مَا لَمْ أُنْهَ عَنْكَ»

Important issues of the Chapter

1) The explanation of the Verse,

﴿إِنَّكَ لَا تَهْدِى مَنْ أَحْبَبْتَ﴾

"Verily you (O Muhammad ﷺ) do not guide he whom you like." (28:56)

2) The explanation of the Verse,

﴿مَا كَانَ لِلنَّبِيِّ﴾ الآية

"It is not (proper) for the Prophet..." (9:113)

3) And it is the major issue: The explanation of his (the Prophet's ﷺ) saying,

---

"Verily I will seek forgiveness for you as long as I am not prohibited from (seeking it for) you."

Then Allâh revealed,

﴿مَا كَانَ لِلنَّبِيِّ وَالَّذِينَ ءَامَنُوٓا أَن يَسْتَغْفِرُوا لِلْمُشْرِكِينَ وَلَوْ كَانُوٓا أُو۟لِى قُرْبَىٰ مِنۢ بَعْدِ مَا تَبَيَّنَ لَهُمْ أَنَّهُمْ أَصْحَٰبُ ٱلْجَحِيمِ﴾

"It is not (proper) for the Prophet and those who believe, to ask Allâh's forgiveness for the *Mushrikeen* (polytheists, idolaters), even if they are close relatives, after it has become clear to them that they are companions of Hell." (9:113)

This is clear in the position that Allâh, the Mighty and Majestic, forbade the Prophet ﷺ to seek forgiveness for the *Mushrikūn* (polytheists, idolaters). If this is the case, even if he was able to seek forgiveness in the transitory grave state (*Al-Barzakh*), he would never seek forgiveness for a *Mushrik* who turned to him for intercession, assistance, with a sacrifice, a vow, deifying him, placing trust in him, or placing his needs with him instead of Allâh. Then the Shaikh (Ibn Taymiyyah) said, "And Allâh revealed regarding Abu Ṭâlib,

﴿إِنَّكَ لَا تَهْدِى مَنْ أَحْبَبْتَ وَلَٰكِنَّ ٱللَّهَ يَهْدِى مَن يَشَآءُ﴾

'Verily you (O Muhammad ﷺ) do not guide he whom you like, but Allâh guides whom He wills.'(28:56)"

«لَا إِلَهَ إِلَّا اللهُ»

"Lā ilāha illallāh."

This is contrary to what some people are upon, who claim to have knowledge.

4) That Abu Jahl and those who were with him knew what the Prophet ﷺ meant when he told the man (his uncle), *"Lā ilāha illallāh."* So may Allâh disgrace the person who knows less about the foundation of is Islam than Abu Jahl.

5) The intensity and eagerness of the Prophet ﷺ for his uncle to accept Islam.

6) The refutation against whoever claims that 'Abdul-Muṭṭalib and his ancestors where Muslims.

7) The fact that the Prophet ﷺ sought forgiveness for him but he was not forgiven. Rather, the Prophet ﷺ was prohibited from doing so.

8) The harm of evil companions upon the person.

9) The harm of exalting ancestors and important people.

10) The error of the falsifiers in that is the same as Abu Jahl in using that (the way of the ancestors) as an argument.

11) The witness for the fact that actions are according to the final deeds, because if he (Abu Ṭâlib) had said it, it would have benefited him.

12) The consideration of the magnitude of this false argument in the hearts of those who are misguided, because in the story they did not argue against him except with it, even with the Prophet's eagerness and his repetition. Thus, because of its tremendous nature and its distinction with them, they limited their argument to it (i.e. ancestral pride).

Chapter 18

What has been Narrated Regarding the Cause of the Disbelief of the Children of Aadam and Their Leaving Their Religion is Exaggeration Concerning the Righteous People*

The Statement of Allâh,

﴿يَٰٓأَهۡلَ ٱلۡكِتَٰبِ لَا تَغۡلُواْ فِي دِينِكُمۡ﴾

* In this chapter and what comes after it, the Shaikh explains that the cause of the greatest *Shirk* is exaggeration which Allâh and His Messenger ﷺ forbade. It makes no difference whether it is in this nation or the previous nations. This is a way of mentioning the causes after mentioning the foundations and the beliefs.

The word *Ghuloo* (exaggeration) is taken from Ghalaa (exaggerating) regarding something when one exceeds its limits. Hence, the meaning is that the cause of the disbelief of the children of Aadam and their leaving their religion, which Allâh commanded them with, is exceeding the limit that He allowed regarding the righteous people. The righteous people include the Prophets, the Messengers, the *Awliyaa'* (pious believers), and everyone who has the characteristic of righteousness and sincerity to Allâh. They are among those who are foremost in doing good deeds or among the people who adhere to what is required of them. And all of the levels (of righteousness) are known with Allâh.

Regarding the righteous people, it is allowed to love them for the sake of Allâh, and they should be respected, and followed in their righteousness and their deeds. If they were among the Messengers and Prophets, their Laws and that which they commanded are to be taken from. What they have left behind is to be followed. This is the limit that has been allowed. They have the right to respect, love, loyalty, defense, support and similar things. From that which occurs from exaggeration regarding the righteous people is that some of them are given special divine characteristics. It is said about some of them that they know the secrets of the Preserved Tablet (*Al-Lawḥ ul-Mahfooḍḥ*) and the Pen (*Al-Qalam*), and that he is from the goodness of this world and its harm. This is as Al-Boosayree said in his well-known poem,

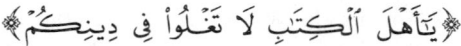

"O People of the Scripture (Jews and Christians)! Do not exaggerate in your religion." (4:171)[1]

"If I compare his (Prophet Muhammad ﷺ) status with his *Ayaat* (Verses, signs or miracles) his status is greater,

His name brings life to the rotting decay (i.e. a corpse) when it is called upon."

He is saying (in this poem) that the Prophet ﷺ was not given an *Ayah* (miracle, sign or Verse) that was comparable to his status. The explainer of the poem said, "Even the Qur'ān is not comparable to the status of the Prophet ﷺ. (We seek refuge in Allâh from this.) Nothing is appropriate for his status except if his name is mentioned over a dead person who has decayed and his ashes have faded away in the earth, and his bones have deteriorated, these bones come back together and are revived due to the Prophet's name being mentioned over him." This is from the types of exaggeration that occur from those who worship other than Allâh and turn to Prophets and Messengers instead of Allâh. They give them special characteristics of godliness that they have not been allowed. Rather, this is a form of major *Shirk* with Allâh, and likening the creation to the creator and this is disbelief (*Kufr*) - we seek refuge in Allâh from this. Thus, there is the permitted limit, exaggeration and the third situation, which is *Al-Jafaa'* (aversion). Aversion in reference to the righteous people is a lack of loyalty to them, not respecting them, not giving them their rights and abandoning love of the righteous. Thus, every deficiency in this matter is considered *Al-Jafaa'* (aversion, abhorrence), and every increase (beyond the limit) is considered *Al-Ghuloo* (exaggeration).

﴿يَٰٓأَهۡلَ ٱلۡكِتَٰبِ لَا تَغۡلُواْ فِي دِينِكُمۡ﴾

[1] "O People of the Scripture (Jews and Christians)! Do not exaggerate in your religion." (4:171)

Allâh forbade the People of the Scripture from exaggeration. The word *Taghloo* (you exaggerate) in the Verse is a verb that has come in the form of prohibition, and it covers all types of exaggeration in the religion. The one who pays attention to the situation of the People of the Book when Allâh relates their story from what occurred with them, he will find that they exaggerated concerning their righteous people. The Christians exaggerated concerning 'Eesaa (Jesus), his mother (Maryam) and his disciples. The Jews also exaggerated concerning 'Uzayr (Ezra), the companions of Moosaa and their rabbis and monks, and so forth. They

And in the Ṣaḥeeḥ, Ibn 'Abbâs رَضِيَ اللهُ عَنْهُمَا said concerning the Statement of Allâh the Most High,

﴿وَقَالُوا۟ لَا تَذَرُنَّ ءَالِهَتَكُمْ وَلَا تَذَرُنَّ وَدًّا وَلَا سُوَاعًا وَلَا يَغُوثَ وَيَعُوقَ وَنَسْرًا﴾

"And they said, 'Do not forsake your gods! Do not forsake Wadd nor Suwaa' nor Yaghooth nor Nasr.'" (71:23)

هَذِهِ أَسْمَاءُ رِجَالٍ صَالِحِينَ مِنْ قَوْمِ نُوحٍ، فَلَمَّا هَلَكُوا أَوْحَى الشَّيْطَانُ إِلَى قَوْمِهِمْ: أَنِ انْصِبُوا إِلَى مَجَالِسِهِمُ الَّتِي كَانُوا يَجْلِسُونَ فِيهَا أَنْصَابًا، وَسَمُّوهَا بِأَسْمَائِهِمْ، فَفَعَلُوا وَلَمْ تُعْبَدْ، حَتَّى إِذَا هَلَكَ أُولَئِكَ وَنُسِيَ الْعِلْمُ عُبِدَتْ.

"These were names of righteous men from the people of Nooḥ (Noah). Then, when they passed away, Satan inspired their people to set up statues in their gathering places where they used to sit and to name these statues with their names. They did this but the statues were not worshipped until those people passed away and the knowledge was forgotten. Then they were worshipped."[1]

---

gave them some special qualities of godliness and intercession, and they gave them a share of the sovereignty, or they claimed that they determined the affairs or controlled something of the dominion.

[1] And in the Ṣaḥeeḥ, Ibn 'Abbâs رَضِيَ اللهُ عَنْهُمَا said concerning the Statement of Allâh the Most High,

﴿وَقَالُوا۟ لَا تَذَرُنَّ ءَالِهَتَكُمْ وَلَا تَذَرُنَّ وَدًّا وَلَا سُوَاعًا وَلَا يَغُوثَ وَيَعُوقَ وَنَسْرًا ۝ وَقَدْ أَضَلُّوا۟ كَثِيرًا﴾

"And they said, 'Do not forsake your gods! Do not forsake Wadd nor Suwaa' nor Yaghooth nor Nasr.'" (71:23,24)

"These were names of righteous men from the people of Nooḥ (Noah). Then, when they passed away, Satan inspired their people..."

The Shirk of the people of Nooḥ (Noah) was exaggeration concerning the righteous people and their souls. Then Satan came to them from the aspect of the soul of that righteous servant and the remnants of that soul, and that

Ibn Al-Qayyim said, "More than one of the *Salaf* have said that when they died the people devoted themselves to their graves. Then they made statues of their images their. Then, after a long period passed they began worshipping them."[1]

'Umar narrated that Allâh's Messenger ﷺ said,

«لَا تُطْرُونِي كَمَا أَطْرَتِ النَّصَارَى عِيسَىٰ ابْنَ مَرْيَمَ إِنَّمَا أَنَا عَبْدٌ؛ فَقُولُوا: عَبْدُاللهِ وَرَسُولُهُ».

"Do not exaggerate in praising me as the Christians exaggerated in praising 'Isâ (Jesus), the son of Maryam (Mary). I am only a slave, so say, 'slave of Allâh and His

---

whoever attached himself to it, it would intercede for him. Then, from that glorification, he drove them to pictures, statues, idols and images. This is as Ibn 'Abbaas رَضِيَ اللهُ عَنْهُمَا said here in explaining the origin and occurrence of this *Shirk*: "Then, when they passed away, Satan inspired their people to set up statues in their gathering places where they used to sit and to name these statues with their names. They did this but the statues were not worshipped until those people passed away and the knowledge was forgotten. Then they were worshipped."

[1] Ibn Al-Qayyim said, "More than one of the *Salaf* have said that when they died the people devoted themselves to their graves. Then they made statues of their images their. Then, after a long period passed they began worshipping them." The evidence from this is that these people turned to images of the righteous people and the people of knowledge used to teach them that if they made images they were not supposed to worship them. However, these images of the righteous and revered people were a means, way and cause (of *Shirk*), because they were (eventually) worshipped in the future when the knowledge was forgotten. Maybe Satan came to the image and made it seem to the one who was looking at it or speaking to it that it spoke, and that the mouth of the fashioned image could speak. And maybe Satan made it seem that he heard some voice coming from it and other similar things from the types of action that make the hearts become attached to these souls. Thus, these people become attached to them (the statues), and this is what happens to the people who devote themselves to graves and worship the people in them along with Allâh. Therefore, it is a cause of *Shirk* with Allâh.

Messenger.''[1]   They (Al-Bukhari and Muslim) both recorded it.

And Umar رَضِيَ اللهُ عَنْهُ also narrated that Allâh's Messenger ﷺ said,

«إِيَّاكُمْ وَالْغُلُوَّ فَإِنَّمَا أَهْلَكَ مَنْ كَانَ قَبْلَكُمُ الْغُلُوُّ».

"Beware of exaggeration, for it was only exaggeration that destroyed those who were before you.''[2]

Muslim recorded from Ibn Mas'ud رَضِيَ اللهُ عَنْهُ that Allâh's Messenger ﷺ said,

---

[1] 'Umar رَضِيَ اللهُ عَنْهُ narrated that Allâh's Messenger ﷺ said,

«لَا تُطْرُونِي كَمَا أَطْرَتِ النَّصَارَى عِيسَىٰ ابْنَ مَرْيَمَ»

"Do not exaggerate in praising me as the Christians exaggerated in praising 'Eesaa (Jesus), the son of Maryam (Mary)."

Al-Iṭraa' also means to exceed the limit in praising. In the statement "as the Christians exaggerated", the letter Kaaf here is the Kaaf of comparison. In other words, "Do not exceed the limits in praising me like the Christians exceeded the limits in praising the son of Maryam." This is comparing one incident with another incident. It means that there should be no likeness made or prohibition of this type of exaggerated praising. Thus, he forbade exaggerated praising of himself because the Christians over exalted the son of Maryam and that led them to Al-Kufr (disbelief), Ash-Shirk and claiming that he (Jesus) was the son of Allâh. For this reason he said,

«إِنَّمَا أَنَا عَبْدٌ؛ فَقُولُوا: عَبْدُاللهِ وَرَسُولُهُ»

"I am only a slave, so say, 'slave of Allâh and His Messenger.'"

[2] And he ('Umar رَضِيَ اللهُ عَنْهُ) narrated that Allâh's Messenger ﷺ said,

«إِيَّاكُمْ وَالْغُلُوَّ فَإِنَّمَا أَهْلَكَ مَنْ كَانَ قَبْلَكُمُ الْغُلُوُّ»

"Beware of exaggeration, for it was only exaggeration that destroyed those who were before you."

This is a prohibition of exaggeration in all of its forms. Exaggeration is a cause of every evil, and moderation is a cause of every success and goodness.

«هَلَكَ الْمُتَنَطِّعُونَ - قَالَهَا ثَلَاثًا -»

"The excessive are destroyed." He said it three times.[1]

Important issues of the Chapter

1) That whoever understands this chapter and the two chapters after it, then it will become clear to him the strangeness of Islam. He will see some of the Power of Allâh and His amazing ability to change (and turn) the hearts.

2) Knowledge of the first act of *Shirk* that occurred on the face of the earth was concerning confusion regarding the righteous people.

3) Knowledge of the first thing that was changed of the religion of the Prophets and the cause of that, along with knowing that Allâh sent them.

---

[1] Muslim recorded from Ibn Mas'ud رَضِيَ اللهُ عَنْهُ that Allâh's Messenger ﷺ said,

«هَلَكَ الْمُتَنَطِّعُونَ - قَالَهَا ثَلَاثًا -»

"The excessive are destroyed."

He said it three times. This means those who are excessive in what they bring in their actions or their statements, and they desire knowledge of something or they burden themselves with something that Allâh did not permit. The words *At-Tanaṭṭu', Al-Iṭraa'* and *Al-Ghuloo* are close in meaning, and *Al-Ghuloo* (exaggeration) gathers all of their meanings.

Thus, the Shaikh - may Allâh have mercy upon him - explains in this chapter that the reason for the disbelief of the children of Aadam and the reason for their abandoning their religion is exaggeration concerning the righteous people. The people of Nooḥ transgressed the limit regarding the righteous people, and they devoted themselves to their graves and worshipped them, so they became gods. The Christians exaggerated concerning their Messenger, 'Eesaa (Jesus), the disciples and the clergymen (priests) until they made them gods along with Allâh. Likewise, in this nation, the Prophet has been given a share of the special characteristics of a god. And this is exactly what he forbade.

4) Knowing the cause of accepting innovations (i.e. religious heresies) even though the divine Laws and the innate natures reject them.

5) That the cause of all of that mixing the truth with falsehood. The first thing was the love of the righteous people. The second thing was that some people from the people of knowledge and religion did something that they intended to be good. But then those who came after them thought that they intended something else.

6) The explanation of the Verse in *Surah Nooḥ* (71:23).

7) Knowledge of the nature of the human being in that truth decreases in his heart while falsehood increases.

8) It contains a proof for what has been related from the *Salaf* that innovation (*Al-Bid'ah*) is a cause of disbelief (*Al-Kufr*).

9) Satan's knowledge of what innovation (*Al-Bid'ah*) leads to, even if the intention of the doer is good.

10) Knowledge of the general principle, which is the prohibition of exaggeration and knowing what it leads to.

11) The harm of devotion to graves for the sake of a righteous deed.

12) Knowledge of the prohibition of statues and the wisdom behind removing them.

13) Knowledge of the tremendous status of this story and the intense need for it with the (people's) heedlessness of it.

14) And it is the most amazing thing. Their - the people of innovations - reading this story in the books of *Tafseer* and *Hadith*, and their knowing the meaning of the discussion, and yet Allâh has placed a barrier between them and their hearts. This is to such an extent that they believe that the deed of the people of Nooḥ is the best

form of worship, and they believe that what Allâh and His Messenger has forbidden is only the disbelief (*Al-Kufr*) that makes the blood and the wealth lawful.

15) The declaration that they only are seeking intercession.

16) Their thinking that the scholars who made the images intended that.

17) The great clarification in the Prophet's statement,

«لا تُطْرُونِي كَمَا أَطْرَتِ النَّصَارَى ابْنَ مَرْيَمَ»

"Do not exaggerate in praising me as the Christians exaggerated in praising 'Isâ (Jesus), the son of Maryam (Mary)."

May the blessings of Allâh and His peace be upon the one who conveyed the clear message (i.e. Prophet Muhammad ﷺ).

18) His advising us about the destruction of those who are excessive.

19) The declaration that they (the statues) were not worshipped until the knowledge was forgotten. This contains an explanation regarding the awareness of the value of its presence and the harm in its being lost.

20) That the cause of the loss of knowledge is the death of the scholars.

Chapter 19

What has been Narrated Regarding the Condemnation of Whoever Worships Allâh at the Grave of a Righteous Man — So How About if He Worships the Man in the Grave?*

In the *Ṣaḥeeḥ* it is narrated from 'Aishah رَضِيَ الله عَنْهَا that Umm Salamah رَضِيَ الله عَنْهَا mentioned a church that she saw in the land of Abyssinia to Allâh's Messenger ﷺ and what pictures it contained. He said,

---

* This chapter, along with the chapters that come after it, contains a clarification that the Prophet ﷺ was concerned with this *Ummah*. From the completeness of his concern is that he warned them about every means and he closed every way that led to *Ash-Shirk*. An example of what has come in regard to this condemnation is that a person will come to the grave of a righteous man, whose righteousness is known, in order to worship Allâh Alone at it. He does this hoping for the blessing of this spot. This has spread among many of the people - that is the belief that whatever is around the graves of the righteous people is blessed, and that worship performed at such places is not like worship performed anywhere else.

His Statement (in the chapter heading), "So How About if He Worships the Man in the Grave?" This means that the person worships the grave or he worships the man (in the grave). This is because the worship of the *Quboориyyoon* (grave worshippers) sometimes is directed to the grave and sometimes to the person in the grave. Sometimes it is directed to what is around the grave. Thus, the structures that surround the grave at the gravesites of the righteous people have become shrines. Sometimes these metal walls are taken to be gods! Hence, the people wipe them hoping to get blessings from it, and they take them as a means of mediation to Allâh. They devote themselves to them, worship them, hope in them and fear them.

أُولئِكِ إِذَا مَاتَ فِيهِمُ الرَّجُلُ الصَّالِحُ أَوِ الْعَبْدُ الصَّالِحُ بَنَوْا عَلَىٰ قَبْرِهِ مَسْجِدًا، وَصَوَّرُوا فِيهِ تِلْكَ الصُّوَرَ أُولئِكَ شِرَارُ الْخَلْقِ عِنْدَ اللهِ»

"These are people that when a righteous man dies among them or a righteous worshipper, they build a Masjid (place of worship) over his grave and they make these images in it. These people are the worst of creation with Allâh."[1]

---

[1] In the *Ṣaḥeeḥ* it is narrated from 'Aishah رَضِيَ اللهُ عَنْهَا that Umm Salamah رَضِيَ اللهُ عَنْهَا mentioned a church that she saw in the land of Abyssinia to Allâh's Messenger ﷺ and what pictures it contained. He said,

«أُولئِكِ إِذَا مَاتَ فِيهِمُ الرَّجُلُ الصَّالِحُ أَوِ الْعَبْدُ الصَّالِحُ بَنَوْا عَلَىٰ قَبْرِهِ مَسْجِدًا، وَصَوَّرُوا فِيهِ تِلْكَ الصُّوَرَ»

"These are people that when a righteous man dies among them or a righteous worshipper, they build a Masjid (place of worship) over his grave and they make these images in it."

Masjid is generally used to mean every place that is taken for the worship of Allâh. Therefore, the churches were built over the graves of these righteous people and they placed an image of that slave on his grave or over his grave on the wall. They did this to guide the people to the worship of Allâh by honoring that righteous man and his grave.

In his statement, "These people", he is addressing Umm Salamah رَضِيَ اللهُ عَنْهَا.

«أُولئِكَ شِرَارُ الْخَلْقِ عِنْدَ اللهِ»

"Are the worst of creation with Allâh."

This means, those who exalt the righteous people and build Mosques over their graves. There is nothing in the *Hadith* that says that they turned in worship to these righteous people. They only honored their graves and placed images in them.

So these people have combined two *Fitnahs* (trials, evils): The *Fitnah* of the graves and the *Fitnah* of the statues. The word "statues" here means images. Both of these things are means from those things that lead to the occurrence of the major *Shirk*. We understand from this the warning of this *Ummah* against building a Masjid over the grave of anyone.

So these people have combined two *Fitnahs* (trials, evils): The *Fitnah* of the graves and the *Fitnah* of the statues.

They (Al-Bukhari and Muslim) both recorded from her ('Aishah) that she said, "When it (death) came to Allâh's Messenger ﷺ he began to draw a *Khameeṣah* (a garment having markings on it) over his face. When he was covered with it he would then remove it. While he was in this state he said,

«لَعْنَةُ اللهِ عَلَى الْيَهُودِ وَالنَّصَارَى، اتَّخَذُوا قُبُورَ أَنْبِيَائِهِمْ مَسَاجِدَ»

'The Curse of Allâh is upon the Jews and the Christians. They took the graves of their Prophets as Masjids.'

He was warning against what they had done. Were it not for that his grave would have been placed outside (at the graveyard), but it was feared that it would be taken as a Masjid (place of worship)."[1]

---

[1] "They (Al-Bukhari and Muslim) both recorded from her..." Her here means 'Aishah رَضِيَ اللهُ عَنْهَا. "That she said, 'When it came to Allâh's Messenger ﷺ...'" This means that death came to him. "He began to draw a *Khameeṣah* (a garment having markings on it) over his face." This *Hadith* is from the greatest *Ahadith* that contain a rebuke of the means of *Ash-Shirk*, building Mosques over graves and taking the graves of the Prophets and righteous people as Mosques. The point of this comes from the fact that when the Prophet ﷺ was in that state of distress and difficulty and the pangs of death had descended upon him, he was not heedless. Rather, he was extremely concerned, even in that condition, with warning the *Ummah* about one of the things that leads to *Ash-Shirk*, and directing the curse and supplication against the Jews and Christians with the curse of Allâh. The reason for this was that they took the graves of their Prophets as Mosques. So in that situation the Prophet ﷺ feared that his grave would be taken as a Masjid just as the graves of the Prophets before him were taken as Mosques. His curse upon whoever takes the graves as Mosques was a warning for the Companions against that, and a proof that such people had committed a major sin. Taking the graves as Mosques comes in three forms:

The first form: That the person prostrates on the grave, and this is the most hideous of the types.

The second form: That the person prays (*Aṣ-Ṣalaah*) to the grave. This is by him being in front of the grave and praying towards it. Then verily he takes the grave - and whatever is around it has the same ruling - as a place for humility and submission. And the meaning of the word Masjid is a place of humility and submission. For this reason the Prophet ﷺ forbade praying towards graves, as prayer performed towards a grave is a means of glorification, and this corresponds with the chapter heading of the Shaikh.

The third form: That the grave is placed inside of the Masjid. So when the Prophet would be buried, these people would begin building structures over him. They would make that which was around his grave a Masjid and they would take that place as a place of worship and the performance of prayer (*Aṣ-Ṣalaaḥ*).

'Aishah رَضِيَ اللهُ عَنْهَا then said, "Were it not for that his grave would have been placed outside." This means that it would have been placed in the open and his grave would have been placed with the rest of the graves in the graveyard known as Al-Baqee' or something similar. This is one of the two reasons (for not burying the Prophet ﷺ outside of 'Aishah's house). The other reason is the statement of Abu Bakr رَضِيَ اللهُ عَنْهُ. Verily he heard the Prophet ﷺ saying,

«إِنَّ الْأَنْبِيَاءَ يُقْبَرُونَ حَيْثُ يُقْبَضُونَ»

"Verily the Prophets are buried in the place where they die."

Then she said, "but it was feared that it would be taken as a Masjid (place of worship)." This means that the Prophet ﷺ or the Companions feared that his grave would be taken as a Masjid. This is a notice concerning one of the two reasons (that his grave was not made outside) as we have mentioned. The Companions accepted his warning and acted according to the Prophet ﷺ final advice. From that which proves this is that they took three meters from *Ar-Rawdhah Ash-Shareefah* (the Noble Garden area) so that the second wall could be placed and then the third wall. Then a metal wall was placed there. This took up even more than three meters. This is the greatest application of the Prophet's command, in that they took away from *Ar-Rawdhah Ash-Shareefah* and they did even more by taking away from the Masjid in order to protect the Prophet's grave from being taken as a Masjid. There is no doubt that this is from the greatest understanding of those who did this. However, with one who

They (Al-Bukhari and Muslim) both recorded it.

Muslim recorded that Jundub bin 'Abdullah رَضِيَ اللهُ عَنْهُ said, "I heard the Prophet ﷺ, saying five days before he died,

«إِنِّي أَبْرَأُ إِلَى اللهِ أَنْ يَكُونَ لِي مِنْكُمْ خَلِيلٌ، فَإِنَّ اللهَ قد اتَّخَذَنِي خَلِيلًا كَمَا اتَّخَذَ إِبْرَاهِيمَ خَلِيلًا، وَلَوْ كُنْتُ مُتَّخِذًا مِنْ أُمَّتِي خَلِيلًا لَاتَّخَذْتُ أَبَا بَكْرٍ خَلِيلًا، أَلَا وَإِنَّ مَنْ كَانَ قَبْلَكُمْ كَانُوا يَتَّخِذُونَ قُبُورَ أَنْبِيَائِهِمْ مَسَاجِدَ أَلَا فَلَا تَتَّخِذُوا الْقُبُورَ مَسَاجِد فَإِنِّي أَنْهَاكُم عَنْ ذٰلِكَ»

'I am innocent before Allâh of having a *Khaleel* (intimate and most beloved companion) from among you. For verily Allâh took me as a *Khaleel* just as He took Ibrâhîm as a *Khaleel*. And if I had taken a *Khaleel* from among my *Ummah* (nation, followers) I would have taken Abu Bakr as a *Khaleel*. Verily those who were before you used to take the graves of their Prophets as Masjids. Do not take the graves as Masajid, for verily I forbid you from that.'"

Verily he forbade this at the end of his life. Then he cursed - while he was in the throws of death - whoever did this. Prayer (*Aṣ-Ṣalaah*) at them (the graves) is from this, even if a Masjid is not built. This is the meaning of her statement, "it was feared that it would be taken as a Masjid (place of worship)."

For verily the Companions did not build a Masjid around his grave. Every place where prayer (*Aṣ-Ṣalaah*) is meant to be performed is called a Masjid, as the Prophet ﷺ said,

---

does not look carefully and who does not understand, he will think that the grave is inside of the Masjid. Yet, in reality, it is actually not a grave inside of a Masjid, because of the presence of the different walls that separate the Masjid from the grave. Also, the eastern side of it is not a part of the Masjid. The important point here is that the Prophet's grave was not taken as a Masjid.

«جُعِلَتْ لِيَ الأَرْضُ مَسْجِدًا وَطَهُورًا»

"The earth was made a Masjid for me and a (source of) purification."[1]

---

[1] Muslim recorded that Jundub bin 'Abdullah said, "I heard the Prophet ﷺ saying five days before he died...

«أَلَا وَإِنَّ مَنْ كَانَ قَبْلَكُمْ كَانُوا يَتَّخِذُونَ قُبُورَ أَنْبِيائِهِمْ مَسَاجِدَ»

'Verily those who were before you used to take the graves of their Prophets as Mosques.'"

This is that which has occurred in this *Ummah*, and it is a means from the things that lead to *Ash-Shirk*. The means lead to that which comes after them. Indeed it is affirmed in the principles of Islamic Law and that which the researchers have agreed upon, that it is obligatory to block the means that lead to *Ash-Shirk* and the forbidden things. For this reason, it is not correct to pray (*Aṣ-Ṣalaah*) in a Masjid that is built over a grave, because it contradicts the Prophet's prohibition.

Then he said,

«أَلَا فَلَا تَتَّخِذُوا الْقُبُورَ مَسَاجِدَ»

"Do not take the graves as Mosques."

This is by building over them and praying (*Aṣ-Ṣalaah*) around them.

Then the Shaikh said, "Verily he forbade this at the end of his life. Then he cursed - while he was in the throws of death - whoever did this. Prayer (*Aṣ-Ṣalaah) at them (the graves) is from this, even if a Masjid is not built. This is the meaning of her statement, 'it was feared that it would be taken as a Masjid (place of worship).'" This means that prayer (Aṣ-Ṣalaah*) at graves is not permissible. It makes no difference whether one prays at them seeking the blessing of that place, or he prays an optional prayer at them, other than the funeral prayer (*Ṣalaat ul-Janaazah*). All of this is not permissible, regardless of whether there is a building over the grave, like a Masjid, or it is not in a building. For this reason it has been related in *Al-Bukhari* with an incomplete chain of narration (*Mu'allaq*) from the statement of 'Umar رَضِيَ اللهُ عَنْهُ that he saw Anas praying at a grave and he said to him, "The grave, the grave!" He meant, "Beware of the grave." This proves that the prayer at the graves is not permissible, because it is a means from the things that lead to the major *Shirk*.

Then the Shaikh said, "This is the meaning of her statement, 'it was feared that it would be taken as a Masjid (place of worship).' For verily the

Aḥmad recorded with a good chain of narration from Ibn Mas'ud رَضِيَ اللهُ عَنْهُ a statement, which he attributed to the Prophet ﷺ,

«إِنَّ مِنْ شِرَارِ النَّاسِ مَن تُدْرِكُهُمُ السَّاعَةُ وَهُمْ أَحْيَاءٌ، والَّذِينَ يَتَّخِذُونَ الْقُبُورَ مَسَاجِدَ»

"Verily from the worst of the people are those whom the Hour comes upon them while they are living, and those who take the graves as Masajid."[1] [Abu Ḥaatim (Ibn Ḥibbaan) recorded it in his Ṣaḥîḥ]

Companions did not build a Masjid around his grave. Every place where prayer (*Aṣ-Ṣalaah*) is meant to be performed is called a Masjid, as the Prophet ﷺ said, 'The earth was made a Masjid for me and a (source of) purification.'" And this is obvious.

[1] The Shaikh then said, "Aḥmad recorded with a good chain of narration from Ibn Mas'ud رَضِيَ اللهُ عَنْهُ a statement, which he attributed to the Prophet ﷺ,

«إِنَّ مِنْ شِرَارِ النَّاسِ. . . »

'Verily from the worst of the people...'

Abu Ḥaatim recorded it in his *Ṣaḥeeḥ*." Abu Haatim here means Ibn Hibbaan. Concerning the Prophet's statement,

«وَالَّذِينَ تَتَّخِذُونَ الْقُبُورَ مَسَاجِدَ»

"and those who take the graves as Mosques."

This includes every person who takes a grave as a Masjid (i.e. place of worship). It makes not difference whether he took it as a place to pray on, to or at. Thus, this intention of praying at a grave makes the one who intends it among the worst of people, whom the Prophet ﷺ described as such.

Take note of this, along with what has spread in the lands of the Muslims of constructing buildings and domes over graves. Also, there is the construction of shrines and the honor given to it, and directing people to them. Then there is the mention of long stories regarding the virtues of these righteous people (in the graves) and their answering of supplications, helping to relieve worries and similar things. Hence, the extreme strangeness of Islam will become apparent to in these times and that

Important issues of the Chapter

1) What the Messenger mentioned about whoever builds a Masjid where Allâh is worshipped at the grave of a righteous person, even if the intention of the person who does so is correct.

2) The prohibition of images and the severity of the matter.

3) Consideration of his intense concern about this, firstly how he explained it to them, and then what he said five days before his death. Then, while he was in the throws of death, he did not suffice with what has preceded.

4) He forbade doing this at his grave before his grave existed.

5) That this is from the ways of the Jews and Christians regarding the graves of their Prophets.

6) His cursing them for that.

7) That his intent was to warn us about his grave.

8) The reason for not placing his grave in the open.

9) The meaning of taking it as a Masjid.

10) That he mentioned those who take graves as Masajid and those upon whom the Hour would be established together. Thus, he mentioned the means that leads to *Ash-Shirk* before it occurred while he was in his final moments of life.

11) His mentioning in his address five days before his death the refutation against the two groups, who are the worst of the people of innovation. Some of the scholars have

---

which was before it. Then how about if they (the people) say, "Verily this is permissible! And this is *Tauḥid*!" Rather, how about if they accuse whoever forbids them from this of lacking knowledge and understanding?! He is calling them to Allâh and they are calling him to the Fire. We ask Allâh for safety and wellbeing.

expelled them from the seventy-two sects. They (these two groups) are the *Raafidhah* and the *Jahmiyyah*. This is because *Shirk* and the worship of graves occurred due to the *Raafidhah,* and they were the first to construct Masajid over graves.

12) What the Prophet ﷺ was tested by of the agony of death.

13) How he was honored by Allâh making him a *Khaleel.*

14) A clear declaration that intimate friendship (*Khullah*) is more exalted than love.

15) 'A clear declaration that Aṣ-Ṣiddiq رَضِيَ اللهُ عَنْهُ was the best of the Companions.

16) 'The indication of his (Abu Bakr's) succession (as the *Khaleefah* after the Prophet ﷺ).

Chapter 20

What has been narrated Regarding Exaggeration Concerning the Graves of the Righteous People making them Idols that are worshipped besides Allâh*

Maalik recorded in *Al-Muwaṭṭa'* that Allâh's Messenger ﷺ said,

«اللَّهُمَّ لَا تَجْعَلْ قَبْرِي وَثَنًا يُعْبَدُ، اشْتَدَّ غَضَبُ اللهِ عَلَى قَوْمٍ اتَّخَذُوا قُبُورَ أَنْبِيَائِهِمْ مَسَاجِدَ».

"O Allâh do not make my grave an idol that is worshipped. May the anger of Allâh be severe upon a people who take the graves of their Prophets as Masajid."[1]

---

* The description of the grave in the Islamic Law is one. The Islamic Law has not made a distinction and no evidence has come in the Islamic Law that the grave of the righteous person should be distinct from the grave of others. Rather, the description (of the grave) is one, which is that it is either a grave that is *Musannam* (arched) or *Murabba'* (squared). Therefore, transgressing the limit concerning the graves of the righteous is a transgression in what has been commanded or prohibited regarding the graves. This occurs by righting upon them, or elevating them, or building structures over them, or taking them as Masjids, or by making the grave a means of drawing nearer to Allâh. This may also be in making the grave or the person in the grave a means of intercession for them with Allâh. The person will give the grave the right to be vowed to, or sacrificed to, or he will seek intercession by its dirt. They do this believing that it is a means of mediation with Allâh. They do other acts that are similar to these from the forms of major *Shirk* with Allâh, blessed be He the Most High.

[1] Maalik recorded in *Al-Muwaṭṭa'* that Allâh's Messenger ﷺ said,

«اللَّهُمَّ لَا تَجْعَلْ قَبْرِي وَثَنًا يُعْبَدُ»

"Oh Allâh do not make my grave an idol that is worshipped."

This is seeking refuge and supplication due to fear that this matter would

Ibn Jareer recorded with his chain of narration from Sufyaan, who narrated from Mansoor, who narrated from Mujâhid concerning the Verse,

﴿أَفَرَءَيْتُمُ ٱللَّٰتَ وَٱلْعُزَّىٰ﴾

"Have you seen Al-Laat and Al-'Uzzaa?" (53:19)

"He (Laat) used to serve them (the pilgrims) *As-Saweeq*.[1] So he died and they (the people) devoted themselves to his grave." Abu Al-Jawzaa' narrated the same thing from Ibn 'Abbaas رَضِيَ اللهُ عَنْهُ, that he said, "He (Laat) used to serve *As-Saweeq* to the

---

occur. This means that it is possible for the grave to be an idol that is worshipped. Thus, the goal is that the grave is taken as an idol that is worshipped, and the means that leads to that is what comes after it. The Prophet ﷺ said,

«اشْتَدَّ غَضَبُ اللهِ عَلَى قَوْمٍ اتَّخَذُوا قُبُورَ أَنْبِيَائِهِمْ مَسَاجِدَ».

"May the anger of Allâh be severe upon a people who take the graves of their Prophets as Mosques."

This is exaggeration that is known as exaggeration of the means (*Ghulul-Wasaa'il*). In this *Hadith* the Prophet ﷺ combined between the mention of the means (that lead to *Ash-Shirk*), the deterrence from it and the severity of the anger of Allâh upon whoever commits it. He also mentioned the result of what this means will lead its practitioners to, which is that the graves will become idols that are worshipped besides Allâh. This *Hadith* contains a clarification that it is possible for the grave to become an idol.

[1] Ibn Jareer recorded with his chain of narration from Sufyaan, who narrated from Mansoor, who narrated from Mujâhid concerning the Verse,

﴿أَفَرَءَيْتُمُ ٱللَّٰتَ وَٱلْعُزَّىٰ﴾

"Have you seen Al-Laat and Al-'Uzzaa?" (53:19)

The proof here is in the statement of Mujâhid, "He died and they (the people) devoted themselves to his grave." This was because he was a man who benefited them by serving them *As-Saweeq*. Thus, the righteousness of that man made them exaggerate concerning his grave. *Al-'Ukoof* (devotion) here means adhering to the grave by honoring it, believing in the blessings, the reward and the benefit that come from adhering to it, and its repelling of harms. Devotion to graves make them become idols that are worshipped.

Ḥajj pilgrim."

Ibn 'Abbaas رَضِيَ اللهُ عَنْهُ said, "Allâh's Messenger ﷺ cursed the women who visit the graves and those who set up Masajid and lights over them (the graves)." (Recorded by the *Sunan* compilers)[1]

Important issues of the Chapter

1) The explanation of idols.
2) The explanation of worship.
3) That the Prophet ﷺ did not seek refuge except from that which is feared will occur.
4) His combining with this the taking of the Prophet's graves as Masajid.
5) Mention of the intense anger of Allâh.
6) And it is from the most important of these points - knowing the description of the worship of Al-Laat (i.e. how it started), which was one of the major idols.
7) Knowing that it was the grave of a righteous man.
8) That it was the name of the person in the grave and a mention of the meaning of (the idol) being named such.
9) His cursing the women who frequently visited the graves.
10) His cursing whoever placed lights at graves.

---

[1] Ibn 'Abbaas رَضِيَ اللهُ عَنْهُ said, " Allâh's Messenger ﷺ cursed..." We have already discussed the issue of the Masajids. The prohibition of placing lights upon the graves is because it is a means of glorifying these graves and a type of exaggeration concerning them. Lights are placed at the graves and in the previous times candles were placed on them. In these days huge lights are placed over them that make it clear that this place is intended and sought after, and arrangements of lights are placed on them and illuminations that shine. These lights lead the people to exalt this grave. Thus, these people are cursed by the curse of Allâh's Messenger ﷺ. Therefore, it is not permissible that these lights be placed upon the graves.

Chapter 21

What has been Narrated Regarding Al-Muṣtafaa's ﷺ Protection of *At-Tauhid* and His Closing Every Path that Leads to *Ash-Shirk*

The Statement of Allâh the Most High,

﴿لَقَدْ جَآءَكُمْ رَسُولٌ مِّنْ أَنفُسِكُمْ عَزِيزٌ عَلَيْهِ مَا عَنِتُّمْ﴾ الآية

"Verily, there has come to you a Messenger (Muhammad ﷺ) from among yourselves. It grieves him that you should receive any injury or difficulty." (9:128)[1]

---

[1] The Statement of Allâh the Most High,

﴿لَقَدْ جَآءَكُمْ رَسُولٌ مِّنْ أَنفُسِكُمْ عَزِيزٌ عَلَيْهِ مَا عَنِتُّمْ﴾

"Verily there has come to you a Messenger (Muhammad ﷺ) from among yourselves. It grieves him that you should receive any injury or difficulty." (9:128)

This means that he does not desire for you all to be in any hardship and distress.

Allâh continues,

﴿حَرِيصٌ عَلَيْكُم﴾

"He (Muhammad ﷺ) is anxious over you."

From his anxiousness over us and our distress being something that he was concerned with the fact that he protected *At-Tauhid* and the honor of *At-Tauhid*, and that he closed off every path that would lead us to *Ash-Shirk*.

﴿بِالْمُؤْمِنِينَ رَءُوفٌ رَّحِيمٌ ○ فَإِن تَوَلَّوْا فَقُلْ حَسْبِيَ اللَّهُ لَآ إِلَٰهَ إِلَّا هُوَ عَلَيْهِ تَوَكَّلْتُ وَهُوَ رَبُّ الْعَرْشِ الْعَظِيمِ﴾

"To the believers (he ﷺ is) full of pity, kind and merciful. But if they turn away, say (O Muhammad ﷺ): 'Allâh is sufficient for me. *Lâ ilâha illa Huwa* (none has the right to be worshipped but He), in Him I put my trust and He is the Lord of the Mighty Throne." (9:128,129)

Abu Hurayrah رَضِيَ اللهُ عَنْهُ narrated that Allâh's Messenger ﷺ said,

«لَا تَجْعَلُوا بُيُوتَكُمْ قُبُورًا، وَلَا تَجْعَلُوا قَبْرِي عِيدًا وَصَلُّوا عَلَيَّ فَإِنَّ صَلَاتَكُمْ تَبْلُغُنِي حَيْثُ كُنْتُمْ»

"Do not make your houses graves and do not make my grave a place of celebration. And send *Ṣalâh* (prayers for blessings, graces and mercy) upon me, for verily your *Ṣalaah* reaches me wherever you may be."[1]

Recorded by Abu Daawood with a good chain of narration and its narrators are reliable.

'Ali bin Al-Ḥusayn رَضِيَ اللهُ عَنْهُ narrated that he saw a man coming to a space that was at the grave of the Prophet ﷺ, and the man would enter that space and supplicate. So he ('Ali) forbade him and said, "Shall I not tell you a *Hadith* that I heard from my father (Al-Ḥusayn), who related it from my grandfather ('Ali bin Abi Ṭâlib), who related it from Allâh's Messenger ﷺ? He said,

---

[1] Abu Hurayrah رَضِيَ اللهُ عَنْهُ narrated that Allâh's Messenger ﷺ said,

«لَا تَجْعَلُوا بُيُوتَكُمْ قُبُورًا . . .»

"Do not make your houses graves..."

In reference to the word *'Eed* (used in the *Hadith*) then it may be an *'Eed* that is related to a particular place, as it is used here, or it may also be an *'Eed* that is related to a particular time.

«لَا تَجْعَلُوا قَبْرِي عِيدًا»

"Do not make my grave an *'Eed.*"

This means a place that you all return to (to visit) at a known time during the year, or at known times you all make it a custom to come to the grave. Verily this leads to glorifying the Prophet ﷺ as Allâh is glorified. For verily taking the graves as a place of *'Eed* is from the means that lead to *Ash-Shirk*. For this reason the Prophet ﷺ said,

«وَصَلُّوا عَلَيَّ فَإِنَّ صَلَاتَكُمْ تَبْلُغُنِي حَيْثُ كُنْتُمْ»

"And send *Ṣalaah* (prayers for blessings, graces and mercy) upon me, for verily your *Ṣalâh* reaches me wherever you may be."

«لَا تَتَّخِذُوا قَبْرِي عِيدًا، وَلَا بُيُوتَكُمْ قُبُورًا، وَصَلُّوا عَلَيَّ فَإِنَّ تَسْلِيمَكُمْ يَبْلُغُنِي حَيْثُ كُنْتُمْ»

'Do not take my grave as a place of celebration nor your houses as graves. And send *Ṣalâh* (prayers for blessings, graces and mercy) upon me, for verily your salutations (asking for safety and peace for me) reach me wherever you may be.'"[1]

He recorded it in *Al-Mukhtaarah*.

Important issues of the Chapter

1) Explanation of the Verse in *Surah Baraa'ah* (*At-Tawbah*) (9:128-129).

2) The Prophet's ﷺ keeping his *Ummah* as far away as possible from transgressing this sacred boundary.

---

[1] 'Ali bin Al-Ḥusayn رَضِيَ اللهُ عَنْهُ narrated that he saw a man coming to a space that was at the grave of the Prophet ﷺ..." Likewise, the *Hadith* of 'Ali bin Al-Ḥusayn has this same meaning (as the previous *Hadith*). Thus, the protection of the Prophet ﷺ was the protecting of *At-Tauhid* and its honor and closing every path that leads to *Ash-Shirk*, even concerning his grave. If the matter is such, then this applies even more so to the graves of others besides him. That which has occurred is that this *Ummah* has not accepted - in many of its groups - the protection of the Prophet ﷺ in this. They have taken the graves as Mosques and places of celebrations (*'Eeds*). They have even constructed shrines over the graves, decorated them with lights, and accepted that sacrifices and vows should be directed to them, and that circuits (i.e. *Aṭ-Ṭawaaf*) should be made around them. Thus, they (the graves) have been made like the *Ka'bah*, and the places around them have been made holy to a greater extent than the sanctity of the blessed sites of Allâh. Verily you find that the worshippers of the graves have humbleness, humility, devotion, hope, and fear when they come to the grave of the Prophet, or the grave of the righteous man, or the grave of the pious believer (*Waliyy*). Yet, you do not find these things in their hearts when they are alone with Allâh. This is precisely what opposition to Allâh and His Messenger, Muhammad ﷺ is.

3) Mention of his concern for us, and his kindness and mercy.
4) His prohibition of visiting his grave in a particular manner, even though visiting it is from the best of deeds.
5) His prohibition of excessive visits (to his grave).
6) His encouraging the performance of optional prayers in the house.
7) That it was established with them (the Companions) that prayer (*Aṣ-Ṣalaah*) should not be offered in the cemetery.
8) The reason for this is that the prayer of a man and his sending peace upon him (the Prophet ﷺ) reaches him even if the person is far away. Therefore, there is no need for one to believe that he must be close (to the grave).
9) The fact that in his being in *Al-Barzakh* (transitory grave state) the deeds of his *Ummah* are presented to him in their *Ṣalaah* (sending prayers of blessings and mercy) and *Salaam* (prayers for peace and safety) upon him.

Chapter 22

What has been Narrated Regarding the Fact that Some of this *Ummah* (Nation) will Worship Idols*

The Statement of Allâh the Most High,

﴿أَلَمْ تَرَ إِلَى ٱلَّذِينَ أُوتُوا۟ نَصِيبًا مِّنَ ٱلْكِتَٰبِ يُؤْمِنُونَ بِٱلْجِبْتِ وَٱلطَّٰغُوتِ﴾

---

* After explaining the obligation of being aware of *At-Tauhid* and having knowledge of it, fearing *Ash-Shirk,* explaining some of the particular aspects of *At-Tauhid* and major and minor *Shirk* and the things that lead to them, the Shaikh presents the issue that someone might say, "All of this is correct. However, this *Ummah* is safe from falling into major *Shirk*. This is due to the Prophet's statement,

«إِنَّ الشَّيْطَانَ أَيِسَ أَنْ يَعْبُدَهُ الْمُصَلُّونَ فِي جَزِيرَةِ الْعَرَبِ وَلَكِنْ فِي التَّحْرِيشِ بَيْنَهُمْ»

'Verily Satan has given up hope that those who pray (*Aṣ-Ṣalaah*) *would worship him in the Arabian Peninsula, but (he hopes for) discord among them.*'''

The answer to this is that this argument is out of place. Satan despairs, but Allâh has not made him despair of being worshipped (at all) in the Arabian Peninsula. Then, in his statement, "has given up hope that those who pray (*Aṣ-Ṣalaah*) would worship him'', there is no doubt that those who pray are commanders of the good and forbidders of evil. And the greatest evil that the person who prays will reject is *Ash-Shirk* with Allâh. For verily Satan gives up hope that one who establishes the prayer in its true manner will ever worship him. Therefore, we say, "This *Hadith* does not mention that the worship of Satan will not occur in this *Ummah*.'' This is why shortly after the Prophet ﷺ died a group of the Arabs reverted from Islam, and that was from the worship of Satan, because worshipping Satan is by obeying him, as Allâh said,

﴿أَلَمْ أَعْهَدْ إِلَيْكُمْ يَٰبَنِىٓ ءَادَمَ أَن لَّا تَعْبُدُوا۟ ٱلشَّيْطَٰنَ إِنَّهُۥ لَكُمْ عَدُوٌّ مُّبِينٌ﴾

"Did I not command you, O children of Aadam, that you should not

"Have you not seen those who were given a portion of the Scripture? They believe in *Al-Jibt* and *At-Tâghût*." (4:51)[1]

---

worship Satan? Verily he is a clear enemy to you." (36:60)

The worship of Satan, as is mentioned in the explanation of the Verse, is by obeying him in commands and prohibitions. It is obeying him in the commission of *Ash-Shirk*, obeying him abandoning faith and abandoning its necessities.

The word *Awthaan* (idols) is the plural of the word *Wathn*, and the *Wathn* is everything that people turn to in worship or seeking assistance along with Allâh. It is also that which people believe brings benefit or harm without the permission of Allâh, or that the person internally fears just as he fears Allâh. It makes no difference whether that idol is a statue, meaning an image of a human figure or something else, or it is not an image. For example, it could be that the person worships a wall, or a grave or a dead person.

[1] The Statement of Allâh the Most High,

﴿أَلَمْ تَرَ إِلَى ٱلَّذِينَ أُوتُوا۟ نَصِيبًا مِّنَ ٱلْكِتَٰبِ يُؤْمِنُونَ بِٱلْجِبْتِ وَٱلطَّٰغُوتِ﴾

"Have you not seen those who were given a portion of the Scripture? They believe in *Al-Jibt* and *At-Tâghût*." *(4:51)*

Al-Jibt is a general name for everything that contains an opposition to the command of Allâh and the command of His Messenger ﷺ in beliefs. *Al-Jibt* may be magic, fortune telling or something evil that harms its practitioner.

At-Tâghût is a word that is derived from the word *Ṭughyaan*, which is that by which the slave transgresses his limit, such as something that is worshipped or followed. The limit of someone who is followed in the religion is that he commands what the Islamic Law commands and forbids whatever the Islamic Law forbids. *At-Tâghût* also includes those who are worshipped, those who are followed and those who are obeyed. The appropriate point for this chapter that is taken from this Verse is that this happened with those who were given a portion of the Scripture from the Jews and Christians. The Prophet ﷺ informed that what happened among the nations before us will happen in this *Ummah*. This will be mentioned in the *Hadith* of Abu Sa'eed رَضِيَ اللهُ عَنْهُ. From this *Ummah* are those who believe in Magic and from them there are those who believe in the worship of other than Allâh. Thus, in this they are following the ways of

And His Statement,

﴿قُلْ هَلْ أُنَبِّئُكُم بِشَرٍّ مِّن ذَٰلِكَ مَثُوبَةً عِندَ ٱللَّهِ ۚ مَن لَّعَنَهُ ٱللَّهُ وَغَضِبَ عَلَيْهِ وَجَعَلَ مِنْهُمُ ٱلْقِرَدَةَ وَٱلْخَنَازِيرَ وَعَبَدَ ٱلطَّٰغُوتَ ۚ﴾

"Say (O Muhammad ﷺ), 'Shall I inform you of something worse than that, regarding the recompense from Allâh: those (Jews) whom Allâh cursed and His anger is upon them, and He transformed some of them into monkeys and swine, and they worshipped *At-Tâghût*. (5:60)[1]

And His Statement,

﴿قَالَ ٱلَّذِينَ غَلَبُوا۟ عَلَىٰٓ أَمْرِهِمْ لَنَتَّخِذَنَّ عَلَيْهِم مَّسْجِدًا﴾

"Those who won their point said: 'Verily we shall build a place of worship over them.'" (18:21)[2]

---

those who were before them.

[1] And His Statement,

﴿قُلْ هَلْ أُنَبِّئُكُم بِشَرٍّ مِّن ذَٰلِكَ مَثُوبَةً عِندَ ٱللَّهِ ۚ مَن لَّعَنَهُ ٱللَّهُ وَغَضِبَ عَلَيْهِ وَجَعَلَ مِنْهُمُ ٱلْقِرَدَةَ وَٱلْخَنَازِيرَ وَعَبَدَ ٱلطَّٰغُوتَ ۚ﴾

"Say (O Muhammad ﷺ), 'Shall I inform you of something worse than that, regarding the recompense from Allâh: those (Jews) whom Allâh cursed and His anger is upon them, and He transformed some of them into monkeys and swine, and they worshipped *At-Tâghût*.'" (5:60)

This is referring to whoever Allâh has cursed and whoever worships *At-Tâghût*. The worship of *At-Tâghût* is general and it includes the worship of idols, such as worshipping graves, deifying the people in them and seeking mediation through them to Allâh. This has occurred with some people from the *Ummah* of Muhammad ﷺ. The worship of idols, such as graves, shrines, trees, stones and similar things, has occurred (among the Muslims).

[2] And His Statement,

﴿قَالَ ٱلَّذِينَ غَلَبُوا۟ عَلَىٰٓ أَمْرِهِمْ لَنَتَّخِذَنَّ عَلَيْهِم مَّسْجِدًا﴾

"Those who won their point said: 'Verily we shall build a place of

Abu Sa'eed ﷺ narrated that Allâh's Messenger said,

«لَتَتَّبِعُنَّ سَنَنَ مَنْ كَانَ قَبْلَكُمْ حَذْوَ الْقُذَّةِ بِالْقُذَّةِ حَتَّى لَوْ دَخَلُوا جُحْرَ ضَبٍّ لَدَخَلْتُمُوهُ»

"You will certainly follow the way of those who were before you just as the feather of an arrow is equal to another feather,[1] so much so that if they entered the hole of a lizard, you all would also enter it."

---

worship over them.'" (18:21)

The statement, "Those who won their point" means those were victorious in the matter. They glorified those righteous people and they said,

﴿لَنَتَّخِذَنَّ عَلَيْهِم مَّسْجِدًا﴾

"Verily we shall build a place of worship (Masjid) over them."

Just as it happened in that *Ummah* (nation), it will certainly happen in this *Ummah*. The reason is that there is nothing that occurred of *Ash-Shirk* in the nations before us except that it has occurred in this *Ummah*.

[1] Abu Sa'eed رَضِيَ اللهُ عَنْهُ narrated that Allâh's Messenger ﷺ said,

«لَتَتَّبِعُنَّ سَنَنَ مَنْ كَانَ قَبْلَكُمْ»

"You will certainly follow the way of those who were before."

The word *Sanan* is singular and it is way and path. In other words, you all will certainly follow the path of those who were before you. The letter *Laam* in his statement, *Latattbi 'anna* (you will certainly follow) is the occurrence in the answer of an oath. Why did the Prophet ﷺ swear an oath? He did so in order to give tremendous emphasis to this matter that this *Ummah* is going to follow the way and path of those who were before them from the previous nations. This is a warning.

His Statement, "just as the feather of an arrow is equal to another feather" means due to the equality. The feather and another feather are on the arrow, and one is equal to the other. There is no difference between one and the other.

Then he said,

«حَتَّى لَوْ دَخَلُوا جُحْرَ ضَبٍّ لَدَخَلْتُمُوهُ»

"so much so that if they entered the hole of a lizard, you all would also enter it."

They said, "O Messenger of Allâh, are they the Jews and the Christians?" He replied,

«فَمَنْ؟»

"Who else?"

They (Al-Bukhari and Muslim) both recorded it.[1]

Muslim recorded from Thawbaan that Allâh's Messenger said,

«إِنَّ اللهَ زَوَى لِيَ الْأَرْضَ، فَرَأَيْتُ مَشَارِقَهَا وَمَغَارِبَهَا، وَإِنَّ أُمَّتِي سَيَبْلُغُ مُلْكُهَا مَا زُوِيَ لِي مِنْهَا، وأُعْطِيتُ الْكَنْزَيْنِ: الْأَحْمَرَ وَالْأَبْيَضَ، وَإِنِّي سَأَلْتُ رَبِّي لِأُمَّتِي أَنْ لَا يُهْلِكَهَا بِسَنَةٍ بِعَامَّةٍ، وَأَنْ لَا يُسَلِّطَ عَلَيْهِمْ عَدُوًّا مِنْ سِوَى أَنْفُسِهِمْ فَيَسْتَبِيحَ بَيْضَتَهُمْ، وإِنَّ رَبِّي قَالَ: يَا مُحَمَّدُ إِنِّي إِذَا قَضَيْتُ قَضَاءً فَإِنَّهُ لَا يُرَدُّ، وَإِنِّي أَعْطَيْتُكَ لِأُمَّتِكَ أَنْ لَا أُهْلِكَهُمْ بِسَنَةٍ بِعَامَّةٍ، وَأَنْ لَا أُسَلِّطَ عَلَيْهِمْ عَدُوًّا مِنْ سِوَىٰ أَنْفُسِهِمْ فَيَسْتَبِيحَ بَيْضَتَهُمْ، وَلَوِ اجْتَمَعَ عَلَيْهِمْ مَنْ بِأَقْطَارِهَا، حَتَّى يَكُونَ بَعْضُهُمْ يُهْلِكُ بَعْضًا، وَيَسْبِي بَعْضُهُمْ بَعْضًا».

"Verily Allâh gathered the earth for me and I saw its east and its west. And verily the dominion of my *Ummah* will reach all of what was gathered for me of it (the earth). The two treasures were given to me: the red (gold) and the white (silver). Indeed I asked my Lord to

[1] They said, "O Messenger of Allâh, are they the Jews and the Christians?" He replied,

«فَمَن؟»

"Who else?"

They (Al-Bukhari and Muslim) both recorded it.

The pillars of this chapter rest upon this *Hadith*, as every disbelief (*Kufr*) and association of partners (with Allâh) (*Shirk*) that occurred in the previous nations will occur in this *Ummah*.

not destroy my *Ummah* with drought or by allowing their enemy to overpower them — from other than themselves — who would wipe them all out, even if people from all sides of the earth collectively attack them. This (safety) would remain until some of them (the Muslims) destroy others and some of them take others as captives."[1]

Al-Barqaanee recorded this same narration in his *Ṣaḥeeḥ* and he added (that the Prophet ﷺ said),

«وَإِنَّمَا أَخَافُ عَلى أُمَّتِي الأَئِمَّةَ الْمُضِلِّينَ وَإِذَا وَقَعَ عَلَيْهِمُ السَّيْفُ لَمْ يُرفَعْ إِلَى يَوْمِ الْقِيَامَةِ، وَلَا تَقُومُ السَّاعَةُ حَتَّى يَلْحَقَ حَيٌّ مِنْ أُمَّتِي بِالْمُشْرِكِينَ. وَحَتَّى تَعْبُدَ فِئَامٌ مِنْ أُمَّتِي الأَوْثَانَ وَإِنَّهُ سَيَكُونُ فِي أُمَّتِي كَذَّابُونَ ثَلَاثُونَ كُلُّهُمْ يَزْعُمُ أَنَّهُ نَبِيٌّ وَأَنَا خَاتَمُ النَّبِيِّينَ لَا نَبِيَّ بَعْدِي، وَلَا تَزَالُ طَائِفَةٌ مِنْ أُمَّتِي عَلى الْحَقِّ مَنْصُورَةً، لَا يَضُرُّهُمْ مَنْ خَذَلَهُمْ وَلَا مَنْ خَالَفَهُمْ حَتَّى يَأْتِيَ أَمْرُ اللهِ تَبَارَكَ وَتَعَالَى» .

"I only fear for my *Ummah*, the *Imaams* (leaders) who lead (them) astray.[2] And when the sword falls upon

---

[1] Muslim recorded from Thawbaan رَضِيَ اللهُ عَنْهُ that Allâh's Messenger ﷺ said,

«إِنَّ اللهَ زَوَى لِيَ الْأَرْضَ، فَرَأَيْتُ مَشَارِقَهَا وَمَغَارِبَهَا، وَإِنَّ أُمَّتِي سَيَبْلُغُ مُلْكُهَا مَا زُوِيَ لِي»

"Verily Allâh gathered the earth for me and I saw its east and its west. And verily the dominion of my *Ummah* will reach all of what was gathered for me..."

[2] Al-Barqaanee recorded this same narration in his *Ṣaḥeeḥ* and he added (that the Prophet ﷺ said),

«وَإِنَّمَا أَخَافُ عَلَى أُمَّتِي الأَئِمَّةَ الْمُضِلِّينَ»

"I only fear for my *Ummah*, the *Imaams* (leaders) who lead (them) astray."

them it will not be removed until the Day of Resurrection. The Hour will not be established until a tribe from my *Ummah* joins the polytheists (*Al-Mushrikūn*), and groups of my *Ummah* worships the idols.[1] Verily there will be thirty liars in my *Ummah*, all of them claiming that he is a Prophet. Yet, I am the last of the Prophets — there will be no Prophet after me. There will always be a group from my *Ummah* upon the truth, victorious.[2] Whoever abandons them and opposes them will not harm them until the command of Allâh, the Blessed and Most High, comes."

The Imams (leaders) who lead astray are those whom the people take as leaders. It includes those who are leaders in the religion and those who are in charge of governing. They are those who control the rein of power of the people, thus they lead the people astray with innovations and acts of *Ash-Shirk*, and they make these things seem good to them until they come to be the truth in the people's eyes.

[1] Then he said,

«وَإِذَا وَقَعَ عَلَيْهِمُ السَّيْفُ لَمْ يُرفَعْ إِلَى يَوْمِ الْقِيَامَةِ، وَلَا تَقُومُ السَّاعَةُ حَتَّى يَلْحَقَ حَيٌّ مِنْ أُمَّتِي بِالْمُشْرِكِينَ»

"And when the sword falls upon them it will not be removed until the Day of Resurrection. The Hour will not be established until a tribe from my *Ummah* joins the polytheists (*Al-Mushrikūn*)."

This means by abandoning the lands of Islam and going to the lands of the polytheists (*Al-Mushrikūn*), being pleased with them and their religion. It could also mean in reference to characteristics. Hence, they would commit *Ash-Shirk* just as the *Mushrikūn* commit *Ash-Shirk* and they would turn back apostates (from Islam).

[2] Then he said, "and groups of my *Ummah* worships the idols." The word *Fi'aam* means large groups, and this is clearly appropriate for the chapter.

Then he said,

«وَإِنَّهُ سَيَكُونُ فِي أُمَّتِي كَذَّابُونَ ثَلَاثُونَ كُلُّهُمْ يَزْعُمُ أَنَّهُ نَبِيٌّ وَأَنَا خَاتَمُ النَّبِيِّينَ لَا نَبِيَّ بَعْدِي، وَلَا تَزَالُ طَائِفَةٌ مِنْ أُمَّتِي عَلَى الْحَقِّ مَنْصُورَةً، لَا يَضُرُّهُمْ مَنْ خَذَلَهُمْ وَلَا مَنْ خَالفهُمْ حَتَّى يَأْتِيَ أَمْرُ اللهِ تَبَارَكَ وَتَعَالى»

Important issues of the Chapter

1) Explanation of the verse of *Surah An-Nisaa'* (4:51).
2) Explanation of the verse of *Surah Al-Maa'idah* (5:60).
3) Explanation of the verse of *Surah Al-Kahf* (18:21).
4) The most important issues, which is the meaning of belief in Al-Jibt and *At-Tâghût* in this place. Is it a belief of the heart or is it agreeing with its people while hating it and knowing that it is false?
5) Their (the Jews) statement that the disbelievers, whom they knew were disbelievers, were on a more guided path than the believers.
6) This is the goal of this issue: That this will definitely occur in this *Ummah*, as is confirmed in the *Hadith* of Abu Sa'eed, among large groups.
7) His (the Prophet's ﷺ) declaration of its occurrence - meaning the worship of idols - in this *Ummah*.
8) The most amazing thing is the appearance of those who will claim Prophethood like Al-Mukhtaar (Al-Mukhtaar bin Abi 'Ubaid Ath-Thaqafee who conquered Kufah at the

---

"Verily there will be thirty liars in my *Ummah*, all of them will claimed that he is a Prophet. Yet, I am the last of the Prophets - there will be no Prophet after me. There will always be a group from my *Ummah* upon the truth, victorious. Whoever abandons them and opposes them will not harm them until the command of Allâh, the Blessed and Most High, comes."

This group has been named *Manṣoorah* (victorious) because Allâh will aid it against whoever struggles against it with proofs and evidences. This aid and victory is not referring to the spearheads (i.e. war). For even though they may be beaten in some battles or the rule may pass away from them sometimes, they are victorious and aided by what Allâh has given them of proof, texts, correctness and truth against others besides them. For they are upon the truth and others besides them are upon falsehood.

beginning of the caliphate of Ibn Zubair), while still pronouncing the two testimonies of faith (*Ash-Shahaadatayn*). Also, the person will declare that he is from this *Ummah* and that the Messenger (Muhammad ﷺ) is true and the Qur'ān is true. It also contains the point that Muhammad is the last of the Prophets. Yet, with all of this the liar will be believed in all of this, even with his clear contradiction. Al-Mukhtaar came out at the end of the time of the Companions and large groups of people followed him.

9) The good news that the truth will not perish completely as it did in the previous times. Rather, there will always be a group upon it.

10) The great sign is that even with their few numbers they will not be harmed by whoever abandons them or opposes them.

11) That this will be the condition until the establishment of the Hour.

12) What it contains of tremendous signs. From them is the Prophet's informing that Allâh gathered the east and the west for him, and he told what that meant. So it happened just as he informed, as opposed to the situation of the north and the south. He informed that he was given the two treasures and he informed of the acceptance of his supplication for his *Ummah* in the two things that he asked for. He informed that he was not granted the third thing. He informed of the occurrence of the sword and that it would not be lifted once it occurred. He informed of some of them destroying others and some of the taking others as captives. He mentioned his fear for his *Ummah* from the *Imaams* (leaders) who lead astray. He informed of the appearance of those who will claim Prophethood in this *Ummah*. He informed that the Victorious Group

(*Aṭ-Ṭaa'ifat ul-Manṣoorah*) would always remain. All of this occurred just as he informed, even though each of these things seems the most farfetched to the intellects.

13) The restricting of his fear for his *Ummah* to the *Imams* who lead astray.

14) Drawing attention to the meaning of idol worship.

Chapter 23

What has been narrated Regarding *As-Siḥr* (Sorcery or Magic)*

The Statement of Allâh the Most High,

﴿وَلَقَدْ عَلِمُوا۟ لَمَنِ ٱشْتَرَىٰهُ مَا لَهُۥ فِى ٱلْـَٔاخِرَةِ مِنْ خَلَـٰقٍ﴾

"And indeed they knew that whoever purchased it (magic) would have no share in the Hereafter." (2:102)[1]

---

* Magic is one of the types of major *Shirk* with Allâh and it is opposed to the foundation of *At-Tauhid*. The reality of magic is that it is using the devils to effect people. It is not possible for the magician to achieve the performance of his magic until he becomes close to the devils. Thus, when he becomes close to them the devils among the *jinns* serve him by effecting the body of the bewitched person. Therefore, it is not possible for the magician to become a real magician unless he draws near to the devils. Therefore, we say that magic is *Ash-Shirk* with Allâh. Allâh, the Mighty and Majestic says,

﴿وَمِن شَرِّ ٱلنَّفَّـٰثَـٰتِ فِى ٱلْعُقَدِ﴾

"And (we seek refuge with the Lord) from the evil of the *Naffaathaat* (those women who blow) into the knots." (113:4)

An-Naffaathaat is the plural of the word *Naffaathah*, and it comes in a way that expresses intensity in its meaning of blowing. Here it (*Naffaathah*) means the witch. She has been called that because she often blows into the knot (of a string or something similar). She also blows with incantations, spells and charms of protection. To do this she uses the jinn to serve the purpose of this knot that contains something from the body of the bewitched person or something attached to him, so that it will have an effect on him.

[1] The Statement of Allâh the Most High,

﴿وَلَقَدْ عَلِمُوا۟ لَمَنِ ٱشْتَرَىٰهُ﴾

"And indeed they knew that whoever purchased it (magic)..." (2:102)

His Statement,

﴿يُؤْمِنُونَ بِٱلْجِبْتِ وَٱلطَّٰغُوتِ﴾

"They believe in *Al-Jibt* and *At-Tâghût.*" *(4:51)*

'Umar رَضِيَ الله عَنْهُ said, "*Al-Jibt* is magic and *At-Tâghût* is the devil (Satan)."[1]

Jaabir رَضِيَ الله عَنْهُ said, "*Aṭ-Ṭawaagheet* (the plural of *At-Tâghût*) are fortunetellers. The devil (Satan) used to descend to them and one of them is in every tribe."[2]

This means that the magician purchases the magic and he does so at the expense of *At-Tauhid*. Thus, the price is At-Tauhid and that which is purchased (in its place) is magic.

Then he said,

﴿مَا لَهُۥ فِى ٱلْءَاخِرَةِ مِنْ خَلَٰقٍ﴾

"would have no share in the Hereafter." (2:102)

This means any portion. Thus, the *Mushrik* (polytheist, idolater) will have no portion (of good) in the hereafter.

[1] His Statement,

﴿يُؤْمِنُونَ بِٱلْجِبْتِ وَٱلطَّٰغُوتِ﴾

"They believe in *Al-Jibt* and *At-Tâghût.*" *(4:51)*

'Umar رَضِيَ الله عَنْهُ said, "*Al-Jibt* is magic." This is a rebuke of the People of the Scripture (Jews and Christians) due to their believing in magic, and this is abundant among the Jews. Since Allâh has rebuked them, cursed them and is angry with them because of that, then this shows that it is from the forbidden things and the major sins. If it contains anything of associating a partner with Allâh, then it is obvious that it is *Shirk* with Allâh, the Mighty and Sublime. This applies to all of its types. 'Umar رَضِيَ الله عَنْهُ then said, "and *At-Tâghût* is the devil (Satan)." This means that *Al-Jibt* is a general noun that includes many things - as we have mentioned - and from the most prominent and apparent of them with the Jews is magic. So they believe in *Al-Jibt*, meaning magic, and they believe in *At-Tâghût*, meaning the devil (Satan). And it (*At-Tâghût*) is everything that they turn to in obedience and being far away from the truth and what is right.

[2] Jaabir رَضِيَ الله عَنْهُ said, "*Aṭ-Ṭawaagheet* (the plural of *At-Tâghût*) are fortunetellers. The devil (Satan) used to descend to them and one of them

Abu Hurayrah رَضِيَ اللهُ عَنْهُ narrated that Allâh's Messenger ﷺ said,

«اجْتَنِبُوا السَّبْعَ الْمُوبِقَاتِ»

"Avoid the seven destroyers."

They said, "O Messenger of Allâh, what are they?" He said,

«الشِّرْكُ بِاللهِ، وَالسِّحْرُ، وَقَتْلُ النَّفْسِ الَّتِي حَرَّمَ اللهُ إِلَّا بِالْحَقِّ، وَأَكْلُ الرِّبَا، وَأَكْلُ مَالِ الْيَتِيمِ، وَالتَّوَلِّي يَوْمَ الزَّحْفِ، وَقَذْفُ الْمُحْصَنَاتِ الْغَافِلَاتِ الْمُؤْمِنَاتِ»

"*Ash-Shirk* (associating partners) with Allâh, magic, killing a soul that Allâh has made sacred except with a right to do so, taking interest (usury), taking the wealth of the orphan, fleeing on the day battle, and making a false accusation against the chaste, believing women who do not even think of doing any act of lewdness."[1]

---

is in every tribe." Jaabir is Jaabir bin 'Abdullah رَضِيَ اللهُ عَنْهُمَا. The explanation of this is forthcoming.

[1] Abu Hurayrah رَضِيَ اللهُ عَنْهُ narrated that Allâh's Messenger ﷺ said,

«اجتنبوا السبع الموبقات»

"Avoid the seven destroyers."

They said, "O Messenger of Allâh, what are they?" He said,

«الشرك بالله، والسحر. . .»

"*Ash-Shirk* (associating partners) with Allâh, magic..."

The word *Al-Mawbiqaat* are those things that destroy the one who practices them and they place him in destruction and loss in this life and in the hereafter. They are the greatest of the major sins. The attachment of magic to *Ash-Shirk* (with a conjunction) is a connection that distinguishes between the specific and the general. Thus, magic is one of the particular aspects of *Ash-Shirk* with Allâh.

Jundub رَضِيَ اللهُ عَنْهُ narrated a *Hadith* that he attributed to the Prophet (i.e. *Marfoo'*) which states,

«حَدُّ السَّاحِرِ ضَرْبُهُ بِالسَّيْفِ»

"The punishment of the magician (sorcerer) is striking him with the sword."

Jundub رَضِيَ اللهُ عَنْهُ narrated a *Hadith* that he attributed to the Prophet (i.e. *Marfoo'*) which states,

«حَدُّ السَّاحِرِ ضَرْبُهُ بِالسَّيْفِ»

"The punishment of the magician (sorcerer) is striking him with the sword."[1]

Recorded by At-Tirmithi who said, "It is authentic (*Ṣaḥeeḥ*) as *Mawqoof* (i.e. only a statement of Jundub and not attributed to the Prophet ﷺ)."

It is recorded in *Ṣaḥeeḥ Al-Bukhari* that Bajaalah bin 'Abadah said, "Umar bin Al-Khattaab رَضِيَ اللهُ عَنْهُ wrote (commanding us) to kill every male and female magician (i.e. sorcerers and witches). So we killed three sorcerers."[2]

It is authentically reported from Ḥafṣah رَضِيَ اللهُ عَنْهَا that she commanded that a slave girl of hers who worked magic on her be killed, so she was killed. This has also been authentically reported from Jundub. Aḥmad said, "This (killing of sorcerers) has been related from three of the Companions of the Prophet ﷺ."[3]

---

[1] Recorded by At-Tirmithi who said, "It is authentic (*Ṣaḥeeḥ*) as *Mawqoof* (i.e. only a statement of Jundub and not attributed to the Prophet ﷺ). It has been narrated like this, using the statement "striking him", and it is the most authentic wording. Here it does not distinguish between one magician and another. Rather, every magician, regardless of what type of magician he is, his punishment is that he should be killed. The correct view is that the punishment here is the punishment of apostasy. This is because the reality of magic is that it must contain the association of partners with Allâh. Hence, whoever associates partners with Allâh, then he has apostatized (from Islam) and his blood and wealth are lawful.

[2] It is recorded in *Ṣaḥeeḥ ul-Bukhari* that Bajaalah bin 'Abadah said, "Umar bin Al-Khattaab رَضِيَ اللهُ عَنْهُ wrote (commanding us) to kill every male and female magician (i.e. sorcerers and witches). So we killed three sorcerers." This is clear in the command to kill the male and female magicians without making any distinction between them.

[3] It is authentically reported from Ḥafṣah رَضِيَ اللهُ عَنْهَا that she commanded that a slave girl of hers who worked magic on her be killed, so she was

Important issues of the Chapter

1) The explanation of the Verse of *Surah Al-Baqarah* (2:102).
2) The explanation of the Verse of *Surah An-Nisâ'* (4:51).
3) The explanation of *Al-Jibt* and *At-Tâghût* and the difference between them.
4) That *At-Tâghût* may be from the jinn and it may be from men.
5) Knowledge of the seven destroyers that have been particularly forbidden.
6) That the magician is to be declared a disbeliever.
7) That the magician is to be killed and his is not requested to repent.
8) That this (magic) existed among the Muslims in the time of 'Umar, رَضِيَ اللهُ عَنْهُ so how about after him?!

---

killed. This has also been authentically reported from Jundub. Aḥmad said, "This (killing of sorcerers) has been related from three of the Companions of the Prophet ﷺ." This means that it is obligatory for the magician to be killed. The Companions ruled that he should be killed and they commanded his execution without any distinction (i.e. concerning the type of magic or the sex of the magician, etc.). It is obligatory that no distinction be made between one type and another. It is obligatory for the Muslims to beware of magic in all of its types, and that they help each other in informing (about it) in order to be free of any responsibility. It is also in order to reject the evil of every person whom they know to be practicing witchcraft. This is as the Imaams have said, "Magicians do not enter any land except that corruption, wrongdoing, enmity and transgression spread in it."

Chapter 24

A Clarification of Some of the Types of *As-Siḥr* (Sorcery or Magic)*

Aḥmad said that Muhammad bin Ja'far told them that 'Awf told them that Ḥayyaan bin Al-'Alaa' informed them that Qaṭn bin Qabeeṣah told them on the authority of his father that he heard the Prophet ﷺ saying,

«إِنَّ الْعِيَافَــةَ وَالطَّرْق وَالطِّيَرَة مِنَ الْجِبْتِ»

"Verily *Al-'Iyaafah, Aṭ-Ṭarq* and *Aṭ-Ṭiyarah* are from *Al-Jibt*."[1]

---

* The word *Siḥr* (magic) is general in the (Arabic) language. It contains the specific word, which includes seeking the help of the devils, drawing near to them and worshipping them, so that they may serve the magician. Other meanings also enter into this word that the Islamic legislation has also considered as magic. These other things are not like the first true magic, neither in actuality nor in ruling. Magic is in varying degrees and the distinction between these types is important. For this reason the *Imaam* mentioned this chapter so that a distinction is made between these types.

[1] The Prophet ﷺ said,

«إِنَّ الْعِيَافَــةَ وَالطَّرْقَ وَالطِّيَرَةَ مِنَ الْجِبْتِ»

"Verily *Al-'Iyaafah, Aṭ-Ṭarq* and *Aṭ-Ṭiyarah* are from *Al-Jibt*."

Al-'Iyaafah is as 'Awf explained it, "To drive away the birds." This is that one scatters some birds so that he can see where the birds will move (fly). In the person's movement he drives away the birds, and he understands from that driving away whether this matter that he is going to do is something that is praiseworthy or blameworthy. Or the driving away of the birds allows him to see the reality of the future situation. This is a type of *Al-Jibt* and it is magic. Why? We mentioned that the meaning of *Al-Jibt* is something evil and wicked that causes one to deviate from the truth. This explanation is one of the interpretations of the word *Al-'Iyaafah*. *Al-'Iyaafah* is from that which has an effect. It effects from the aspect causing a person to proceed forth or hold back. Thus, because of that it becomes a form of magic. *Aṭ-Ṭiyarah* is more general than *Al-'Iyaafah* because *Al-*

'Awf said, "Al-'Iyaafah is to drive away the birds and *Aṭ-Ṭarq* is the line that is drawn on the ground." Al-Ḥasan said concerning *Al-Jibt*, "It is the screaming of Satan."[1] The chain of this narration is good (*Jayyid*). This *Hadith* with its chain was recorded by Abu Daawood, An-Nasaa'ee and Ibn Ḥibbaan in his *Ṣaḥeeḥ*.

Ibn 'Abbaas رَضِيَ اللهُ عَنْهُ narrated that Allâh's Messenger ﷺ said,

«مَنِ اقْتَبَسَ شُعْبَةً مِنَ النُّجُومِ فَقَدِ اقْتَبَسَ شُعْبَةً مِنَ السِّحْرِ، زَادَ مَا زَادَ»

> "Whoever learns a branch of knowledge of the stars, then he has learned a branch of magic; the more he learns (of the stars), the more he learns (of magic)."

Recorded by Abu Dâwûd with an authentic (*Ṣaḥeeḥ*) chain of narration.[2]

'Iyaafah — according to the statement of 'Awf, which is one of its interpretations — is related only to birds. However, *Aṭ-Ṭiyarah* is general name for whatever contains ill-fortune or good luck (i.e. omens in general) by anything. The explanation of this will come in a separate chapter. In reference to *Aṭ-Ṭarq*, it is derived from placing paths on the ground, which are numerous lines having no specific number. Then the fortuneteller, who is using the lines, begins to quickly wipe away the lines, one by one, or two by two. Then he looks at what remains and he says, "This that is left shows such-and-such." This is a type of fortune telling and fortune telling is a type of magic.

Here he ('Awf) says, "And Aṭ-Ṭarq is the line that is drawn on the ground."

[1] Al-Ḥasan said concerning *Al-Jibt*, "It is the screaming of Satan." This is one of the types of magic, because Satan calls to it with his voice and his wailing.

[2] Ibn 'Abbaas رَضِيَ اللهُ عَنْهُ narrated that Allâh's Messenger ﷺ said,

«مَنِ اقْتَبَسَ شُعْبَةً مِنَ النُّجُومِ فَقَدِ اقْتَبَسَ شُعْبَةً مِنَ السِّحْرِ، زَادَ مَا زَادَ»

"Whoever learns a branch of knowledge of the stars, then he has learned a branch of magic; the more he learns (of the stars), the more he learns (of magic)."

An-Nasaa'ee recorded a *Hadith* of Abu Hurayrah رَضِيَ اللهُ عَنْهُ (that the Prophet ﷺ said),

«مَنْ عَقَدَ عُقْدَةً ثُمَّ نَفَثَ فِيهَا فَقَدْ سَحَرَ، وَمَنْ سَحَرَ فَقَدْ أَشْرَكَ، وَمَنْ تَعَلَّقَ شَيْئًا وُكِلَ إِلَيْهِ»

"Whoever ties a knot and then blows into it, then he has practiced magic, and whoever practices magic has committed *Ash-Shirk*. And whoever hangs something, then he is entrusted to it."[1]

Recorded by Abu Daawood with an authentic (*Ṣaḥeeḥ*) chain of narration. This contains a clarification that learning knowledge of the stars is actually learning magic. This will be discussed in a forthcoming chapter that specifically deals with the types of knowledge of the stars and what is the purpose for which Allâh made the stars.

[1] An-Nasaa'ee recorded a *Hadith* of Abu Hurayrah رَضِيَ اللهُ عَنْهُ (that the Prophet ﷺ said),

«مَنْ عَقَدَ عُقْدَةً ثُمَّ نَفَثَ فِيهَا»

"Whoever ties a knot and then blows into it..."

Blowing here means the blowing that contains seeking refuge and help from the devils, and words that bring (summon) the jinn when they are recited. Such jinn then serve the purpose of this magic knot. However, every blowing into a not is related to magic.

Then he said, "then he has practiced magic." This is because the jinn serves this magic with the blowing into the knot. The benefit of the knot with the magicians is that the magic cannot be broken as long as the knot remains tied. Therefore, the matter that the magician wants is tied to two things: the knot and the blowing. From the matters that are important for you to know from this chapter is that this time the knot may be clearly visible and another time it may extremely small.

Then he said,

«وَمَنْ سَحَرَ فَقَدْ أَشْرَكَ»

"and whoever practices magic has committed Ash-Shirk."

This is general.

«وَمَنْ تَعَلَّقَ شَيْئًا وُكِلَ إِلَيْهِ»

Ibn Mas'ud رَضِيَ اللهُ عَنْهُ narrated that Allâh's Messenger ﷺ said,

«أَلَا هَلْ أُنَبِّئُكُمْ مَا الْعَضْهُ؟ هِيَ النَّمِيمَةُ، الْقَالَةُ بَيْنَ النَّاسِ»

"Shall I not inform you all of what *Al-'Adhh* is? It is slanderous, malicious gossip among the people."[1] (*Muslim*).

They both (Al-Bukhari and Muslim) recorded from Ibn 'Umar رَضِيَ اللهُ عَنْهُ that Allâh's Messenger ﷺ said,

«إِنَّ مِنَ الْبَيَانِ لَسِحْرًا»

"Indeed some eloquent speech is magic."[2]

"And whoever hangs something, then he is entrusted to it."

Thus, whoever is attached to Allâh, then Allâh is sufficient for him. Whenever the slave is attached to other than Allâh, then he is entrusted to whomever he is attached to. And everyone other than Allâh is in need of Him, and Allâh is the Giver of favor and He is the Giver of bounty. Allâh says,

﴿يَٰٓأَيُّهَا ٱلنَّاسُ أَنتُمُ ٱلْفُقَرَآءُ إِلَى ٱللَّهِ ۖ وَٱللَّهُ هُوَ ٱلْغَنِىُّ ٱلْحَمِيدُ﴾

"O mankind! You all are in need of Allâh and Allâh is the Most Wealthy (Free of all needs), Worthy of all praise." (35:15)

[1] Ibn Mas'ud رَضِيَ اللهُ عَنْهُ narrated that Allâh's Messenger ﷺ said,

«أَلَا هَلْ أُنَبِّئُكُمْ مَا الْعَضْهُ؟ هِيَ النَّمِيمَةُ، الْقَالَةُ بَيْنَ النَّاسِ»

"Shall I not inform you all of what *Al-'Adhh* is? It is slanderous, malicious gossip among the people."

Muslim recorded it. The basis of the word *'Adh-h* in the (Arabic) language is used for different things, and among them is magic. The aspect of similarity between slander and magic is that the effect of magic is in separating between those who love each other or bringing together those who are divided. Its effect upon the hearts is hidden. This act of the slanderer divides those who love each other simply due to some speech that he (the gossiper) takes to this person and speech that he takes to that person.

[2] They both (Al-Bukhari and Muslim) recorded from Ibn 'Umar رَضِيَ اللهُ عَنْهُ that Allâh's Messenger ﷺ said,

Important issues of the Chapter

1) That *Al-'Iyaafah, Aṭ-Ṭarq* and *Aṭ-Ṭiyarah* are all kinds of *Al-Jibt* (sorcery/magic).
2) The explanation of *Al-'Iyaafah, Aṭ-Ṭarq* and *Aṭ-Ṭiyarah*.
3) That knowledge of the stars is a kind of magic.
4) That tying knots along with blowing (into them) is from this (magic).
5) That *An-Nameemah* (gossiping, slandering) is from this (magic).
6) That some eloquent speech is also from this (magic).

«إِنَّ مِنَ الْبَيَانِ لَسِحْرًا»

"Indeed some eloquent speech is magic."

He said about speech that from it is that which is magic. The intent of the word speech here is explaining that which is in the soul with eloquent, clear words that take the listeners and the hearts and puts a spell on them. Thus, it may be that it turns the truth into falsehood or falsehood into truth. The correct view from the statements of the people of knowledge is that this contains a rebuke of speech and it is not a commendation for it. This is why the Shaikh - may Allâh have mercy upon him - brings it in this chapter that contains various types of forbidden things.

Chapter 25

What has been Related Concerning the Fortunetellers (Soothsayers) and the like*

Muslim recorded in his *Ṣaḥeeḥ* from some of the wives of the Prophet ﷺ that he said,

«مَنْ أَتَىٰ عَرَّافًا فَسَأَلَهُ عَنْ شَيْءٍ فَصَدَّقَهُ، لَمْ تُقبَلْ لَهُ صَلَاةُ أَرْبَعِينَ يَوْمًا»

---

* The like means from the diviners, the psychic astrologers and so forth. Fortune telling is a practice that opposes the foundation of *At-Tauhid*. The fortuneteller is a *Mushrik* (one who associates partners) with Allâh, because he uses the jinn and draws near to them with acts of worship so that the jinn will serve him and inform him of matters of the unseen. This is not possible unless the person draws near to the jinn with various types of worship. The original fortunetellers in the pre-Islamic days of ignorance were a people who were considered virtuous and righteous. It was claimed that they had knowledge of the unseen matters that would happen to the people or in the land. For this reason the Arabs used to exalt the fortunetellers and fear them.

The jinn reached the point of acquiring knowledge of the unseen matters that they were truthful about by way of eavesdropping. The situations regarding eavesdropping are three:

1) Before Prophet Muhammad's Prophethood and it took place very often.

2) After the Prophet ﷺ received his Prophethood the jinn were in able to eavesdrop. Even if they did, it would be rare and only regarding matters that were not from Allâh's revelation of His Book (the Qur'ān) to His Prophet. This was so that there would be no confusion in the foundation of the revelation and the Prophethood.

3) After the Prophet's death eavesdropping (by the jinn) returned but it was not as often as it was before that, because the heaven was filled with stern guards and shooting stars (as missiles).

Once this becomes clear, then the *Kaahin* is also referred to as *Al-'Arraaf*, for they are two names that are interrelated. One of them means the other. The same is true for the *Rammaal* and the *Munajjim*.

Muslim recorded in his *Ṣaḥeeḥ* from some of the wives of the Prophet ﷺ

"Whoever goes to a fortuneteller and asks him about something and believes him, his prayer will not be accepted from him for forty days."[1]

Abu Hurayrah رَضِيَ اللهُ عَنْهُ narrated that the Prophet ﷺ said,

---

that the Prophet ﷺ said,

«مَنْ أَتَىٰ عَرَّافًا فَسَأَلَهُ عَنْ شَيْءٍ فَصَدَّقَهُ، لَمْ تُقبَلْ لَهُ صَلَاةُ أَرْبَعِينَ يَوْمًا»

"Whoever goes to a fortuneteller and asks him about something and believes him, his prayer will not be accepted from him for forty days."

Regarding this *Hadith*, the explainers have drawn attention to the fact that the wording of it in Muslim is without the statement, "and believes him." The statement, "and believes him" is present in this *Hadith* in the *Musnad* of Imaam Aḥmad. The Shaikh — may Allâh have mercy upon him - mentioned this wording and attributed it to Muslim according to a methodology of the people of knowledge in attributing a *Hadith* to one of the two *Ṣaḥeeḥ* compilers if its basis is found in them. This is in order to unite the route of transmission or similar reasons. We said that the word *Al-'Arraaf* includes the word *Al-Kaahin* and similar words. The intent of his statement, "his prayer will not be accepted from him for forty days" is that it counts and he does not have to make it up, but there is no blessing in it for him. This is because the sin and the wrongdoing that he did when he went to the *'Arraaf* and asked him about something counters against the reward of the prayer (*Aṣ-Ṣalaah*) for forty days. Therefore, this negates that. This proves the tremendous nature of the sin of the one who goes to the *'Arraaf* and asks him about something — even if he does not believe him - seeking to know something.

[1] Abu Hurayrah رَضِيَ اللهُ عَنْهُ narrated that the Prophet ﷺ said,

«مَنْ أَتَىٰ كَاهِنًا فَصَدَّقَهُ بِمَا يَقُولُ فَقَدْ كَفَرَ بِمَا أُنْزِلَ عَلَىٰ مُحَمَّدٍ ﷺ»

"Whoever goes to a soothsayer or a fortuneteller and believes him in what he says, then he has disbelieved in what was revealed to Muhammad ﷺ."

This (what was revealed to Muhammad ﷺ) is the Qur'ān. This is because it has come in the Qur'ān and what the Prophet ﷺ has explained in the *Sunnah* that the fortuneteller, the magician and the diviner will not be successful, and that they only lie and they do not tell the truth. The disbelief here is the minor disbelief (*Kufr*), according to the correct view,

«مَنْ أَتَىٰ كَاهِنًا فَصَدَّقَهُ بِمَا يَقُولُ فَقَدْ كَفَرَ بِمَا أُنْزِلَ عَلَىٰ مُحَمَّدٍ ﷺ»

"Whoever goes to a soothsayer or a fortuneteller and believes him in what he says, then he has disbelieved in what was revealed to Muhammad ﷺ." (Abu Dâwûd).

Another narration was recorded by the four (*Sunan* compilers), and Al-Ḥaakim, who said, "It is authentic (*Ṣaḥeeḥ*) according to their (Al-Bukhari and Muslim) conditions", from Abu Hurayrah رَضِيَ اللهُ عَنْهُ that the Prophet ﷺ said,

«مَنْ أَتَى عَرَّافًا أَوْ كَاهِنًا فَصَدَّقَهُ بِمَا يَقُولُ فَقَدْ كَفَرَ بِمَا أُنْزِلَ عَلَىٰ مُحَمَّدٍ ﷺ»

"Whoever goes to a fortuneteller or soothsayer and believes him in what he says, then he has disbelieved in what was revealed to Muhammad ﷺ."

Abu Ya'laa recorded a similar narration with a good (*Jayyid*) chain that is *Mawqoof* (a statement of Abu Hurayrah رَضِيَ اللهُ عَنْهُ only).

'Imraan bin Huṣayn narrated a *Hadith* that he attributed to the Prophet ﷺ (*Marfoo'*) which states,

«لَيْسَ مِنَّا مَنْ تَطَيَّرَ أَوْ تُطُيِّرَ لَهُ أَوْ تَكَهَّنَ أَوْ تُكُهِّنَ لَهُ أَوْ سَحَرَ أَوْ سُحِرَ لَهُ، وَمَنْ أَتَىٰ كَاهِنًا فَصَدَّقَهُ بِمَا يَقُولُ فَقَدْ كَفَرَ بِمَا أُنزِلَ عَلَىٰ مُحَمَّدٍ ﷺ»

"He is not of us who seeks omens, or has omens interpreted for him, or who practices fortune telling, or has his fortune told to him, or practices magic or has magic performed for him. And whoever goes to a

---

due to the implication of the *Ahadith* and the appearance of an explanatory cause in it (i.e. that he believes him).

fortuneteller and believes him in what he says, then verily he has disbelieved in what was revealed to Muhammad ﷺ."

Recorded by Al-Bazzaar with a good (*Jayyid*) chain of narration.

Aṭ-Ṭabaraanee recorded the same *Hadith* in *Al-Awsaṭ* with a good (*Ḥasan*) chain of narration from Ibn 'Abbaas without his statement, "And whoever goes..." to the end of the *Hadith*.[1]

Al-Baghawee said, "*Al-'Arraaf* is the one who claims to have knowledge of the matters by fore signs that he uses to guide to the stolen object, the place of the lost item and similar things. It is said that he is the *Kaahin*. And the *Kaahin* is the one who informs about matters of the unseen that will occur in the future. It has also been said that he is the one who informs about what is in the inner thoughts (i.e. mind reader)."[2]

---

[1] 'Imraan bin Huṣayn narrated a *Hadith* that he attributed to the Prophet ﷺ (*Marfoo'*) which states, "He is not of us..." This proves that the deed is forbidden. Some of the people of knowledge say, "Verily this statement proves that it is from the major sins."

Then he said, "who seeks omens, or has omens interpreted for him." The discussion concerning this will come in its chapter.

Then he said, "or who practices fortune telling." This means that he claims knowledge of the unseen and he claims that he is a fortuneteller.

Then he said, "or has his fortune told to him." This means that he is pleased to have his fortune told to him, so he goes to the fortuneteller and asks him about something.

Then he said, "or practices magic or has magic performed for him. And whoever goes to a fortuneteller and believes him in what he says, then verily he has disbelieved in what was revealed to Muhammad ﷺ." All of this is because believing the fortuneteller contains a form of assisting him in major *Shirk* with Allâh. This is the ruling concerning the one who goes to the fortuneteller to ask him (about something). In reference to the fortuneteller, we have already mentioned his ruling, and it is that he is a *Mushrik* who is committing major *Shirk* with Allâh.

[2] Al-Baghawee said, "*Al-'Arraaf* is the one who claims to have knowledge of the matters by fore signs that he uses to guide to the stolen object, the place

Abu Al- 'Abbâs Ibn Taymiyyah said, "*Al-'Arraaf* is a name for the *Kaahin*, the *Munajjim* (psychic astrologer), the *Rammaal* (diviner who uses figures or lines in the sand) and people similar to them from those who speak of knowledge of the affairs by these means."[1]

Ibn 'Abbaas said about people who write *Abaa Jaad* (Abjad, numerology) and gaze at the stars (i.e. using the Zodiac), "Whoever does that will not fine any share (of good) for himself with Allâh."[2]

---

of the lost item and similar things. It is said that he is the Kaahin." In other words they are two names for the same thing. "And the *Kâhin* is the one who informs about matters of the unseen that will occur in the future. It has also been said that he is the one who informs about what is in the inner thoughts (i.e. mind reader)."

[1] Abu Al-'Abbaas Ibn Taymiyyah said, "*Al-'Arraaf* is a name for the *Kaahin*, the *Munajjim* (astrologer who makes predictions), the *Rammaal* (diviner who uses figures or lines in the sand)." The definition of the Munajjim will come later. *Ar-Rammaal* is the person who performs *Aṭ-Ṭarq*, or the one who draws lines in the sand, or uses stones on the sand to inform about unseen matters. An explanation of this will come later. Then he said, "and people similar to them from those who speak of knowledge of the affairs by these means." Meaning, like those who read palms and those who read teacups (i.e. interpreting signs in a teacup).

[2] Ibn 'Abbaas said about people who write *Abaa Jaad* (Abjad, numerology) and gaze at the stars (i.e. using the Zodiac), "Whoever does that will not fine any share (of good) for himself with Allâh." This is because the writing of *Abaa Jaad* (Abjad) and gazing at the stars - meaning for divination - is a type of fortune telling.

What remains is that we say that the types of fortune telling are extremely numerous. That which combines them is that the fortuneteller uses an apparent means (i.e. lines, stars, palms, etc.) that he has to convince the questioner that knowledge has come to him by way of clear matters. In this way the fortuneteller deceives whoever comes to him. In reality these means cannot acquire that knowledge (that they claim). Rather the knowledge has come to him by way of the jinn. This means (i.e. cards, tealeaves, lines, etc.) is only for mockery of the people, but the person

Important issues of the Chapter

1) That belief in the fortuneteller and faith in the Qur'ān cannot coexist.
2) The declaration that it (belief in a *Kaahin*) is *Kufr* (disbelief).
3) Mention of whomever has his fortune told to him.
4) Mention of whomever has an omen interpreted for him.
5) Mention of whomever has magic performed for him.
6) Mention of whomever learns *Abaa Jaad* (Abjad, numerology).
7) Mention of the difference between the *Kaahin* and the *'Arraaf.*

---

thinks that it leads to knowledge, and that these people have knowledge and information through these matters, and that the person (soothsayer) is a virtuous person from among the righteous.

Chapter 26

What has been related Concerning Curing Magic Spells (*An-Nushrah*)*

Jaabir رَضِيَ اللهُ عَنْهُ narrated that Allâh's Messenger ﷺ was asked about *An-Nushrah*, so he said,

«هِيَ مِنْ عَمَلِ الشَّيْطَانِ»

"It is an act of Satan."

Recorded by Aḥmad with a *Jayyid* (good) chain, and Abu Dâwûd, who said, "Aḥmad was asked about it (*An-Nushrah*) and he said, 'Ibn Mas'ud رَضِيَ اللهُ عَنْهُ disliked all of this.'"[1]

---

* This means regarding the distinguishing of its types and is all *An-Nushrah* - which is undoing magic - blameworthy? Or is it that there is *An-Nushrah* that is blameworthy and *An-Nushrah* that is allowed? *An-Nushrah* is related to magic and its basis is taken from *An-Nashr*, which is the ill person getting up healthy. It is also a name for the curing of the bewitched person. *An-Nushrah* has two divisions: permissible *Nushrah* and prohibited *Nushrah*. The permissible *Nushrah* is that which is by the Qur'ān, or acceptable supplications or medicines that the doctors may have. This is if the magic effects the body parts. The prohibited *Nushrah* is that the first magic is removed by another magic. This is that the second sorcerer, who is curing the first magic and removing it, must seek help or turn to some of his jinn in removing these jinn that have worked this magic and the effect of their magic. Therefore, this becomes a type of contract, and its initiation can only be by *Ash-Shirk* with Allâh and its removal and curing can only be by *Ash-Shirk* with Allâh. This is why he (Al-Ḥasan) said, "None can break the magic (spell) except a magician (sorcerer)." Meaning, that the magic spell cannot be broken by anything other than the Islamically valid method, except by a magician (sorcerer).

[1] Jaabir رَضِيَ اللهُ عَنْهُ narrated that Allâh's Messenger ﷺ was asked about *An-Nushrah*, so he said, "It is an act of Satan." That which is well known and affirmed among the Arabs is that the name *An-Nushrah* is only used in reference to the magician (sorcerer).

Recorded by Aḥmad with a good (*Jayyid*) chain, and Abu Dâwûd, who

Al-Bukhari recorded from Qataadah that he said to Ibn Al-Musayyab, "If a man is under a spell or he is unable to have sex with his wife, should he be treated to undo the spell or should *An-Nushrah* be used on him?" He said, "There is nothing wrong with it. They only intend to rectify matters (i.e. do good) with it. For that which benefits has not been prohibited."

It has been reported from Al-Ḥasan that he said, "None can break the magic (spell) except a magician (sorcerer)." Ibn Al-Qayyim said, "*An-Nushrah* is removing the magic (spell) from one who is under a spell, and is of two types:

1) Breaking a spell with its like, and it is that which is from the deeds of Satan. The statement of Al-Ḥasan is considered to mean this. So the one who performs the spell of *An-Nushrah* and the one who is being treated with it both draw near to Satan by (doing) what he loves. Thus, he (Satan) removes his working (i.e. magic) from the person under the spell.

2) *An-Nushrah* by *Ar-Ruqyah* (supplications and recitation of Qur'ān), words for seeking refuge with Allâh from evils, medications, and permissible invocations. This method (of *An-Nushrah*) is permissible."[1]

---

said, "Aḥmad was asked about it (*An-Nushrah*) and he said, 'Ibn Mas'ud رَضِيَ اللهُ عَنْهُ disliked all of this.'" This means *An-Nushrah* by way of *At-Tamaa'im* (charms, amulets) that contain (the Verses of) the Qur'ān. In reference to *An-Nushrah* by utilizing blowing and *Ar-Ruqyah* without hanging (or attaching) anything, then it is not possible that Imaam Aḥmad or Ibn Mas'ud would detest that, because the Prophet ﷺ used it and allowed its usage.

[1] Al-Bukhari recorded from Qataadah that he said to Ibn Al-Musayyab, "If a man is under a spell or he is unable to have sex with his wife, should he be treated to undo the spell or should *An-Nushrah* be used on him?" He said, "There is nothing wrong with it. They only intend to rectify matters (i.e. do good) with it. For that which benefits has not been prohibited." Ibn

Important issues of the Chapter

1) The prohibition of *An-Nushrah*.
2) The difference between that which has been prohibited and that which has been allowed (of *An-Nushrah*), that removes the confusion.

Al-Musayyab intends by this, that which benefits of *An-Nushrah* by *At-Ta'awwuthaat* (prayers seeking refuge with Allâh from evil), invocations, the Qur'ān, permissible medication and similar things. However, concerning *An-Nushrah* that is done with magic, then Ibn Al-Musayyab is too esteemed to say that such is permissible. Therefore, the conclusion is that magic in its initial occurrence and to cure other magic is only possible by major *Shirk* with Allâh. Hence, based on this, it is not permissible to break magic spells - not even in the situation of necessity - with magic like it. Rather, the spell should be broken and removed by Islamically legislated *Ruqaa* (plural of *Ruqyah*).

Chapter 27

What has been related Concerning Belief in Omens *(At-Tatayyur)**

The Statement of Allâh the Most High,

﴿أَلَآ إِنَّمَا طَٰٓئِرُهُمْ عِندَ ٱللَّهِ وَلَٰكِنَّ أَكْثَرَهُمْ لَا يَعْلَمُونَ﴾

"Verily, their evil omens are with Allâh, but most of them know not." (7:131)

And His Statement,

﴿قَالُوا۟ طَٰٓئِرُكُم مَّعَكُمْ﴾ الآية

"They (Messengers) said: 'Your evil omens be with you!'" (36:19)[1]

---

* This means what has been related regarding it being *Shirk* with Allâh and a contradiction to the obligatory completion of *At-Tauhid* if it causes one to carry out something or prevents him. This is because it is minor *Shirk*, and it requires expiation if it falls into the heart, and similar rules like this. Its reality is ill-fortune or good luck that is determined by the movement of the birds, either to the right, to the left, or whether they take off or remain sitting. It may also be due to something other than birds, such as some incident that happens to him. He uses these things as a proof of the success of his upcoming matter or its failure.

[1] The Statement of Allâh the Most High,

﴿أَلَآ إِنَّمَا طَٰٓئِرُهُمْ عِندَ ٱللَّهِ وَلَٰكِنَّ أَكْثَرَهُمْ لَا يَعْلَمُونَ﴾

"Verily, their evil omens are with Allâh, but most of them know not." (7:131)

This means that the cause of what comes to them of good things or evil things actually comes from *Al-Qadhaa'* and *Al-Qadar*. (the Preordainment and Decree). Therefore, it is with Allâh.

At-Taṭayyur is a description from the descriptions of the polytheist enemies of the Messengers. Therefore, since this is the case, it is something that is blameworthy. The followers of the Messengers attached that (such occurrences) to what was with Allâh of Preordainment and Decree, or

Abu Hurayrah رَضِيَ اللهُ عَنْهُ narrated that Allâh's Messenger ﷺ said,

«لَا عَدْوَى وَلَا طِيَرَةَ وَلَا هَامَةَ وَلَا صَفَرَ»

"(There is) no *'Adwaa* (contagion of disease without Allâh's permission), nor *Ṭiyarah* (bad omen), nor Haamah (omen from an owl), nor *Ṣafar* (bad luck in the month of *Ṣafar*)."

They (Al-Bukhari and Muslim) both recorded it, and Muslim added (that the Prophet ﷺ said),

«وَلَا نَوْءَ، وَلَا غُولَ»

"...and no *Naw'* (constellation) and no *Ghool* (ghosts, spooks, etc.)."[1]

---

what Allâh gave them of reward for their deeds, or punishment for them. This is as Allâh said,

﴿أَلَآ إِنَّمَا طَٰٓئِرُهُمْ عِندَ ٱللَّهِ﴾

"Verily, their evil omens are with Allâh."

Concerning His Statement,

﴿قَالُوا۟ طَٰٓئِرُكُم مَّعَكُمْ ۚ أَئِن ذُكِّرْتُم﴾

"They (Messengers) said: 'Your evil omens be with you!'" (36:19)

This means that the true cause of evils upon you or the cause of good coming to you is from something in you that is connected to you. It may be an evil deed (that you did) or opposing the Messengers and rejecting them. Thus, *Aṭ-Ṭiyarah* is from the habit of the polytheists (*Mushrikūn*) and the enemies of the Messengers.

[1] Abu Hurayrah رَضِيَ اللهُ عَنْهُ narrated that Allâh's Messenger ﷺ said,

«لَا عَدْوَى وَلَا طِيَرَةَ وَلَا هَامَةَ وَلَا صَفَرَ»

"(There is) no *'Adwaa* (contagion of disease without Allâh's permission), nor *Ṭiyarah* (bad omen), nor *Haamah* (omen from an owl), nor *Ṣafar* (bad luck in the month of *Ṣafar*)."

They (Al-Bukhari and Muslim) both recorded it, and Muslim added (that the Prophet ﷺ said), "...and no *Naw'* (constellation) and no *Ghool* (ghosts, etc.)." This means that there is no *'Adwaa* (contagion) that effects in its nature and in itself. The *'Adwaa* (contagion) only moves (from one place

They (Al-Bukhari and Muslim) both recorded from Anas رَضِيَ اللهُ عَنْهُ that Allâh's Messenger ﷺ said,

«لَا عَدْوَى وَلَا طِيَرَةَ ويُعْجِبُنِي الْفَأْلُ»

"(There is) no *'Adwaa* (contagion), and no *Ṭiyarah* (bad omen), but *Al-Fa'l* pleases me." They said, "What is *Al-Fa'l?*" He said, "The good word."[1]

Abu Dâwûd recorded with an authentic (*Ṣaḥeeḥ) chain that 'Uqbah bin 'Aamir said, "Aṭ-Ṭiyarah* was mentioned before Allâh's Messenger ﷺ and he said,

---

or person to another) by the permission of Allâh. The people of the pre-Islamic times of ignorance believed that the *'Adwaa* moved by itself, so Allâh negated that belief. His Statement, "nor *Ṭiyarah* (bad omen)" means that it also is not effective. For verily *Aṭ-Ṭiyarah* is something imagined that is in the heart and it has no effect in the Preordainment of Allâh and His Decree.

[1] They (Al-Bukhari and Muslim) both recorded from Anas رَضِيَ اللهُ عَنْهُ that Allâh's Messenger ﷺ said,

«لَا عَدْوَى»

"(There is) no *'Adwaa* (contagion)."

This means that there is no *'Adwaa* (contagion) that effects by itself. Rather, it occurs by the permission of Allâh. Then he said, "and no *Ṭiyarah* (bad omen)," which means there is no *Ṭiyarah* that is fundamentally effective. This (the occurrence) only goes back to the Preordainment of Allâh and His Decree (i.e. *Al-Qadhaa'* and *Al-Qadar*). Then he said,

«وَيُعْجِبُنِي الْفَأْلُ»

"but *Al-Fa'l* pleases me."

They said, "What is *Al-Fa'l?*" He said,

«الْكَلِمَةُ الطَّيِّبَةُ»

"The good word."

This is because *Al-Fa'l* is thinking good about Allâh and *At-Tashaa'um* (pessimism, following ill omens) is evil thinking about Allâh. For this reason *Al-Fa'l* becomes commendable and praiseworthy and *At-Tashaa'um* is blameworthy.

«أَحْسَنُهَا الْفَأْلُ وَلَا تَرُدُّ مُسْلِمًا، فَإِذَا رَأَى أَحَدُكُمْ مَا يَكْرَهُ فَلْيَقُلْ: اللَّهُمَّ لَا يَأْتِي بِالْحَسَنَاتِ إِلَّا أَنْتَ وَلَا يَدْفَعُ السَّيِّئَاتِ إِلَّا أَنْتَ، وَلَا حَوْلَ وَلَا قُوَّةَ إِلَّا بِكَ»

'The best of it is *Al-Fa'l*, and it does not prevent the Muslim (from his objective). So if one of you sees what he dislikes, then let him say: O Allâh, none brings the good things but You, and none repels the evils but You, and there is no power, and no might except with You.'''[1]

---

[1] Abu Dâwûd recorded with an authentic (*Ṣaḥeeḥ) chain that 'Uqbah bin 'Aamir said, "Aṭ-Ṭiyarah* was mentioned before Allâh's Messenger ﷺ and he said,

«أَحْسَنُهَا الْفَأْلُ»

'The best of it is *Al-Fa'l*.'''

Aṭ-Ṭiyarah is effecting with words, because we have already mentioned to you that *Aṭ-Ṭiyarah* is general. It includes statements and deeds that take place before the slave. *Al-Fa'l* (the good word) in itself is wanted because it is optimism that expands the chest, delights it and removes the distress that Satan inspires and causes in the slave's heart. Hence, if the slave opens the door of optimism to his heart he removes from his heart the door of Satan's effect upon the soul. Then he said,

«وَلَا تَرُدُّ مُسْلِمًا»

"and it does not prevent the Muslim (from his objective)."

This statement is informative, but it contains prohibition, and this is done to stress the prohibition. Then he said, "So if one of you sees what he dislikes, then let him say:

«اللَّهُمَّ لَا يَأْتِي بِالْحَسَنَاتِ إِلَّا أَنْتَ وَلَا يَدْفَعُ السَّيِّئَاتِ إِلَّا أَنْتَ وَلَا حَوْلَ وَلَا قُوَّةَ إِلَّا بِكَ»

O Allâh, none brings the good things but You, and none repels the evils but You, and there is no power, and no might except with You."

This is a great supplication in repelling what comes to the heart from the types of *At-Tashaa'um* (pessimism, following ill omens) and *Aṭ-Ṭiyarah*.

He (Abu Dâwûd) also recorded a *Marfoo' Hadith* from Ibn Mas'ud رَضِيَ اللهُ عَنْهُ which states (that the Prophet ﷺ said),

«الطِّيَرَةُ شِرْكٌ، الطِّيَرَةُ شِرْكٌ، وَمَا مِنَّا إِلَّا . . وَلٰكِنَّ اللهَ يُذْهِبُهُ بِالتَّوَكُّلِ»

"Aṭ-Ṭiyarah is *Shirk, Aṭ-Ṭiyarah* is *Shirk,* and there is none among us except... but Allâh removes it with trust in Him (*At-Tawakkul*)."

Abu Dâwûd and At-Tirmiṭḥi recorded it. At-Tirmiṭḥi graded it authentic (*Ṣaḥeeḥ*) and he considered the last part of it as the statement of Ibn Mas'ud رَضِيَ اللهُ عَنْهُ.[1]

Aḥmad recorded a *Hadith* of Ibn 'Amr which states (that the Prophet ﷺ said),

«مَنْ رَدَّتْهُ الطِّيَرَةُ عَنْ حَاجَتِهِ فَقَدْ أَشْرَكَ»

"Whoever *Aṭ-Ṭiyarah* prevented from his need, then verily he committed *Shirk.*"

They said, "What is the expiation of that?" He said, "That you say:

---

[1] A *Marfoo' Hadith* is narrated from Ibn Mas'ud رَضِيَ اللهُ عَنْهُ which states (that the Prophet ﷺ said),

«الطِّيَرَةُ شِرْكٌ الطِّيَرَةُ شِرْكٌ»

"Aṭ-Ṭiyarah is *Shirk, Aṭ-Ṭiyarah* is *Shirk.*"

This means that it is minor *Shirk* with Allâh. His (Ibn Mas'ud's) statement,

«وَمَا مِنَّا إِلَّا . . .»

"and there is none among us except..."

this means except that it comes to him. Then he said,

«وَلٰكِنَّ اللهَ يُذْهِبُهُ بِالتَّوَكُّلِ»

"but Allâh removes it with trust in Him (*At-Tawakkul*)."

This is because the goodness of *At-Tawakkul* and the slave coming with the obligation of *At-Tawakkul* will take Satan's plot by *At-Taṭayyur* away from him.

«اللَّهُمَّ لَا خَيْرَ إِلَّا خَيْرُكَ، وَلَا طَيْرَ إِلَّا طَيْرُكَ وَلَا إِلٰهَ غَيْرُكَ»

O Allâh, there is no good except for Your good, and no *Ṭayr* except for your *Ṭayr*, and there is no god (worthy of worship) other than You."

He (Aḥmad) also recorded a *Hadith* of Fadhl bin Al-'Abbaas رَضِيَ اللهُ عَنْهُ which states (that the Prophet ﷺ said),

«إِنَّمَا الطِّيَرَةُ مَا أَمْضَاكَ أَوْ رَدَّكَ»

"*Aṭ-Ṭiyarah* is only that which causes you to carry something out or that turns you back (from your mission)."[1]

Important issues of the Chapter

1) Drawing attention to Allâh's Statement,

﴿أَلَآ إِنَّمَا طَٰٓئِرُهُمْ عِندَ ٱللَّهِ﴾

"Verily their evil omens are with Allâh." (7:131)

Along with His Statement,

[1] Aḥmad recorded a *Hadith* of Ibn 'Amr رَضِيَ اللهُ عَنْهُمَا which states (that the Prophet ﷺ said),

«مَنْ رَدَّتْهُ الطِّيَرَةُ عَنْ حَاجَتِهِ فَقَدْ أَشْرَكَ»

"Whoever *Aṭ-Ṭiyarah* prevented from his need, then verily he committed *Shirk*."

This is the guiding principle that *Aṭ-Ṭiyarah* is a type of *Shirk*. They said, "What is the expiation of that?" He said, "That you say:

«اللَّهُمَّ لَا خَيْرَ إِلَّا خَيْرُكَ، وَلَا طَيْرَ إِلَّا طَيْرُكَ»

O Allâh, there is no good except for Your good, and no *Ṭayr* except for your *Ṭayr*."

This means that nothing will ever occur except your Preordainment that You have ordained, or nothing will ever occur or be destined except what You have decreed for the slave. And the knowledge - knowledge of the unseen matters - is only with Allâh, the Mighty and Majestic.

﴿طَٰٓئِرُكُم مَّعَكُمۡ﴾

"Your evil omens be with you!'" (36:19)

2) Negation of *Al-'Adwaa* (contagion of disease).

3) Negation of *Aṭ-Ṭiyarah* (bad omen).

4) Negation of *Al-Haamah* (omen in the owl).

5) Negation of *Aṣ-Ṣafar* (misfortune associated with the month of *Ṣafar*).

6) That *Al-Fa'l* (a good word of pessimism) is not from this (*At-Taṭayyur*).

7) Explanation of *Al-Fa'l*.

8) That whatever occurs in the hearts of this (ill omen) while it is hated does not harm. Rather, Allâh will remove it with *At-Tawakkul* (reliance upon Him).

9) Mention of the person should say who experiences this.

10) The declaration that *Aṭ-Ṭiyarah* is *Shirk*.

11) Explanation of the blameworthy *Ṭiyarah*.

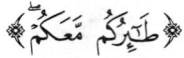

Chapter 28

What has been related Concerning Astrology (*At-Tanjeem)**

Al-Bukhari narrated in his *Ṣaḥeeḥ* that Qataadah said, "Allâh created these stars for three (purposes): adornment (beauty) for the sky, missiles for (i.e. against) the devils, and signs that are used for guidance (during travel). Therefore, whoever interprets them for other than that has erred, lost his share

---

* This means concerning its ruling and its types. There are three types of *At-Tanjeem*:

The first: The *Tanjeem* that is the belief that the stars themselves do things that have an effect (upon this world) and that the things that occur in the land are done as a result of the will of the stars. This is deification of the stars and it is major *Kufr* (disbelief) and major *Shirk* according to the *Ijmaa'* (consensus of the scholars), just like the *Shirk* of the people of Ibrâhîm.

The second type: The *Tanjeem* that is called *'Ilm ut-Ta'theer* (knowledge of effects, i.e. the Zodiac). This is seeking guidance in the movement of the stars, their coming together, their separating, their rising and their setting, for what will occur in the land. The one who does these things is called a *Munajjim* (i.e. psychic astrologer) and it is a type of fortune telling. The devils come to these people and reveal to them what they seek and what will occur. This type of *Tanjeem* is forbidden and it is a major sin. It is also disbelief (*Kufr*) in Allâh, the Mighty and Majestic.

The third type: It is that which is included in the name *At-Tanjeem* (astrology) and it is called *'Ilm ut-Tasyeer* (knowledge of stellar movement). It is that one knows the stars and the movement of the stars in order to know the direction of the *Qiblah*, the times and what is appropriate of the times for planting. Some the scholars have allowed this. The reason for the permission in it is that it makes the stars, their movements, their coming together, their parting, their rising and their setting, a time. It does not make it a cause (of occurrences). If the situation is like this, then there is no problem with speaking about it or learning it, because it makes the stars, their appearance and their setting, times, and that is allowed.

(of reward) and taken upon himself that which he has no knowledge of."[1]

Qataadah disliked learning the positions of the moon, and Ibn 'Uyaynah did not allow it. *Ḥarb* mentioned this from both of them.

Aḥmad and Ishaaq allowed learning the positions (of the moon and stars). [2]

Abu Mûsâ رَضِيَ اللهُ عَنْهُ narrated that Allâh's Messenger ﷺ said,

«ثَلَاثَةٌ لَا يَدْخُلُونَ الْجَنَّةَ: مُدْمِنُ الْخَمْرِ، وَقَاطِعُ الرَّحِمِ، وَمُصَدِّقٌ بِالسِّحْرِ»

---

[1] Al-Bukhari narrated in his *Ṣaḥeeḥ* that Qataadah said, "Allâh created these stars for three (purposes): adornment (beauty) for the sky..." This is as Allâh said,

﴿وَزَيَّنَّا ٱلسَّمَآءَ ٱلدُّنْيَا بِمَصَٰبِيحَ وَحِفْظًا ۚ﴾

"And We adorned the nearest (lowest) heaven with lamps (stars) and to guard (from the devils as missiles)." (4:12)

Then he said, "...missiles for (i.e. against) the devils." The Verses concerning this are numerous. Then he said, "...and signs that are used for guidance (during travel)." This means guidance to directions. Then he said, "Therefore, whoever interprets them for other than that has erred, lost his share (of reward) and taken upon himself that which he has no knowledge of." And this is correct, because the stars are a creation from the creation of Allâh. We do not understand their secret except for what Allâh has informed us of.

[2] Qataadah disliked learning the positions of the moon, and Ibn 'Uyaynah did not allow it. *Ḥarb* mentioned this from both of them.
Aḥmad and Ishaaq allowed learning the positions (of the moon and stars). And this is the correct view, because Allâh has favored His slaves with this. He said,

﴿وَٱلْقَمَرَ نُورًا وَقَدَّرَهُۥ مَنَازِلَ لِتَعْلَمُوا۟ عَدَدَ ٱلسِّنِينَ وَٱلْحِسَابَ ۚ﴾

"And the moon as a light, and He measured out for it stages that you may know the number of the years and the seckoning." (10:5)

The obvious meaning of the Verse is that attaining the blessing in this is by learning it and that is the proof of its permissibility.

"Three (types of people) will not enter Paradise: The one who is addicted to *Al-Khamr* (alcohol, intoxicants), the one who severs the ties of kinship and the one who believes in magic."[1]

Recorded by Aḥmad and Ibn Ḥibbaan in his *Ṣaḥeeḥ*.

Important issues of the Chapter

1) The wisdom behind the creation of the stars.

---

[1] Abu Moosaa narrated that Allâh's Messenger ﷺ said,

«ثَلَاثَةٌ لَا يَدْخُلُونَ الْجَنَّةَ: مُدْمِنُ الْخَمْرِ، وَقَاطِعُ الرَّحِمِ، وَمُصَدِّقٌ بِالسِّحْرِ»

"Three (types of people) will not enter Paradise: The one who is addicted to *Al-Khamr* (alcohol, intoxicants), the one who severs the ties of kinship and the one who believes in magic."

We have already discussed that *At-Tanjeem* is a type of magic, as the Prophet ﷺ said,

«مَنِ اقْتَبَسَ شُعْبَةً مِنَ النُّجُومِ فَقَدِ اقْتَبَسَ شُعْبَةً مِنَ السِّحْرِ . .»

"Whoever learns a branch from (the knowledge of) the stars, then verily he has learned a branch of magic."

From that which is clearly included in *At-Tanjeem* in these times, even though the people are unaware of it, is what often appears in the magazines and is called the Horoscopes (*Al-Burooj*). This is *At-Tanjeem* that is *At-Ta'theer* (see the second type above). It is a type of fortune telling that must be openly rejected. One should not let it enter into his house, he should not read it, nor should he even look at it. This is because if he looks at these Horoscopes then he has entered into the prohibition from the aspect of him going to the fortuneteller without rejecting him. So if he comes and reads (the horoscopes), and he knows his Zodiac sign that he was born in or that fits him, and he reads what is in it, this is asking the fortuneteller, which is prohibited. Then, if he believes in what he read, he has disbelieved in what was revealed to Muhammad ﷺ.

Hence, these Horoscope people are among the fortunetellers. This shows you the strangeness of *At-Tauhid* among its people and the strange understanding of the reality of this book - *Kitaab ut-Tauhid* - even with the people of the *Fiṭrah* (Islamic religion) and the people of this call (i.e. the call to Islam).

2) The refutation against whoever claims other than that.
3) Mention of the difference of opinion regarding learning the positions (of the moon and stars).
4) The threat regarding whoever believes in any magic, even though he knows it is false.

Chapter 29

What has been related Concerning Seeking Rain by the Stars (*Al-Anwaa'*)*

The Statement of Allâh the Most High,

﴿وَتَجْعَلُونَ رِزْقَكُمْ أَنَّكُمْ تُكَذِّبُونَ﴾

"And instead (of thanking Allâh) for the provision He gives you, you deny (Him by disbelief)?" (56:82)[1]

Abu Malik Al-Ash'ari رَضِيَ الله عَنْهُ narrated that Allâh's Messenger ﷺ said,

«أَرْبَعٌ فِي أُمَّتِي مِنْ أَمْرِ الْجَاهِلِيَّةِ لَا يَتْرُكُونَهُنَّ: الْفَخْرُ بِالْأَحْسَابِ، وَالطَّعْنُ فِي الْأَنْسَابِ، وَالِاسْتِسْقَاءُ بِالنُّجُومِ، وَالنِّيَاحَةُ»

"Four things are in my *Ummah* from the affairs of pre-Islamic ignorance that they will not abandon: Pride

---

* Meaning they attribute provision of rainwater to the stars. The star is called *Naw'*. This is contradictory to the completion of *At-Tauhid*. For verily the necessary completion of *At-Tauhid* obligates the slave to attribute all blessings to Allâh Alone, and to not attribute anything of them to other than Allâh, even if that other was a means (of their occurrence). This contains two types of transgression:

First: That they (the stars) are not the causes (of rain).

Second: That they are made means (or causes) that Allâh did not make causes, yet blessings, bounty and rain is attributed to them.

[1] The Statement of Allâh the Most High,

﴿وَتَجْعَلُونَ رِزْقَكُمْ أَنَّكُمْ تُكَذِّبُونَ﴾

"And instead (of thanking Allâh) for the provision He gives you, you deny (Him by disbelief)?" (56:82)

The scholars of *Tafseer* have said, "The meaning of this Verse is that you all make it your livelihood that you reject that the blessings are from Allâh by attributing them to other than Allâh, the Mighty and Majestic.

(boasting) about the family lineages, defaming the family lineages (of others), seeking rain by the stars and wailing (over the dead).''

He further said,

«النَّائِحَةُ إِذَا لَمْ تَتُبْ قَبْلَ مَوْتِهَا تُقَامُ يَوْمَ الْقِيَامَةِ وَعَلَيْهَا سِرْبَالٌ مِنْ قَطِرَانٍ، وَدِرْعٌ مِنْ جَرَبٍ»

"If the woman who wails (in mourning) does not repent before her death she will be raised on the Day of Resurrection and a garment of tar and a shirt of mange.''[1] (Muslim recorded it).

---

[1] Abu Maalik Al-Ash'aree رَضِيَ اللهُ عَنْهُ narrated that Allâh's Messenger ﷺ said,

«أَرْبَعٌ فِي أُمَّتِي مِنْ أَمْرِ الْجَاهِلِيَّةِ لَا يَتْرُكُونَهُنَّ»

"Four things are in my *Ummah* from the affairs of pre-Islamic ignorance that they will not abandon.''

This is an evidence for the condemnation of these things and that they are from the branches of the pre-Islamic ignorance. In *Ṣaḥeeḥ Al-Bukhari* there is a *Hadith* recorded from Ibn 'Abbaas رَضِيَ اللهُ عَنْهُمَا that the Prophet ﷺ said,

«أَبْغَضُ الرِّجَالِ إِلَى اللهِ ثَلَاثَةٌ: . . وَمُبْتَغٍ فِي الْإِسْلَامِ سُنَّةَ الْجَاهِلِيَّةِ»

"The most hated men to Allâh are three... and the one who desires the *Sunnah* (way) of pre-Islamic ignorance in Islam."

He continued saying,

«لَا يَتْرُكُونَهُنَّ: الْفَخْرُ بِالْأَحْسَابِ»

"they will not abandon: Pride (boasting) about the family lineages.''

This means in regard to arrogance and lofty status. Then he said,

«وَالطَّعْنُ فِي الْأَنْسَابِ»

"defaming the family lineages (of others).''

This is by reviling the lineage of so-and-so and so-and-so, and denying the lineage of so-and-so and so-and-so without any Islamically valid evidence and without an Islamically sanctioned necessity. Then he said,

«وَالْاسْتِسْقَاءُ بِالنُّجُومِ»

They (Al-Bukhari and Muslim) both recorded from Zayd bin Khalid رَضِيَ الله عَنْهُ that he said, "Allâh's Messenger ﷺ led us in the morning prayer at Al-Ḥudaybiyah after a night of rain. When he completed the prayer he faced the people and said, 'Do you know what your Lord has said?' They replied, 'Allâh and His Messenger know best.'[1] He said that He (Allâh) said, 'This morning someone became a believer in Me among

---

"seeking rain by the stars."

This is attributing rain to the stars. It also includes that which is even worse, which is seeking rain from the star. Next he said,

«وَالنِّيَاحَةُ»

"and wailing (over the dead)."

He further said,

«وَالنَّائِحَةُ إِذَا لَمْ تَتُبْ قَبْلَ مَوْتِهَا تُقَامُ يَوْمَ الْقِيَامَةِ وَعَلَيْهَا سِرْبَالٌ مِنْ قَطِرَانٍ وَدِرْعٌ مِنْ جَرْبٍ»

"If the woman who wails (in mourning) does not repent before her death she will be raised on the Day of Resurrection and a garment of tar and a shirt of mange."

Muslim recorded it. *An-Niyaaḥah* (wailing over the dead) is from the major sins and it is raising the voice during calamities, tearing the clothes, and similar to that. This is contrary to the patience that is obligatory and it is from the characteristics of pre-Islamic ignorance.

[1] They (Al-Bukhari and Muslim) both recorded from Zayd bin Khaalid رَضِيَ الله عَنْهُ that he said, "Allâh's Messenger ﷺ led us in the morning prayer at Al-Ḥudaybiyah after a night of rain. When he completed the prayer he faced the people and said,

«هَلْ تَدْرُونَ مَاذَا قَالَ رَبُّكُمْ؟»

'Do you know what your Lord has said?'

They replied, 'Allâh and His Messenger know best.'" Mentioning the knowledge of the Prophet ﷺ (i.e. saying Allâh and His Messenger know best) is restricted to his noble life. In other words, this should not be said in this way except during his life. However, after his death, if a person is asked about something that he does not know, he should say, "Allâh knows best."

my slaves and someone became a disbeliever. As for whoever said: we were given rain by the bounty of Allâh and His mercy, then that is a believer in Me and a disbeliever in the star.[1] As for whoever said: We were given rain by such-and-such star, then that is a disbeliever in Me and a believer in the star.''' [2]

They (Al-Bukhari and Muslim) both recorded a *Hadith* with same meaning from Ibn 'Abbaas and it says, "Some of them said, 'Verily such-and-such star was truthful.' So Allâh revealed these Verses,

﴿فَلَآ أُقْسِمُ بِمَوَٰقِعِ ٱلنُّجُومِ ○ وَإِنَّهُۥ لَقَسَمٌ لَّوْ تَعْلَمُونَ عَظِيمٌ ○ إِنَّهُۥ لَقُرْءَانٌ كَرِيمٌ ○ فِى كِتَٰبٍ مَّكْنُونٍ ○ لَّا يَمَسُّهُۥٓ إِلَّا ٱلْمُطَهَّرُونَ ○ تَنزِيلٌ مِّن رَّبِّ ٱلْعَٰلَمِينَ ○ أَفَبِهَٰذَا ٱلْحَدِيثِ أَنتُم مُّدْهِنُونَ ○ وَتَجْعَلُونَ رِزْقَكُمْ أَنَّكُمْ تُكَذِّبُونَ﴾

'So nay! I swear by the setting of the stars. And verily, it

---

[1] He said that He (Allâh) said,

«أَصْبَحَ مِنْ عِبَادِي مُؤْمِنٌ بِي وَكَافِرٌ، فَأَمَّا مَنْ قَالَ: مُطِرْنَا بِفَضْلِ اللهِ وَرَحْمَتِهِ، فَذٰلِكَ مُؤْمِنٌ بِي كَافِرٌ بِالْكَوْكَبِ»

"This morning someone became a believer in Me among my slaves and someone became a disbeliever. As for whoever said: we were given rain by the bounty of Allâh and His mercy, then that is a believer in Me and a disbeliever in the star.'

[2] This is because attributing blessings to Allâh alone proves his faith. Then He (Allâh) said,

«وَأَمَّا مَنْ قَالَ: مُطِرْنَا بِنَفْءِ كَذَا وَكَذَا، فَذٰلِكَ كَافِرٌ بِي مُؤْمِنٌ بِالْكَوكَبِ»

"As for whoever said: We were given rain by such-and-such star, then that is a disbeliever in Me and a believer in the star."

Like I have already mentioned to you, the letter *Baa'* in his statement, "We were given rain *Bi-Naw'i kaṭḥaa* (by such-and-such star)'', if it means that the star was a means of causing the rain, then this is minor *Shirk*. However, if it (the *Baa'*) means that the star is the one who brought the rain in response to the supplication of its worshippers or due to its mercy to mankind, then this is major *Shirk* with Allâh.

is a tremendous oath if you but knew. That (this) is indeed an honored Qur'ān. In a protected Book (*Al-Lawḥ ul-Mahfooḍḥ*), which (that Book) none touches it except the pure. A Revelation (this Qur'ān) from the Lord of the *'Aalameen* (the worlds, all that exists). Is this the discussion (this Qur'ān) that you deny, and you make it your livelihood that you should reject it?''' (56:75-82)[1]

Important issues of the Chapter

1) The explanation of the verse of *Surah Al-Waaqi'ah* (56:82).
2) Mentioning the four things that are from the matters of pre-Islamic ignorance.
3) Mentioning the disbelief in some of them.
4) That from disbelief (*Al-Kufr*) there is that which does not expel one from the religion (of Islam).
5) His (Allâh's) Statement, "This morning someone became

---

[1] They (Al-Bukhari and Muslim) both recorded a Hadith with same meaning from Ibn 'Abbaas and it says, "Some of them said, 'Verily such-and-such star was truthful.' So Allâh revealed these Verses,

﴿فَلَا أُقْسِمُ بِمَوَاقِعِ النُّجُومِ ○ وَإِنَّهُ لَقَسَمٌ لَّوْ تَعْلَمُونَ عَظِيمٌ ○ إِنَّهُ لَقُرْآنٌ
كَرِيمٌ ○ فِي كِتَابٍ مَّكْنُونٍ ○ لَّا يَمَسُّهُ إِلَّا الْمُطَهَّرُونَ ○ تَنزِيلٌ مِّن رَّبِّ
الْعَالَمِينَ ○ أَفَبِهَٰذَا الْحَدِيثِ أَنتُم مُّدْهِنُونَ ○ وَتَجْعَلُونَ رِزْقَكُمْ أَنَّكُمْ تُكَذِّبُونَ﴾

'So nay! I swear by the setting of the stars. And verily, it is a tremendous oath if you but knew. That (this) is indeed an honored Qur'ān. In a protected Book (*Al-Lawḥ ul-Mahfooḍḥ*), which (that Book) none touches it except the pure. A Revelation (this Qur'ān) from the Lord of the *'Aalameen* (the worlds, all that exists). Is this the discussion (this Qur'ān) that you deny, and you make it your livelihood that you should reject it?''' (56:75-82) The meaning of this is clear.

a believer in Me among my slaves and someone became a disbeliever", was due to the descent of blessing (i.e. rain).

6) The understanding of faith (*Al-Eemaan*) in this context.
7) The understanding of disbelief (*Al-Kufr*) in this context.
8) The understanding of his statement, "Verily such-and-such star was truthful."
9) The scholar bringing up the issue for the student by asking about it. This is due to the Prophet's statement, "Do you all know what your Lord has said?"
10) The threat against the woman who wails.

Chapter 30

The Statement of Allâh the Most High*

﴿وَمِنَ ٱلنَّاسِ مَن يَتَّخِذُ مِن دُونِ ٱللَّهِ أَندَادًا يُحِبُّونَهُمْ كَحُبِّ ٱللَّهِ﴾

"And of mankind are some who take others besides Allâh as rivals (to Allâh). They love them as they love Allâh." (2:165)

The Statement of Allâh,

﴿قُلْ إِن كَانَ ءَابَآؤُكُمْ وَأَبْنَآؤُكُمْ وَإِخْوَٰنُكُمْ وَأَزْوَٰجُكُمْ وَعَشِيرَتُكُمْ وَأَمْوَٰلٌ ٱقْتَرَفْتُمُوهَا وَتِجَٰرَةٌ تَخْشَوْنَ كَسَادَهَا وَمَسَٰكِنُ تَرْضَوْنَهَآ أَحَبَّ إِلَيْكُم

---

* The Statement of Allâh,

﴿وَمِنَ ٱلنَّاسِ مَن يَتَّخِذُ مِن دُونِ ٱللَّهِ أَندَادًا يُحِبُّونَهُمْ كَحُبِّ ٱللَّهِ﴾

"And of mankind are some who take others besides Allâh as rivals (to Allâh). They love them as they love Allâh." (2:165)

This is where the *Imaam* begins to mention the acts of worship of the heart and how to single out Allâh with them. This is from the obligations of *At-Tauhid* and the things that complete it. He begins these (acts of worship of the heart) with the chapter of love and that it is obligatory that Allâh be more beloved to the slave that everything, even his own self. What is intended by this love is the love of worship, and it is the love that contains attachment to the beloved by carrying out (his) commands with a desire to do so, and by choice, and turning to the beloved with requests. Also the person avoids (his) prohibitions, with a desire to do so, and by choice. This is the love of worship, which directing it to other than Allâh is major *Shirk* with Him. So this (love of worship) is the support of the religion and pillar of the hearts righteousness. Singling out Allâh with this is obligatory.

His Statement,

﴿وَمِنَ ٱلنَّاسِ مَن يَتَّخِذُ مِن دُونِ ٱللَّهِ أَندَادًا يُحِبُّونَهُمْ كَحُبِّ ٱللَّهِ﴾

"And of mankind are some who take others besides Allâh as rivals (to Allâh)."

This means as equals, peers and counterparts. "They love them as they love Allâh." This means love them the same as they love Him.

﴿مِّنَ ٱللَّهِ وَرَسُولِهِۦ﴾

"Say: If your fathers, your sons, your brothers, your wives, your kindred, the wealth that you have gained, the business in which you fear a decline, and the dwellings in which you delight are more beloved to you than Allâh and His Messenger." (9:24)[1]

Anas رَضِيَ اللهُ عَنْهُ narrated that Allâh's Messenger ﷺ said,

«لَا يُؤْمِنُ أَحَدُكُمْ حَتَّى أَكُونَ أَحَبَّ إِلَيْهِ مِنْ وَلَدِهِ وَوَالِدِهِ وَالنَّاسِ أَجْمَعِينَ»

"None of you believes until I become more beloved to him than his child (children), his father (parents) and all of mankind." (*Al-Bukhari* and *Muslim* both recorded it)[2]

---

[1] His Statement,

﴿قُلْ إِن كَانَ ءَابَآؤُكُمْ وَأَبْنَآؤُكُمْ﴾ إلى قوله: أَحَبَّ إِلَيْكُم مِّنَ ٱللَّهِ وَرَسُولِهِۦ﴾

"Say: If your fathers, your sons, your brothers, your wives, your kindred, the wealth that you have gained, the business in which you fear a decline, and the dwellings in which you delight are more beloved to you than Allâh..."

This is a threat and it proves that loving other than Allâh more than loving Allâh is of the major sins and the things that are forbidden. This is because has made a threat for doing so. The obligation for completing *At-Tauhid* is that the slave loves Allâh and His Messenger above all else that is loved. Loving the Prophet ﷺ is love for the sake of Allâh and not loving him along with (i.e. equally with) Allâh. This is because Allâh is the One Who commanded us to love the Prophet ﷺ.

[2] Anas رَضِيَ اللهُ عَنْهُ narrated that Allâh's Messenger ﷺ said,

«لَا يُؤْمِنُ أَحَدُكُمْ»

"None of you believes..."

This means the complete faith (*Al-Eemaan ul-Kaamil*). Then he said,

«حَتَّى أَكُونَ أَحَبَّ إِلَيْهِ مِنْ وَلَدِهِ وَوَالِدِهِ وَالنَّاسِ أَجْمَعِينَ»

They (Al-Bukhari and Muslim) both recorded from him (Anas رَضِيَ اللهُ عَنْهُ) that Allâh's Messenger ﷺ said,

«ثَلَاثٌ مَنْ كُنَّ فِيهِ وَجَدَ بِهِنَّ حَلَاوَةَ الْإِيمَانِ؛ أَنْ يَكُونَ اللهُ وَرَسُولُهُ أَحَبَّ إِلَيْهِ مِمَّا سِوَاهُمَا، وَأَنْ يُحِبَّ الْمَرْءَ لَا يُحِبُّهُ إِلَّا للهِ، وَأَنْ يَكْرَهَ أَنْ يَعُودَ فِي الْكُفْرِ بَعْدَ إِذْ أَنْقَذَهُ اللهُ مِنْهُ كَمَا يَكْرَهُ أَنْ يُقْذَفَ فِي النَّارِ»

"Whoever has three things in him has found with them the sweetness of faith (*Al-Eemaan*): That Allâh and His Messenger are more beloved to him than anything else besides them, that he loves a person and he only loves him for Allâh, and that he hates to return to disbelief after Allâh saved him from it, just as he hates to be thrown into the Fire."

In another narration it states,

«لَا يَجِدُ أَحَدٌ حَلَاوَةَ الْإِيمَانِ حَتَّى . . »

"None of you finds the sweetness of faith (*Al-Eemaan*) until..." The rest is the same.[1]

"...until I become more beloved to him than his child (children), his father (parents) and all of mankind."

This means loving me (the Prophet ﷺ) is given precedence over loving others besides me, until I become more beloved to him in his soul and more important than his child and his father and all of mankind. This becomes apparent with action. So the one who loves Allâh with the love of worship, hope, and fear, then he is active in seeking His pleasure, and he is active in avoiding what angers the Lord. Likewise, is the case of whoever really loves the Prophet ﷺ.

[1] They (Al-Bukhari and Muslim) both recorded from him (Anas رَضِيَ اللهُ عَنْهُ) that Allâh's Messenger ﷺ said,

«ثَلَاثٌ مَنْ كُنَّ فِيهِ وَجَدَ بِهِنَّ حَلَاوَةَ الْإِيمَانِ. . . »

"Whoever has three things in him has found with them the sweetness of faith (*Al-Eemaan*)..."

Ibn 'Abbaas رَضِيَ اللهُ عَنْهُمَا said, "Whoever loves for Allâh, hates for Allâh, befriends for Allâh, and makes enmity for Allâh, then the *Walaayah* (closeness, friendship, support) of Allâh is only achieved by that[1] . A Slave will never find the taste of faith (*Al-Eemaan*), even if his prayers (*Aṣ-Ṣalaah*) and fasting (*Aṣ-Ṣawm) is abundant, until he becomes like this. The general brotherhood of the people has become based upon worldly matters, and that will not benefit its people at all (in the hereafter). "Recorded by Ibn Jareer.*

Concerning Allâh's Statement,

﴿وَتَقَطَّعَتْ بِهِمُ ٱلْأَسْبَابُ﴾

"And all of their relations will be cut off from them." (2:166)[2]

Ibn 'Abbaas said (it means), "Love."

The intent of the word sweetness here is the sweetness that results from attaining its completion, because faith (*Al-Eemaan*) has a sweetness that is present in the soul.

[1] Ibn 'Abbaas رَضِيَ اللهُ عَنْهُمَا said, "Whoever loves for Allâh, hates for Allâh, befriends for Allâh, and makes enmity for Allâh, then the *Walaayah* (closeness, friendship, support) of Allâh is only achieved by that." This means that the slave can only be a *Waliyy* among the *Awliyaa'* (righteous believers and friends) of Allâh by this action. *Al-Walaayah* is love and support. Then he continued, "A slave will never find the taste of faith (*Al-Eemaan*)..." to the end of the *Hadith*.

Concerning Allâh's Statement,

﴿وَتَقَطَّعَتْ بِهِمُ ٱلْأَسْبَابُ﴾

"And all of their relations will be cut off from them." (2:166)

[2] Ibn 'Abbaas رَضِيَ اللهُ عَنْهُمَا said (it means), "Love." This is because the *Mushrikūn* (polytheists, idolaters) were making *Shirk* by their gods and they loved them and thought that they would interceded for them on the Day of Resurrection due to their love and adoration of them.

Important issues of the Chapter

1) The explanation of the Verse of *Surah Al-Baqarah* (2:165).
2) The explanation of the verse of *Surah Baraa'ah (At-Tawbah)* (9:24).
3) The obligation of loving him more than the self, the family and the wealth.
4) That the negation of faith (*Al-Eemaan*) does not mean going out of Islam.
5) That faith (*Al-Eemaan*) has a sweetness that the person may find or may not find.
6) The four deeds of the heart that the *Walaayah* (love, friendship and support) of Allâh can only be attained by them, and no one finds the taste of faith (*Al-Eemaan*) except with them.
7) The Companion's (Ibn 'Abbaas's) understanding of the current happening, that general brotherhood among the people was based upon worldly matters.
8) The explanation of the Verse,

   ﴿وَتَقَطَّعَتْ بِهِمُ ٱلْأَسْبَابُ﴾

   "Then all of the relations will be cut off from them." (2:166).
9) That among the *Mushrikūn* (polytheists, idolaters) are those who love Allâh very much.
10) The threat against whoever the eight (things) are more beloved to him than his religion. (The eight are mentioned in the *Surah At-Tawbah*, Verse 24.)
11) That whoever takes a rival god and his love for it is equal to the love of Allâh, then this is the major *Shirk*.

Chapter 31

The Statement of Allâh the Most High,*

﴿إِنَّمَا ذَٰلِكُمُ ٱلشَّيْطَٰنُ يُخَوِّفُ أَوْلِيَآءَهُۥ فَلَا تَخَافُوهُمْ وَخَافُونِ إِن كُنتُم مُّؤْمِنِينَ﴾

"It is only Satan who suggests to you the fear of his *Awliyaa'* (supporters and friends), so do not fear them, but fear Me if you are believers." (3:175)

---

* This chapter concerns the explanation of the worship of fear of Allâh, and that it is from the obligatory acts of worship of the heart. Its completion is the completion of *At-Tauhid* and deficiency in it is a deficiency in the completion of *At-Tauhid*. Fearing other than Allâh is divided into that which is *Shirk*, that which is forbidden (*Ḥaraam*) and that which is permissible (*Mubaaḥ*).

Al-Khawf ush-Shirk (Fear that is *Shirk*): This is related to fear of the inner self in this life. It is that a person fears that some great thing will harm him, whether that great one is a Prophet, a *Waliyy* (person beloved by Allâh), or a jinn. This is *Shirk*. The fear that is *Shirk* is related to the hereafter because the person fears that this great one will not help him in the hereafter. Due to his desire that this great one benefits him in the hereafter, intercedes for him, draws him near to him in the hereafter, and keeps the torment away from him in the hereafter, he fears him and he places his fear with him.

Al-Khawf ul-Muḥarram (Forbidden fear): This is that a person fears the creation in carrying out an obligatory act or refraining from a forbidden act from that which Allâh has obligated or forbidden.

Al-Khawf uṭ-Ṭabee'ee (Natural fear): This is the allowed fear and it is something that is natural. For instance, one's fear of an enemy, or a vicious animal, or fire, or anything similar.

﴿إِنَّمَا ذَٰلِكُمُ ٱلشَّيْطَٰنُ يُخَوِّفُ أَوْلِيَآءَهُۥ﴾

"It is only Satan who suggests to you the fear of his *Awliyaa'* (supporters and friends)." (3:175)

The correct meaning of this is that Satan makes the people of *At-Tauhid* afraid of their enemies. Allâh then says,

﴿فَلَا تَخَافُوهُمْ﴾

His Statement,

﴿إِنَّمَا يَعْمُرُ مَسَٰجِدَ ٱللَّهِ مَنْ ءَامَنَ بِٱللَّهِ وَٱلْيَوْمِ ٱلْءَاخِرِ وَأَقَامَ ٱلصَّلَوٰةَ وَءَاتَى ٱلزَّكَوٰةَ وَلَمْ يَخْشَ إِلَّا ٱللَّهَ﴾ الآية

"The Mosques of Allâh shall be maintained only by those who believe in Allâh and the Last Day, perform the *Aṣ-Ṣalâh, give Az-Zakât* and fear none but Allâh." (9:18)[1]

And His Statement,

﴿وَمِنَ ٱلنَّاسِ مَن يَقُولُ ءَامَنَّا بِٱللَّهِ فَإِذَآ أُوذِىَ فِى ٱللَّهِ جَعَلَ فِتْنَةَ ٱلنَّاسِ كَعَذَابِ ٱللَّهِ﴾ الآية

"Of mankind are some who say: 'We believe in Allâh', but if they are made to suffer for the sake of Allâh, they

---

"so do not fear them."

This is a prohibition and the prohibition is that of forbiddance (*At-Taḥreem*). This is a prohibition of applying the act of worship of fear to other than Him (Allâh). This proves that it is a prohibition of one of the particular aspects of *Ash-Shirk*. Then He says,

﴿وَخَافُونِ إِن كُنتُم مُّؤْمِنِينَ﴾

"but fear Me if you are believers."

Here He commands fear, so this proves that fear is one of the acts of worships.

[1] And His Statement,

﴿إِنَّمَا يَعْمُرُ مَسَٰجِدَ ٱللَّهِ مَنْ ءَامَنَ بِٱللَّهِ وَٱلْيَوْمِ ٱلْءَاخِرِ وَأَقَامَ ٱلصَّلَوٰةَ وَءَاتَى ٱلزَّكَوٰةَ وَلَمْ يَخْشَ إِلَّا ٱللَّهَ﴾

"The Mosques of Allâh shall be maintained only by those who believe in Allâh and the Last Day, perform the *Aṣ-Ṣalâh, give Az-Zakât* and fear none but Allâh." (9:18)

This Verse clearly proves that it is obligatory to fear Allâh, and that Allâh commends these people because they make their fear for Allâh Alone besides all else. The word for fear used here (*Khashyah*) is more specific than the previous word (*Khawf*).

consider the *Fitnah* (trial, evil) of mankind as Allâh's punishment." [1] (29:10)

Abu Sa'eed رَضِيَ اللهُ عَنْهُ narrated a *Marfoo'Hadith* (in which the Prophet ﷺ said),

«إِنَّ مِنْ ضَعْفِ الْيَقِينِ أَنْ تُرضِيَ النَّاسَ بِسَخَطِ اللهِ، وَأَن تَحْمَدَهُمْ عَلَى رِزْقِ اللهِ، وَأَنْ تَذُمَّهُمْ عَلَى مَا لَمْ يُؤْتِكَ اللهُ، إِنَّ رِزْقَ اللهِ لَا يَجُرُّهُ حِرْصُ حَرِيصٍ، وَلَا يَرُدُّهُ كَرَاهِيَةُ كَارِهٍ»

"Verily from the weakness of certainty is that you please the people by what angers Allâh, that you praise them for the sustenance of Allâh, and that you blame them for what Allâh has not given you. Verily the sustenance of Allâh can not be brought by the desire of a covetous person, nor can it be prevented by the dislike of one who detests."[2]

---

[1] And His Statement,

﴿وَمِنَ ٱلنَّاسِ مَن يَقُولُ ءَامَنَّا بِٱللَّهِ فَإِذَآ أُوذِىَ فِى ٱللَّهِ جَعَلَ فِتْنَةَ ٱلنَّاسِ كَعَذَابِ ٱللَّهِ﴾

"Of mankind are some who say: 'We believe in Allâh', but if they are made to suffer for the sake of Allâh, they consider the *Fitnah* (trial, harm, evil) of mankind as Allâh's punishment." (29:10)

This is that a person fears it (the people's harm) and therefore he abandons what Allâh has made obligatory upon him, or he does what Allâh has made forbidden due to fear of the people's talk (i.e. what they might say).

[2] Abu Sa'eed narrated a *Marfoo' Hadith* (in which the Prophet ﷺ said),

«إِنَّ مِنْ ضَعْفِ الْيَقِينِ»

"Verily from the weakness of certainty."

This means from the things that cause weakness of faith (*Al-Eemaan*). That which causes weakness in faith are the forbidden things, because faith increases with obedience (to Allâh) and decreases with disobedience (to Allâh, i.e. forbidden things). Then he said,

«أَنْ تُرضِيَ النَّاسَ بِسَخَطِ اللهِ، وَأَن تَحْمَدَهُمْ عَلَى رِزْقِ اللهِ، وَأَنْ تَذُمَّهُمْ عَلَى مَا لَمْ يُؤْتِكَ اللهُ، إِنَّ رِزْقَ اللهِ لَا يَجُرُّهُ حِرْصُ حَرِيصٍ، وَلَا يَرُدُّهُ كَرَاهِيَةُ كَارِهٍ»

'Aishah رضي الله عنها narrated that Allâh's Messenger ﷺ said,

«مَنِ الْتَمَسَ رِضَا اللهِ بِسَخَطِ النَّاسِ رَضِيَ اللهُ عَنْهُ وَأَرْضَى عَنْهُ النَّاسَ، وَمَنِ الْتَمَسَ رِضَا النَّاسِ بِسَخَطِ اللهِ سَخِطَ اللهُ عَلَيْهِ وَأَسْخَطَ عَلَيْهِ النَّاسَ»

"Whoever seeks to acquire the pleasure of Allâh at the expense of the people's anger, Allâh will be pleased with him and make the people pleased with him. Whoever seeks to acquire the pleasure of the people at the expense of Allâh's anger, Allâh will be angry with him and make the people angry with him."

Ibn Ḥibbaan recorded it in his *Ṣaḥeeḥ*.[1]

Important issues of the Chapter

1) The explanation of the Verse of *Surah Âl-'Imrân* (3:175).

2) The explanation of the Verse of *Surah Baraa'ah (At-Tawbah)* (9:18).

"is that you please the people by what angers Allâh, that you praise them for the sustenance of Allâh, and that you blame them for what Allâh has not given you. Verily the sustenance of Allâh can not be brought by the desire of a covetous person, nor can it be prevented by the dislike of one who detests."

This proves that pleasing the people at the expense of angering Allâh is an act of disobedience, sin and it is forbidden.

[1] 'Aishah رضي الله عنها narrated that Allâh's Messenger ﷺ said,

«مَنِ الْتَمَسَ رِضَا اللهِ بِسَخَطِ النَّاسِ. . . الحديث»

"Whoever seeks to acquire the pleasure of Allâh at the expense of the people's anger..."

This is the reward of whoever singles out Allâh with the worship of fear. It is also the recompense of whoever does not complete *At-Tauhid* in the worship of fear, because he commits a sin due to fear of the people and he makes his fear of the people a reason to do the forbidden or abandon an obligation.

3) The explanation of the Verse of *Surah Al-'Ankaboot* (29:10).
4) That certainty weakens and strengthens.
5) The sign of its weakness and from that are these three things (mentioned in the *Hadith*).
6) That making fear solely for Allâh is from the obligations.
7) Mention of the reward of whoever does this.
8) Mention of the punishment of whoever abandons it.

Chapter 32

The Statement of Allâh the Most High*

﴿وَعَلَى ٱللَّهِ فَتَوَكَّلُوٓا۟ إِن كُنتُم مُّؤْمِنِينَ﴾ الآية

"Put your trust in Allâh if you are believers indeed."(5:23)

---

* The purpose of this chapter is to explain that trust in Allâh is a condition for the correctness of (one's) Islam. The reality of trust in Allâh according to the Islamic Law combines tremendous acts of worship of the heart. It means to turn the affairs over to Allâh while acting according to the means. Thus, the one who trusts in Allâh according to the Islamic Law is the person who acts by the means and entrusts the affairs to Allâh in gaining benefit by the means, in what occurs by that means, and in Allâh's support and aid. For verily there is no power or strength except by Him (Allâh). Therefore, trusting in Allâh is purely an act of worship of the heart.

Trusting in other than Allâh has two situations:

The first: That it is a form of major *Shirk*. This is that a person puts his trust in someone of the creation in what none is able to do but Allâh - like forgiveness of sin, are granting a child to the person or granting the person some job. This occurs often with the worshippers of the graves and the *Awliyaa'* (the beloved friends of Allâh). This is a form of major *Shirk* with Allâh, and it is a contradiction to the foundation of *At-Tauhid*.

The second: That a person trusts in the creation in what Allâh has given him (the creation) the power to do. This is hidden *Shirk* and minor *Shirk*. This is like a person saying, "I put my trust in Allâh and you." Likewise, it is also not permissible to say, "I put my trust in Allâh and then in you." The reason is that the creation has no share in *At-Tawakkul* (entrusting). The true entrusting that we have mentioned is not befitting for any except Allâh. Because it (*At-Tawakkul*) is entrusting the matters to someone who has control over the matters, and the creation does not have control over the matters. Allâh has only made the creation a means, for example by making someone of the creation an intercessor. However, this does not mean that trust should be put in the person. This Verse contains the command to trust in Allâh, and since Allâh has commanded it, we know that it is from the acts of worship. Also, because the preposition and the noun governed by the preposition in His Statement, "And in Allâh (*Wa 'alal-laah*)" precedes what is related to it, which is the verb "put your trust

And His Statement,

﴿إِنَّمَا ٱلْمُؤْمِنُونَ ٱلَّذِينَ إِذَا ذُكِرَ ٱللَّهُ وَجِلَتْ قُلُوبُهُمْ﴾ الأية

"The believers are only those who, when Allâh is mentioned, feel a fear in their hearts." (8:2)[1]

And His Statement,

﴿يَٰٓأَيُّهَا ٱلنَّبِيُّ حَسْبُكَ ٱللَّهُ﴾ الآية

"O Prophet (Muhammad ﷺ)! Allâh is Sufficient for you." (8:64)[2]

(*Fatawakkaloo*)", then this proves the obligation of singling out Allâh with *At-Tawakkul* (trust and reliance). It also proves that *At-Tawakkul* is worship that must be restricted and limited to Allâh. This is the point of evidence from the Verse. Another evidence in this Verse is His Statement, "If you are believers." Allâh has made faith (*Al-Eemaan*) incorrect except with *At-Tawakkul* (trust in Him).

[1] And His Statement,

﴿إِنَّمَا ٱلْمُؤْمِنُونَ ٱلَّذِينَ إِذَا ذُكِرَ ٱللَّهُ وَجِلَتْ قُلُوبُهُمْ﴾ الآية

"The believers are only those who, when Allâh is mentioned their hearts tremble... and they put their trust in their Lord." (8:2)

What is clear from the implication of the Verse - as the preposition and the noun governed by the preposition have come first - is that they single out Allâh for *At-Tawakkul*. Thus, He describes the believers with these characteristics, and this proves that these are the greatest positions of the people of faith (*Al-Eemaan*).

[2] And His Statement,

﴿يَٰٓأَيُّهَا ٱلنَّبِيُّ حَسْبُكَ ٱللَّهُ﴾

"O Prophet! Allâh is sufficient for you." (8:64)

This means is enough for you and He is enough for whoever follows you of the believers. This is because word *Ḥasb* (sufficient) means *Kaafee* (adequate, enough). Therefore, Allâh is sufficient for whoever trusts in Him. For this reason he (the Shaikh) followed this Verse with another Verse in which He said,

﴿وَمَن يَتَوَكَّلْ عَلَى ٱللَّهِ فَهُوَ حَسْبُهُۥٓ﴾

And His Statement,

﴿وَمَن يَتَوَكَّلْ عَلَى ٱللَّهِ فَهُوَ حَسْبُهُۥٓ﴾

"And whoever puts his trust in Allâh, then He (Allâh) will suffice him." (65:3)

Ibn 'Abbaas said (concerning the Verse),

﴿حَسْبُنَا ٱللَّهُ وَنِعْمَ ٱلْوَكِيلُ﴾

"Allâh is sufficient for us, and He is the Best Disposer of affairs (for us)." (3:173)

Ibrâhîm عليه السلام said this when he was cast into the fire and Muhammad ﷺ said it when they said to him,

﴿إِنَّ ٱلنَّاسَ قَدْ جَمَعُوا۟ لَكُمْ فَٱخْشَوْهُمْ فَزَادَهُمْ إِيمَٰنًا﴾ الآية

'Verily the people (polytheist) have gathered against you (a great army), therefore, fear them. But it only increased them in Faith.' (3:173)" (Recorded by Al-Bukhari and An-Nasâ'i).[1]

"And whoever puts his trust in Allâh, then He (Allâh) will suffice him." (65:3)

Trusting in Allâh, the Mighty and Majestic, as we have mentioned, goes back to understanding *Tauhid ur-Ruboobiyyah* (the *Tauhid* of Lordship) and the importance of belief in *Tauhid ur-Ruboobiyyah*. For verily some of the *Mushrikūn* (polytheists, idolaters) may have great reliance upon Allâh.

Therefore we say that creating *At-Tawakkul* in the heart goes back to contemplating the effects of *Ar-Ruboobiyyah* (Allâh's Lordship). For the more the slave contemplates upon the dominion of Allâh, the heavens, the earth and other things, it teaches him that Allâh is the Owner of the dominion, that He is in control and that His helping His slave is something extremely easy in reference to what Allâh causes to happen in His dominion. Therefore, with this reflection the believer magnifies Allâh and he magnifies trust in Him (*At-Tawakkul*).

[1] Ibn 'Abbaas رضي الله عنهما said (concerning the Verse),

﴿حَسْبُنَا ٱللَّهُ وَنِعْمَ ٱلْوَكِيلُ﴾

Important issues of the Chapter

1) That *At-Tawakkul* (trust in Allâh) is from the obligatory duties.
2) That it is from the conditions of faith (*Al-Eemaan*).
3) The explanation of the Verse of *Surah Al-Anfaal* (8:2).
4) The explanation of the Verse at the end of *Surah Al-Anfâl*. (8:64).
5) The explanation of the Verse of *Surah Aṭ-Ṭalaaq* (65:3).
6) The great status of this statement (Allâh is sufficient for us, and He is the Best Disposer of affairs) and that it was the saying of Ibrâhîm and Muhammad ﷺ in times of distress.

"Allâh is sufficient for us, and He is the Best Disposer of affairs (for us)." (3:173)

Ibrâhîm عَلَيْهِ السَّلَام said this when he was cast into the fire and Muhammad ﷺ said it when they said to him,

﴿إِنَّ ٱلنَّاسَ قَدْ جَمَعُوا۟ لَكُمْ فَٱخْشَوْهُمْ فَزَادَهُمْ إِيمَـٰنًا﴾

'Verily the people (polytheist) have gathered against you (a great army), therefore, fear them. But it only increased them in Faith.' (3:173)"

This clarifies the greatness of this statement and it is the believer's saying, "Allâh is sufficient for us, and He is the Best Disposer of affairs." For verily when the greatest hope of the slave is in Allâh and his trust is in Allâh, even if the heavens and the earth and whoever is in them plots against him, Allâh will give him ease in his affair and He will make a way out for him.

Chapter 33

The Statement of Allâh the Most High*

﴿أَفَأَمِنُوا۟ مَكْرَ ٱللَّهِ ۚ فَلَا يَأْمَنُ مَكْرَ ٱللَّهِ إِلَّا ٱلْقَوْمُ ٱلْخَٰسِرُونَ﴾

"Did they feel secure against the Plan of Allâh? None feels secure from the Plan of Allâh except the people who are the losers." (7:99)

Allâh's Statement,

﴿وَمَن يَقْنَطُ مِن رَّحْمَةِ رَبِّهِۦٓ إِلَّا ٱلضَّآلُّونَ﴾

"Who despairs of the Mercy of his Lord except those who are astray."[1] (15:56)

---

* This chapter is connected to both of these Verses due to their related issues. The first Verse contains a discussion that from the characteristics of the *Mushrikūn* is that they believe in the punishment of Allâh but they do not fear (it). Feeling secure from the Plan of Allâh results from lack of fear and abandoning the worship of fear. The worship of fear of Allâh is an act of worship of the heart. The reality of the Plan of Allâh and the meaning of this attribute is that He makes matters easy for the slave until he thinks that he is totally safe, but that is only a gradual alluring concerning him. This is as the Prophet ﷺ said,

«إِذَا رَأَيْتُمُ اللهَ يُعْطِي الْعَبْدَ وَهُوَ مُقِيمٌ عَلَى مَعَاصِيهِ فَاعْلَمُوا أَنَّ ذَلِكَ اسْتِدْرَاجٌ»

"If you see that Allâh gives the slave while he is continuing in his acts of disobedience, then know that that is gradual alluring."

Allâh has plans for whoever plans against His *Awliyaa'* (beloved friends and believers), His Prophets and His religion (Islam). Here it is an attribute of perfection, because at that time (when His Plan occurs) it is a manifestation of might, strength and dominance.

[1] Allâh's Statement,

﴿وَمَن يَقْنَطُ مِن رَّحْمَةِ رَبِّهِۦٓ إِلَّا ٱلضَّآلُّونَ﴾

"Who despairs of the Mercy of his Lord except those who are astray." (15:56)

Ibn 'Abbaas رَضِيَ اللهُ عَنْهُمَا narrated that Allâh's Messenger ﷺ was asked about the major sins and he said,

«الشِّرْكُ بِاللهِ، وَالْيَأْسُ مِنْ رَوْحِ اللهِ، وَالأَمْنُ مِنْ مَكْرِ اللهِ»

"Associating partners (*Ash-Shirk*) with Allâh, despairing of hope in Allâh and feeling secure against the Plan of Allâh."[1]

This contains a discussion that from the characteristics of those who are astray is that they despair of the Mercy of Allâh. The implied meaning of this is that the characteristic of the pious and those who are guided is that they do not despair of Allâh's Mercy. Combining fear and hope is an Islamically sanctioned obligation so that the worship will be correct. Which of them is dominant in the heart? The aspect of fear is dominant over hope in regards to the healthy person who is a disobedient sinner, and the aspect of hope is dominant over fear in regards to the sick person who fears destruction or death. Hope and fear are equal in the situation of the balanced people who hasten to do acts of goodness.

﴿إِنَّهُمْ كَانُوا يُسَارِعُونَ فِي الْخَيْرَاتِ وَيَدْعُونَنَا رَغَبًا وَرَهَبًا وَكَانُوا لَنَا خَاشِعِينَ﴾

"Verily, they used to hasten to do good deeds, and they used to call on Us with hope and fear, and used to themselves before Us." (21:90)

[1] Ibn 'Abbaas رَضِيَ اللهُ عَنْهُمَا narrated that Allâh's Messenger ﷺ was asked about the major sins and he said,

«أَكْبَرُ الْكَبَائِرِ: الإِشْرَاكُ بِاللهِ وَالْيَأْسُ مِنْ رَوْحِ اللهِ وَ الأَمْنُ مِنْ مَكْرِ اللهِ»

"Associating partners (*Ash-Shirk*) with Allâh despairing of hope in Allâh and feeling secure against the Plan of Allâh."

Despair refers to abandoning the worship of hope (in Allâh). Feeling secure against the Plan of Allâh refers to abandoning the worship of fear (of Allâh). Combining them is an obligation from the obligatory duties, and their leaving or deficiency in them is a deficiency in the completion of *At-Tauhid* of whoever has that in his heart.

Ibn Mas'ud رَضِيَ اللهُ عَنْهُمَا said,

"أَكْبَرُ الْكَبَائِرِ: الإِشْرَاكُ بِاللهِ، وَالأَمْنُ مِنْ مَكْرِ اللهِ، وَالْقُنُوطُ مِنْ رَحْمَةِ اللهِ، وَالْيَأْسُ مِنْ رَوْحِ اللهِ"

Ibn Mas'ud رَضِيَ اللهُ عَنْهُمَا said, "The greatest of the major sins are associating partners with Allâh (*Ash-Shirk*), feeling secure against the Plan of Allâh, despairing of Allâh's Mercy, and giving up hope in Allâh." ('Abdur-Razzaaq recorded it).[1]

Important issues of the Chapter

1) The explanation of the Verse of *Surah Al-A'raaf* (7:99).
2) The explanation of the Verse of *Surah Al-Ḥijr* (15:56).
3) The severity of the threat regarding whoever feels secure against the Plan of Allâh.
4) The severity of the threat regarding despair.

'The greatest of the major sins are associating partners with Allâh (*Ash-Shirk*), feeling secure against the Plan of Allâh, despairing of Allâh's Mercy, and giving up hope in Allâh.''

Despairing of the Mercy of Allâh is general and the word *Ar-Raḥmah* (Mercy) includes bringing blessings and averting vengeance. The *Rawh* of Allâh is usually used with regards to ending calamities (or afflictions).

Chapter 34

A Part of Faith in Allâh is Being Patient with the Decrees of Allâh and the Statement of Allâh the Most High*

﴿وَمَن يُؤْمِنۢ بِٱللَّهِ يَهْدِ قَلْبَهُۥ﴾

"And Whoever believes in Allâh, He guides his heart." (64:11)

'Alqamah said, "This is the man who is afflicted by a calamity and he knows that it is from Allâh, so he is pleased and submits."[1]

---

* This means that from the characteristics and branches of faith (*Al-Eemaan*) is patience with the Decrees of Allâh. This is from the great stations and sublime acts of worship. The obligatory acts require patience, the prohibitions require patience and the decrees of existence require patience. Therefore, patience is of three types. The reality of patience is keeping the tongue from complaining, keeping the heart from being displeased and keeping the limbs from showing anger by tearing clothes or similar to that.

[1] The Statement of Allâh the Most High,

﴿وَمَن يُؤْمِنۢ بِٱللَّهِ﴾

"And whoever believes in Allâh."

This means whoever magnifies Allâh, carries out His commands and avoids His prohibitions. Then He says,

﴿يَهْدِ قَلْبَهُۥ﴾

"He guides his heart."

Meaning to the acts of worship, patience and avoiding becoming angry. 'Alqamah said, "This is the man who is afflicted by a calamity and he knows that it is from Allâh, so he is pleased", meaning with the preordainment of Allâh. Then he said, "and submits", meaning to his knowledge that it is from Allâh. This explanation of 'Alqamah is clearly correct and right. Afflictions are from the Decree and the Decree refers back to the Wisdom of Allâh. Allâh's Wisdom is placing matters in their

It is recorded in *Ṣaḥeeḥ Muslim* from Abu Hurayrah رَضِيَ اللهُ عَنْهُ that Allâh's Messenger ﷺ said,

«اثْنَتَانِ فِي النَّاسِ هُمَا بِهِمْ كُفْرٌ: الطَّعْنُ فِي النَّسَبِ وَالنِّيَاحَةُ عَلَى الْمَيِّتِ»

"There are two things among the people that are disbelief with them: Defaming the family lineage and wailing over the deceased."[1]

They (Al-Bukhari and Muslim) both recorded a *Marfoo' Hadith* from Ibn Mas'ud رَضِيَ اللهُ عَنْهُ (that the Prophet ﷺ said),

---

proper places that agree with the praiseworthy objectives from them. By this we know that the when the calamity afflicts the slave there is good for him in it. Either he will be patient and be rewarded or he will become angry and be condemned for that.

[1] It is recorded in *Ṣaḥeeḥ Muslim* from Abu Hurayrah رَضِيَ اللهُ عَنْهُ that Allâh's Messenger ﷺ said,

«اثْنَتَانِ فِي النَّاسِ هُمَا بِهِمْ كُفْرٌ»

"There are two things among the people that are disbelief with them."

Meaning two characteristics are from the branches of *Kufr* (disbelief) that are established among the people and they will remain among the people. Then he continued,

«الطَّعْنُ فِي النَّسَبِ وَالنِّيَاحَةُ عَلَى الْمَيِّتِ»

"Defaming the family lineage and wailing over the deceased."

This is complaining and lamenting, and wailing is opposed to patience. The obligatory patience includes restraining the limbs from striking the cheeks and tearing the garments and similar acts. It also includes restraining the tongue from complaining and lamenting. The fact that it is from the branches of disbelief does not prove that whoever performs it is a *Kaafir* (disbeliever) with the absolute disbelief that expels one from the religion. Rather, it proves that whoever performs it has with him a characteristic from the characteristics of the disbelievers and a branch from the branches of disbelief.

«لَيْسَ مِنَّا مَنْ ضَرَبَ الْخُدُودَ، وَشَقَّ الْجُيُوبَ، وَدَعَا بِدَعْوَى الْجَاهِلِيَّةِ»

"He is not of us who strikes the cheeks, tears the garments and calls with the call of pre-Islamic ignorance."[1]

Anas رَضِيَ اللهُ عَنْهُ narrated that Allâh's Messenger ﷺ said,

«إِذَا أَرَادَ اللهُ بِعَبْدِهِ الْخَيْرَ عَجَّلَ لَهُ الْعُقُوبَةَ فِي الدُّنْيَا، وَإِذَا أَرَادَ بِعَبْدِهِ الشَّرَّ أَمْسَكَ عَنْهُ بِذَنْبِهِ حَتَّى يُوَافِيَ بِهِ يَوْمَ الْقِيَامَةِ»

"When Allâh wants good for His slave He hastens his punishment for him in this life, and when He wants evil for His slave He holds back from him (i.e. punishing him) for his sin until He comes with it on the Day of Resurrection."[2]

---

[1] They (Al-Bukhari and Muslim) both recorded a *Marfoo' Hadith* from Ibn Mas'ud رَضِيَ اللهُ عَنْهُ (that the Prophet ﷺ said),

«لَيْسَ مِنَّا مَنْ ضَرَبَ الْخُدُودَ، وَشَقَّ الْجُيُوبَ، وَدَعَا بِدَعْوَى الْجَاهِلِيَّةِ»

"He is not of us who strikes the cheeks, tears the garments and calls with the call of pre-Islamic ignorance."

The statement, "He is not of us", proves that the deed is from the major sins. For this reason we say abandoning patience and showing anger is a major sin from the major sins, and acts of disobedience (sins) decrease faith. This is because faith increases with obedience and it decreases with disobedience (sins). The decrease of faith takes away from the completion of *At-Tauhid*. Verily abandoning patience is contrary to the obligatory completion of *At-Tauhid*.

[2] Anas رَضِيَ اللهُ عَنْهُ narrated that Allâh's Messenger ﷺ said,

«إِذَا أَرَادَ اللهُ بِعَبْدِهِ الْخَيْرَ عَجَّلَ لَهُ الْعُقُوبَةَ فِي الدُّنْيَا، وَإِذَا أَرَادَ بِعَبْدِهِ الشَّرَّ أَمْسَكَ عَنْهُ بِذَنْبِهِ حَتَّى يُوَافِيَ بِهِ يَوْمَ الْقِيَامَةِ»

"When Allâh wants good for His slave He hastens his punishment for him in this life, and when He wants evil for His slave He holds back from him (i.e. punishing him) for his sin until He comes with it on the Day of Resurrection."

The Prophet ﷺ said,

«إِنَّ عِظَمَ الْجَزَاءِ مَعَ عِظَمِ الْبَلَاءِ، وَإِنَّ اللهَ تَعَالَىٰ إِذَا أَحَبَّ قَوْمًا ابْتَلَاهُمْ فَمَنْ رَضِيَ فَلَهُ الرِّضَا، وَمَنْ سَخِطَ فَلَهُ السَّخَطُ»

"Verily the greater reward is with the greater trial. Verily when Allâh the Most High loves a people He tests them. Therefore, whoever is pleased, then he will have the pleasure (of Allâh), and whoever is angry, then for him is the anger (of Allâh)."[1] (It was graded *Ḥasan* (good) by At-Tirmiṭḥi).

Important issues of the Chapter

1) The explanation of the Verse of *Surah At-Taghaabun* (64:11).
2) That this (i.e. accepting Allâh's Decree) is a part of faith in Allâh.
3) Abusing family lineage.
4) The severity of the threat concerning whoever strikes the

This contains an explanation of the Wisdom of Allâh, that if the afflicted person realizes it (this Wisdom), his patience will become greater and he will taste the sweetness of this great worship of the heart. This worship is avoiding becoming angry and being pleased with the action of Allâh and His Preordainment. For this reason some of the *Salaf* blamed themselves if they saw themselves not being afflicted with any trial or not becoming sick and similar things.

[1] And the Prophet ﷺ said,

«إِنَّ عِظَمَ الْجَزَاءِ مَعَ عِظَمِ الْبَلَاءِ، وَإِنَّ اللهَ تَعَالَىٰ إِذَا أَحَبَّ قَوْمًا ابْتَلَاهُمْ فَمَنْ رَضِيَ فَلَهُ الرِّضَا، وَمَنْ سَخِطَ فَلَهُ السَّخَطُ»

"Verily the greater reward is with the greater trial. Verily when Allâh the Most High loves a people He tests them. Therefore, whoever is pleased, then he will have the pleasure (of Allâh), and whoever is angry, then for him is the anger (of Allâh)."

cheeks, tears the garment (in lamenting) and calls with the call of pre-Islamic ignorance.

5) The sign of Allâh intending good for His slave.

6) The sign of Allâh intending bad for His slave.

7) The sign of Allâh's love for the slave.

8) The forbiddance of being displeased (with Allâh's decree).

9) The reward of being pleased (with Allâh's decree) during trials (i.e. afflictions).

Chapter 35

What has been Related Concerning Showing Off (*Ar-Riyaa'*) *

The Statement of Allâh the Most High,

﴿قُلْ إِنَّمَآ أَنَا۠ بَشَرٌ مِّثْلُكُمْ يُوحَىٰٓ إِلَيَّ أَنَّمَآ إِلَٰهُكُمْ إِلَٰهٌ وَٰحِدٌ﴾ الآية

"Say (O Muhammad ﷺ): 'I am only a man like you. It has been revealed to me that your god is One God (Allâh).'"(18:110)[1]

---

* This is referring to the threat and that it is *Shirk* with Allâh. The reality of it comes from the optical vision, and that is that a person does an act of worship so that the people may see him in that and praise him for it. Showing off has two levels.

The first level: The showing off of the hypocrites. This is that the person exhibits Islam and hides disbelief (*Al-Kufr*) because the creation (other people; Muslims) sees him. This is contrary to *At-Tauhid* from its foundation and it is major disbelief in Allâh.

The second type of showing off: That the Muslim shows off his deed or some of his deed. This is hidden *Shirk*, and this *Shirk* is contrary to the completion of *At-Tauhid*.

[1] And the Statement of Allâh the Most High,

﴿قُلْ إِنَّمَآ أَنَا۠ بَشَرٌ مِّثْلُكُمْ يُوحَىٰٓ إِلَيَّ أَنَّمَآ إِلَٰهُكُمْ إِلَٰهٌ وَٰحِدٌ فَمَن كَانَ يَرْجُوا۟ لِقَآءَ رَبِّهِۦ فَلْيَعْمَلْ عَمَلًا صَٰلِحًا وَلَا يُشْرِكْ بِعِبَادَةِ رَبِّهِۦٓ أَحَدًۢا﴾

"Say (O Muhammad ﷺ): 'I am only a man like you. It has been revealed to me that your god is One God (Allâh). So whoever hopes for the Meeting with his Lord, let him work righteousness deeds and not associate anyone as a partner in the worship of his Lord.'" (18:110)

This is a prohibition against associating partners (with Allâh). The prohibition here is generally inclusive of all the types of *Shirk*, among which is the *Shirk* of showing off (*Ar-Riyaa'*). For this reason the *Salaf* used this Verse as an evidence for the issues of showing off, just as the *Imaam* has presented it here - may Allâh have mercy on him. His Statement,

Abu Hurayrah رَضِيَ اللهُ عَنْهُ narrated a *Marfoo' Hadith* from the Prophet ﷺ that Allâh the Most High said,

«أَنَا أَغْنَى الشُّرَكَاءِ عَنِ الشِّرْكِ، مَنْ عَمِلَ عَمَلًا أَشْرَكَ مَعِيَ فِيهِ غَيْرِي تَرَكْتُهُ وَشِرْكَهُ»

"I am the freest of partners having no need of association (*Ash-Shirk*). Whoever does a deed associating something in it other than Me, I have forsaken him and his association." (*Muslim*)[1]

"anyone" includes all of the creation, whether it is by wanting them to look, or making them hear, or other than that.

[1] Abu Hurayrah رَضِيَ اللهُ عَنْهُ narrated a *Marfoo' Hadith* from the Prophet ﷺ that Allâh the Most High said,

«أَنَا أَغْنَى الشُّرَكَاءِ عَنِ الشِّرْكِ، مَنْ عَمِلَ عَمَلًا أَشْرَكَ مَعِيَ فِيهِ غَيْرِي تَرَكْتُهُ وَشِرْكَهُ»

"I am the freest of partners having no need of association (*Ash-Shirk*). Whoever does a deed associating something in it other than Me, I have forsaken him and his association."

This *Hadith* proves that (act of) showing off is rejected back to the one who does it. If the showing off is presented in the act of worship from its beginning, then the entire act of worship is nullified and he is at fault for his showing off. He is also guilty of committing the hidden *Shirk*, which is minor *Shirk*. However, if the worship was originally intended for Allâh but the worshipper mixed his deed with showing off - meaning he did what was required and added to it, like lengthening the bowing or words of glorification for the people - then this added amount of worship is worthless and he is sinful for it. This is in the physical acts of worship. In reference to the acts of worship with wealth, then the case is different from this. The Prophet ﷺ said, "Whoever does a deed", meaning he begins it. The word *'Amilan* (a deed) is in the indefinite case and it comes in the form of a conditional statement. Thus, it includes all deeds. Then he said, "associating something in it other than Me." This means the person made the deed for both Allâh and other than Allâh. For verily He, the Mighty and Majestic, is freest of partners from needing association (*Ash-Shirk*). He does not except anything except what is for Him Alone.

Abu Sa'eed narrated a *Marfoo' Hadith* (in which the Prophet ﷺ said),

«أَلَا أُخْبِرُكُمْ بِمَا هُوَ أَخْوَفُ عَلَيْكُمْ عِنْدِي مِنَ الْمَسِيحِ الدَّجَّالِ؟»

"Shall I not inform you all of what I fear more for you all than *Al-Maseeḥ Ad-Dajjaal* (the False Messiah)?"

They said, "Of course, O Allâh's Messenger ﷺ." He said,

«الشِّرْكُ الْخَفِيُّ يَقُومُ الرَّجُلُ فَيُصَلِّي فَيُزَيِّنُ صَلَاتَهُ؛ لِمَا يَرَى مِنْ نَظَرِ رَجُلٍ»

"The hidden *Shirk* (*Ash-Shirk ul-Khafiyy*). The man stands and prays (*Aṣ-Ṣalaah*), and he beautifies his prayer because he sees another man looking (at him)." Aḥmad recorded it.[1]

---

[1] Abu Sa'eed narrated a *Marfoo' Hadith* (in which the Prophet ﷺ said),

«أَلَا أُخْبِرُكُمْ بِمَا هُوَ أَخْوَفُ عَلَيْكُمْ عِنْدِي مِنَ الْمَسِيحِ الدَّجَّالِ؟»

"Shall I not inform you all of what I fear more for you all than *Al-Maseeḥ Ad-Dajjaal* (the False Messiah)?"

They said, "Of course, O Messenger of Allâh." He said,

«الشِّرْكُ الْخَفِيُّ»

"The hidden *Shirk* (*Ash-Shirk ul-Khafiyy*)."

This is because the matter of the False Messiah is something clear and obvious, and the Prophet ﷺ clarified his situation. However, showing off is often presented to the heart and this *Shirk*, little by little, leads the slave to disregard Allâh's watching and direct his attention to the watching of the creatures. For this reason the Prophet ﷺ considered it a greater cause of fear for us that the *Al-Maseeḥ Ad-Dajjaal* (the False Messiah). Then he explained it with his statement,

«يَقُومُ الرَّجُلُ فَيُصَلِّي فَيُزَيِّنُ صَلَاتَهُ لِمَا يَرَى مِنْ نَظَرِ رَجُلٍ»

"The man stands and prays (*Aṣ-Ṣalaah*), and he beautifies his prayer because he sees another man looking (at him)."

Important issues of the Chapter

1) The explanation of the Verse of *Surah Al-Kahf* (18:110).
2) The great issue is in the rejection of the righteous deed if anything enters it that is for other than Allâh.
3) Mention of the reason that necessitates this, which is the complete lack of need (of Allâh).
4) That among the reasons is that He (Allâh) is better everything that is associated as a partner.
5) The Prophet's fear of showing off for his Companions.
6) That he explained as being when the person prays (*Aṣ-Ṣalaah*) for Allâh but he beautifies it because he notices someone looking at him.

Chapter 36

It is from *Ash-Shirk* that a Person Seeks Worldly Gain by his Deeds*

The Statement of Allâh the Most High,

﴿مَن كَانَ يُرِيدُ ٱلْحَيَوٰةَ ٱلدُّنْيَا وَزِينَتَهَا نُوَفِّ إِلَيْهِمْ أَعْمَٰلَهُمْ فِيهَا﴾ الآيتان

"Whosoever desires the life of the world and its glitter, to them we shall pay in full (the wages of) their deeds therein." (two *Ayât*) (11:15-16)[1]

In the *Ṣaḥeeḥ* it is recorded from Abu Hurayrah رَضِيَ اللهُ عَنْهُ that

* This means that which has caused him to perform an action is worldly reward, and this is a form of *Shirk* with Allâh that is minor *Shirk*.

[1] And the Statement of Allâh the Most High,

﴿مَن كَانَ يُرِيدُ ٱلْحَيَوٰةَ ٱلدُّنْيَا وَزِينَتَهَا نُوَفِّ إِلَيْهِمْ أَعْمَٰلَهُمْ فِيهَا وَهُمْ فِيهَا لَا يُبْخَسُونَ أُوْلَٰٓئِكَ ٱلَّذِينَ لَيْسَ لَهُمْ فِي ٱلْءَاخِرَةِ إِلَّا ٱلنَّارُ وَحَبِطَ مَا صَنَعُواْ فِيهَا وَبَٰطِلٌ مَّا كَانُواْ يَعْمَلُونَ﴾

"Whoever desires the life of the world and its glitter we will pay them in full (the wages of) their deeds in it (i.e. this world) and they will have no diminishing therein. They are those for whom there is nothing in the hereafter but the Fire. And vain are the deeds they did therein and what they did therein is nullified." (11:15-16)

This means from those whom Allâh intends this for and from those for whom Allâh wills it. This general statement here is made specific by the Verse in *Surah Al-Israa'*. Those who seek the life of this world, fundamentally, intently and actively are the disbelievers. For this reason this Verse revealed concerning them. However, its wording includes everyone who seeks the worldly life with his righteous deeds.

The deeds that the slave does seeking to gain the reward of this world are of two types.

The first: That the deed that he does and gains by it the reward of this world, and he seeks it while not seeking the reward of the hereafter, and the Islamic Law does not encourage it by mentioning the reward of this world. Examples are prayer (*Aṣ-Ṣalaah*), fasting (*Aṣ-Ṣiyaam*) and similar things from the deeds and acts of obedience. It is not permissible to seek worldly gains in these deeds. If a person intends worldly gains with these

Allâh's Messenger ﷺ said,

«تَعِسَ عَبْدُ الدِّينَارِ، تَعِسَ عَبْدُ الدِّرْهَمِ، تَعِسَ عَبْدُ الْخَمِيصَةِ، تَعِسَ عَبْدُ الْخَمِيلَةِ، إِنْ أُعطِيَ رَضِيَ، وَإِنْ لَمْ يُعطَ سَخِطَ، تَعِسَ وَانْتَكَسَ، وَإِذَا شِيكَ فَلَا انْتَقَشَ، طُوبَىٰ لِعَبْدٍ آخَذٍ بِعِنَانِ فَرَسِهِ فِي سَبِيلِ اللهِ، أَشْعَثَ رَأْسُهُ، مُغْبَرَّةٍ قَدَمَاهُ، إِنْ كَانَ فِي الْحِرَاسَةِ كَانَ فِي الْحِرَاسَةِ وَإِنْ كَانَ فِي السَّاقَةِ كَانَ فِي السَّاقَةِ، إِنِ اسْتَأْذَنَ لَمْ يُؤْذَنْ لَهُ، وَإِنْ شَفَعَ لَمْ يُشَفَّعْ»

"Ruined is the worshipper of the dinar, ruined is the worshipper of the dirham, ruined is the worshipper of the *Khameeṣah*, ruined is the worshipper of the *Khameelah*. If he is given he is pleased and if he is not given he is upset. May he be ruined and suffer relapse, and if he is pricked with a thorn, may he not find anyone

---

deeds, then he is a *Mushrik*.

The second type: Deeds that the Islamic Law has granted a reward for in this life and encourages it by mentioning a reward for it in this life. Examples are keeping family relations, kind treatment of parents and deeds similar to this. This type, if the person seeks some gain in his deed when he does that deed, seeking to gain that worldly reward and at the same time doing his deed solely for Allâh, but not seeking the reward of the hereafter, then this is included in this threat. For it is from this type of *Shirk*. However, if the person seeks to gain both the worldly reward and the reward of the hereafter, then there is no harm in that. This is because the Islamic Law has only encouraged it by mentioning the reward in this in order to encourage its performance.

From that which is included under this Verse is the person who does a righteous deed for the sake of wealth. For example, that a person studies the religious knowledge only to get a job, and he is not concerned with removing ignorance from himself, seeking Paradise and fleeing from the Fire. This is included in that. Also included in that are those who do deeds for the sake of showing off, and those who do righteous deeds while they have with them one of the things that nullifies Islam. This person, even though he says that he is a believer, he is in not truthful in that, because if he is truthful, he would single out Allâh for his deed.

to remove it for him. *Ṭoobaa* (a huge tree in Paradise) is for a Slave who takes hold of the reins of his horse in the Way of Allâh with his hair becoming disheveled and his feet becoming dusty. If he is assigned the watch, then he remains on watch. If he is assigned the rear guard, he guards the rear. If he seeks permission (to come before an authority figure), he is not permitted and if he intercedes, his intercession is not accepted (due to his seemingly low status)."[1]

Important issues of the Chapter

1) The person's seeking worldly gains with deeds of the hereafter.
2) The explanation of the Verse of *Surah Hood* (11:15-16).
3) Calling the Muslim person worshipper of the dinar, the dirham and the *Khameeṣah*.
4) The explanation of that in that if he is given he is pleased and if he is not given he is upset.
5) His (the Prophet's ﷺ) statement, "May he be ruined and suffer relapse."
6) His (the Prophet's ﷺ) statement, "and if he is pricked with a thorn, may he not find anyone to remove it for him."
7) The commendation of the *Mujaahid* (fighter in the Way of Allâh) who is described with these characteristics.

[1] In the *Ṣaḥeeḥ* it is recorded from Abu Hurayrah that Allâh's Messenger ﷺ said,

«تَعِسَ عَبْدُ الدِّينَارِ»

"Ruined is the worshipper of the dinar..."

Hence, the person intends the deed and he does the deed for the sake of this world (i.e. worldly gain). The Prophet ﷺ has called him a worshipper of the dinar. This proves that it is from *Ash-Shirk*, because worship is in levels. From these levels is the worship that is minor *Shirk*. It is said, "He worshipped this thing", because it is what activated his concern. It is known that the slave is obedient to his master. He is obedient to him and he turns in whatever direction he directs him.

Chapter 37

Whoever Obeys the Scholars and the Rulers in Forbidding what Allâh has Allowed or Allowing what He has Forbidden, then He has Taken Them as Lords Besides Allâh *

Ibn 'Abbaas رَضِيَ اللهُ عَنْهُمَا said, "Stones are about to descend upon you from the heavens! I say, 'Allâh's Messenger ﷺ said', and you all say (in reply), 'Abu Bakr and 'Umar رَضِيَ اللهُ عَنْهُمَا said.'"[1]

Aḥmad bin Ḥanbal said, "I am amazed at some people who know the chain of narration (of a *Hadith*) and its authenticity, yet they go with the opinion of Sufyaan (Ath-Thawree), while

---

* This chapter and the chapters after it are related to the explanation of the necessities of *At-Tauhid* and the requirements of the realization of the testimony (*Shahaadah*) that none has the right to be worshipped but Allâh (*Lā ilāha illallāh*). The scholars are tools and means for understanding the texts of the Book (the Qur'ān) and the *Sunnah*. Thus, their obedience is from the aspect of obedience that is subjective to Allâh and His Messenger. In reference to the independent (absolute) obedience, then it is not for anyone other than Allâh, and it is a form of worship. Concerning the matters of *Ijtihaad* (independent deduction by a qualified scholar) that do not contain a text from the Book (Al-Qur'ān) and the *Sunnah*, then they are obeyed in that. This is due to Allâh's permission for that and what it contains of benefits that are established in the Islamic Law.

[1] Ibn 'Abbaas رَضِيَ اللهُ عَنْهُمَا said, "Stones are about to descend upon you from the heavens! I say, 'Allâh's Messenger ﷺ said', and you all say (in reply), 'Abu Bakr and 'Umar رَضِيَ اللهُ عَنْهُمَا said.'"

Imaam Aḥmad recorded this narration with an authentic (*Ṣaḥeeḥ*) chain of narration. The understanding of the statement of Ibn 'Abbaas is that he would not oppose the statement of the Prophet ﷺ that was clear in its meaning with the statement of anyone else who had no evidence for his statement. It made no difference whether the statement was made by Abu Bakr or 'Umar, so how about others who are less than them?

Allâh the Most High says,

﴿فَلْيَحْذَرِ ٱلَّذِينَ يُخَالِفُونَ عَنْ أَمْرِهِۦٓ أَن تُصِيبَهُمْ فِتْنَةٌ أَوْ يُصِيبَهُمْ عَذَابٌ أَلِيمٌ﴾

'Let those who oppose his (the Messenger's) command beware, lest some *Fitnah* befall them or a painful torment be inflicted upon them.' (24:63)

Do you know what the *Fitnah* is? The *Fitnah* is *Ash-Shirk*. Maybe if the person rejects some of his (the Prophet's) words something of deviation will fall into his heart and thus he would be destroyed."[1]

---

[1] Aḥmad bin Ḥanbal said, "I am amazed at some people who know the chain of narration (of a *Hadith*) and its authenticity, yet they go with the opinion of Sufyaan (Ath-Thawree), while Allâh the Most High says,

﴿فَلْيَحْذَرِ ٱلَّذِينَ يُخَالِفُونَ عَنْ أَمْرِهِۦٓ أَن تُصِيبَهُمْ فِتْنَةٌ﴾

'Let those who oppose his (the Messenger's) command beware, lest some *Fitnah* should befall them...''' (24:63)

Meaning a type of *Shirk*, which may reach the level of major *Shirk*.

﴿أَوْ يُصِيبَهُمْ عَذَابٌ أَلِيمٌ﴾

"...or a painful torment be inflicted upon them."

Aḥmad continued, "Do you know what the *Fitnah* is? The *Fitnah* is *Ash-Shirk*. Maybe if the person rejects some of his (the Prophet's) words something of deviation will fall into his heart and thus he would be destroyed." This means if he rejects some statement of the Prophet ﷺ for the statement of someone else. Allâh, the Mighty and Majestic said about the Jews,

﴿فَلَمَّا زَاغُوٓا۟ أَزَاغَ ٱللَّهُ قُلُوبَهُمْ﴾

"So when they deviated, Allâh caused their hearts to deviate." (61:5)

Thus, they deviated solely by their will and choice, even with the explanation of the arguments, and the appearance of evidences and proofs. But when they deviated, Allâh caused their hearts to deviate as a punishment from Him upon them for that (willful deviation).

'Adiyy bin Ḥaatim رَضِيَ اللهُ عَنْهُ narrated that he heard the Prophet ﷺ reciting this verse,

﴿اتَّخَذُوٓا۟ أَحْبَارَهُمْ وَرُهْبَـٰنَهُمْ أَرْبَابًا مِّن دُونِ ٱللَّهِ﴾ الآية

"They (the Jews and Christians) took their rabbis and their monks as lords besides Allâh." (9:31)

('Adiyy said) "So I said to him, 'We did not worship them.' He replied,

«أَلَيْسَ يُحَرِّمُونَ مَا أَحَلَّ اللهُ فَتُحَرِّمُونَهُ، وَيُحِلُّونَ مَا حَرَّمَ اللهُ فَتُحِلُّونَهُ؟!»

'Did they not prohibit what Allâh allowed, so you prohibited it, and did they not allow what Allâh prohibited, so you allowed it?!'

I said, 'Yes.' He said,

«فَتِلْكَ عِبَادَتُهُمْ»

'That was your worship of them.'"

Reported by Ahmad and At-Tirmithi, who graded it good (*Hasan*).[1]

Important issues of the Chapter

1) The explanation of the Verse of *Surah An-Noor* (24:63).

2) The explanation of the Verse of *Surah Baraa'ah (At-*

---

[1] 'Adiyy bin Ḥaatim رَضِيَ اللهُ عَنْهُ narrated that he heard the Prophet ﷺ reciting this Verse,

﴿اتَّخَذُوٓا۟ أَحْبَارَهُمْ وَرُهْبَـٰنَهُمْ أَرْبَابًا مِّن دُونِ ٱللَّهِ﴾ الآية

"They (the Jews and Christians) took their rabbis and their monks as lords besides Allâh." (9:31)

('Adiyy said) "So I said to him, 'We did not worship them.'..." Obeying the rabbis in declaring what is lawful and forbidden has two levels.

The first level: That one obeys the scholars or the leaders in changing the

Tawbah) (9:31).

3) Pointing out the meaning of worship that 'Adiyy denied.
4) Ibn 'Abbaas رَضِيَ اللهُ عَنْهُمَا making an example of Abu Bakr and 'Umar رَضِيَ اللهُ عَنْهُمَا and Aḥmad making an example of Sufyaan.
5) The changing of the conditions to this extent until the worship of the monks had become the best of deeds with most of the people. This became known as *Al-Walaayah* and worship of the rabbis became know as knowledge and understanding (*'Ilm and Fiqh*). Then the conditions changed to where those who were not of the righteous being worshipped besides Allâh. Then, in reference to the second meaning, those who were from the ignorant began being worshipped.

---

religion, due to exalting them. Hence, the person declares lawful what they make lawful. This means that he believes that it (the thing) is lawful due to his obedience to them and exalting them, yet he knows that the thing is forbidden. This is the person who has taken them as lords, which is major disbelief and major *Shirk* with Allâh. This is the person who directs the worship of obedience to other than Allâh.

The second level: That the person obeys the scholar or the leader in making the lawful forbidden or making the forbidden lawful in reference to deeds. Yet, he knows that he is disobedient (to Allâh) in that and he confesses that it is disobedience, but he obeys them due to his love for the sin or love for being in conformity with them. This person has the same ruling as those like him from the sinful people.

The Shaikh intends by mentioning the monks and that obedience also occurs through the monks - who are the devout worshippers - to draw attention to what *Sufism* contains, and the *Sufi* orders, and the people of extremism in *Sufism* and the exaggeration in exalting the *Sufi* leaders. For verily they obey their Shaikhs, devout worshippers and *Awliyaa'* (beloved friends of Allâh), whom they claim are *Awliyaa'*. They obey them in changing the religion and this is a form of taking these worshippers as lords besides Allâh.

Chapter 38

The Statement of Allâh the Most High*

﴿أَلَمْ تَرَ إِلَى ٱلَّذِينَ يَزْعُمُونَ أَنَّهُمْ ءَامَنُوا۟ بِمَآ أُنزِلَ إِلَيْكَ وَمَآ أُنزِلَ مِن قَبْلِكَ يُرِيدُونَ أَن يَتَحَاكَمُوٓا۟ إِلَى ٱلطَّٰغُوتِ وَقَدْ أُمِرُوٓا۟ أَن يَكْفُرُوا۟ بِهِۦ وَيُرِيدُ ٱلشَّيْطَٰنُ أَن يُضِلَّهُمْ ضَلَٰلًۢا بَعِيدًا﴾ الآيات

"Have you not seen those (hypocrites) who claim that they believe in that which has been sent down to you, and that which was sent down before you, and they wish to go for judgement (in their disputes) to the *Ṭâghût* while they have been ordered to reject them? But Satan wishes to lead them far astray." (4:60) [1]

---

* Singling out Allâh for oneness in His Lordship and in His Godship contains, necessitates and requires that He be singled out in Ruling. The *Tauhid* of Allâh in obedience and realization of the testimony that none has the right to be worshipped but Allâh and Muhammad is Allâh's Messenger (*Lā ilāha illallāh wa Muhammadur-Rasoolul-laah*) cannot occur unless the worshippers judge according to what Allâh revealed to His Messenger. Leaving off ruling according to what Allâh revealed to His Messenger ﷺ for the ruling of pre-Islamic ignorance, or man-made systems of government, or opinions is major disbelief in Allâh and from that which nullifies the statement of *At-Tauhid*. The *Imaam*, Shaikh Muhammad bin Ibrâhîm said in the beginning of his treatise, *Taḥkeem ul-Qawaaneen*, "Verily the clear major disbelief is placing the cursed, man-made laws in place of what the Trustworthy Spirit (Jibreel) descended with upon the heart of the leader of the Messengers. This is so that it (the man-made law) will be a law among the *'Aalameen* (the worlds, all that exists) that is contradictory and opposed to what descended from the Lord of the *'Aalameen*."

[1] The Statement of Allâh the Most High,

﴿أَلَمْ تَرَ إِلَى ٱلَّذِينَ يَزْعُمُونَ أَنَّهُمْ ءَامَنُوا۟ بِمَآ أُنزِلَ إِلَيْكَ وَمَآ أُنزِلَ مِن قَبْلِكَ﴾

"Have you not seen those (hypocrites) who claim that they believe in that which has been sent down to you, and that which was sent

And the Statement of Allâh,

﴿وَإِذَا قِيلَ لَهُمْ لَا تُفْسِدُوا۟ فِى ٱلْأَرْضِ قَالُوٓا۟ إِنَّمَا نَحْنُ مُصْلِحُونَ﴾

"And when it is said to them, 'Make not mischief on the earth.' They say, 'We are only peace-makers.'"[1] (2:11)

---

down before you?" (4:60)

This proves that they are liars, for faith does not come together with seeking judgement and ruling from *At-Ṭâghût* (all false deities and those who rule by other than Allâh's law). Allâh then says,

﴿يُرِيدُونَ أَن يَتَحَاكَمُوٓا۟ إِلَى ٱلطَّـٰغُوتِ﴾

"they wish to go for judgement (in their disputes) to the *Ṭaaghoot*."

His Statement, "they wish", is an important point and a condition in the nullification of the foundation of faith from whoever seeks judgement from *At-Tâghût*. That condition is that it must be by the person desire, which means voluntarily, by choice, and desiring that while not detesting it. Thus, the desire (or wish) is a condition. Then He says,

﴿وَقَدْ أُمِرُوٓا۟ أَن يَكْفُرُوا۟ بِهِۦ﴾

"while they have been ordered to reject them?"

The command to reject taking judgements to *At-Tâghût* is an obligatory command and it is from the particular aspects of *At-Tauhid* and magnifying Allâh in His Lordship. Then He says,

﴿وَيُرِيدُ ٱلشَّيْطَـٰنُ أَن يُضِلَّهُمْ ضَلَـٰلًۢا بَعِيدًا﴾

"But Satan wishes to lead them far astray."

This proves that this (ruling by other than what Allâh ruled) is from the inspiration of Satan and his temptation.

[1] And the Statement of Allâh,

﴿وَإِذَا قِيلَ لَهُمْ لَا تُفْسِدُوا۟ فِى ٱلْأَرْضِ قَالُوٓا۟ إِنَّمَا نَحْنُ مُصْلِحُونَ﴾

"And when it is said to them, 'Make not mischief on the earth.' They say, 'We are only peace — makers.'" (2:11)

Mischief in the land is by ruling by other than the Law of Allâh and associating partners with Allâh. Making things right in the land is by the *Sharee'ah* (Islamic Law) and *At-Tauhid*. Corrupting it is by *Ash-Shirk* in its various types, among which is *Shirk* in obedience. This Verse is clear in its

And His Statement,

﴿وَلَا تُفْسِدُوا فِي الْأَرْضِ بَعْدَ إِصْلَاحِهَا﴾

"And do not do mischief on the earth after it has been set in order." (7:56)

And His Statement,

﴿أَفَحُكْمَ الْجَاهِلِيَّةِ يَبْغُونَ﴾ الآية

"Do they then seek the judgement of (the Days of) Ignorance?" (5:50)

'Abdullah bin 'Umar narrated that Allâh's Messenger ﷺ said,

«لَا يُؤْمِنُ أَحَدُكُمْ حَتَّى يَكُونَ هَوَاهُ تَبَعًا لِمَا جِئْتُ بِهِ»

"None of you believes until his desire follows that which I have come with."

An-Nawawee said, "An authentic (*Ṣaḥeeḥ*) *Hadith*. We have recorded it in *Kitâb ul-Ḥajj* with an authentic (*Ṣaḥeeḥ*) chain."

Ash-Sha'bee said, "There was a dispute between a man from the hypocrites and a man from the Jews. So the Jew said, 'We will take the matter to Muhammad for decision.' The Jew said this because he knew that he (Muhammad ﷺ) would not take any bribery. The hypocrite said, 'We will take the matter to the Jews for decision.' He said this because he knew that the Jews would take a bribe. Therefore, they agreed to go to a fortuneteller in Juhaynah and seek the decision from him. Thus, Allâh revealed the Verse,

﴿أَلَمْ تَرَ إِلَى الَّذِينَ يَزْعُمُونَ﴾

'Do you not see those who claim...' (4:60)"

It has been said that this Verse was revealed concerning two

---

pointing out that from the characteristics of the hypocrites is that they strive for *Ash-Shirk*, its means and its particular aspects, and they say, "We only seek to make things right."

men who disputed, so one of them said, "We will refer the matter to the Prophet ﷺ." The other said, "We will take it Ka'b bin Al-Ashraf." Then they referred the matter to 'Umar رَضِيَ اللهُ عَنْهُ. So one of them mentioned the story to him ('Umar) and he said to the one who was not pleased with (the decision of) Allâh's Messenger ﷺ, "Is it so?" The man said, "Yes." So he struck him with the sword and killed him.[1]

Important issues of the Chapter

1) The explanation of the Verse of *Surah An-Nisaa'* (4:60) and what it contains of assisting in understanding *At-Tâghût*.

2) The explanation of the Verse of *Surah Al-Baqarah* (2:11),

﴿وَإِذَا قِيلَ لَهُمْ لَا تُفْسِدُوا فِي الْأَرْضِ﴾

"And when it is said to them, 'Do not make mischief on the earth.'" (2:11)

3) The explanation of the Verse of *Surah Al-A'raaf* (7:56),

﴿وَلَا تُفْسِدُوا فِي الْأَرْضِ بَعْدَ إِصْلَاحِهَا﴾

"And do not make mischief on the earth after it has been set in order." (7:56)

---

[1] And His Statement,

﴿أَفَحُكْمَ الْجَاهِلِيَّةِ يَبْغُونَ وَمَنْ أَحْسَنُ مِنَ اللَّهِ حُكْمًا لِقَوْمٍ يُوقِنُونَ﴾

"Do they then seek the judgement of (the Days of) Ignorance? And who is better in judgement than Allâh for a people who have firm faith?" (5:50)

The pre-Islamic ignorance is that some of them make others the judge. This means that man makes a code of law and makes it the ruling judgement. Therefore, whoever seeks judgement in the laws of pre-Islamic ignorance, then he makes man the decision-maker. This means that he takes man as someone to be obeyed besides Allâh or makes him a partner for Allâh in the worship of obedience.

4) The explanation of,

﴿أَفَحُكْمَ ٱلْجَٰهِلِيَّةِ يَبْغُونَ﴾

"Do they then seek the judgement of (the Days of) Ignorance?" (5:50)

5) What Ash-Sha'bee said regarding the reason for the revelation of the first Verse.

6) The explanation of true faith and false faith.

7) The story of 'Umar with the hypocrite.

8) The fact that faith is not attained by anyone until his desires follow that which Muhammad ﷺ was sent with.

Chapter 39

Whoever Denies Anything from the Names and Attributes (of Allâh) and the Statement of Allâh the Most High*

﴿وَهُمْ يَكْفُرُونَ بِالرَّحْمَٰنِ﴾

"And they disbelieve in *Ar-Raḥmaan* (the Most Beneficent)."[1] (13:30)

---

* The relationship of this chapter to Kitâb ut-Tauhid is from two aspects:
The first: That *Tauḥid ul-Asmaa' waṣ-Ṣifaat* (*Tauḥid* in Allâh's Names and Attributes) is from the evidences of the *Tauḥid* of worship.
The second: That denying anything from the Names and Attributes (of Allâh) is *Shirk* and disbelief (*Kufr*) that expels one from the religion. If the Name is confirmed, or the Attribute is confirmed, and the person knows that Allâh has affirmed them for Himself or His Messenger ﷺ has affirmed them for Him, then he denies them, by basically negating them, then this is disbelief. The reason is that this is rejection of the Book (the Qur'ān) and the *Sunnah*.

[1] And the Statement of Allâh the Most High,

﴿وَهُمْ يَكْفُرُونَ بِالرَّحْمَٰنِ﴾

"And they disbelieve in Ar-Raḥman (the Most Beneficent)." (13:30) Ar-Raḥman is one of the Names of Allâh, and the *Mushrikūn* (polytheist, idolaters) and the disbelievers in Makkah said, "We do not know *Ar-Raḥmaan* except for the *Raḥmaan* of Al-Yamaamah." Thus, they disbelieved in the Name of Allâh, *Ar-Raḥman*. This is disbelief in itself. For this reason Allâh said,

﴿وَهُمْ يَكْفُرُونَ بِالرَّحْمَٰنِ﴾

"And they disbelieve in Ar-Raḥman (the Most Beneficent)." (13:30) Meaning the Name of Allâh, Ar-Raḥmaan. It also includes the understanding that they disbelieved in the Attribute of *Ar-Raḥmaan*. Every Name from the Names of Allâh includes an Attribute. Thus, a Name from the Names of Allâh alludes to both of two things in congruity. They are the Name itself and the Attribute that the Name includes (in its meaning). For this reason we say that every Name from the Names of Allâh

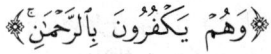

In *Ṣaḥeeḥ Al-Bukhari* 'Ali رَضِيَ اللهُ عَنْهُ said, "Speak to people according to what they know. Do you want Allâh and His Messenger ﷺ to be rejected?!"[1]

'Abdur-Razzaaq recorded from Ma'mar, who reported from Ibn Taawoos, who reported from his father, who reported from Ibn 'Abbaas رَضِيَ اللهُ عَنْهُمَا that he saw a man rising up in rejection when he heard a *Hadith* from the Prophet ﷺ regarding the Attributes (of Allâh). So he (Ibn 'Abbaas) said, "What are these people so afraid of? They find ease in accepting its clear laws and they are destroyed with its unclear matters."[2]

---

includes an Attribute from the Attributes of Allâh. Even the Magnificent Name, Allâh, which is the proper Name for He who is rightfully worshipped, is derived — according to the correct view from the two opinions of the scholars — from the word *Ilaahah*, which means worship.

[1] In *Ṣaḥeeḥ Al-Bukhari* 'Ali رَضِيَ اللهُ عَنْهُ said, "Speak to people according to what they know. Do you want Allâh and His Messenger to be rejected?!" This contains an evidence that some knowledge is not suitable for everyone. For example, some particulars of *Tauhid ul-Asmaa' waṣ-Ṣifaat* are not appropriate for everyone (to know). Thus, some fine points concerning the Names and Attributes should not be thrown out (before everyone). However, they (the people) have been commanded to believe in that in a comprehensive manner, according to what is well known in the Book and the *Sunnah*. This is because from the causes of denying the Names and Attributes is that a person tells the people that which they do not understand from the Names and Attributes. Thus, it is obligatory upon the Muslim, and particularly the student of knowledge, to not make the people reject anything from what Allâh has said, or what His Messenger ﷺ has informed of. A cause of that rejection is that people are told what they do not know and what their intellects do not grasp.

[2] 'Abdur-Razzaaq recorded from Ma'mar, who reported from Ibn Ṭaawoos, who reported from his father, who reported from Ibn 'Abbaas رَضِيَ اللهُ عَنْهُمَا that he saw a man rising up in rejection when he heard a *Hadith* from the Prophet ﷺ regarding the Attributes (of Allâh). This was because he understood that some resemblance was being made (for Allâh with the creation) or anthropomorphization from this Attribute. Therefore, he was

When the Quraysh heard Allâh's Messenger ﷺ mentioning *Ar-Raḥmaan* (the Most Beneficent) they denied that. Thus, concerning them Allâh revealed,

﴿وَهُمْ يَكْفُرُونَ بِالرَّحْمَٰنِ﴾

"And they disbelieve in *Ar-Raḥmaan* (the Most Beneficent)."[1] (13:30)

Important issues of the Chapter

1) The lack of faith by denying anything from the Names and Attributes (of Allâh).
2) The explanation of the Verse of *Surah Ar-Ra'd* (13:30).
3) Avoiding speaking about that which the listener does not understand.

---

afraid of this Attribute. It is obligatory upon the Muslim that when he hears an Attribute from the Attributes of Allâh that is mentioned in the Book of Allâh or the Sunnah of the Prophet ﷺ that he treats it in the manner of all of the Attributes. This is that he affirms the Attribute for Allâh without a description of how or any resemblance to the creation. This is why Ibn 'Abbaas said here, "What are these people so afraid of?" Meaning what is the reason of these people's fear? "They find ease in accepting its clear laws." Meaning when they are told of what they know, they find ease in their hearts concerning that. Then he said, "and they are destroyed with its unclear matters." So when they hear something in the Book or the *Sunnah* that their intellects do not understand, they are destroyed by it, they become afraid, they become terrified, they interpret, they negate or they deny. And this is from the causes of misguidance. He intends here by his saying "the unclear matters" that which the knowledge of it is not clear to some of the listeners.

[1] When the Quraysh heard Allâh's Messenger ﷺ mentioning *Ar-Raḥmaan* (the Most Beneficent) they denied that. Thus, concerning them Allâh revealed, "And they disbelieve in *Ar-Raḥmaan* (the Most Beneficent)." (13:30) Thus, rejecting the Attribute or rejecting the Name means a lack of belief in that, and this is denial and disbelief. This is different than interpretation (*At-Ta'weel*). Interpretation and deviation have levels that will be explained if Allâh wills.

4) Mentioning the reason, which is that to do so leads to the rejection Allâh and His Messenger, even though evil is not intended.

5) The statement of Ibn 'Abbaas to the person who denied something from that (i.e. Allâh's Names and Attributes) and that it (his denial) would destroy him.

Chapter 40

The Statement of Allâh the Most High,*

﴿يَعْرِفُونَ نِعْمَتَ ٱللَّهِ ثُمَّ يُنكِرُونَهَا وَأَكْثَرُهُمُ ٱلْكَٰفِرُونَ﴾ الآية

"They recognize the Favor of Allâh, yet they deny it and most of them are disbelievers." (16:83)

Mujaahid said, "This is the man's statement, 'This is my wealth, I inherited it from my forefathers.'"[1]

'Awn bin 'Abdullah said, "They say, 'Were it not for so-and-so it would not be like this.'"[2]

---

* What is obligatory upon the slave is that he knows that all favors are from Allâh and that the completion of *At-Tauhid* cannot occur except by attributing every favor to Allâh. And attributing favors to other than Allâh is a deficiency in the completion of *At-Tauhid* and minor *Shirk* with Allâh. This is because it contains attributing favors to other than Allâh, and Allâh said,

﴿وَمَا بِكُم مِّن نِّعْمَةٍ فَمِنَ ٱللَّهِ﴾

"And whatever favor you have, then it is from Allâh." (16:53)

[1] Mujaahid said, "This is the man's statement, 'This is my wealth, I inherited it from my forefathers.'" This statement is contrary to the completion of *At-Tauhid* and it is a type of *Shirk*, because the person has attributed this wealth to himself and he has attributed it to his forefathers. However, the reality is that Allâh favored his forefathers with this wealth and then He favored this believer with it, as Allâh made the division of the inheritance reach him. This is all from the bounty of Allâh and His favor. The father is a means of the wealth reaching you. For this reason, in the division of inheritance, it is not permissible for the father or the owner of the wealth to divide inheritance however he wishes. This is because the wealth is in reality not his.

[2] 'Awn bin 'Abdullah said, "They say, 'Were it not for so-and-so it would not be like this." This is like the person saying, "Were it not for the pilot we would have been destroyed", and similar statements from the words that contain attaching the occurrence of a matter to this means. It makes no difference whether this means is a person, an inanimate object, a spot, or a

Ibn Qutaybah said, "They say, 'This (wealth, favor) is due to the intercession of our gods.'"[1]

Abul-'Abbaas said after the *Hadith* of Zayd bin Khaalid that contains the statement of Allâh,

«أَصْبَحَ مِنْ عِبَادِي مُؤْمِنٌ بِي وَكَافِرٌ»

> "From my Slaves this morning someone has become as a believer in Me and someone a disbeliever..."

and the Hadith was mentioned previously, "This is mentioned often in the Book and the *Sunnah*. Allâh rebukes whoever attributes His bounties to other than Him and associates partners with Him."

Some of the *Salaf* said, "This is like their saying, 'The wind was good', and 'The sailor was skillful', and similar statements that run upon the tongues of many people."[2]

---

creation from the creations of Allâh, such as rain, water or wind.

[1] Ibn Qutaybah said, 'They say, "This (wealth, favor) is due to the intercession of our gods."' This means that if they acquire some favorable thing they remember that they had turned to the *Awliyaa'* (beloved friends of Allâh), or the Prophets, or the idols, or the statues, and they directed something of worship to them. Thus, they say, "The gods interceded for us, so due to that, this good has come to us. Hence, they reflect upon their gods and they forget that the One Who granted that (favor) is Allâh, and Allâh does not accept the intercession of *Shirk* from these intercessions that they mention.

[2] Abul-'Abbaas said after the *Hadith* of Zayd bin Khaalid that contains the Statement of Allâh,

«أَصْبَحَ مِنْ عِبَادِي مُؤْمِنٌ بِي وَكَافِرٌ فَأَمَّا مَنْ قَالَ: مُطِرْنَا بِفَضْلِ اللهِ وَرَحْمَتِهِ فَذَلِكَ مُؤْمِنٌ بِي كَافِرٌ بِالْكَوْكَبِ، وَأَمَّا مَنْ قَالَ: مُطِرْنَا بِنَوْءِ كَذَا وَكَذَا فَذَلِكَ كَافِرٌ بِي مُؤْمِنٌ بِالْكَوْكَبِ»

> "From my slaves this morning someone has become as a believer in Me and someone a disbeliever..."

and the *Hadith* was mentioned previously, "This is mentioned often in the Book and the *Sunnah*. Allâh rebukes whoever attributes His bounties to

Important issues of the Chapter

1) The explanation of acknowledging the favor and denying it.
2) Knowing that this runs upon the tongues of many people.
3) Calling this type of speech a denial of the favor.
4) The combination of two opposites in the heart.

---

other than Him and associates partners with Him."

Some of the *Salaf* said, "This is like their saying, 'The wind was good', and 'The sailor was skillful', and similar statements that run upon the tongues of many people." This is a chapter that it is necessary to be concerned with and alert the people to, because the favors of Allâh upon them are numerous and unlimited. For this reason, it is obligatory to attribute the favors to Allâh and that the person mentions them and is thankful. This is because from the levels of thankfulness for a favor is that it (the favor) is imputed to whoever conferred it. This is the first of the levels. Allâh says,

﴿وَأَمَّا بِنِعْمَةِ رَبِّكَ فَحَدِّثْ﴾

"And therefore, proclaim the favor of your Lord." (93:11)

This is that you say, "This is from the bounty of Allâh", or "This is the favor of Allâh." If the heart turns to the creation, then it has committed this type of *Shirk* that is contrary to the completion of *At-Tauhid*.

Chapter 41

The Statement of Allâh the Most High,*

﴿فَلَا تَجْعَلُوا لِلَّهِ أَندَادًا وَأَنتُمْ تَعْلَمُونَ﴾

"Then do not set up rivals (*Andaad*) to Allâh while you know." (2:22)

Ibn 'Abbaas رضي الله عنهما said concerning this Verse, "The *Andaad* means *Shirk*. It is more inconspicuous than a black ant on a black stone in the dark of night. And it is that you say, 'By Allâh and by your life, O so-and-so', and 'By my life.' And it is that you say, 'Were it not for this little dog, the thieves would have come to us', or 'Were it not for the duck in the house, the thieves would have come to us.' And it is the saying of the man to his friend, 'What Allâh has willed and what you willed.' And it is the saying of the man, 'Were it not for Allâh and so-and-so.' Do not put so-and-so into it. All of this is *Shirk*." [1] (Ibn Abi Ḥâtim recorded this).

---

* The reality of *At-Tauhid* is that there is not in the heart anything except Allâh. He has no partner, nor any rival. This is like the person who swears by other than Allâh, or like the person who says, "What Allâh willed and what so-and-so willed", and similar statements. That which is wanted when using such statements is that they are attributed (only) to Allâh.

Thus, it becomes clear to us hear that there are two levels:

The first is the statement and it is that the person says, "Were it not for Allâh, such-and-such would not have occurred.

The second is that it is permissible to say, "Were it not for Allâh, and then so-and-so, such-and-such would not have occurred." This is *Tauhid* due to its making the level of so-and-so beneath the level of Allâh's favoring. However, this is not the complete (faith and *Tauhid*). For this reason, Ibn 'Abbaas رضي الله عنهما said here, "Do not put so-and-so into it."

[1] In reference to that which is not permissible, and that which Ibn 'Abbaas said about it, "All of this is *Shirk*", it is that one says, "Were it not for Allâh and so-and-so", using the letter *Waaw* (and). This is because the conjunction *Waaw* (and) denotes association between the added object

'Umar bin Al-Khaṭṭaab رَضِيَ اللهُ عَنْهُ said that Allâh's Messenger ﷺ said,

«مَنْ حَلَفَ بِغَيْرِ اللهِ فَقَدْ كَفَرَ أَوْ أَشْرَكَ»

"Whoever swears by other than Allâh, then he has disbelieved or committed *Shirk*."

Recorded by At-Tirmiṭḥee, who graded it good (*Ḥasan*), and Al-Ḥaakim graded it authentic (*Ṣaḥiḥ*).[1]

Ibn Mas'ud رَضِيَ اللهُ عَنْهُ said, "That I swear by Allâh while lying is more beloved to me than that I swear by other than Him while telling the truth."[2]

---

and that which it is added to without any difference in their status or time. For this reason it becomes a form of minor *Shirk*.

[1] 'Umar bin Al-Khaṭṭab رَضِيَ اللهُ عَنْهُ said that Allâh's Messenger said,

«مَنْ حَلَفَ بِغَيْرِ اللهِ»

"Whoever swears by other than Allâh..."

This is referring to swearing to an oath by other than Allâh. The oath is stress upon a statement by something that magnifies it between the speaker and the person being addressed. It takes place by (adding) one of the three participles of swearing: *Waaw, Baa'* or *Taa'*. It is obligatory that no speech should be emphasized except by (the Name of) Allâh. This is because Allâh is the true exalter. This is why he (the Prophet ﷺ) said here,

«فَقَدْ كَفَرَ أَوْ أَشْرَكَ»

"then he has disbelieved or committed *Shirk*."

Why? Because he has exalted this creation like the exalting of Allâh in swearing by it. His disbelief (*Kufr*) and his *Shirk* are of the minor form. However, it may reach the major *Shirk*, and that is if he exalts the creation in it like the exalting of Allâh in worship. There is also the oath by other than Allâh in wording (only), and it is also *Shirk*, even if the heart is not tied to the oath. This is like the person who always has upon his tongue the usage of swearing by the Prophet, or the *Ka'bah*, or trust, or a *Waliyy* (righteous, beloved friend of Allâh), and similar things. However, the person actually does not intend to swear an oath. It is merely something that runs upon his tongue with the flow of light speech. This is also *Shirk*, because it is an exalting of other than Allâh.

[2] Ibn Mas'ud رَضِيَ اللهُ عَنْهُ said, "That I swear by Allâh while lying is more

Huṭhayfah رَضِيَ اللهُ عَنْهُ narrated that Allâh's Messenger ﷺ said,

«لَا تَقُولُوا: مَا شَاءَ اللهُ وَشَاءَ فُلَانٌ وَلَكِنْ قُولُوا: مَا شَاءَ اللهُ ثُمَّ شَاءَ فُلَانٌ»

"Do not say, 'What Allâh willed and what so-and-so willed.' Rather, say, 'What Allâh willed, then what so-and-so willed.'"[1]

Abu Dâwûd recorded it with an authentic (*Ṣaḥeeḥ*) chain.

It has been related from Ibrâhîm An-Nakha'ee that he hated for someone to say, "I seek refuge with Allâh and with you." Yet, he permitted that someone says, "With Allâh and then with you." He said, "And they say, 'Were it not for Allâh, then so-and-so.' And do not say, 'Were it not for Allâh and so-and-so.'"[2]

---

beloved to me than that I swear by other than Him while telling the truth." This is due to the tremendous sin in swearing by other than Allâh, and that swearing by other than Allâh is *Shirk*. In reference to lying, it is a major sin, and minor *Shirk* is worse than the major sins. For this reason he (Ibn Mas'ud) preferred to lie with *At-Tauhid* and not to be truthful with *Ash-Shirk*. This is because the goodness of *At-Tauhid* is greater than the evil of lying and the evil of *Ash-Shirk* is more despicable than the evil of lying.

[1] Huṭhayfah رَضِيَ اللهُ عَنْهُ narrated that Allâh's Messenger ﷺ said,

«لَا تَقُولُوا: مَا شَاءَ اللهُ وَشَاءَ فُلَانٌ وَلَكِنْ قُولُوا: مَا شَاءَ اللهُ ثُمَّ شَاءَ فُلَانٌ»

"Do not say, 'What Allâh willed and what so-and-so willed.'"

This is the prohibition that is for making something forbidden, because to associate partners in the will is minor *Shirk* with Allâh. Then he said, "Rather, say, 'What Allâh willed, then what so-and-so willed.'" This is because the conjunction *Thumma* (then) denotes a lower level in the will, and this is because the will of the slave is subordinate to the will of Allâh. Allâh the Most High said,

﴿وَمَا تَشَآءُونَ إِلَّآ أَن يَشَآءَ ٱللَّهُ رَبُّ ٱلْعَٰلَمِينَ﴾

"And you all do not will except that Allâh, the Lord of *Al-'Aalameen* (the worlds, all that exists) wills." (81:29)

[2] It has been related from Ibrâhîm An-Nakha'ee that he hated for

Important issues of the Chapter

1) The explanation of the Verse of *Surah Al-Baqarah* (2:22) concerning the *Andaad* (rivals).
2) That the Companions interpreted the Verse that was revealed concerning major *Shirk* as including minor *Shirk* as well.
3) That swearing by other than Allâh is *Shirk*.
4) That if someone swears by other than Allâh while being truthful, this is a greater sin than the false oath.
5) The difference between the conjunctions *Waaw* (and) and *Thumma* (then) in word usage.

---

someone to say, "I seek refuge with Allâh and with you." This is because the letter *Waaw* (and) necessitates association of partners in seeking refuge. Seeking refuge, as we have mentioned, has two aspects: The apparent aspect and the hidden aspect. Seeking refuge is seeking shelter, protection, having hope, fear and the turning of the heart to the one whom refuge is sought with, and this is not suitable for anyone but Allâh. Dislike in the (word) usage of the *Salaf* usually means that it is forbidden. It (their dislike) has also been related concerning that which is not forbidden, yet they would only use it (the wording disliked) regarding that for which there was no text. Then he said, "Yet, he permitted that someone says, 'With Allâh and then with you.'" This is due to what this contains of depreciation (in the levels). He said, "And they say, 'Were it not for Allâh, then so-and-so.' And do not say, 'Were it not for Allâh and so-and-so.'"

Chapter 42

What has been related concerning Whoever is not Satisfied with the Oath taken by Allâh's Name

Ibn 'Umar رَضِيَ اللهُ عَنْهُمَا narrated that Allâh's Messenger ﷺ said,

«لَا تَحْلِفُوا بِآبَائِكُمْ، مَنْ حَلَفَ بِاللهِ فَلْيَصْدُقْ، وَمَنْ حُلِفَ لَهُ بِاللهِ فَلْيَرْضَ وَمَنْ لَمْ يَرْضَ فَلَيْسَ مِنَ اللهِ»

"Do not swear by your fathers. Whoever swears by Allâh, then let him speak the truth, and whoever is given an oath by Allâh (i.e. in Allâh's Name), then let him be pleased with it. And whoever is not pleased (with the oath by Allâh), then he is not of Allâh."

Ibn Maajah recorded it with a good (*Ḥasan*) chain.[1]

---

[1] Ibn 'Umar رَضِيَ اللهُ عَنْهُمَا narrated that Allâh's Messenger ﷺ said,

«لَا تَحْلِفُوا بِآبَائِكُمْ، مَنْ حَلَفَ بِاللهِ فَلْيَصْدُقْ، وَمَنْ حُلِفَ لَهُ بِاللهِ فَلْيَرْضَ»

"Do not swear by your fathers. Whoever swears by Allâh, then let him speak the truth, and whoever is given an oath by Allâh (i.e. in Allâh's Name), then let him be pleased with it."

This *Hadith* is general concerning every oath, regardless of whether it is with a judge (*Qaadhee*) or if it is not with a judge. This is because the cause of being pleased with the statement that was sworn to is exaltation of Allâh, the Mighty and Majestic. For verily the exalting of Allâh in the heart of the slave makes him believe whoever swore to him by Allâh, even if the person was lying. However, he may still not depend upon it (the oath), but he should not display rejection of it due to honoring Allâh. This is so that he may make his *Tauḥid* and his exalting Allâh for himself, and the lie of that person in swearing by Allâh against him (the liar). Then he said, "And whoever is not pleased", meaning with the oath, "then he is not of Allâh." This proves that his deed is from the major sins.

Important issues of the Chapter

1) The prohibition of swearing by the forefathers.
2) The command for the one to whom an oath is sworn to be pleased (or satisfied) with it.
3) The threat against whoever is not pleased (with the oath sworn by Allâh).

Chapter 43

The Statement, "What Allâh willed and (what) you willed." *

Qutaylah narrated that a Jew came to the Prophet ﷺ and said, "Verily you all commit *Shirk*. You say, 'What Allâh willed and (what) you willed', and you say, 'By the *Ka'bah*.' So the Prophet ﷺ commanded them that if they wanted to swear, they should say, 'By the Lord of the *Ka'bah*', and that they should say, 'What Allâh willed, then (what) you willed.'"

An-Nasaa'ee recorded it and he graded it authentic (*Ṣaḥeeḥ*).

He (An-Nasaa'ee) also recorded from Ibn 'Abbaas رَضِيَ اللهُ عَنْهُمَا that a man said to the Prophet ﷺ, "What Allâh willed and (what) you willed." So the Prophet ﷺ said,

«أَجَعَلْتَنِي للهِ نِدًّا؟ بَلْ مَا شَاءَ اللهُ وَحْدَهُ»

> "Have you made me a rival with Allâh? Rather, what Allâh Alone willed."[1]

Ibn Maajah recorded from Aṭ-Ṭufayl — the brother of 'Aishah رَضِيَ اللهُ عَنْهَا through her mother — that he said, "I dreamed that I came upon a group of Jews and said to them, 'Indeed you would be the people (you claim) had you not said 'Uzayr is the son of Allâh.' Then they said, 'You too would be the people (you claim) if you did not say: What Allâh willed and

---

* This (statement) is *Shirk* in wording and it is associating partners in will, which is a form of minor *Shirk*.

[1] Qutaylah narrated that a Jew came to the Prophet ﷺ... This narration contains points of benefit: That the person who follows desires (i.e. deviation) may understand what is correct. So if he has the correct understanding (in a matter), it is obligatory to accept it from him, because it is mandatory for the Muslim to accept the truth from whoever brings it, even if he is a Jew or a Christian.

He (An-Nasaa'ee) also recorded from Ibn 'Abbaas رَضِيَ اللهُ عَنْهُمَا that a man said...

(what) Muhammad willed.' Then I passed by a group of Christians and said to them, 'You would be the people (you claim) had you not said Christ is the son of Allâh.' Then they said, 'You too would be the people (you claim) if you did not say, 'What Allâh willed and (what) Muhammad willed.' When I awoke the following morning I narrated the above dream to some people, and then I came to the Prophet ﷺ and narrated it to him. He asked, 'Have you told this to anybody else?' I said, 'Yes.' Then he praised and glorified Allâh and said, 'To proceed: Verily Ṭufayl saw a dream, which he has already told some of you. You used to say a statement, which I was prevented by such-and-such from prohibiting you from. So (henceforth), do not say, 'What Allâh willed and (what) Muhammad willed', but say, 'What Allâh Alone willed.'''[1]

---

[1] Ibn Maajah recorded from Aṭ-Ṭufayl — the brother of 'Aishah رَضِيَ الله عَنْهَا through her mother — that he said, "I dreamed that I came upon a group of Jews and said to them, 'Indeed you would be the people (you claim) had you not said 'Uzayr is the son of Allâh.' Then they said, 'You too would be the people (you claim) if you did not say: What Allâḥ willed and (what) Muhammad willed.''' This contains the point that the person of desires (i.e. deviation) or the person who follows the false religion may refute the follower of the truth in that he also has some falsehood, just as he has falsehood. If the person (who is a follower of truth) is faced with that, he must submit to the truth. He must not reject the truth simply because the person who brings it is follower of falsehood. These matters (mentioned in this narration) are from the minor *Shirk* and this is alluded to by his statement at the end of the narration, "You used to say a statement, which I was prevented by such-and-such from prohibiting you from." *Ash-Shirk* in words comes in different stages (depending upon people's level of understanding). However, the major *Shirk* is negated from the beginning of the Message (Islam). It is not permissible to delay its rejection. However, concerning the *Shirk* in words, it may be for a benefit - such as understanding the propagation (*Fiqh ud-Da'wah*) and understanding the order of importance - that some of it may be delayed in order to complete the greater benefit. In reference to the major *Shirk*, no benefit remains with its presence.

Important issues of the Chapter

1) The Jews awareness of minor *Shirk*.
2) The person's understanding if he has a desire.
3) The Prophet's statement,

«أَجَعلْتَنِي للهِ ندًّا؟»

"Have you made me a rival with Allâh?"

So how about the person who says,

"O *Imaam* (leader) of the Messengers, O my support,
You are the door of Allâh and my reliance,
In my worldly affairs and my hereafter,
O Messenger of Allâh, take my hand,
No difficulty seems easy to me,
Except by you, O crown of the existence."

4) That this (saying as Allâh and Muhammad willed) is not from the major *Shirk* due to the Prophet's statement, "I was prevented by such-and-such."
5) That the righteous dream is from the types of revelation.
6) That it is a cause of the legislation of some of the Islamic laws.

Chapter 44

Whoever Curses Time, Then He has Offended Allâh*

The Statement of Allâh the Most High,

﴿وَقَالُوا۟ مَا هِىَ إِلَّا حَيَاتُنَا ٱلدُّنْيَا نَمُوتُ وَنَحْيَا وَمَا يُهْلِكُنَآ إِلَّا ٱلدَّهْرُ﴾ الآية

"And they say, 'There is nothing but our life of this world, we die and we live, and nothing destroys us except *Ad-Dahr* (the time).'"[1] (45:24)

---

* Cursing time is from the words that are not permissible and it is obligatory to abandon such. Using such words is contrary to the completion of *At-Tauhid*, and this occurs often with the ignorant people. For verily if something happens to them at a certain time that does not please them, they curse that time, degrade it and attribute evil to it. They will curse that day, year or month. There is no doubt that this (what occurred) is not related to the time, because time is a thing that does not act. Deeds are only done in it (time). The One Who controls it and decrees it is Allâh, so therefore, the person who curses it is actually offending Allâh. Cursing time is in differing levels, the highest of which is to actually curse the time. It is not considered cursing time to describe the years as difficult or to describe the day as black (i.e. dreary, sad), or the months as unfortunate, and similar statements. The reason is that this is restricted, meaning this is the day that he (the person) was unfortunate, or this is the day that he was bleak or dismal. Thus, the meaning of this is to describe what happened in that time, and that from his description was such-and-such, meaning this person who is speaking. So actually, he is describing his condition and he is not describing the time with praise or reviling.

[1] The Statement of Allâh the Most High,

﴿مَا هِىَ إِلَّا حَيَاتُنَا ٱلدُّنْيَا نَمُوتُ وَنَحْيَا وَمَا يُهْلِكُنَآ إِلَّا ٱلدَّهْرُ﴾

"And they say, 'There is nothing but our life of this world, we die and we live, and nothing destroys us except *Ad-Dahr* (the time)." (45:24)

Attributing things to time is from the characteristics of the *Mushrikūn* (polytheist, idolaters), who are the enemies of *At-Tauhid*. Thus, we

In the *Ṣaḥiḥ*, Abu Hurayrah رَضِيَ اللهُ عَنْهُمَا narrated that the Prophet ﷺ said,

«قَالَ اللهُ تَعَالىٰ: يُؤْذِينِي ابْنُ آدَمَ يَسُبُّ الدَّهْرَ وَأَنَا الدَّهْرُ أُقَلِّبُ اللَّيْلَ وَالنَّهَارَ»

"Allâh the Most High said, 'The son of Aadam offends Me. He curses time and I am *Ad-Dahr* (the Time). I turn the night and the day.'"

In another narration (he said),

«لَا تَسُبُّوا الدَّهْرَ، فَإِنَّ اللهَ هُوَ الدَّهْرُ»

"Do not curse time, for verily Allâh is *Ad-Dahr* (the Time)."[1]

---

understand from this that the characteristic of the *Muwaḥḥidoon* (people of *At-Tauhid*) is that they attribute things to Allâh, the Mighty and Majestic.

[1] In the *Ṣaḥeeḥ*, Abu Hurayrah رَضِيَ اللهُ عَنْهُ narrated that the Prophet ﷺ said,

«قَالَ اللهُ تَعَالىٰ: يُؤْذِينِي ابْنُ آدَمَ يَسُبُّ الدَّهْرَ وَأَنَا الدَّهْرُ»

"Allâh the Most High said, 'The son of Aadam offends Me. He curses time and I am *Ad-Dahr* (the Time).'"

His Statement,

«وَأَنَا الدَّهْرُ»

"I am *Ad-Dahr* (the Time)",

does not mean that *Ad-Dahr* (the Time) is from the Names of Allâh, but he arranged it (this statement) according to what came before it. Thus, he said, "He curses time and I am *Ad-Dahr* (the Time)." This is because the reality of the matter is that *Ad-Dahr* (time) does not possess anything, nor does it do anything. Therefore, cursing time is cursing Allâh, because in time Allâh does whatever He wills for a wisdom. Then he said,

«أُقَلِّبُ اللَّيْلَ وَالنَّهَارَ»

"I turn the night and the day."

The night and the day are both time, and Allâh is the One Who rotates them. Thus, they do not control anything of the affairs, and cursing them is actually cursing the One Who causes their rotation.

Important issues of the Chapter

1) The prohibition of cursing time.
2) Calling it offending Allâh.
3) Contemplation upon his statement, "For verily Allâh is *Ad-Dahr* (the Time)."
4) That a person may curse or revile even though he does not intend it in his heart.

Chapter 45

Using the Name "Judge of Judges"*

In the *Ṣaḥeeḥ*, Abu Hurayrah رَضِيَ اللهُ عَنْهُ narrated that the Prophet ﷺ said,

«إِنَّ أَخْنَعَ اسْمٍ عِنْدَ اللهِ رَجُلٌ تَسَمَّىٰ مَلِكَ الْأَمْلَاكِ، لَا مَالِكَ إِلَّا اللهُ»

"Verily the most awful name with Allâh is a man who names himself king of kings. There is no king except Allâh."[1]

---

* The Shaikh draws attention to the fact that using names that have meanings that are only for Allâh is not permissible. *At-Tauhid* necessitates that none should be described with these names except Allâh, and none should be given these names except Allâh.

[1] In the *Ṣaḥeeḥ*, Abu Hurayrah رَضِيَ اللهُ عَنْهُ narrated that the Prophet ﷺ said,

«إِنَّ أَخْنَعَ»

"Verily the most awful",

meaning the lowest and the most disgraceful. Then he continued,

«اسْمٍ عِنْدَ اللهِ رَجُلٌ تَسَمَّىٰ مَلِكَ الْأَمْلَاكِ»

"name with Allâh is a man who names himself king of kings. There is no king except Allâh." This is for restriction.

«لَا مَالِكَ إِلَّا اللهُ»

"There is no king except Allâh",

means the true king is only Allâh Alone. This contains the sin of naming the person with what is exclusively for Allâh. For verily the One Who possesses the kings is Allâh. The kings are numerous. The human being is only described as being the king of something specific and he is not a king of everything. Likewise, is dominion (*Al-Mulk*), which is the execution of authority, domination and supremacy. For verily it is in some parts of the earth and it is not in all of the earth. Thus, the one who owns is called a king if he owns a possession, or he is called a king if he possesses a dominion, which means execution of authority. Thus, the king is attached

Sufyaan said, "This is like the title *Shaahaan Shaah.*"

In another version he (the Prophet ﷺ) said,

«أَغْيَظُ رَجُلٍ عَلَى اللهِ يَوْمَ الْقِيَامَةِ وَأَخْبَثُهُ»

"The man that Allâh is most angry with on the Day of Judgement and the most despicable man..."

His saying *Akhna'* means the lowest.[1]

Important issues of the Chapter

1) The prohibition of using the name king of kings.
2) That anything that has its meaning is like it, just as Sufyaan said.
3) Unerstanding the gravity of this matter and similar matters, even though it may be certain that the heart does not intend its meaning.
4) Understanding that this is due to reverence of Allâh.

---

to his place, and hence, it is said, "He is the king of such-and-such country, or the king of such-and-such, and so forth. However, the absolute, comprehensive title king of kings, this is only Allâh. Thus, *At-Tauhid* necessitates that no one takes this name, nor should anyone be pleased with being named this name. Even if you find this in some of the books, do not convey it as you found it.

[1] Sufyaan said, "This is like the title *Shaahaan Shaah.*" In another version he (the Prophet ﷺ) said, "The man that Allâh is most angry with on the Day of Judgement and the most despicable man..."

The cause of him being the one whom Allâh is most angry with, and the most despicable man is that in reality he made himself similar to Allâh by using this name.

Chapter 46

Respecting the Names of Allâh and Changing One's Name for the Sake of that*

It is narrated from Abu Shurayḥ that he was given the *Kunyah* (nickname) Abul-Ḥakam, so the Prophet ﷺ said to him,

«إِنَّ اللهَ هُوَ الْحَكَمُ وَإِلَيْهِ الْحُكْمُ»

"Verily Allâh is Al-Ḥakam (the Judge) and the judgement is for Him."

He (Abu Shurayḥ) said, "Verily whenever my people differed in anything they would come to me, and I would judge between them and both parties would be pleased." The Prophet ﷺ said,

«مَا أَحْسَنَ هَذَا! فَمَالَكَ مِنَ الْوَلَدِ؟»

"How excellent this is! Do you have any children?"

He replied, "Shurayḥ, Muslim and 'Abdullah." The Prophet ﷺ said, "Who is the oldest of them?" I said, "Shurayḥ." He said,

«فَأَنْتَ أَبُو شُرَيْحٍ»

"Then you are Abu Shurayḥ."

Abu Dâwûd and others recorded it.[1]

---

* This chapter contains guidance to the conduct with Allâh that must emanate from the heart of the person who believes in *At-Tauhid* and his tongue. This respect may be recommended and it may also be obligatory. The respect for these Names (of Allâh) is that they should not be misused, nor should anyone other than Him be described with them.

[1] It is narrated from Abu Shurayh that he was given the *Kunyah* (nickname) Abul-Ḥakam. Al-Ḥakam is one of the Names of Allâh and Allâh does not give birth nor is He born. Therefore, his (Abu Shurayḥ) using the nickname Abul-Ḥakam (Father of the Judge) is not appropriate.

From another angle, Al-Ḥakam - which means achieving the ultimate perfection in judgement - contains the meaning of making a decision between litigants, and this goes back to whoever possesses the authority of judgement, Who is Allâh. The human being may be a judge on a subordinate level only. For this reason, the Prophet ﷺ refused to allow him to use this name. So the Prophet ﷺ said to him,

«إِنَّ اللهَ هُوَ الْحَكَمُ»

"Verily Allâh is Al-Ḥakam (the Judge)."

In the Arabic the pronoun *Huwa* (he) is used and it is a supporting pronoun (*Dhameer 'Imaad*) or a pronoun of distinction (*Dhameer Faṣl*) and it is not subject to the rules of *Al-I'raab* (the change that takes place at the end of some 'Arabic words based upon grammar usage). Its purpose is that it is made specific by the first (noun that preceded it). Then the Prophet ﷺ said, "and the judgement is for Him." This means that the judgement is for Him and no one else. For this reason the word *Al-Ḥukm* (the judgement), which means to all of the characteristics of judgement, is not for anyone other than Allâh. Then that man (Abu Shurayḥ) gave his reason and he said, "Verily whenever my people differed in anything they would come to me, and I would judge between them and both parties would be pleased." The Prophet ﷺ said, "How excellent this is!" Meaning rectifying matters between litigants. Then there is the question, did he judge between them according to the Islamic Law or did he judge between them according to his opinion? The answer is that he judged between them according to his opinion. So the Prophet ﷺ said, "How excellent this is! Do you have any children?" He replied, "Shurayḥ, Muslim and 'Abdullah." The Prophet ﷺ said, "Who is the oldest of them?" I said, "Shurayḥ." He said, "Then you are Abu Shurayḥ." For this reason we say that it is from proper etiquette that no one is called Al-Ḥakam, or Al-Ḥaakim or similar names, except if it is for the executing the laws of Allâh. This is because such a person is judging according to the judgement of the One Who possesses the absolute judgement, Who is Allâh. Therefore, it is permissible to use that title in such a case and there is no harm in it, because Allâh describes whoever judges according to His Law as being a *Ḥaakim* (judge).

Important issues of the Chapter

1) Respecting the Attributes and Names of Allâh, even if one does not intend (by using them) the actual meaning.
2) Changing the name on account of that.
3) Choosing the eldest child's name as the *Kunyah*.

Chapter 47

Whoever Makes Fun of Anything that Contains the Mention of Allâh or the Qur'ān or the Messenger*

The statement of Allâh the Most High,

﴿وَلَئِن سَأَلْتَهُمْ لَيَقُولُنَّ إِنَّمَا كُنَّا نَخُوضُ وَنَلْعَبُ﴾

"If you ask them, (about this), they declare: 'We were only talking idly and joking.'"[1] (9:65)

---

* *At-Tauhid* is submission, compliance, acceptance and honoring, and mocking and making fun of anything that contains the mention of Allâh or the Qur'ān or the Messenger is opposed to this because it is contrary to honoring. For this reason it is major disbelief in Allâh, however with its principle condition, which is that mocking - degrading, making fun and teasing - is at Allâh or His Messenger or the Qur'ān. If the mocking is at the religion, then that is excluded from this, as mocking the religion contains different classifications. Is the intent of the mocking actually the religion of Islam? If so, then this is disbelief (*Kufr*). It could be that this reviler, or curser or mocker of the religion intends the religious (practice) of the person who is being mocked and he does not fundamentally mean to mock the Islamic religion. In this case his mocking is not directed at one of the three (Allâh, the Qur'ān or Allâh's Messenger ﷺ).

[1] The Statement of Allâh the Most High,

﴿وَلَئِن سَأَلْتَهُمْ لَيَقُولُنَّ إِنَّمَا كُنَّا نَخُوضُ وَنَلْعَبُ قُلْ أَبِاللَّهِ وَءَايَٰتِهِۦ وَرَسُولِهِۦ كُنتُمْ تَسْتَهْزِءُونَ ۝ لَا تَعْتَذِرُوا۟ قَدْ كَفَرْتُم بَعْدَ إِيمَٰنِكُمْ﴾

"If you ask them they will certainly say, 'We were only talking idly and joking.' Say, 'Was it at Allâh, and His *Ayaat* and His Messenger that you were mocking? Do not make excuses. Verily you have disbelieved after your (acceptance of) faith.'" (9:65-66)

This Verse is a textual proof that the person who mocks Allâh, the Messenger and the *Ayaat* of Allâh - meaning the legislative revelations of Allâh, i.e. the Qur'ān - then this mocker is a disbeliever (*Kaafir*) and his making excuses that he was just joking and playing does not benefit him.

Ibn 'Umar, Muhammad bin Ka'b, Zayd bin Aslam, Qataadah - they all had input in the narration of this *Hadith* - narrated that a man said during the expedition of Tabuk, "We have not seen the likes of these reciters of ours. They have the greatest appetites, the most lying tongues, and they are the most cowardly when meeting the enemy." They were referring to Allâh's Messenger ﷺ and his reciting Companions. 'Awf bin Maalik said to him, "You have lied; rather you are a hypocrite. I will certainly inform Allâh's Messenger ﷺ." So 'Awf went to Allâh's Messenger ﷺ to inform him, but he found that the Qur'ān had preceded him (i.e. Allâh already had revealed Verses about it to the Prophet ﷺ). Then that man came to Allâh's Messenger ﷺ who had already mounted his she camel and was riding it. He said, "O Messenger of Allâh, we were only talking idly and speaking the talk of riding so that we could overcome the weariness along the way." Ibn 'Umar رضي الله عنهما said, "It is as if I can still see him now clinging to the saddle strap of Allâh's Messenger ﷺ she camel and the stones were striking his feet while he was saying, 'We were only talking idly and joking.' So Allâh's Messenger ﷺ said to him,

﴿أَبِٱللَّهِ وَءَايَٰتِهِۦ وَرَسُولِهِۦ كُنتُمْ تَسْتَهْزِءُونَ﴾

'Was it at Allâh and His *Ayaat* (proofs, evidences, verses, signs, revelations, etc.) and His Messenger that you were mocking.?'

Important issues of the Chapter

1) It is the major issue, and it is that whoever mocks in this manner then he is a disbeliever (*Kaafir*).

Verily he is a disbeliever (*Kaafir*). This Verse was revealed concerning the hypocrites. In reference to the people of *At-Tauhid*, this basically does not come from them.

2) That this is the explanation of the Verse concerning whoever does this, whoever he may be.
3) The difference between *An-Nameemah* (tale-carrying, gossiping) and *An-Naṣeeḥah* (sincerity) to Allâh and His Messenger.
4) The difference between the pardoning that Allâh loves and harshness against the enemies of Allâh.
5) That there are excuses that should not be accepted.

Chapter 48

The Statement of Allâh the Most High,

﴿وَلَئِنْ أَذَقْنَٰهُ رَحْمَةً مِّنَّا مِنۢ بَعْدِ ضَرَّآءَ مَسَّتْهُ لَيَقُولَنَّ هَٰذَا لِى﴾ الآية

"And truly, if We give him taste of mercy from Us, after some adversity has touched him, he is sure to say, 'This due to my (merit).'" (41:50)

Mujâhid said, "(Meaning) this is due to by works and I deserve it."[1]

Ibn 'Abbâs رَضِيَ اللهُ عَنْهُمَا said, "He means from myself."

And the Statement of Allâh,

﴿قَالَ إِنَّمَآ أُوتِيتُهُۥ عَلَىٰ عِلْمٍ عِندِىٓ﴾

"He (Qaaroon) said, 'I have only been given this (vast wealth) due to knowledge that I possess.'" (28:78)

Qataadah said, "(Meaning) due to knowledge that I possess of the different methods of earning."

Others said, "(Meaning) due to knowledge from Allâh that I deserve." This is the meaning of the statement of Mujâhid,

---

[1] Mujâhid said, "(Meaning) this is due to by works and I deserve it." This means that he was deserving of that and that Allâh did not favor him with this thing, or He favored him with it because he deserved this favoring. Two kinds of people are included in this description that has been mentioned in the Verse: the person who attributes something to himself and he basically does not attribute it to Allâh. The second is the person attributes something to himself from the aspect of deserving and that he sees himself as deserving that thing from Allâh, as occurs with some of those who have been deceived. The action of the slave is a means and this means differs. It may be effective by the permission of Allâh, and thus, the matter goes back to the fact that it is the bounty of Allâh that He gives to whomever He wishes.

"(Meaning) I have been given it due to (my) nobility."[1]

Abu Hurayrah رَضِيَ اللهُ عَنْهُ narrated that he heard Allâh's Messenger ﷺ saying,

«إِنَّ ثَلَاثَةً مِنْ بَنِي إِسْرَائِيلَ: أَبْرَصَ وَأَقْرَعَ وَأَعْمَىٰ، فَأَرَادَ اللهُ أَنْ يَبْتَلِيَهُمْ، فَبَعَثَ إِلَيْهِمْ مَلَكًا فَأَتَى الْأَبْرَصَ فقَالَ: أَيُّ شَيْءٍ أَحَبُّ إِلَيْكَ؟ قَالَ: لَوْنٌ حَسَنٌ، وَجِلْدٌ حَسَنٌ، وَيَذْهَبُ عَنِّي الَّذِي قَدْ قَذِرَنِي النَّاسُ بِهِ، قَالَ فَمَسَحَهُ فَذَهَبَ عَنْهُ قَذَرُهُ، وَأُعْطِيَ لَوْنًا حَسَنًا وَجِلْدًا حَسَنًا. قَالَ: فَأَيُّ الْمَالِ أَحَبُّ إِلَيْكَ؟ قَالَ: الْإِبِلُ أَوِ الْبَقَرُ - شَكَّ إِسْحَاقُ - فَأُعْطِيَ نَاقَةً عُشَرَاءَ، وَقَالَ: بَارَكَ اللهُ لَكَ فِيهَا. قَالَ: فَأَتَى الْأَقْرَعَ فقَالَ: أَيُّ شَيْءٍ أَحَبُّ إِلَيْكَ؟ قَالَ: شَعْرٌ حَسَنٌ، وَيَذْهَبُ عَنِّي الَّذِي قَدْ قَذِرَنِي النَّاسُ بِهِ، قَالَ: فَمَسَحَهُ فَذَهَبَ عَنْهُ، وَأُعْطِيَ شَعْرًا حَسَنًا وَجِلْدًا حَسَنًا، قَالَ: أَيُّ الْمَالِ أَحَبُّ إِلَيْكَ؟ قَالَ: الْبَقَرُ - أَوِ الْإِبِلُ - فَأُعْطِيَ بَقَرَةً حَامِلًا، وَقَالَ: بَارَكَ اللهُ لَكَ فِيهَا. فَأَتَى الْأَعْمَىٰ فَقَالَ: أَيُّ شَيْءٍ أَحَبُّ إِلَيْكَ؟ قَالَ: أَنْ يَرُدَّ اللهُ إِلَيَّ بَصَرِي فَأُبْصِرَ النَّاسَ، فَمَسَحَهُ فَرَدَّ اللهُ إِلَيْهِ بَصَرَهُ، قَالَ: فَأَيُّ الْمَالِ أَحَبُّ إِلَيْكَ؟ قَالَ: الْغَنَمُ، فَأُعْطِيَ شَاةً وَالِدًا، فَأُنْتِجَ هَذَانِ وَوَلَّدَ هَذَا، فَكَانَ لِهَٰذَا وَادٍ مِنَ الْإِبِلِ، وَلِهَٰذَا وَادٍ مِنَ الْبَقَرِ، وَلِهَٰذَا وَادٍ مِنَ الْغَنَمِ. قَالَ: ثُمَّ إِنَّهُ أَتَى الْأَبْرَصَ فِي صُورَتِهِ وَهَيْئَتِهِ فَقَالَ: رَجُلٌ مِسْكِينٌ وَابْنُ سَبِيلٍ قَدِ انْقَطَعَتْ بِيَ الْحِبَالُ فِي سَفَرِي فَلَا بَلَاغَ لِيَ الْيَوْمَ إِلَّا بِاللهِ ثُمَّ

[1] And the Statement of Allâh, "He (Qaaroon) said, 'I have only been given this (vast wealth) due to knowledge that I possess.'' (28:78) Qataadah said, "(Meaning) due to knowledge that I possess of the different methods of earning.'' This happens to many people from those whom Allâh has enriched and they have begun making tremendous business. Such a person attributes something to himself and says, "I have knowledge of the different methods of earning'', and similar statements, or if he is given a position (job), he says, "This is due to my efforts.''

بِكَ، أَسْأَلُكَ - بِالَّذِي أَعْطَاكَ اللَّوْنَ الْحَسَنَ وَالْجِلْدَ الْحَسَنَ وَالْمَالَ - بَعِيرًا أَتَبَلَّغُ بِهِ فِي سَفَرِي، فَقَالَ: الْحُقُوقُ كَثِيرَةٌ فَقَالَ لَهُ: كَأَنِّي أَعْرِفُكَ، أَلَمْ تَكُنْ أَبْرَصَ يَقْذَرُكَ النَّاسُ، فَقِيرًا فَأَعْطَاكَ اللهُ عَزَّ وَجَلَّ الْمَالَ؟ فَقَالَ: إِنَّما وَرِثْتُ هَذَا الْمَالَ كَابِرًا عَنْ كَابِرٍ، فَقَالَ: إِنْ كُنْتَ كَاذِبًا فَصَيَّرَكَ اللهُ إِلَىٰ مَا كُنْتَ، قَالَ: ثُمَّ إِنَّهُ أَتَى الْأَقْرَعَ فِي صُورَتِهِ فَقَالَ لَهُ مِثْلَ مَا قَالَ لِهٰذَا، وَرَدَّ عَلَيْهِ مِثْلَ مَا رَدَّ عَلَيْهِ هَذَا، فَقَالَ: إِنْ كُنْتَ كَاذِبًا فَصَيَّرَكَ اللهُ إِلَىٰ مَا كُنْتَ، قَالَ: وَأَتَى الْأَعْمَىٰ فِي صُورَتِهِ فَقَالَ: رَجُلٌ مِسْكِينٌ وَابْنُ سَبِيلٍ، قَدِ انْقَطَعَتْ بِيَ الْحِبَالُ فِي سَفَرِي فَلَا بَلَاغَ لِيَ الْيَوْمَ إِلَّا بِاللهِ ثُمَّ بِكَ، أَسْأَلُكَ بِالَّذِي رَدَّ عَلَيْكَ بَصَرَكَ شَاةً أَتَبَلَّغُ بِهَا فِي سَفَرِي، فَقَالَ: قَدْ كُنْتُ أَعْمَىٰ فَرَدَّ اللهُ إِلَيَّ بَصَرِي، فَخُذْ مَا شِئْتَ، وَدَعْ مَا شِئْتَ فَوَاللهِ لَا أَجْهَدُكَ الْيَوْمَ بِشَيْءٍ أَخَذْتَهُ للهِ، فَقَالَ: أَمْسِكْ مَالَكَ، فَإِنَّمَا ابْتُلِيتُمْ فَقَدْ رَضِيَ اللهُ عَنْكَ وَسَخِطَ عَلَىٰ صَاحِبَيْكَ»

"Verily there were three (men) from the Children of Israel - a leper, a bald man and a blind man - whom Allâh wanted to test. So He sent an angel to them. The angel came to the leper and said, 'What thing do you like the most?' He replied, 'A nice color, nice skin and that this, which has caused the people to have an aversion to me, leaves me.' So the angel touched him and his disgusting disease left him, and he was given a nice color and nice skin. The angel said, 'Which wealth do you like the most?' He said, 'Camels or cows' - the narrator, Isḥaaq was uncertain - so he was given a pregnant she-camel. Then the angel said, 'May Allâh bless you in her.' Then the angel came to the bald man and said, 'What thing do you like the most?' He replied, 'Nice hair and that this, which has caused the people to have an aversion to me, leaves me.' So the angel touched him and it (his baldness) left him, and he was given beautiful hair beautiful hair. The angel said, 'Which wealth do you like the most?' He said, 'Cows or camels.' So he was given a pregnant cow. Then the angel said, 'May Allâh bless you in her." Then the angel came to the blind man and he said, 'What thing do you like the most?' He replied, 'That Allâh returns my sight to me so that I can see the people.' So the angel touched him and Allâh returned his sight to him. Then the angel said, 'Which wealth do you like the most?' He said, 'Sheep.' So he was given a pregnant sheep. Afterwards, these two (the camel and the cow) gave birth and this (sheep) gave birth. This man had a valley full of camels, this one had a valley full of cows, and this one had a valley full of sheep. Then the angel came to the leper in his (previous) form and shape (i.e. as a leper) and said, 'I am a poor man and a wayfarer, and I have lost all of my wealth on my journey. There is no way for me to reach my destination today except by Allâh and then you. I ask you by the One Who gave you the beautiful color, beautiful skin and wealth, to give me a single camel by which I may reach my destination on my journey.' The man said, 'I have many obligations.' So the angel said to him, 'I think I know you. Weren't you a leper whom the people used to avoid? Weren't you poor and then Allâh gave you wealth?' The man replied, 'I only inherited this wealth from my forefathers.' The angel said, 'If you are lying, may Allâh make you the way that you were.' Then the angel went to the bald man in his (previous) form and he told him the same thing he told this (first man), and he responded to him in the same manner as this (first man). So the angel said, 'If you are lying, may Allâh make you the way that you were.' Then the angel went to the blind man in his (previous) form and said, 'I am a poor man and a wayfarer, and I have lost all of my wealth on my journey. There is no way for me to reach my destination today except by Allâh and then you. I ask you by the One Who returned your sight to you, to give me a single sheep by which I may reach my destination on my journey.' The man replied, 'Verily I was blind and Allâh returned my sight to me, so take whatever you wish and leave what you wish. By Allâh, I will not stop you from taking anything today that you take for Allâh's sake.' The angel said, 'Keep your wealth, for verily you all have only been tested, and Allâh is pleased with you and angry with your two companions.'"[1]

They (Al-Bukhari and Muslim) both recorded it.

Important issues of the Chapter

1) The explanation of the Verse [*Surah Al-Fuṣṣilat* (41:50)].
2) What is the meaning of,

﴿لَيَقُولَنَّ هَٰذَا لِي﴾

"He is sure to say, 'This is for me (due to my merit).'" (41:50)

---

[1] Then he brings the lengthy *Hadith* of Abu Hurayrah رَضِيَ اللهُ عَنْهُ and the implication of it is obvious. So that Allâh cured these people, but when he cured them, two of them attributed the favor to themselves and the third attributed it to Allâh. Thus, Allâh rewarded the last one with good and made his favor last for him, and He punished the sinfulness of the two men. This is the bounty of Allâh that He favors with, then He affirms the favor for whomever He wills and removes it from whomever He wills. From the causes of securing the favor is that the slave magnifies his Lord, knows that the bounty is in the Hand of Allâh and that the favor is the favor of Allâh. The perfection of *At-Tauhid* is that the slave knows that he is in need of Allâh and he is not deserving of anything from Allâh. Rather, Allâh is the Lord, Who deserves to be worshipped, thanked and honored by His slaves. He deserves that they remember Him and attribute favors to Him.

3) What is the meaning of His Statement,

﴿إِنَّمَآ أُوتِيتُهُۥ عَلَىٰ عِلْمٍ عِندِىٓ﴾

"I have only been given this (vast wealth) due to knowledge that I possess." (28:78)

4) What great lessons this wonderful story contains.

Chapter 49

The Statement of Allâh the Most High,

﴿فَلَمَّآ ءَاتَىٰهُمَا صَٰلِحًا جَعَلَا لَهُۥ شُرَكَآءَ فِيمَآ ءَاتَىٰهُمَا فَتَعَٰلَى ٱللَّهُ عَمَّا يُشْرِكُونَ﴾

"But when He gave them a *Ṣâliḥ* (good in every aspect) child, they ascribed partners with Him (Allâh) in that which He had given to them. High is Allâh, Exalted above all that they ascribe as partners to Him." (7:190)

Ibn Hazm said, "They (the scholars) have agreed upon the forbiddance of every name that insinuates worship of other than Allâh, like 'Abdu 'Amr (slave of 'Amr), 'Abdul-Ka'bah (slave of the *Ka'bah*) and names similar to that, except 'Abdul-Muṭṭalib."[1]

---

[1] Ibn Hazm said, "They (the scholars) have agreed upon the forbiddance of every name that insinuates worship of other than Allâh, like 'Abdu 'Amr (slave of 'Amr), 'Abdul-Ka'bah (slave of the *Ka'bah*) and names similar to that, except 'Abdul-Muṭṭalib."

Ibn Hazm's statement "They have agreed", means that the people of knowledge have reached a consensus - as far as he knew - that names insinuating worshipping of other than Allâh is forbidden. Rather, it is forbidden in the Laws of all of the Prophets, because it contains the attributing of favors to other than Allâh. It also contains ill manners (i.e. disrespect) with Allâh in reference to Lordship (*Ruboobiyyah*) and Worship (*Ilaahiyyah*). People's using names that insinuate worship of other than Allâh is also despised in reference to meaning. His Statement, "except 'Abdul-Muṭṭalib", means that they have not agreed upon it. For verily there are among the people of knowledge those who said, "It is disliked to use the name 'Abdul-Muṭṭalib and it is not forbidden." However, this statement is not correct. That which they use as a proof concerning it is not acceptable. That is because the Prophet's statement (that they use as a proof),

«أَنَا النَّبِيُّ لَا كَذِبْ أَنَا ابْنُ عَبْدِ الْمُطَّلِبْ»

Ibn 'Abbâs رَضِيَ اللهُ عَنْهُمَا said concerning this Verse, "When Aadam had sexual intercourse with her (Eve), she became pregnant. Then Iblees (Satan) came to them and said, 'I am your companion who got you all put out of Paradise. Obey me, otherwise I will cause him (your child) to have two horns like a deer, and he will come out of your womb and tear it up! I will do it! I will do it!' Thus, he frightened them (Aadam and Eve) and he told them to name the child 'Abdul-Ḥaarith. However, they refused to obey him and the baby came out dead. Then she became pregnant again and he came to them and said to them the same as he had said before. However, they refused to obey him and the baby came out dead. Then she became pregnant again and he came to them and he spoke to them and they were overcome by love of the child. So they named it 'Abdul-Ḥaarith. And that is Allâh's Statement,

﴿جَعَلَا لَهُۥ شُرَكَآءَ فِيمَآ ءَاتَىٰهُمَآۚ﴾

"They ascribed partners to Him (Allâh) in that which He had given them." (7:190)

Ibn Abi Ḥaatim recorded it.

"I am the Prophet, that is no lie. I am the son of 'Abdul-Muṭṭalib", is only giving information. And giving information does not contain a direct insinuation of worship simply by the addition of that created thing to other than its creator. It is only his giving information. And the matter of giving information is broader than the matter of initiating, as is well known.

In reference to some of the companions having the name 'Abdul-Muṭṭalib, the researchers among the reporters have said, "That whoever was named 'Abdul-Muṭṭalib, his correct name was Al-Muṭṭalib without the addition of the word 'Abd (implying worship). However it (the name) was merely recorded as 'Abdul-Muṭṭalib due to the usage of the name 'Abdul-Muṭṭalib being more widespread than the name Al-Muṭṭalib. Therefore, an error occurred in that."

He (Ibn Abi Ḥatim) also recorded from Qataadah with an authentic (*Ṣaḥeeḥ*) chain that he said, "They ascribed partners (to Allâh) in His obedience and not in His worship.

He (Ibn Abi Ḥatim) also recorded from Mujaahid with an authentic (*Ṣaḥeeḥ*) chain that he said concerning Allâh's Statement,

﴿لَئِنْ ءَاتَيْتَنَا صَٰلِحًا﴾

"If you give us a *Ṣaalih* (good and healthy child)." (7:189)

"They feared that the child might not be human." This meaning was also mentioned from Al-Ḥasan, Sa'eed and others.[1]

---

[1] Ibn 'Abbaas رَضِيَ اللهُ عَنْهُمَا said concerning this Verse, "When Aadam had sexual intercourse with her (Eve), she became pregnant..." That which most of the *Salaf* are upon is that this story is about Aadam and Ḥawaa' (Eve), and this is what the Shaikh has relied upon - may Allâh have mercy upon him. Concerning his statement, "*Ṣaalih*", this means in reference to his physical creation (i.e. healthy) and in reference to his being beneficial for them. The word *Shurakaa'''* (partners) is the plural of *Shareek* (partner), and the meaning of Sharikah in the Arabic language is that two people share in something. Thus, they made partners with Allâh in what He had given them. This was in their obeying Satan and naming that child 'Abdul-Ḥaarith. Al-Haarith is Iblees (Satan). This was not the first time. Verily disobedience had occurred (from them) before that just as has been mentioned in the *Hadith* that the Prophet ﷺ said,

«خَدَعَهُمَا مَرَّتَيْنِ»

"He (Satan) deceived them (Aadam and Ḥawaa') twice."

This was well known with the *Salaf*. Therefore, His Statement, "partners in that which He had given them", is from the aspect of association of partners in obedience. It is known that every disobedient person is obedient to Satan, and that every act of disobedience (sin) does not come from the slave except that there is a type of association of partners that has occurred in obedience. This does not necessitate a deficiency in the status of Aadam and Ḥawaa', nor does it necessitate *Shirk* with Allâh. It is only a

Important issues of the Chapter

1) The forbiddance of every name that insinuates worship of other than Allâh.
2) The explanation of the verse [*Surah Al-A'raaf* (7:190)].
3) That this was only *Shirk* in name and the actual *Shirk* is not what is meant.
4) That Allâh's gift of a healthy girl to a man is among his favors.
5) The *Salaf's* mentioning of the difference between *Ash-Shirk* in obedience and *Ash-Shirk* in worship.

---

type of giving a share (association) in obedience. The minor sins were allowed to the Prophets, as is known among the people of knowledge. This is because they do not remain upon them. Rather they make haste to turn to Allâh, and their condition (of piety) after the sin become greater than their condition before. This is a matter that is known with the people of knowledge. *Ash-Shirk* here means association (giving a share) in obedience and not minor *Shirk*, may Allâh forbid that for them.

Chapter 50

The Statement of Allâh the Most High,*

﴿وَلِلَّهِ ٱلْأَسْمَآءُ ٱلْحُسْنَىٰ فَٱدْعُوهُ بِهَا ۖ وَذَرُوا۟ ٱلَّذِينَ يُلْحِدُونَ فِىٓ أَسْمَٰٓئِهِۦ ۚ﴾ الآية

"And (all) the Most Beautiful Names belong to Allâh, so call on Him by them, and leave the company of those who belie or deny His Names." (7:180)

Ibn Abi Ḥâtim mentioned that Ibn 'Abbâs رَضِيَ اللهُ عَنْهُمَا said,

﴿يُلْحِدُونَ فِىٓ أَسْمَٰٓئِهِۦ ۚ﴾

---

* The Statement of Allâh the Most High,

﴿وَلِلَّهِ ٱلْأَسْمَآءُ ٱلْحُسْنَىٰ فَٱدْعُوهُ بِهَا ۖ وَذَرُوا۟ ٱلَّذِينَ يُلْحِدُونَ فِىٓ أَسْمَٰٓئِهِۦ ۚ﴾

"And (all) the Most Beautiful Names belong to Allâh, so call on Him by them, and leave the company of those who belie or deny His Names." (7:180)

"And (all) the most Beautiful Names belong to Allâh." The letter *Laam* here in His Statement "to Allâh" is the *Laam* of *Istiḥqaaq* (deserving or having the right). It means that the most Beautiful Names that are the most extensive in goodness are rightfully for Allâh and Allâh deserves that. Then He said, "so call on Him by them." This is a command, and supplication here is interpreted as praise and worship. Thus, we worship Him seeking a means to Him by these Beautiful Names and what they contain of Lofty Attributes. It is also interpreted as meaning asking and requesting. This means that if we have a request, we direct it to Allâh and we ask Him by these Names according to what agrees with the requested thing. Both of these interpretations are correct. The letter *Baa'* in His Statement "by them" is the *Baa'* of *Waseelah* (means or mediations). In other words seek a means of mediation with them. Then He said, "And leave those who make *Ilḥaad* in His Names." This means abandon. This means that it is obligatory upon the Muslim to stay away from the condition of those who make *Ilḥaad* (heresy or deviation) in the Names of Allâh. *Ilḥaad* in Allâh's Names is to incline or deviate with them away from their realities to that which is not befitting of Allâh. This *Ilḥaad* is in different levels.

"Those who make *Ilḥaad* in His Names. (7:180) "(means) those who commit *Shirk*."[1]

It is also reported from him (Ibn 'Abbâs رَضِيَ اللهُ عَنْهُمَا) that they derived the name Al-Laat from Al-Ilaah (the God) and Al-'Uzzaa from Al-'Azeez (the Most Mighty).

It is reported from Al-A'mash that he said, they included in them (the Names of Allâh) that which was not of them.

---

[1] Ibn Abi Ḥâtim mentioned that Ibn 'Abbâs رَضِيَ اللهُ عَنْهُمَا said, "Those who make *Ilḥaad* in His Names." (7:180) "(Means) those who commit *Shirk*." It is also reported from him (Ibn 'Abbaas) that they derived the name Al-Laat from Al-Ilaah (the God) and Al-'Uzzaa from Al-'Azeez (the Most Mighty). It is reported from Al-A'mash that he said, they included in them (the Names of Allâh) that which was not of them. From the levels of *Ilḥaad* in Allâh's Names and Attributes is that people give the things that are worshipped the Names of Allâh. This is like the pagans naming Al-Laat (their idol) from Al-Ilaah (the God), and Al-'Uzzaa (another idol) from the name Al-'Azeez (the Most Mighty), and similar to that. From *Ilḥaad* in the Names of Allâh is that a son is attributed to Allâh, like the situation of the Christians. From Ilḥaad is to reject the Names and Attributes of Allâh, or to reject some of them, as the extreme *Jahmiyyah* sect did. Verily they do not believe in a single Name from the Names of Allâh nor a single one of His Attributes, except for existence and presence. Also from *Ilhaad* and deviating with it away from the confirmed right that is obligatory for Allâh regarding these Names, is that they are interpreted and changed from their apparent meanings to meanings that are not permissible to change them to. The principle of the *Salaf* is to believe in them and not change them from their real meanings with interpretations, or allegories or similar things. This is like what the *Mu'tazilah*, the *Ashaa'irah*, the *Maatooreediyyah* and other groups did. These are some of the types of *Ilḥaad*. If this is understood, then from *Ilḥaad* there is that which is disbelief and that which is innovation (*Bid'ah*), depending upon the situations that we have mentioned. The last situation (interpretations and changes in meaning) is innovation and *Ilḥaad* that does not take its practitioner to the level of disbelief (*Kufr*). The studies of this matter are lengthy due to their being related to the Names and Attributes (of Allâh), and this is known in the study of the Names and Attributes.

Important issues of the Chapter

1) Affirmation of the Names (of Allâh).
2) That they are Beautiful.
3) The command to supplicate with them.
4) Abandoning whoever opposes this from the ignorant deviant people.
5) The explanation of *Ilḥaad* in them (the Names of Allâh).
6) The threat against whoever makes *Ilḥaad*.

Chapter 51

The statement "*As-Salaam* (Peace and Security) be upon Allâh" Should not be Said*

It is recorded in the *Ṣaḥeeḥ* that Ibn Mas'ud رَضِيَ اللهُ عَنْهُ said, "When we were with the Prophet ﷺ in prayer we used to say, '*As-Salaam* (Peace and Security) be upon Allâh from His Slaves. *As-Salaam* (Peace and Security) be upon so-and-so and so-and-so.' Thus, the Prophet ﷺ said,

«لَا تَقُولُوا السَّلَامُ عَلَى اللهِ، فَإِنَّ اللهَ هُوَ السَّلَامُ»

'Do not say peace be upon Allâh, for verily Allâh is *As-Salaam* (the Peace).'"[1]

---

* This is because of deficiency in the realization of *At-Tauhid*. Realizing the obligatory *Tauhid* is in not saying this statement, because Allâh is truly in no need of worship, and the slaves are truly poor (needy of Him). Allâh says,

﴿يَـٰٓأَيُّهَا ٱلنَّاسُ أَنتُمُ ٱلْفُقَرَآءُ إِلَى ٱللَّهِ ۖ وَٱللَّهُ هُوَ ٱلْغَنِىُّ ٱلْحَمِيدُ﴾

"O mankind! You are in need of Allâh and Allâh is Rich (Free of all needs), Worthy of all praise." (35:15)

Therefore, they are the ones who need *As-Salaam* (Peace and Security).

[1] It is recorded in the *Ṣaḥeeḥ that Ibn Mas'ud* رَضِيَ اللهُ عَنْهُ said, "When we were with the Prophet ﷺ in prayer we used to say, '*As-Salaam* (Peace and Security) be upon Allâh from His slaves. *As-Salaam* (Peace and Security) be upon so-and-so and so-and-so.'" They said this thinking that it was a greeting and the greeting in this *Sharee'ah* (Islamic Law) is attached to the meaning. Thus, (their saying) *As-Salaam* upon Allâh from His slaves is as if they were saying, "Greetings to Allâh from His slaves." This meaning, even if it is correct in reference to its intent, it is not correct in its wording. The meaning of *As-Salaam* upon Allâh is peace and safety be upon Allâh from His slaves. There is no doubt that this is false and misconduct with what is obligatory for Allâh in His Lordship and His Names and Attributes. For this reason the Prophet ﷺ said to them, "Do not say peace be upon Allâh, for verily Allâh is *As-Salaam* (the Peace)." He prohibited them and this prohibition is for making something forbidden.

Important issues of the Chapter

1) The explanation of *As-Salaam*.
2) That it is a greeting.
3) That it is not appropriate for Allâh.
4) The reason for that.
5) The Prophet ﷺ teach them the greeting that is not appropriate for Allâh.

Chapter 52

The Person's saying, "O Allâh, forgive me if You wish."*

It is recorded in the *Saheeh* from Abu Hurayrah رَضِيَ اللهُ عَنْهُ that Allâh's Messenger ﷺ said,

«لَا يَقُلْ أَحَدُكُمْ: اللَّهُمَّ اغْفِرْ لِي إِنْ شِئْتَ، اللَّهُمَّ ارْحَمْنِي إِنْ شِئْتَ، لِيَعْزِمِ الْمَسْأَلَةَ فَإِنَّ اللهَ لَا مُكْرِهَ لَهُ»

"None of you should say, 'O Allâh, forgive me if You wish. O Allâh, have mercy upon me if You wish.' Let him ask for what he wants with determination. [1]

---

* It is understand from this statement that the speaker does not need to be forgiven. It is as if he does not want to humble himself and he is not in need. This is the deed of the people of arrogance and those who turn away from Allâh. For this reason it contains a lack of realization of *At-Tauhid* and it is contrary to what is obligatory upon the slave in reference to Allâh's Lordship. It is obligatory that the slave manifests his poverty and his need of His Lord, and that he cannot do without the forgiveness of Allâh, and He cannot do without Allâh, His pardoning, His generosity and His favor. This is the reason that the Shaikh brought the *Hadith*.

[1] It is recorded in the *Saheeh* from Abu Hurayrah رَضِيَ اللهُ عَنْهُ that Allâh's Messenger ﷺ said,

«لَا يَقُلْ أَحَدُكُمْ: اللَّهُمَّ اغْفِرْ لِي إِنْ شِئْتَ، اللَّهُمَّ ارْحَمْنِي إِنْ شِئْتَ، لِيَعْزِمِ الْمَسْأَلَةَ فَإِنَّ اللهَ لَا مُكْرِهَ لَهُ»

"None of you should say, 'O Allâh, forgive me if You wish. O Allâh, have mercy upon me if You wish. Let him ask for what he wants with determination.'"

This means that he should ask his request with determination, neediness and humility. He should not ask as one who is not in need and is arrogant. Then he said, "For verily there is none who can force Allâh." This means that no one can compel Him due to His perfect lack of need, might, dominance and power. This is from the effects of the Names and Attributes.

For verily there is none who can force Allâh."

Muslim recorded,

«وَلْيُعْظِمِ الرَّغْبَةَ، فَإِنَّ اللهَ لَا يَتَعَاظَمُهُ شَيْءٌ أَعْطَاهُ»

"And one should have great hope (in asking), for verily nothing that Allâh gives too much for Him."[1]

Important issues of the Chapter

1) The prohibition of making a statement of exception (i.e. if You wish) in supplication.
2) Clarifying the reason for that.
3) The Prophet's statement, "Let him ask for what he wants with determination."
4) Increasing the hopes for what is desired (in asking Allâh).
5) (The Prophet's ﷺ) giving the reason for this command.

[1] Muslim recorded, "And one should have great hope (in asking), for verily nothing that Allâh gives is too much for Him." In reference to the Prophet's saying, "It (the illness) is a purification if Allâh wills." This is basically not a supplication, but it is a form of informing. It means, "The sickness will be a purification if Allâh wills." Thus, it is separate from the fundamental of beseeching.

Chapter 53

The Person's Should not Say, "My male slave (*'Abdee*) or my female slave (*Amatee*)." *

It is recorded in the *Ṣaḥeeḥ* from Abu Hurayrah رَضِيَ اللهُ عَنْهُ that Allâh's Messenger ﷺ said,

«لَا يَقُل أَحَدُكُمْ: أَطْعِمْ رَبَّكَ، وَضِّىءْ رَبَّكَ وَلْيَقُلْ: سَيِّدِي ومَوْلَايَ وَلَا يَقُلْ أَحَدُكُمْ: عَبْدِي وَأَمَتِي، وَلْيَقُلْ: فَتَايَ وَفَتَاتِي وَغُلَامِي»

"None of you should say, 'Feed your lord (*Rabbaka*)' and 'help your lord perform ablution.' Rather, he should say, 'My master (*Sayyidee*) or my guardian (*Mawlaayaa*).' And none of you should say, 'My male slave ('Abdee)' and 'My female slave (*Amatee*).' Let him say (instead), My young man (*Fataaya*), my young lady (*Fataatee*) and my boy (*Ghulaamee*).''' [1]

---

* The reason for the prohibition is that the servitude of the human being for Allâh is true servitude, either by force or by choice. This is obvious because He is the Lord and the Controller. Thus, the man's statement to his bondsman (slave), "This is my slave ('Abdee) and this is my female slave (Amatee)", contains ascribing servitude to himself. This is contrary to the completion of the obligatory etiquette with Allâh, and it is contrary to honoring Allâh's Lordship and making the servitude of the creation for Allâh. For this reason, this wording is not permissible according to many of the people of knowledge, and it is disliked according to other groups (of scholars).

[1] It is recorded in the *Ṣaḥeeḥ* from Abu Hurayrah رَضِيَ اللهُ عَنْهُ that Allâh's Messenger ﷺ said,

«لَا يَقُلْ أَحَدُكُمْ: أَطْعِمْ رَبَّكَ وَضِّىءْ رَبَّكَ»

"None of you should say, 'Feed your lord (*Rabbaka*)' and 'help your lord perform ablution.'''

The people of knowledge have differed concerning this prohibition in this

Important issues of the Chapter

1) The prohibition of saying, "My male slave (*'Abdee*) and my female slave (*Amatee*)."
2) The slave should not say to his master, "My lord (*Rabbee*)", and it should not be said to him, "Feed your lord (*Rabbaka*)."
3) Teaching the first (the master) to say, "My young man

Hadith. Some of them said that it is for forbiddance and others said that it is a prohibition suggesting dislike. This is because it is an aspect of etiquette. The correct view is that it is not permissible for someone to say my slave (*'Abdee*) and my slave woman (*Amatee*), or feed your lord (*Rabbaka*) and so forth. In reference to attaching lordship to one who is not responsible, such as saying the lord of the house (*Rabb ud-Daar*), there is no problem with that. This is because the true servitude is not envisioned in that. Then he said, "Rather, he should say,

«وَلْيَقُلْ : سَيِّدِي وَمَوْلَايَ»

'My master (*Sayyidee*) or my guardian (*Mawlaayaa*).'"

Mastership - even though Allâh is the Master - when used in attached possessive case, there is no harm in it. This is because the human being has mastership that is appropriate for him. However, Allâh has the complete mastery over all of His creations. Concerning the statement *Mawlaayaa*, the word *Mawlaa* has many different meanings, and addressing a person with the saying *Mawlaayaa* has been allowed by a group of the people of knowledge based upon this *Hadith*. The correct view is that it is permissible to use the expression *Mawlaayaa* (my guardian), and *Sayyidee* (my master) and similar statements for people, because mastery here is mastery and guardianship that is appropriate for humans. Thus, these expressions do not hold the status of the titles *Rabbaka* (your Lord), *'Abdee* (my slave) or *Amatee* (my slave woman). Then he said,

«وَلَا يَقُلْ أَحَدُكُمْ : عَبْدِي وَأَمَتِي، وَلْيَقُلْ : فَتَايَ وَفَتَاتِي وَغُلَامِي»

"And none of you should say, 'My male slave (*'Abdee*)' and 'My female slave (*Amatee*).' Let him say (instead), 'My young man (*Fataaya*), my young lady (*Fataatee*) and my boy (*Ghulaamee*).'"

(*Fataaya*), my young lady (*Fataatee*) and my boy (*Ghulaamee*)."

4) Teaching the second (the slave) to say, "My master (*Sayyidee*) and my guardian (*Mawlaayaa*)."

5) Drawing attention to the intent, which is the realization of *At-Tauhid* even in the expressions.

Chapter 54

Whoever Asks by Allâh Should not be Denied*

Ibn 'Umar رَضِيَ اللهُ عَنْهُ narrated that Allâh's Messenger ﷺ said,

«مَنِ اسْتَعَاذَ بِاللهِ فَأَعِيذُوهُ وَمَنْ سَأَلَ بِاللهِ فَأَعْطُوهُ وَمَنْ دَعَاكُمْ فَأَجِيبُوهُ وَمَنْ صَنَعَ إِلَيْكُمْ مَعْرُوفًا فَكَافِئُوهُ، فَإِنْ لَمْ تَجِدُوا مَا تُكَافِئُونَهُ فَادْعُوا لَهُ حَتَّى تَرَوْا أَنَّكُمْ قَدْ كَافَأْتُمُوهُ»

"Whoever seeks refuge by Allâh, then give him refuge, whoever asks by Allâh, then give him, whoever invites, then accept his invitation, and whoever does some good to you, then compensate him. If you do not find anything to give him in compensation, then supplicate for him until you think that you have compensated him."

Abu Dâwûd and An-Nasâ'i recorded it with an authentic (*Ṣaḥeeḥ*) chain.[1]

---

* If someone asks a question and makes Allâh his intermediary (in asking), then it is not permissible to deny him, due to honoring and exalting Allâh. Shaikh ul-Islam Ibn Taymiyyah and a number of the researchers have said, "It is forbidden (*Ḥaraam*) to deny the one who asks by Allâh if he directs a request to a specific person regarding a specific matter." This means that the person has specified you in this request, and he asks you by Allâh to help him, and you are able to give him what he requests. It is recommended to give him if the request is not directed to a specific person, for instance if he asks so-and-so, so-and-so and so-and-so. It is allowed to give if the person who asks by Allâh is known to be lying.

[1] Ibn 'Umar رَضِيَ اللهُ عَنْهُمَا narrated that Allâh's Messenger ﷺ said,

«مَنِ اسْتَعَاذَ بِاللهِ فَأَعِيذُوهُ»

"Whoever seeks refuge by Allâh, then give him refuge."

This is because whoever seeks refuge by Allâh, then he has sought refuge with the Greatest by Whom refuge may be sought.

Important issues of the Chapter

1) Giving refuge to whomever seeks refuge by Allâh.
2) Giving to whomever asks by Allâh.
3) Accepting the invitation.
4) Compensating for the act of kindness.
5) That supplicating is compensation for whoever is not able to give anything other than it.
6) His Statement,

«حَتَّى تَرَوْا أَنَّكُمْ قَدْ كَافَأْتُمُوهُ»

"until you think that you have compensated him."

«وَمَنْ سَأَلَ بِاللهِ فَأَعْطُوهُ وَمَنْ دَعَاكُمْ فَأَجِيبُوهُ»

"Whoever asks by Allâh, then give him, whoever invites, then accept his invitation."

The majority of people of knowledge hold the view that this is specifically for the wedding invitation and not all invitations. Regarding the other invitations, it is recommended to accept them (i.e. not mandatory).

«وَمَنْ صَنَعَ إِلَيْكُمْ مَعْرُوفًا فَكَافِئُوهُ»

"And whoever does some good to you, then compensate him."

This means with the same kind of goodness (that he gave you). This is in order to clear the heart, so that there will not be in his heart any declination, lowliness and submissiveness from seeing that good. For this reason the Prophet ﷺ said,

«فَإِنْ لَمْ تَجِدُوا مَا تُكَافِئُونَهُ فَادْعُوا لَهُ حَتَّى تَرَوا أَنَّكُمْ قَدْ كَافَأْتُمُوهُ»

"If you do not find anything to give him in compensation, then supplicate for him until you think that you have compensated him."

These are levels that none reaches except the masters of *Ikhlaaṣ* (purity of faith) and realization of *At-Tauhid*. May Allâh make both you and us among them.

Chapter 55

Nothing but Paradise Should be Asked for by Allâh's Face

Jaabir رَضِيَ اللهُ عَنْهُ narrated that Allâh's Messenger ﷺ said,

«لَا يُسْأَلُ بِوَجْهِ اللهِ إِلَّا الْجَنَّةُ»

"Nothing except Paradise should be asked for by Allâh's Face." (Abu Dâwûd recorded it).[1]

---

* This is due to revering and honoring Allâh, His Names and His Attributes.

[1] Jaabir رَضِيَ اللهُ عَنْهُ narrated that Allâh's Messenger ﷺ said,

«لَا يُسْأَلُ بِوَجْهِ اللهِ إِلَّا الْجَنَّةُ»

"Nothing except Paradise should be asked for by Allâh's Face."
This prohibition contains the stressed prohibition and the Face of Allâh is an Attribute of Allâh's Self from among His Attributes, and it is according to what is befitting His Majesty and Magnificence. We know the basis of the meaning, but the complete meaning or the modality of it we entrust that to its Knower (Allâh) and the One Who is described with it (Allâh). However, we affirm the attribute upon the basis of avoiding comparing it to creation (*At-Tamtheel*) and rejecting it entirely (*At-Ta'teel*). This is as Allâh said,

﴿لَيْسَ كَمِثْلِهِ شَيْءٌ وَهُوَ ٱلسَّمِيعُ ٱلْبَصِيرُ﴾

"There is nothing like Him, and He is the All Hearing, the All Seeing." (42:11)
He said,

«إِلَّا الْجَنَّةُ»

"except Paradise",
because it is the greatest thing that may be requested. For this reason it is not permissible to ask Allâh for lowly, despicable things by seeking a means to Him by Himself, or His Face, or any Attribute from His Attributes, or any Name from His Beautiful Names. Rather, one should ask for the greatest request, like Paradise and the type of question that is related to it or those things that necessitate it. This is so that the question

Important issues of the Chapter

1) The prohibition of asking Allâh by the Face of Allâh, except for the utmost aim (Paradise).
2) Affirmation of the Attribute of the Face (of Allâh).

---

will be suitable for the means of the question. This is the meaning of this chapter concerning honoring the Attributes of Allâh, the Mighty and Majestic.

Chapter 56

What has Been Related Concerning Saying Law (If only...)*

The Statement of Allâh the Most High,

﴿يَقُولُونَ لَوْ كَانَ لَنَا مِنَ ٱلْأَمْرِ شَىْءٌ مَّا قُتِلْنَا هَـٰهُنَا﴾

"They say, 'If we had anything to do with the affair, none of us would have been killed here.'" (3:154)

And His Statement,

﴿ٱلَّذِينَ قَالُوا۟ لِإِخْوَٰنِهِمْ وَقَعَدُوا۟ لَوْ أَطَاعُونَا مَا قُتِلُوا۟﴾ الآية

"(They are) the ones who said about their killed brethren while they themselves sat (at home), 'If only they had listened to us, they would not have been killed.'"[1] (3:168)

---

* The author included this chapter because many people reject the Decree in respect to their actions. They think that if they had done some things the situation would change. Yet, Allâh has decreed the deed and its result, so everything is according to His Wisdom.

The Statement of Allâh the Most High,

﴿يَقُولُونَ لَوْ كَانَ لَنَا مِنَ ٱلْأَمْرِ شَىْءٌ مَّا قُتِلْنَا هَـٰهُنَا﴾

"They say, 'If we had anything to do with the affair, none of us would have been killed here.'" (3:154)

[1] And His Statement,

﴿ٱلَّذِينَ قَالُوا۟ لِإِخْوَٰنِهِمْ وَقَعَدُوا۟ لَوْ أَطَاعُونَا مَا قُتِلُوا۟﴾

"(They are) the ones who said about their killed brethren while they themselves sat (at home), 'If only they had listened to us, they would not have been killed.'" (3:168)

The statement *Law* (if only) concerning a matter that occurred in the past is not permissible and it is forbidden. The proof of this is that using the word *Law* (if only) is from the characteristics of hypocrisy. This proves its forbiddance.

It is recorded in the *Ṣaḥeeḥ* from Abu Hurayrah رَضِيَ اللهُ عَنْهُ that Allâh's Messenger ﷺ said,

«احْرِصْ عَلَى مَا يَنْفَعُكَ، وَاسْتَعِنْ بِاللهِ، وَلَا تَعْجِزَنْ، وَإِنْ أَصَابَكَ شَيْءٌ فَلَا تَقُلْ: لَوْ أَنِّي فَعَلْتُ لَكَانَ كَذَا وَكَذَا، وَلٰكِنْ قُلْ: قَدَّرَ اللهُ وَمَا شَاءَ فَعَلَ، فَإِنَّ لَوْ تَفْتَحُ عَمَلَ الشَّيْطَانِ»

"Seek that which will benefit you, and seek Allâh's help. Do not lose heart. If some adversity (misfortune) befalls you, do not say, 'If only I had done so, such-and-such would have occurred.' Instead, say, 'Allâh decreed and He did what He willed.' For verily 'If' begins the work of Satan."[1]

---

[1] It is recorded in the *Ṣaḥeeḥ from Abu Hurayrah* رَضِيَ اللهُ عَنْهُ that Allâh's Messenger ﷺ said,

«احْرِصْ عَلَى مَا يَنْفَعُكَ، وَاسْتَعِنْ بِاللهِ، وَلَا تَعْجِزَنْ، وَإِنْ أَصَابَكَ شَيْءٌ فَلَا تَقُلْ...»

"Seek that which will benefit you, and seek Allâh's help. Do not lose heart. If some adversity (misfortune) befalls you, do not say..."

This is the prohibition that is for forbiddance (*Tahreem*).

لَوْ أَنِّي فَعَلْتُ لَكَانَ كَذَا وَكَذَا، وَلٰكِنْ قُلْ: قَدَّرَ اللهُ وَمَا شَاءَ فَعَلَ، فَإِنَّ لَوْ تَفْتَحُ عَمَلَ الشَّيْطَانِ»

"'If only I had done so, such-and-such would have occurred.' Instead, say, 'Allâh decreed and He did what He willed.' For verily 'If' opens the work of Satan."

Also, if one uses it (the statement 'if only'), it will weaken his heart and dissuade it. The forbiddance refers to the usage of the term *Law* (if only) and *Layta* (if only, I wish) and whatever expressions are similar to them in regretting what has past. However, using the term *Law* (if only) in the future tense, if it is regarding something good, with hope for what Allâh has, and seeking help by the means of goodness, then this is permissible. But if it is in a manner of haughtiness and arrogance, then it is not permissible, because it contains a form of making oneself the judge or decider over the Decree.

Important issues of the Chapter

1) The explanation of the two Verses in *Surah Âl-'Imrân* (3:154 and 3:168).
2) The clear prohibition of saying *Law* (if only) if some calamity befalls you.
3) Giving the reason for this matter, which is that it begins the work of Satan.
4) Giving guidance to good speech.
5) The command to seek what will benefit while seeking the assistance of Allâh.
6) The prohibition of the opposite of that, which is being discouraged.

Chapter 57

The Prohibition of Cursing the Wind*

Ubayy bin Ka'b رَضِيَ الله عَنْهُ narrated that Allâh's Messenger ﷺ said,

«لَا تَسُبُّوا الرِّيحَ فَإِذَا رَأَيْتُم مَا تَكْرَهُونَ فَقُولُوا: اللَّهُمَّ إِنَّا نَسْأَلُكَ مِنْ خَيْرِ هٰذِهِ الرِّيحِ وَخَيْرِ مَا فِيهَا وَخَيْرِ مَا أُمِرَتْ بِهِ. وَنَعُوذُ بِكَ مِنْ شَرِّ هٰذِهِ الرِّيحِ وَشَرِّ مَا فِيهَا وَشَرِّ مَا أُمِرَتْ بِهِ»

"Do not curse the wind. If you see that which you dislike, then say, 'O Allâh, verily we ask You for the good of this wind, the good of what it contains and the good of what it has been commanded. We seek refuge with you from the evil of this wind, the evil of what it contains and the evil of what it has been commanded." At-Tirmiṭhi graded it authentic (*Ṣaḥeeḥ*).[1]

---

* Cursing the wind is like cursing the time. In reality it goes back to offending Allâh, because Allâh is the One Who directs the wind however He wills. The prohibition (here) is for forbiddance. Cursing the wind is by abusing it reviling it with evil. It is not considered cursing it that it is described as being harsh or with characteristics that contain evil for whomever it (the wind) comes to.

[1] Ubayy bin Ka'b رَضِيَ الله عَنْهُ narrated that Allâh's Messenger ﷺ said,

«لَا تَسُبُّوا الرِّيحَ»

"Do not curse the wind."

This proves that Allâh sends the wind however He wills and also diverts it away from whomever He wills. Hence, it is directed by His command. For this reason the Prophet ﷺ said,

«فَإِذَا رَأَيْتُم مَا تَكْرَهُونَ فَقُولُوا: اللَّهُمَّ إِنَّا نَسْأَلُكَ مِنْ خَيْرِ هٰذِهِ الرِّيحِ وَخَيْرِ مَا فِيهَا وَخَيْرِ مَا أُمِرَتْ بِهِ. وَنَعُوذُ بِكَ مِنْ شَرِّ هٰذِهِ الرِّيحِ وَشَرِّ مَا فِيهَا وَشَرِّ مَا أُمِرَتْ بِهِ»

"If you see that which you dislike, then say, 'O Allâh, verily we ask

Important issues of the Chapter

1) The prohibition of cursing the wind.
2) Giving guidance to beneficial speech if the person sees what he dislikes.
3) Giving guidance to fact that it (the wind) is commanded (by Allâh).
4) 'That it (the wind) has been commanded with good and commanded with evil.

You for the good of this wind, the good of what it contains and the good of what it has been commanded. We seek refuge with you from the evil of this wind, the evil of what it contains and the evil of what it has been commanded." (At-Tirmiṭḥi graded it authentic *Ṣaḥeeḥ*).

Chapter 58

The Statement of Allâh the Most High,*

﴿يَظُنُّونَ بِٱللَّهِ غَيْرَ ٱلْحَقِّ ظَنَّ ٱلْجَٰهِلِيَّةِ يَقُولُونَ هَل لَّنَا مِنَ ٱلْأَمْرِ مِن شَيْءٍ قُلْ إِنَّ ٱلْأَمْرَ كُلَّهُۥ لِلَّهِ﴾ الآية

"They thought wrongly of Allâh — the thought of ignorance. They said, 'Have we any part in the affair?' Say (O Muhammad ﷺ), 'Indeed the affair belongs wholly to Allâh.'" (3:154)

And His Statement,

﴿ٱلظَّآنِّينَ بِٱللَّهِ ظَنَّ ٱلسَّوْءِ عَلَيْهِمْ دَآئِرَةُ ٱلسَّوْءِ﴾ الآية

"Those who think evil thoughts about Allâh, for them is a disgraceful torment."[1] (48:6)

---

* From the perfection of Allâh in His Lordship and in His Names and Attributes is that He does not do anything except for a profound wisdom. The wisdom in that is that He places the matters in their proper places that agree with their praiseworthy purposes. For this reason it is mandatory for His perfection that He is thought of with truthful thinking, such as (Him having) completion and perfection of wisdom, mercy and justice. Also, He should not be thought evil of and as deficient like the people of ignorance think of Him, and that which is contrary to the foundation of *At-Tauhid* in some of its conditions, or contrary to the completion of *At-Tauhid*. Thus, they believe, or it comes to their minds with what is with them of *Ash-Shirk*, that the actions of Allâh are not actions of truth. Allâh explains this with His Statement,

﴿يَقُولُونَ هَل لَّنَا مِنَ ٱلْأَمْرِ مِن شَيْءٍ﴾

"They said, 'Have we any part in the affair?'"

This contains a rejection of the Wisdom or the Decree.

[1] And His Statement,

﴿ٱلظَّآنِّينَ بِٱللَّهِ ظَنَّ ٱلسَّوْءِ عَلَيْهِمْ دَآئِرَةُ ٱلسَّوْءِ﴾

"Those who think evil thoughts about Allâh, for them is a disgraceful torment." (48:6)

Ibn Al-Qayyim said concerning the first verse, "This thinking is interpreted to mean that Allâh would not help His Messenger, and that his mission would soon fail. It is also interpreted as their thinking that what befell them was not by the Decree of Allâh and His Wisdom. Thus, it is interpreted to mean a rejection of the Wisdom (of Allâh), the Decree, that the affair of His Messenger ﷺ would be fulfilled and that He would make His religion victorious over all religions. This is the evil thinking that the hypocrites and polytheists thought in *Surah Al-Fatḥ*. This evil thinking only occurred because it was thinking other than what was appropriate for Him, His Wisdom, His Praise and His Truthful Promise. Whoever thinks that Allâh will make falsehood dominant over the truth in a permanent manner with which the truth will vanish, or denies that whatever happens occurs by His Preordainment and Decree, or denies that His Decree is for a profound wisdom that makes Him deserving of praise, and claims that this (what occurs) is due to an abstract will, then that is the thinking of those who disbelieve. Woe to those who

---

Ibn Al-Qayyim mentioned that the *Salaf* interpreted this evil thinking that the ignorant people thought as one of three things and all of them are correct. (1) Denying the Decree, (2) denying the Wisdom, and (3) denying Allâh's helping His Messenger ﷺ or His religion (Islam) or His righteous slaves. Ibn Al-Qayyim said, "Most people think evil of Allâh concerning that which He particularly affects them with and what He does to other than them. None is safe from this except the person who knows Allâh, His Names, His Attributes, and the necessity of His Wisdom and Praise. Let the intelligent, sincere person look closely at himself in this and repent to Allâh. Let him seek His forgiveness from evil thinking about His Lord. If you inspect whomever you wish to inspect, you would see that he is distressed over the Decree and that he blames it, and he thinks that it should have been like this or that. There are those who are effected more or less, so examine yourself. Are you safe? If you are saved from it, then you are saved from something great, and if not, then I cannot regard you as saved."

disbelieve from the Fire. Most people think evil of Allâh concerning that which He particularly affects them with and what He does to other than them. None is safe from this except the person who knows Allâh, His Names, His Attributes, and the necessity of His Wisdom and Praise. Let the intelligent, sincere person look closely at himself in this and repent to Allâh. Let him seek His forgiveness from evil thinking about His Lord. If you inspect whomever you wish to inspect, you would see that he is distressed over the Decree and that he blames it, and he thinks that it should have been like this or that. There are those who are effected more or less, so examine yourself. Are you safe? If you are saved from it, then you are saved from something great, and if not, then I cannot regard you as saved."[1]

Important issues of the Chapter

1) The explanation of the Verse of *Surah Âl- 'Imrân* (3:154).
2) The explanation of the Verse of *Surah Al-Fatḥ* (48:6).
3) Informing that this (evil thinking of Allâh) is of numerous types that are unlimited.
4) That none is safe from this except for whoever knows the Names and Attributes (of Allâh) and he knows himself.

---

[1] Therefore, the cause of this is a lack of knowledge concerning what Allâh deserves and what He has obligated of patience, perseverance and similar to that from the obligations. Many people submit outwardly, but inwardly there is the thinking of ignorance in their hearts and evil belief. For this reason it is obligatory upon the believer to purify her heart from every thought about Allâh other than the truth. He must learn the Names of Allâh and His Attributes. He must learn the effects of that in the dominion of Allâh so there is nothing in his heart, except Allâh is the truth and His action is true, even if the person is afflicted by the greatest calamity.

Chapter 59

What has been related concerning the Deniers of *Al-Qadar* (Decree)*

Ibn 'Umar رَضِيَ اللهُ عَنْهُمَا said, "I swear by the One in Whose Hand is the soul of Ibn 'Umar! If one of them had the like of (Mount) Uḥud in gold, then he spent it in the Way of Allâh, Allâh would not accept it from him until he believes in *Al-Qadar* (Divine Decree)." Then he cited as evidence the statement of Prophet ﷺ,

«الْإِيمَانُ أَنْ تُؤْمِنَ بِاللهِ، وَمَلَائِكَتِهِ، وَكُتُبِهِ، وَرُسُلِهِ، وَالْيَوْمِ الآخِرِ، وَتُؤْمِنَ بِالْقَدَرِ خَيْرِه وَشَرِّهِ»

"*Al-Eemaan* (faith) is that you believe in Allâh, His angels, His Books (Scriptures), His Messengers, the Last Day, and that you believe in *Al-Qadar* (Divine Decree),

---

* *Al-Qadar* (the Decree) is Allâh's knowledge that precedes all things, His writing it in the Preserved Tablet, the comprehensiveness of His Will and His creating all things in particular and the characteristics that they have. From this is the creation of the deeds of the slaves. This is due to His Statement,

﴿ٱللَّهُ خَٰلِقُ كُلِّ شَيْءٍ﴾

"Allâh is the Creator of everything." (39:62)

This includes the slaves (i.e. creatures) and their actions. Thus, it is not said about anyone that he is a believer in the Decree unless he submits and believes in all of these things and the implication of the texts concerning them.

Denial of the Decree may be disbelief that expels one from *At-Tauhid* and the religion (of Islam). This is if the person denies that Allâh's knowledge precedes all things or denies Allâh's writing of all things in the Preserved Tablet (*Al-Lawḥ ul-Maḥfooḍḥ*). There is denial of the Decree that is less than this (i.e. not disbelief), but rather it is heretical innovation (*Bid'ah*) that is contrary to the completion of *At-Tauhid*. This is if the person denies the comprehensive nature of Allâh's will and His creating.

the good of it and the bad of it." (Muslim)[1]

'Ubaadah bin Aṣ-Ṣaamit رَضِيَ اللهُ عَنْهُ said to his son, "O my little boy! You will never find the taste of faith until you know that whatever happened to you was not going to miss you, and whatever missed you was not going to happen to you. I heard Allâh's Messenger ﷺ saying,

«إِنَّ أَوَّلَ مَا خَلَقَ اللهُ الْقَلَمَ، فَقَالَ لَهُ: اكْتُبْ، فَقَالَ: رَبِّ وَمَاذَا أَكْتُبُ؟ قَالَ: اكْتُبْ مَقَادِيرَ كُلِّ شَيْءٍ حَتَّى تَقُومَ السَّاعَةُ»

"Verily the first of what Allâh created was the Pen and He said to it, 'Write.' The Pen said, 'My Lord, what should I write?' He said, 'Write the Decrees of everything until the Hour is established.'"

"O my little son! I heard Allâh's Messenger ﷺ saying,

«مَنْ مَاتَ عَلَى غَيْرِ هٰذَا فَلَيْسَ مِنِّي»

"Whoever dies on other than this, then he is not of me."

---

[1] Ibn 'Umar رَضِيَ اللهُ عَنْهُمَا said, "I swear by the One in Whose Hand is the soul of Ibn 'Umar! If one of them had the like of (Mount) Uhud in gold, then he spent it in the Way of Allâh, Allâh would not accept it from him until he believes in Al-Qadar (Divine Decree)." Why? Because Allâh only accepts the righteous deeds from the Muslim, and whoever denies the Decree and does not believe in the Decree, then he is not a Muslim. Allâh does not accept (deeds) from him even if he spent the like of (Mount) Uhud in gold. Thsen he cited as evidence the statement of Prophet ﷺ,

«الْإِيمَانُ أَنْ تُؤْمِنَ بِاللهِ، وَمَلَائِكَتِهِ، وَكُتُبِهِ، وَرُسُلِهِ، وَالْيَوْمِ الآخِرِ، وَتُؤْمِنَ بِالْقَدَرِ خَيْرِهِ وَشَرِّهِ»

"Al-Eemaan (faith) is that you believe in Allâh, His angels, His Books (Scriptures), His Messengers, the Last Day, and that you believe in Al-Qadar (Divine Decree), the good of it and the bad of it."

This means the good in relation to the son of Aadam (i.e. humans) and the bad in relation to him. In reference to the action of Allâh, then all of Allâh's actions are good because they are in agreement with His Great Wisdom.

In another version recorded by Aḥmad he ﷺ said,

«إِنَّ أَوَّلَ مَا خَلَقَ اللهُ تَعَالَىٰ الْقَلَمُ، فَقَالَ لَهُ: اكْتُبْ فَجَرَى فِي تِلْكَ السَّاعَةِ بِمَا هُوَ كَائِنٌ إِلَىٰ يَوْمِ الْقِيَامَةِ»

"Verily the first of what Allâh the Most High created was the Pen and He said to it, 'Write.' So in that very hour it wrote all that would be until the Day of Resurrection."

In another version recorded by Ibn Wahb, Allâh's Messenger ﷺ said,

«فَمَنْ لَمْ يُؤْمِنْ بِالْقَدَرِ خَيْرِهِ وَشَرِّهِ أَحْرَقَهُ اللهُ بِالنَّارِ»

"So whoever does not believe in the Decree, the good and bad of it, Allâh will burn him with the Fire."

It is recorded in *Al-Musnad* and the *Sunan* collections from Ibn Ad-Daylamee that he said, "I came to Ubayy bin Ka'b and said to him, 'I have some (doubt) within myself about the Decree. Tell me something so that perhaps Allâh might remove it from my heart.' So he said, 'If you spent the like of (Mount) Uhud in gold, Allâh would not accept it from you until you believe in the Decree and know that what happened to you was not going to miss you, and what missed you was not going to happen to you. If you died on other than this you would be of the people of the Fire.' Then I went to 'Abdullah bin Mas'ud, Ḥuthayfah bin Al-Yamaan and Zayd bin Thâbit رضي الله عنهم, and all of them told me the same as that from the Prophet ﷺ."[1]

[1] 'Ubaadah bin Aṣ-Ṣaamit said to his son, "O my little boy! You will never find the taste of faith until you know that whatever happened to you was not going to miss you, and whatever missed you was not going to happen to you." This is because the decreeing of matters has already been completed, and from belief in the Decree is to believe that Allâh has given you a choice and that you are not compelled, be overburdening occurs with that.

This is an authentic (*Ṣaḥeeḥ*) *Hadith* and Al-Ḥaakim recorded it in his *Ṣaḥeeḥ*.

Important issues of the Chapter

1) Explaining the obligation of belief in the Decree.
2) Explaining how to believe in it.
3) Nullification of the deeds of whomever does not believe in it.
4) Informing that one will not find the taste of faith (*Al-Eemaan*) until he believes in it.
5) Mentioning the first of what Allâh created.
6) That it (the Pen) wrote all the decrees of events until the establishment of the (Final) Hour in this hour.
7) The Prophet's disavowal from whoever does not believe in it.
8) The habit of the *Salaf* in removing doubts by asking the scholars.
9) That the scholars answered him with what removed his doubt and that is that they attributed the statement to Allâh's Messenger ﷺ only.

I heard Allâh's Messenger ﷺ saying,

«إِنَّ أَوَّلَ مَا خَلَقَ اللهُ الْقَلَمَ، فَقَالَ لَهُ: اكْتُبْ، فَقَالَ: رَبِّ وَمَاذَا أَكْتُبُ؟ قَالَ: اكْتُبْ مَقَادِيرَ كُلِّ شَيْءٍ حَتَّى تَقُومَ السَّاعَةُ»

"Verily the first of what Allâh created was the Pen and He said to it, 'Write.' The Pen said, 'My Lord, what should I write?' He said, 'Write the Decrees of everything until the Hour is established.'"

This contains an evidence for the position of the Writing. And his statement, "Verily the first thing that Allâh created was the Pen" means - according to the correct view with the researchers - is when Allâh created the Pen. So the statement *Awwal* (first) here is a participle meaning when. In reference to the first thing that Allâh created, it was the *'Arsh* (Throne).

Chapter 60

What has been related concerning Those Who Make Pictures*

Abu Hurayrah رَضِيَ اللهُ عَنْهُ narrated that Allâh's Messenger ﷺ said,

«قَالَ اللهُ تَعَالىٰ: وَمَنْ أَظْلَمُ مِمَّنْ ذَهبَ يَخْلُقُ كَخَلْقِي فَلْيَخْلُقُوا ذَرَّةً، أَوْ لِيَخْلُقُوا حَبَّةً، أَوْ لِيَخْلُقُوا شَعِيرَةً»

"Allâh the Most High said, 'And who is more unjust than he who tries to create like my creation. Let them create an atom, or let them create a seed or let them create a grain of barley.'" (*Al-Bukhari* and *Muslim*)[1]

---

* This is referring to the threat. The picture maker is a person who designs something with his hand in the form of a customary picture.

Picture making has two aspects:

The first: The aspect of mimicking the creation of Allâh, imitating the creation of Allâh, and His Attribute and Name (i.e. the Creator).

The second: That it is a cause of associating partners, because *Shirk* with many of the polytheists was due to images. So from the realization of *At-Tauhid* is that pictures are not allowed to remain because the image is a means from the means of the polytheists in their acts of worship.

[1] Abu Hurayrah رَضِيَ اللهُ عَنْهُ narrated that Allâh's Messenger ﷺ said,

«قَالَ اللهُ تَعَالىٰ: وَمَنْ أَظْلَمُ مِمَّنْ ذَهبَ يَخْلُقُ كَخَلْقِي»

"Allâh the Most High said, 'And who is more unjust than he who tries to create like my creation.'"

Then He said in declaring (their) inability,

«فَلْيَخْلُقُوا ذَرَّةً، أَوْ لِيَخْلُقُوا حَبَّةً، أَوْ لِيَخْلُقُوا شَعِيرَةً»

"Let them create an atom, or let them create a seed or let them create a grain of barley."

Therefore, the one who creates like the creation of Allâh is referring to his thinking. However, in reference to the reality, no one creates like the creation of Allâh. For this reason this person is likening himself to Allâh, and thus, he is the most unjust of creation.

They (Al-Bukhari and Muslim) also recorded from 'Aishah رَضِيَ اللهُ عَنْهَا that Allâh's Messenger ﷺ said,

«أَشَدُّ النَّاسِ عَذَابًا يَوْمَ القِيَامَةِ الَّذِينَ يُضَاهِئُونَ بِخَلْقِ اللهِ»

"The people whose punishment will be the most severe on the Day of Resurrection will be those who tried to imitate Allâh's creation."[1]

They (Al-Bukhari and Muslim) also recorded from Ibn 'Abbâs رَضِيَ اللهُ عَنْهُمَا that he heard Allâh's Messenger ﷺ saying,

«كُلُّ مُصَوِّرٍ فِي النَّارِ يُجْعَلُ لَهُ بِكُلِّ صُورَةٍ صَوَّرَهَا نَفْسٌ يُعَذَّبُ بِهَا فِي جَهَنَّمَ»

"Every picture maker will be in the Fire, and for every picture he made a soul will be made for him and he will be punished by it in Hell."[2]

They (Al-Bukhari and Muslim) also recorded from him (Ibn

---

[1] They (Al-Bukhari and Muslim) also recorded from 'Aishah رَضِيَ اللهُ عَنْهَا that Allâh's Messenger ﷺ said,

«أَشَدُّ النَّاسِ عَذَابًا يَوْمَ الْقِيَامَةِ الَّذِينَ يُضَاهِئُونَ بِخَلْقِ اللهِ»

"The people whose punishment will be the most severe on the Day of Resurrection will be those who tried to imitate Allâh's creation."

Imitation in image making is major disbelief (*Kufr*) in two instances:

The first: That the person makes an image of a statue so that it may be worshipped while he knows that it will be worshipped. This is disbelief in Allâh.

The second level: That the person makes an image and claims that it is better than the creation of Allâh, and this is what is meant by this *Hadith*. Also, included in this (*Hadith's* meaning) is whoever mimics by making an image - like the one who draws with his hand or carves a statue - of what generally does not take him out of the religion. This is a major sin from the major sins, and the person who does it is cursed and threatened with the Fire.

[2] They (Al-Bukhari and Muslim) also recorded from Ibn 'Abbaas رَضِيَ اللهُ عَنْهُمَا that he heard Allâh's Messenger ﷺ saying,

'Abbâs) a *Marfoo' Hadith* which states,

«مَنْ صَوَّر صُورَةً فِي الدُّنْيَا كُلِّف أَنْ يَنْفُخَ فِيهَا الرُّوحَ، وَلَيْسَ بِنَافِخٍ»

"Whoever makes a picture in this world will be burdened with blowing a soul into it and he will not be able to blow it.[1]

Muslim recorded from Abu Al-Hayyaaj that 'Ali رَضِيَ اللهُ عَنْهُ said, "Shall I not dispatch you on the same mission that Allâh's Messenger ﷺ dispatched me? (It is) that you do not leave any picture except that you erase it, and no elevated grave except that you level it."[2]

«كُلُّ مُصَوِّرٍ فِـي النَّارِ يُجْعَلُ لَهُ بِكُلِّ صُورَةٍ صَوَّرَهَا نَفْسٌ يُعذَّبُ بِهَا فِي جَهَنَّمَ»

"Every picture maker will be in the Fire, and for every picture he made a soul will be made for him and he will be punished by it in Hell."

His Statement "soul" conveys the meaning that this picture making was of something that had a soul, which are animals or humans. For this reason, the threat is against this type of picture making.

[1] They (Al-Bukhari and Muslim) also recorded from him (Ibn 'Abbaas) a *Marfoo' Hadith* which states, "Whoever makes a picture in this world will be burdened with blowing a soul into it and he will not be able to blow it." This is because the soul belongs only to Allâh.

[2] Muslim recorded from Abu Al-Hayyaaj that 'Ali رَضِيَ اللهُ عَنْهُ said, "Shall I not dispatch you on the same mission that Allâh's Messenger ﷺ dispatched me? (It is) that you do not leave any picture except that you erase it, and no elevated grave except that you level it." This *Hadith* contains a notice of the second cause from the two causes of forbiddance of picture making, which is that it is a means from the means of *Ash-Shirk*. The point of evidence from this *Hadith* is that it combines the matter of the picture and the elevated grave. Leaving the elevated grave is a means from the means of *Ash-Shirk*, and likewise - due to the combination in the *Hadith* - leaving the picture is also a means from the means of *Ash-Shirk*.

Important issues of the Chapter

1) Severe condemnation regarding the picture makers.

2) Drawing attention to the reason, which is abandoning proper behavior with Allâh. This is due to His Statement,

«وَمَنْ أَظْلَمُ مِمَّنْ ذَهبَ يَخْلُقُ كَخَلْقِي»

"And who is more unjust than he who tries to create like my creation."»

3) Drawing attention to His (Allâh's) power and their inability. This is due to His Statement, "Let them create an atom, or let them create a seed or let them create a grain of barley."

4) The declaration that they will receive the severest punishment.

5) That Allâh will create a soul according to the number every picture and He will punish the picture maker with them in Hell.

6) That he (the picture maker) will be burdened with the task of blowing a soul into it (the picture).

7) The command to erase the picture if it is present.

Chapter 61

What has been related Concerning Swearing Oaths Frequently*

The Statement of Allâh the Most High,

﴿وَٱحۡفَظُوٓاْ أَيۡمَٰنَكُمۡۚ﴾

"And guard your oaths." (5:89)

Abu Hurayrah رَضِيَ اللهُ عَنْهُ narrated that he heard Allâh's Messenger ﷺ saying,

«الْحَلِفُ مَنْفَقَةٌ لِلسِّلْعَةِ مَمْحَقَةٌ لِلْكَسْبِ»

"The swearing of an oath will cause the item to be purchased, and it wipes away the earning (of Allâh's blessing)." (*Al-Bukhari* and *Muslim* both recorded it).[1]

Salmaan رَضِيَ اللهُ عَنْهُ narrated that Allâh's Messenger ﷺ said,

«ثَلَاثَةٌ لَا يُكَلِّمُهُمُ اللهُ، وَلَا يُزَكِّيهِمْ، وَلَهُمْ عَذَابٌ أَلِيمٌ: أُشَيْمِطٌ زَانٍ، وَعَائِلٌ مُسْتَكْبِرٌ، وَرَجُلٌ جَعَلَ اللهَ بِضَاعَتَهُ، لَا يَشْتَرِي إِلَّا بِيَمِينِهِ، وَلَا يَبِيعُ إِلَّا بِيَمِينِهِ»

"There are three (people) whom Allâh will not speak to, He will not purify them and they will have a painful torment: the old man who commits adultery (or fornication), the poor man who is arrogant, and the

---

* Frequently swearing oaths does not accompany the completion of *At-Tauhid*. For verily whoever has complete *Tauhid* in his heart or is near to complete *Tauhid*, he would not make place Allâh in his oaths. This means the oath that the person who swore it meant to be binding. However, the oath that occurs during loose speech is pardoned, even though it is recommended for the person who believes in *At-Tauhid* to purify his tongue and his heart from abundant swearing in showing respect and similar things with loose oaths.

[1] Abu Hurayrah رَضِيَ اللهُ عَنْهُ narrated that he heard Allâh's Messenger ﷺ saying,

man who makes Allâh (as) his merchandise. He does not buy except by his swearing an oath and he does not buy except by his swearing an oath."[1]

At-Ṭabaraanee recorded it with an authentic (*Ṣaḥeeḥ*) chain.

In the *Ṣaḥeeḥ* it is reported from 'Imraan bin Ḥuṣayn رَضِيَ اللهُ عَنْهُ that Allâh's Messenger ﷺ said,

«خَيْرُ أُمَّتِي قَرْنِي ثُمَّ الَّذِينَ يَلُونَهُمْ، ثُمَّ الَّذِينَ يَلُونَهُمْ، ثُمَّ الَّذِينَ يَلُونَهُمْ»

"The best of my *Ummah* is my generation, then those who come after them, then those who come after them, then those who come after them."

'Imraan said, "I do not know whether he mentioned this two or three times after his generation."

The Prophet ﷺ then said,

«ثُمَّ إِنَّ بَعْدَكُمْ قَوْمٌ يَشْهَدُونَ وَلَا يُسْتَشْهَدُونَ، وَيَخُونُونَ وَلَا يُؤْتَمَنُونَ، وَيَنْذِرُونَ وَلَا يُوفُونَ، وَيَظْهَرُ فِيهِمُ السِّمَنُ»

"Then after you all will be a people who will testify but they will not be asked to testify, they will be treacherous and they will not be trustworthy, they will make vows and not fulfill them, and obesity will appear among them."[2]

«الحَلِفُ مَنْفَقَةٌ لِلسِّلْعَةِ مَمْحَقَةٌ لِلْكَسْبِ»

[1] "The swearing of an oath will cause the item to be purchased, and it wipes away the earning (of Allâh's blessing)."

The reason for this is that it is a type of punishment because he does not do what is obligatory of honoring Allâh.

Salmaan رَضِيَ اللهُ عَنْهُ narrated that Allâh's Messenger ﷺ said,

«ثَلَاثَةٌ لَا يُكَلِّمُهُمُ اللهُ، وَلَا يُزَكِّيهِمْ، وَلَهُمْ عَذَابٌ أَلِيمٌ»

[2] "There are three (people) whom Allâh will not speak to, He will not purify them and they will have a painful torment: the old man who

It is also recorded in it (the *Ṣaḥeeḥ*) from Ibn Mas'ud رَضِيَ اللهُ عَنْهُ that the Prophet ﷺ said,

«خَيْرُ النَّاسِ قَرْنِي، ثُمَّ الَّذِينَ يَلُونَهُمْ، ثُمَّ الَّذِينَ يَلُونَهُمْ، ثُمَّ يَجِيءُ قَوْمٌ تَسْبِقُ شَهَادَةُ أَحَدِهِمْ يَمِينَهُ، وَيَمِينُهُ شَهَادَتَهُ»

"The best people are my generation, then those who come after them, then those who come after them. Then there will come a people who the testimony of one of them will precede his oath, and his oath will precede his testimony."[1]

Ibrâhîm said, "They (our parents) used to beat us regarding testimonies and covenants when we were children."

---

commits adultery (or fornication)."

This means the person who has become gray-haired and his heart is attached to *Az-Zinaa* (adultery and fornication). Then he said, "the poor man who is arrogant, and the man who makes Allâh (as) his merchandise. He does not buy except by his swearing an oath and he does not buy except by his swearing an oath." This is clear in expressing that the one who makes Allâh his merchandise is rebuked and he is committing a major sin.

[1] In the *Ṣaḥeeḥ* it is reported from 'Imraan bin Ḥuṣayn رَضِيَ اللهُ عَنْهُ that Allâh's Messenger ﷺ said,

«خَيْرُ أُمَّتِي قَرْنِي»

"The best of my *Ummah* is my generation..."

It is also recorded in it (the *Ṣaḥeeḥ*) from Ibn Mas'ud رَضِيَ اللهُ عَنْهُ that the Prophet ﷺ said,

«خَيْرُ النَّاسِ قَرْنِي، ثُمَّ الَّذِينَ يَلُونَهُمْ، ثُمَّ الَّذِينَ يَلُونَهُمْ، ثُمَّ يَجِيءُ قَوْمٌ تَسْبِقُ شَهَادَةُ أَحَدِهِمْ يَمِينَهُ، وَيَمِينُهُ شَهَادَتَهُ»

"The best people are my generation, then those who come after them, then those who come after them. Then there will come a people who the testimony of one of them will precede his oath, and his oath will precede his testimony."

Ibrâhîm said, "They (our parents) used to beat us regarding testimonies and covenants (i.e. oaths) when we were children." This contains the *Salaf's* training their children and their descendants to honor Allâh.

Important issues of the Chapter

1) The admonishment to guard the oaths.
2) Informing that swearing oaths will cause the item to be purchased, and it wipes away the blessing.
3) The severe threat against whoever does not sell except with his swearing an oath and he does not buy except with his swearing an oath.
4) Alerting that the sin becomes greater with the decrease in the need (cause) for it.
5) Rebuke of those who swear oaths while they have not been requested to swear an oath.
6) The Prophet's commending the first three or four generations, and mentioning what would happen after them.
7) Rebuke of those who testify as witnesses when they have not been asked to give their witness.
8) The fact that the *Salaf* beat the children for (needlessly) bearing witness and taking covenants.

Chapter 62

What has been related concerning the Protection of Allâh and the Protection of His Prophet*

The Statement of Allâh the Most High,

﴿وَأَوْفُوا۟ بِعَهْدِ ٱللَّهِ إِذَا عَـٰهَدتُّمْ وَلَا تَنقُضُوا۟ ٱلْأَيْمَـٰنَ بَعْدَ تَوْكِيدِهَا﴾

"And fulfill the Covenant of Allâh when you have covenanted and break not the oaths after you have appointed."(16:91)[1]

Buraydah said, "Whenever Allâh's Messenger ﷺ would appoint a leader over a army or war party he would advise him particularly to fear Allâh and treat those who were with him from the Muslims in a good manner. He would say,

«اغْزُوا بِسْمِ اللهِ فِي سَبِيلِ اللهِ، قَاتِلُوا مَنْ كَفَرَ بِاللهِ، اغْزُوا وَلَا تَغُلُّوا، وَلَا تَغْدِرُوا، وَلَا تُمَثِّلُوا، وَلَا تَقْتُلُوا وَلِيدًا، وَإِذَا لَقِيتَ عَدُوَّكَ مِنَ الْمُشْرِكِينَ فَادْعُهُمْ إِلَى ثَلَاثِ خِصَالٍ - أَوْ خِلَالٍ -

---

* This means the covenant of Allâh and the covenant of His Prophet ﷺ.

[1] The Statement of Allâh the Most High,

﴿وَأَوْفُوا۟ بِعَهْدِ ٱللَّهِ إِذَا عَـٰهَدتُّمْ وَلَا تَنقُضُوا۟ ٱلْأَيْمَـٰنَ بَعْدَ تَوْكِيدِهَا﴾

"And fulfill the Covenant of Allâh when you have covenanted and break not the oaths after you have appointed." (16:91)

This is explained as being the contracts that are between people. The covenant mentioned here as been explained as being the oath. Thus, it is obligatory to fulfil the contract and the oath due to honoring the right of Allâh. This is because whoever gives an oath by Allâh, then this means that he is affirming its fulfillment by Allâh. So if he breaks the promise and disregards it, this means that he does not honor Allâh in a manner by which he will fear not establishing what is obligatory for Allâh of fulfilling the oath.

فَأَيَّتَهُنَّ مَا أَجَابُوكَ فَاقْبَلْ مِنْهُمْ، ثُمَّ ادْعُهُمْ إِلَى الْإِسْلَامِ، فَإِنْ أَجَابُوكَ فَاقْبَلْ مِنْهُمْ، ثُمَّ ادْعُهُمْ إِلَى التَّحَوُّلِ مِنْ دَارِهِمْ إِلَىٰ دَارِ الْمُهَاجِرِينَ، وَأَخْبِرْهُمْ إِنْ هُمْ فَعَلُوا ذٰلِكَ فَلَهُمْ مَا لِلْمُهَاجِرِينَ وَعَلَيْهِمْ مَا عَلَى الْمُهَاجِرِينَ، فَإِنْ أَبَوْا أَنْ يَتَحَوَّلُوا مِنْهَا فَأَخْبِرْهُمْ أَنَّهُمْ يَكُونُونَ كَأَعْرَابِ الْمُسْلِمِينَ يَجْرِي عَلَيْهِمْ حُكْمُ اللهِ تَعَالَىٰ، وَلَا يَكُونُ لَهُمْ فِي الْغَنِيمَةِ وَالْفَيْءِ شَيْءٌ إِلَّا أَنْ يُجَاهِدُوا مَعَ الْمُسْلِمِينَ، فَإِنْ هُمْ أَبَوْا فَاسْأَلْهُمُ الْجِزْيَةَ، فَإِنْ هُمْ أَجَابُوكَ فَاقْبَلْ مِنْهُمْ وَكُفَّ عَنْهُمْ، فَإِنْ هُمْ أَبَوْا فَاسْتَعِنْ بِاللهِ وَقَاتِلْهُمْ. وَإِذَا حَاصَرْتَ أَهْلَ حِصْنٍ فَأَرَادُوكَ أَنْ تَجْعَلَ لَهُمْ ذِمَّةَ اللهِ وَذِمَّةَ نَبِيِّهِ، فَلَا تَجْعَلْ لَهُمْ ذِمَّةَ اللهِ وَذِمَّةَ نَبِيِّهِ، وَلٰكِنِ اجْعَلْ لَهُمْ ذِمَّتَكَ وَذِمَّةَ أَصْحَابِكَ فَإِنَّكُمْ أَنْ تُخْفِرُوا ذِمَمَكُمْ وَذِمَّةَ أَصْحَابِكُمْ أَهْوَنُ مِنْ أَنْ تُخْفِرُوا ذِمَّةَ اللهِ وَذِمَّةَ نَبِيِّهِ، وَإِذَا حَاصَرْتَ أَهْلَ حِصْنٍ فَأَرَادُوكَ أَنْ تُنْزِلَهُمْ عَلَىٰ حُكْمِ اللهِ فَلَا تُنْزِلْهُمْ عَلَىٰ حُكْمِ اللهِ، وَلٰكِنْ أَنْزِلْهُمْ عَلَىٰ حُكْمِكَ، فَإِنَّكَ لَا تَدْرِي أَتُصِيبُ فِيهِمْ حُكْمَ اللهِ أَمْ لَا»

'Set out for fighting with the Name of Allâh and in the Way of Allâh. Fight against those who disbelieve in Allâh. Go forth for fighting and do not take from the war booty before its division. Do not break treaties, do not mutilate the dead bodies (of enemy soldiers) and do not kill a child. When you meat your enemy among the polytheists call them to three options — or alternatives. Whichever of them that they respond to positively, then accept it from them. Invite them to (accept) Islam. If they respond positively, then accept it from them. Then invite them to move from their land to the land of the *Muhaajireen* (those who migrate to the Muslim lands for the sake of Islam). Inform them that if they do that, they will get what the *Muhaajireen* get (i.e. privileges), and upon them is that which is upon the *Muhaajireen* (i.e.

obligations). If they refuse to move from their land, inform them that they are like the Bedouin Arabs of the Muslims. The law Allâh the Most High applies to them, but they do not have a right to anything of the *Ghaneemah* (war booty captured by fighting) or *Fay'* (war booty captured by surrender and without fighting) unless they fight along with the Muslims. If they refuse (Islam), ask them to pay the *Jizyah* (a tax of protection taken from the non-Muslim citizens in the Islamic State). If they respond to you positively, then accept it from them and leave them alone. If they refuse (to pay the *Jizyah*) then seek Allâh's help and fight them. If you besiege the people of a fortress and they want you to give them the protection of Allâh and the protection of His Prophet ﷺ, do not give them the protection of Allâh and the protection of His Prophet ﷺ. Rather, give them your protection and the protection of your companions. For verily it is a lesser sin if you disregard your word of protection and the protection of your companions than if you disregard the protection of Allâh and the protection of His Prophet. If you besiege the people of a fortress and they want you to allow them to come down (from their fort) according to the law of Allâh, do not let them come down according to Allâh's law. Rather, let them come out based on your law, for verily you do not know whether you will be correct regarding Allâh's law concerning them or not." (*Muslim*)[1]

---

[1] Buraydah رَضِيَ اللهُ عَنْهُ said, "Whenever Allâh's Messenger ﷺ would appoint a leader over a army or war party he would advise him particularly to fear Allâh and treat those who were with him from the Muslims in a good manner. He would say,

«اغْزُوا . . . وَإِذَا حَاصَرْتَ أَهْلَ حِصْنٍ فَأَرَادُوكَ أَنْ تَجْعَلَ لَهُمْ ذِمَّةَ اللهِ وَذِمَّةَ نَبِيِّهِ، فَلَا تَجْعَلْ لَهُمْ ذِمَّةَ اللهِ وَذِمَّةَ نَبِيِّهِ، وَلٰكِنِ اجْعَلْ لَهُمْ ذِمَّتَكَ وَذِمَّةَ

Important issues of the Chapter

1) The difference between the protection of Allâh, the protection

---

أَصْحَابِكَ فَإِنَّكُمْ أَنْ تُخْفِرُوا ذِمَمَكُمْ وَذِمَّةَ أَصْحَابِكُمْ أَهْوَنُ مِنْ أَنْ تُخْفِرُوا ذِمَّةَ اللهِ وَذِمَّةَ نَبِيِّهِ، وَإِذَا حَاصَرْتَ أَهْلَ حِصْنٍ فَأَرَادُوكَ أَنْ تُنْزِلَهُمْ عَلَىٰ حُكْمِ اللهِ فَلَا تُنْزِلْهُمْ عَلَىٰ حُكْمِ اللهِ، وَلٰكِنْ أَنْزِلْهُمْ عَلَىٰ حُكْمِكَ، فَإِنَّكَ لَا تَدْرِي أَتُصِيبُ فِيهِمْ حُكْمَ اللهِ أَمْ لَا»

'...If you besiege the people of a fortress and they want you to give them the protection of Allâh and the protection of His Prophet, do not give them the protection of Allâh and the protection of His Prophet. Rather, give them your protection and the protection of your Companions. For verily it is a lesser sin if you disregard your word of protection and the protection of your Companions than if you disregard the protection of Allâh and the protection of His Prophet. If you besiege the people of a fortress and they want you to allow them to come down (from their fort) according to the law of Allâh, do not let them come down according to Allâh's law. Rather, let them come out based on your law, for verily you do not know whether you will be correct regarding Allâh's law concerning them or not." (Muslim recorded it)

Muslim recorded it. This *Hadith* clearly alludes to honoring Allâh in that the slave should not give the people the protection of Allâh and the protection of His Prophet ﷺ. Rather, he should give his own protection. This contains a great note for the people of *At-Tauhid* and the students of knowledge who are concerned with this knowledge and the people know of them as being concerned with this knowledge. It is a warning to them that no words or deeds should come hastily from them that would show their lack of following this knowledge. You must keep in mind that the people are watching you - particularly in this time, which is the time of doubts and the time of trials. The people are looking at you as being a carrier of the *Sunnah* and *Tauhid*. Therefore, do not deal with them except with something that contains honoring the Lord. Also, you should make these people honor Allâh by your honoring Him. Do not disregard your oath nor be unmindful of the protection of Allâh. You should not be unjust in testifying or dealing, because this will lessen the effect of what you carry of knowledge and religion.

of His Prophet and the protection of the Muslims.

2) Guiding to the less dangerous of two matters.

3) The Prophet's statement,

«اغْزُوا بِسْمِ اللهِ فِي سَبِيلِ اللهِ»

"Set out for fighting with the Name of Allâh and in the Way of Allâh."

4) The Prophet's statement,

«قَاتِلُوا مَنْ كَفَرَ بِاللهِ»

"Fight against those who disbelieve in Allâh."

5) The Prophet's statement,

«فَاسْتَعِنْ بِاللهِ وَقَاتِلْهُمْ»

"Seek Allâh's help and fight them."

6) The difference between the ruling of Allâh and the ruling of the scholars.

7) Concerning the fact that in the case of necessity the companion (of the Prophet ﷺ) might make a judgement and not know whether it agrees with the ruling of Allâh or not.

Chapter 63

What has been related Concerning Declaring an Oath on Allâh*

Jundub bin 'Abdullah رَضِيَ اللهُ عَنْهُ narrated that Allâh's Messenger ﷺ said,

«قَالَ رَجُلٌ: وَاللهِ لَا يَغْفِرُ اللهُ لِفُلَانٍ، فَقَالَ اللهُ عَزَّ وَجَلَّ مَنْ ذَا الَّذِي يَتَأَلَّى عَلَيَّ أَنْ لَا أَغْفِرَ لِفُلَانٍ؟ إِنِّي قَدْ غَفَرْتُ لَهُ وَأَحْبَطْتُ عَمَلَكَ»

"A man said, 'By Allâh, Allâh will not forgive so-and-so.' So Allâh, the Mighty and Majestic said, 'Who is this that swears upon Me that I will not forgive so-and-so? Verily I have forgiven him and I have nullified your deeds.'"[1] (*Muslim*)

---

* Declaring an oath on Allâh is in two aspects:

The first: The aspect of vowing, arrogance and haughtiness to such an extent that the person makes a right for himself upon Allâh and feels that Allâh judges according to the judgement that he himself has chosen. This is contrary to the completion of *At-Tauhid* and it contradicts its foundation.

The second situation: That the person declares an oath upon Allâh in a manner of humility and humbleness towards Allâh, and due to necessity and need for Him, glory be unto Him. This is that which a *Hadith* has been related concerning, "And from the slaves of Allâh are those who, if they vow an oath upon Allâh, He will certainly fulfill it." This is from the aspect of his thinking good about Allâh, the Mighty and Majestic.

[1] Jundub bin 'Abdullah رَضِيَ اللهُ عَنْهُ narrated that Allâh's Messenger ﷺ said,

«قَالَ رَجُلٌ: وَاللهِ لَا يَغْفِرُ اللهُ لِفُلَانٍ، فَقَالَ اللهُ عَزَّ وَجَلَّ مَنْ ذَا الَّذِي يَتَأَلَّى عَلَيَّ أَنْ لَا أَغْفِرَ لِفُلَانٍ؟ إِنِّي قَدْ غَفَرْتُ لَهُ وَأَحْبَطْتُ عَمَلَكَ»

"A man said, 'By Allâh, Allâh will not forgive so-and-so.' So Allâh, the Mighty and Majestic said, 'Who is this that swears upon Me that I will not forgive so-and-so?'"

This person, so-and-so, was a sinful man, so this devout worshipper

In the *Hadith* of Abu Hurayrah رَضِيَ اللهُ عَنْهُ it is mentioned that the speaker was a man who was a devout worshipper. Abu Hurayrah رَضِيَ اللهُ عَنْهُ said, "He spoke a word that destroyed his worldly life and his hereafter."

Important issues of the Chapter

1) Warning against swearing an oath upon Allâh.
2) The fact that the Fire is closer to one of us than the strap of his sandal.
3) That Paradise is similar to that (in nearness).
4) It contains a witness for the Prophet's statement, "Verily the man may speak a word..."
5) That the man may be forgiven due to something that is from the most detested matters to him.

---

vowed, exalted himself and thought that he, with his worship of Allâh, had achieved a level in which he was able to judge the actions of Allâh and that nothing that he requested would be rejected.

This contradicts the reality of servitude (to Allâh). Thus, Allâh punished him and said, "Who is this that swears upon Me?" The word *Eelaa'* (vow) comes from the word *Ulyah*, which is swearing an oath in an arrogant manner. Then He said, "that I will not forgive so-and-so? Verily I have forgiven him and I have nullified your deeds." Thus, He forgave the sinner and nullified the deeds of that devout worshipper. This clarifies for you the serious nature of opposing the honoring of Allâh, and the seriousness of opposing Allâh's *Tauhid*.

Chapter 64

Intercession by Allâh Should not be Sought from His Creation*

Jubayr bin Muṭ'im رَضِيَ اللهُ عَنْهُ said that a Bedouin Arab came to the Prophet ﷺ and said, "O Allâh's Messenger! The souls have been exhausted, the children are hungry and the properties are destroyed. Request rain from your Lord for us, for verily we seek intercession by Allâh from You and by you from Allâh." The Prophet ﷺ said,

«سُبْحَانَ اللهِ، سُبْحَانَ اللهِ!!»

"*Subḥaan Allâh Subḥaan Allâh* (Glorified and exalted is Allâh above imperfections),!!"

And he did not stop glorifying Allâh until the effect of that was apparent in the faces of his Companions. Then the Prophet ﷺ said,

«وَيْحَكَ أَتَدْرِي مَا اللهُ؟! إِنَّ شَأْنَ اللهِ أَعْظَمُ مِنْ ذٰلِكَ، إِنَّهُ لَا يُسْتَشْفَعُ بِاللهِ عَلَىٰ أَحَدٍ»

"Woe unto you! Do you know Who Allâh is?! Verily the status of Allâh is greater than that. Intercession by Allâh is not sought from anyone." (Abu Dâwûd recorded it)[1]

---

* This means that one should not make Allâh a means of mediation to be used for seeking intercession from anyone from the creation. This is contrary to the completion of *At-Tauhid*.

[1] Jubayr bin Muṭ'im رَضِيَ اللهُ عَنْهُ said that a Bedouin Arab came to the Prophet ﷺ and said, "O Messenger of Allâh! The souls have been exhausted, the children are hungry and the properties are destroyed. Request rain from your Lord for us, for verily we seek intercession by Allâh from You and by you from Allâh." This means, "We seek intercession by Allâh by making Allâh a means of mediation that will intercede for us with you so that you will supplicate." The status of Allâh

Important issues of the Chapter

1) Disapproval of whomever says, "We seek intercession by Allâh upon you."
2) The change in Prophet ﷺ such that its effect was recognizable in his companion's faces due to this statement.
3) That he did not disapprove of his statement, "We seek intercession by you upon Allâh."
4) Drawing attention to the explanation of the statement *Subḥaan Allâh*.
5) That the Muslims asked him (the Prophet ﷺ) to pray for rain.

---

is greater than that, as the creation is insignificant and lowly in comparison with the Lord. The Prophet ﷺ said,

«سُبْحَانَ اللهِ، سُبْحَانَ اللهِ!!»

"*Subḥaan Allâh Subḥaan Allâh* (Glorified and exalted is Allâh above imperfections),!!"

And he did not stop glorifying Allâh. This means that he did not cease repeating it in his declaring Allâh's exaltation and magnificence above such, and his declaring Allâh to be far removed from every bad description, or blemish of deficiency, and from every ill thought about Him. Until the effect of that was apparent in the faces of his Companions. Then the Prophet ﷺ said,

«وَيْحَكَ أَتَدْرِي مَا اللهُ؟! إِنَّ شَأْنَ اللهِ أَعْظَمُ مِنْ ذٰلِكَ، إِنَّهُ لَا يُسْتَشْفَعُ بِاللهِ عَلَىٰ أَحَدٍ»

'Woe unto you! Do you know Who Allâh is?! Verily the status of Allâh is greater than that. Intercession by Allâh is not sought from anyone.'"

Chapter 65

What has been Related Concerning the Prophet's Protecting the Sacredness of *At-Tauhid* and His Closing the Paths of *Ash-Shirk*

'Abdullah bin Ash-Shikhkheer رَضِيَ اللهُ عَنْهُ said, "I went with the delegation of Bani 'Aamir to Allâh's Messenger ﷺ and we (the delegation) said, 'You are our master (*Sayyidunaa*).' So he replied,

«السَّيِّدُ اللهُ تَبَارَكَ وَتَعَالَىٰ»

'The Master (*As-Sayyid*) is Allâh, the Blessed and Exalted.'[1]

---

[1] 'Abdullah bin Ash-Shikhkheer رَضِيَ اللهُ عَنْهُ said, "I went with the delegation of Bani 'Aamir to Allâh's Messenger ﷺ and we (the delegation) said, 'You are our master (*Sayyidunaa*).' So he replied, 'The Master (*As-Sayyid*) is Allâh, the Blessed and Exalted.''' In his saying,

«السَّيِّدُ اللهُ تَبَارَكَ وَتَعَالَىٰ»

"The Master (*As-Sayyid*) is Allâh, the Blessed and Exalted",

Even though he is the *Sayyid* (master, leader) of the children of Aadam, which shows that he protected the sacredness of *At-Tauhid* and closed off the paths that led to *Ash-Shirk*. From these (paths that lead to *Ash-Shirk*) is the path of exaggerating in expressions.

Saying to the man that he is a *Sayyid* and similar to that, if it is to address him and show possession of all, then this is the most severe of it. From that which the scholars have mentioned is that it is extremely disliked that it be said to a man that he is *As-Sayyid* (the Master), like this, by adding the letters *Alif* and *Laam*. This is because what is understood from this is the complete meaning of mastery. For this reason you see that those who commit *Shirk* with some of the *Awliyaa'*, like As-Sayyid Al-Badawee, magnify the word *As-Sayyid*. They often use the name 'Abd with *As-Sayyid* (i.e. 'Abdus-Sayyid) and they intend by it As-Sayyid Al-Badawee.

We said, '(You are) the best of us in virtue and the greatest of us in might.' So he replied,

«قُولُوا بِقَوْلِكُمْ أَوْ بَعْضِ قَوْلِكُم وَلَا يَسْتَجْرِيَنَّكُمُ الشَّيْطَانُ»

'Say what you have to say, or part of what you have to say, and do not let Satan get you carried away.'''[1]

Abu Dâwûd recorded it with an authentic (*Ṣaḥeeḥ*) chain.

Anas رَضِيَ اللهُ عَنْهُ narrated that some people said, "O Allâh's Messenger ﷺ! O the best of us and the son of the best of us, and our master and the son of our master." So he said,

«قُولُوا بِقَوْلِكُمْ وَلَا يَسْتَهْوِيَنَّكُمُ الشَّيْطَانُ، أَنَا مُحَمَّدٌ عَبْدُاللهِ وَرَسُولُهُ، مَا أُحِبُّ أَنْ تَرْفَعُونِي فَوقَ مَنْزِلَتِي الَّتِي أَنْزَلَنِي اللهُ عَزَّ وَجَلَّ»

"O people, say what you must say and do not let Satan carry you away. I am Muhammad, the slave of Allâh and His Messenger. I do not like that you elevate me above my status that Allâh, the Mighty and Sublime has given me."[2]

---

[1] "We said, '(You are) the best of us in virtue and the greatest of us in might.' So he replied,

«قُولُوا بِقَوْلِكُمْ أَوْ بَعْضِ قَوْلِكُمْ وَلَا يَسْتَجْرِيَنَّكُمْ الشَّيْطَانُ»

'Say what you have to say, or part of what you have to say, and do not let Satan get you carried away.'''

Abu Dâwûd recorded it with an authentic (*Ṣaḥeeḥ*) chain. That is because this contains praising and lauding when meeting someone, and this is from Satan so that the person will feel great within himself, and then disappointment will come to him. This is because is without *Laa ḥawla wa laa quwwata illaa bil-laah* (There is no might or power except with Allâh) and disdain for the self, humility, and humbleness that Allâh knows from his heart, then he will be disappointed and the matter will take him by surprise.

[2] Anas رَضِيَ اللهُ عَنْهُ narrated that some people said, "O Allâh's Messenger ﷺ! O the best of us and the son of the best of us..." And he is as they described him. However, he closed the door so that no one could enter it

An-Nasâ'i recorded it with a good (*Jayyid*) chain.

Important issues of the Chapter

1) Warning the people against exaggerating.
2) What one should say when it is said to him, "You are our master (*Sayyidunaa*)."
3) The Prophet's saying,

«وَلَا يَسْتَهْوِيَنَّكُمْ الشَّيْطَانُ»

"Do not let Satan get you carried away",
even thought they only said what was true.

4) The Prophet's saying,

«مَا أُحِبُّ أَنْ تَرْفَعُونِي فَوْقَ مَنْزِلَتِي»

"I do not like that you elevate me above my status."

---

by his approval of this deed. For the person may exalt someone and Satan enters that person who is exalted and the one who exalted him, and thus he makes the hearts attached to that exalted one until *Shirk* is committed with him and he is exalted in a manner that is not allowed. This chapter is like the gatherer of what is obligatory of closing off the means that lead to *Ash-Shirk*.

Chapter 66

What has been related Concerning Allâh the Most High's Statement,*

﴿وَمَا قَدَرُوا۟ ٱللَّهَ حَقَّ قَدْرِهِۦ وَٱلْأَرْضُ جَمِيعًا قَبْضَتُهُۥ يَوْمَ ٱلْقِيَـٰمَةِ﴾

"They made not a just estimate of Allâh such as is due to Him. And on the Day of Resurrection." (39:67)

---

* The Imam of this *Da'wah*, Shaikh ul-Islam (Muhammad bin 'Abdul-Wahhaab), concluding this book with this chapter is a magnificent conclusion. This is because whoever knows the reality of what this chapter contains of Allâh's description, then is only able to truly humble himself and make himself submissive in exalting the Lord. "They did not make a just estimate of Allâh as He deserves." This means they did not magnify Him in the manner that He deserves to be magnified. If they had magnified Him in the manner that He deserves to be magnified, they would not have worshipped other besides Him. If you reflect upon your Lord, the Mighty, the Most Wise, Who has the Attributes of Magnificence, and He is above His Throne, commanding and prohibiting in His vast dominion, which the earth is like nothing in that dominion. He pours down His mercy and His favor upon whomever He wills, and He averts trial (calamity) from whomever He wills. He is the Giver of favor and bounty. Thus, you see the actions of Allâh in the heavens, and you see the servitude of the angels in the heavens. You see them turning to this Almighty Lord. Then you look at the fact that Allâh, this Magnificent, Great One, Who has this Attribute of tremendous Sovereignty, turns to You, O lowly, meek slave, and commands you with His Worship. This worship is an honor for you if you only knew. And He commands you to have fear of Him, which is an honor for you if you only knew. For verily if you knew the right of Allâh, and you knew His Attributes, and what He has of absolute loftiness regarding Himself and His Attributes, you would find that you would not be able to do anything except humble yourself to Him will willful humility, and submissiveness. You would only be able to turn to His obedience and draw near to Him with what He loves. If you recited His Speech, then you have recited the Speech of the One Who addressed you with it, and commanded you and prohibited you with it. Then you would

Ibn Mas'ud رَضِيَ اللهُ عَنْهُ narrated that a (Jewish) rabbi from among the rabbis came to Allâh's Messenger ﷺ and said, "O Muhammad! We find (in the knowledge with us) that Allâh will place the heavens on a finger, the earths on a finger, the trees on a finger, the water on a finger, the soil on a finger and the rest of the creation on a finger. Then he will say, 'I am the King.'" So the Prophet ﷺ laughed until his molar teeth became visible, affirming the statement of the rabbi. Then Allâh's Messenger ﷺ recited,

﴿وَمَا قَدَرُوا۟ ٱللَّهَ حَقَّ قَدْرِهِۦ وَٱلْأَرْضُ جَمِيعًا قَبْضَتُهُۥ يَوْمَ ٱلْقِيَـٰمَةِ﴾

"They made not a just estimate of Allâh such as is due to Him. And on the Day of Resurrection." (39:67)

In a narration recorded by Muslim, he (the rabbi) said,

«وَالْجِبَالَ وَالشَّجَرَ عَلَىٰ إِصْبَعٍ ثُمَّ يَهُزُّهُنَّ فَيَقُولُ: أَنَا الْمَلِكُ، أَنَا اللهُ»

"...and the mountains and the trees on a finger, and then He (Allâh) will shake them and say, 'I am the King, I am Allâh.'"

In a narration recorded by Al-Bukhari, he (the rabbi) said,

«يَجْعَلُ السَّماوَاتِ عَلَىٰ إِصْبَعٍ وَالْمَاءَ وَالثَّرَىٰ عَلَىٰ إِصْبَعٍ»

"He (Allâh) will place the heavens on a finger, the water and the soil on a finger..." (*Al-Bukhari* and *Muslim*).

In a narration recorded by Muslim from Ibn 'Umar رَضِيَ اللهُ عَنْهُ (that he attributed to the Prophet ﷺ),

«يَطْوِي اللهُ السَّماوَاتِ يَوْمَ الْقِيَامَةِ ثُمَّ يَأْخُذُهُنَّ بِيَدِهِ الْيُمْنَىٰ، ثُمَّ

---

have reverence beyond reverence and honor beyond honor. For this reason, from the causes of deepness in faith in the heart and magnification of the Lord is that the slave contemplates and thinks about the dominion of the heavens and the earth as Allâh has commanded.

يَقُولُ: أَنَا الْمَلِكُ، أَيْنَ الْجَبَّارُونَ؟ أَيْنَ الْمُتَكَبِّرُونَ؟»

> "Allâh will roll up the heavens on the Day of Resurrection, then He will take them in His Right Hand and say, 'I am the King. Where are the arrogant, where are the prideful?'"

It is reported that Ibn 'Abbâs رَضِيَ اللهُ عَنْهُ said, "The seven heavens and the seven earths in the Palm of the Most Beneficent are only like a mustard seed in one of your palms."

Ibn Jareer said that Yoonus told him that Ibn Wahb informed them that Ibn Zayd said that his father told him that Allâh's Messenger ﷺ said,

«مَا السَّماوَاتُ السَّبْعُ فِي الْكُرْسِيِّ إِلَّا كَدَرَاهِمَ سَبْعَةٍ أُلْقِيَتْ فِي تُرْسٍ»

> "The seven heavens compared to *Al-Kursiyy* (the Footstool) are only like seven dirhams cast into a shield."

And he (Ibn Jareer) said that Abu Ṭḥarr said, "I heard Allâh's Messenger ﷺ saying,

«مَا الْكُرْسِيُّ فِي الْعَرْشِ إِلَّا كَحَلْقَةٍ مِنْ حَدِيدٍ أُلْقِيَتْ بَيْنَ ظَهْرَيْ فَلَاةٍ مِنَ الْأَرْضِ»

> '*Al-Kursiyy* (the Footstool) compared to *Al-'Arsh* (the Throne) is only like an iron ring cast into a desert of the land.'"

Ibn Mas'ud رَضِيَ اللهُ عَنْهُ said, "Between the sky of this world and the one that is next to it (i.e. above it) is five hundred years (i.e. travel distance). And between each heaven and another heaven is five hundred years. And between the seventh heaven and *Al-Kursiyy* (the Footstool) is five hundred years. And between *Al-Kursiyy* and the water is five hundred years. And *Al-'Arsh* (the Throne) is above the water and Allâh is above *Al-'Arsh*. Nothing is hidden from Him from your deeds."

Ibn Mahdiyy recorded it from Ḥammaad bin Salamah, from 'Aaṣim, from Zarr, from 'Abdullah (Ibn Mas'ud). Al-Mas'udee recorded similar to it from 'Aaṣim, from Abi Waa'il, from 'Abdullah (Ibn Mas'ud). This is what Al-Ḥaafiḍḥ Aṭḥ-Ṭḥahabiyy - may Allâh have mercy on him - said, and he said, "And it has many routes."

'Abbâs bin 'Abdul-Muṭṭalib رَضِـيَ اللهُ عَـنْـهُ said that Allâh's Messenger ﷺ said,

«هَلْ تَدْرُونَ كَمْ بَيْنَ السَّمَاءِ وَالأَرْضِ»

"Do you all know how much (distance) is between the sky and the earth?"

We said, "Allâh and His Messenger know best." He said,

«بَيْنَهُمَا مَسِيرَةُ خَمْسِمِائَةِ سَنَةٍ، وَمِنْ كُلِّ سَمَاءٍ إِلَىٰ سَمَاءٍ مَسِيرَةُ خَمْسِمِائَةِ سَنَةٍ، وَكِثَفُ كُلِّ سَمَاءٍ مَسِيرَةُ خَمْسِمِائَةِ سَنَةٍ، وَبَيْنَ السَّمَاءِ السَّابِعَةِ وَالْعَرْشِ بَحْرٌ بَيْنَ أَسْفَلِهِ وَأَعْلَاهُ كَمَا بَيْنَ السَّمَاءِ وَالْأَرْضِ، وَاللهُ عَزَّ وَجَلَّ فَوْقَ ذٰلِكَ، وَلَيْسَ يَخْفَىٰ عَلَيْهِ شَيْءٌ مِنْ أَعْمَالِ بَنِي آدَمَ»

"Between them is the distance of five hundred years (i.e. of travel). And from every heaven to another heaven is the distance of five hundred years. And the thickness of each heaven is the distance of five hundred years. And between the seventh heaven and Al-'Arsh (the Throne) is a sea, and from its bottom to its top is like what is between the heaven (sky) and the earth (i.e. five hundred years). And Allâh, the Mighty and Majestic, is above that and nothing is hidden from Him from the deeds of the children of Aadam." (Abu Dâwûd and others recorded it).

Important issues of the Chapter

1) The explanation of His Statement,

﴿وَٱلْأَرْضُ جَمِيعًا قَبْضَتُهُۥ﴾

"And the entire earth will be in His grasp." (39:67)

2) That these points of knowledge and similar to them remained with the Jews in his time, and they did not reject them or interpret them.

3) That when the rabbi mentioned to the Prophet ﷺ, he affirmed it and the revelation of Qur'ān came to verify that.

4) The occurrence of laughter from him when the rabbi mentioned this great knowledge.

5) The explicit mentioning of the Two Hands and that the heavens are in the Right Hand and the earths in the other.

6) The explicit naming of it (the other Hand) as the left.

7) Mentioning the arrogant and prideful during this.

8) His (Ibn 'Abbâs's) statement, "Like a mustard seed in one of your palms."

9) The greatness of *Al-Kursiyy* (the Footstool) in comparison to the heavens.

10) The greatness of *Al-'Arsh* (the Throne) in comparison to *Al-Kursiyy*.

11) That *Al-'Arsh* is not *Al-Kursiyy*, and (the existence of) the water.

12) How much distance is between each heaven (sky) to another heaven.

13) How much distance is between the seventh heaven and *Al-Kursiyy*.

14) How much distance is between *Al-Kursiyy* and the water.

15) That *Al-'Arsh* is above the water.

16) That Allâh is above *Al-'Arsh*.

17) How much distance is between the heaven (sky) and the earth.

18) The density of every heaven is five hundred years.

19) That the sea is above the heavens has a distance of five hundred years between its bottom and its top, and Allâh knows best.

And all praise is due to Allâh, the Lord of the worlds (all that exists), and may Allâh grant prayers of blessing to our leader Muhammad, his family and all of his Companions.